# YELLOWSTONE HOLIDAY

## Richard A. Bartlett

**MINERVA PRESS**

LONDON

MONTREUX  LOS ANGELES  SYDNEY

YELLOWSTONE HOLIDAY
Copyright © Richard A. Bartlett 1998

ISBN 1 86106 595 7

First Published 1998 by
MINERVA PRESS
195 Knightsbridge
London SW7 1RE

Printed in Great Britain for Minerva Press

# YELLOWSTONE HOLIDAY

# Contents

## Chapter One
# Prelude: by Rail to Wonderland

### I

Over the mantle above the huge stone fireplace at Billner Lodge hangs a most unusual instrument. Mounted on a piece of polished walnut, the device, about eighteen inches long, looks like a shiny old-fashioned bicycle pump. At one end is a crude wooden handle with which to push and pull the piston inside the metal cylinder – but a deep dent about halfway down the cylinder now prevents a full thrust. At the opposite end of the cylinder, cut in half vertically so as to fit smoothly onto the board, is a circular red rubber half-globe, looking exactly like the business end of a plumber's helper.

The device, so different from the usual mounted animal head or rifle that frequents the space above a rustic fireplace, is a wonderful conversation piece.

"What is it?" asked guests of the 1920s vacationing at the Billner Dude Ranch in Montana's Paradise Valley, just north of Yellowstone Park.

The hostess, Lady Prudence Mehitabel Snowden Billner, would flutter her still pretty blue eyes, blush slightly, and reply simply: "It was my brother Rusty's secret weapon. It saved me from – a fate worse than death." And then, always, Lady Billner had work to do in another room. Or one of her two sub-teen sons demanded her attention. Or her husband Stephen, known as Lord Billner to his friends, called her for some matter of business.

The guests in those golden days of dude ranching would exchange glances and begin speculating on the device. What is it? How would it figure in some kind of adventure? A fate worse than death? How would lovely Lady Billner have been threatened by a fate worse than death?

Lady Billner knew it created conversation. That she always smiled, even as she blushed, when the matter came up; that her eyes grew misty at some nostalgic thoughts, just enhanced the riddle. She would never tell and she had sworn Stephen to secrecy. After all, she reasoned, the mystery brought guests back for another year.

But when Stephen and Prudence were snuggled in their feather bed, and the cool, sweet Montana breezes came through the curtained windows, and all was right with the world (perhaps they had made love and were luxuriating for a few minutes before sleep took over) they would reminisce about that wonderful summer of 1909. And if Stephen went to sleep as Prudence talked – a common occurrence – then she would stare blankly at the ceiling and try to complete her reminiscence before Morpheus conquered her.

## II

Any visitor knew immediately that Elm Grove, Michigan, population 4,798 in 1909 but hopeful of 5,000 by the census of 1910, was laid out by migrating Yankees. It had a village common, a prominent Congregational Church, and a Main Street boasting of livery, blacksmith, barber shop, general store, millinery store, drug store with soda fountain, and a few two-story buildings where the village doctors and lawyers practiced their professions.

One of those offices was occupied by the law firm of Snowden and Parker. On this particular evening, Friday, August 13, Judge Philip Snowden – he had served briefly as a local judge – the fortyish junior partner, shook hands with his associate after going over business matters and informing him of a few loose ends still dangling in spite of his working evenings for the past two weeks.

"Philip," retorted Jed Parker, "forget about the loose ends. You and Emily and the family have a wonderful vacation to Yellowstone. I'll see you two weeks from Monday and I guarantee everything will be under control. Now get out of this office!"

Philip took his watch from his vest pocket. "It is nearly six," he mused. "Guess I'd better get home. Emily'll have supper waiting and we've got packing to do. So long, Jed." The partner listened as the sound of footsteps down the stairs ended. Good. Philip Snowden, hard working, decent Phil Snowden, had reached the sidewalk. Now he was walking home, about to begin a long overdue vacation.

The evening sun still shone bright, it had been a hot day, and Philip chose to walk slowly. His route took him through town, then down Second Avenue five blocks to Fifth Street. There he made a right turn and walked three blocks to number 3010, the two-story Victorian house, white with green shutters, that he called home. Determined not to think about the office, now that his vacation had started, his mind turned to his family.

First there was Emily, his wife of twenty-one years. Philip, just setting out his shingle in Oak Grove after graduating from law school at Ann Arbor and passing his state boards, had met her at church. It was love at first sight. He had won the shy girl with the creamy complexion and long brown hair not from rival swains but from Emily's Puritan parents. She had been in their plans for old-age security, expected never to marry but take care of the old folks. Emily had married against her parents' wishes. More, her mother, as Stephen told his partner, had apparently been born frigid and had never thawed. On the night before Emily's wedding she had given her daughter a "what every bride should know" talk that would have prompted a weaker young woman to cancel the wedding. "She ended her talk," Emily later confided to Stephen, "by saying, 'Now, dear, sleep well, for you have a busy day *and night* ahead of you.'" She left poor Emily as tense as a tightrope-walker's rope.

But Philip Snowden, nearly six feet tall, muscular and masculine, proved to be not a beast but a loving, caring mate, gentle as a lamb. Briefly, as Philip Snowden walked slowly toward home, he frowned. Truth was, Emily had never *entirely* got rid of some of that Puritanism. Lately she had turned her back to him in bed several times. Was she all right? Approaching change of life? Tiring of sex? *He* wasn't, Philip told himself. Oh, well.

A couple years after the marriage came Prudence. Philip's smile conveyed his feeling about *that* blessed event. He recalled her giggle at three, her lost baby teeth at four, her irritability at puberty, her blond tresses, clear complexion, blue eyes, pert nose, melodious voice – and her intelligence and vivaciousness. The father frowned. She was nineteen, and in Oak Grove most of the girls in Prudence's graduating class of 1908 were already married, some of them having babies before the requisite nine months. And there was beautiful Prudence, not just unmarried, but not even engaged. He so wanted her to marry the right man.

Was Sam T. Ericson the right one for Prudence? She had known him since first grade. He had been Joseph and she the Virgin Mary in five Christmas plays. He had taken her to the senior prom. His father manufactured structural supports for automobile tops, and Sam was in business with him. Philip nodded his head. He had to admit, Sam was a total boor. But he had good prospects. He'd be a good breadwinner, a member of Elm Grove's elite. And who else was there for Prudence? It bothered him.

And then of course, there was Rusty, eleven years old. Red-headed and freckled, Rusty was the product of Stephen's first night home after the Spanish American War. He was both an embarrassment and a delight, especially for his mother – an embarrassment when he got into mischief, a delight when he did thoughtful, unrequested favors for her. Already Stephen could envision Rusty's future, and it was good. This summer the lad had organized a club made up of the neighborhood boys, the Elklets. The name was probably in deference to the Benevolent and Protective Order of Elks, to which a number of their parents belonged. Rusty, of course, had been elected president. On vacation to Yellowstone he had informed Stephen that he *had* to obtain elk antlers for his club. His father had not discouraged him, thinking they could purchase some along the way.

By now Philip Snowden had turned up Fifth Street, but was still several blocks from home. He waved at neighbors who were watering their lawns or tending to gardens. He observed a sputtering automobile coming down the street and contemplated the purchase of such a contraption. Then the street was quiet. He continued his introspections about his family and his life.

His thoughts came to the last member of his household, his sister Madeline. Poor, dear Madeline. She was thirty on her last birthday, already a spinster in the eyes of the boys and girls struggling through her English classes at Elm Grove High. Stephen frowned and nodded his head negatively. Madeline deserved better. She was petite and definitely attractive, but where were the respectable, educated bachelors in Elm Grove for a thirty year old school teacher? She deserves better, he muttered again, recalling how she had become pregnant by a promising young man who deserted her; how Stephen had arranged her confinement in another city while she was ostensibly at Normal School; how he had then helped pay her expenses through Normal School and, when it was all over, helped land the English teacher's job for her in Elm Grove, where she was invited to live with his family.

As he approached 3010 Fifth Street Philip Snowden mentally wrapped up his reflections with the final sentence, "Everyone's life is a little book – Emily's, Prudence's, Rusty's, Madeline's, even *mine*." Then he heard two screams coming from 3010 Fifth – his house – and his pace quickened. Philip ran up the steps and across the porch through the front door. "Emily, what's wrong?"

In retrospect, he should have known it involved either Prudence or Rusty – and indeed, it was Prudence. It was a simple, innocuous happening, quite understandable, but at the time it was serious and, oh, how embarrassing!

The fourteen months after graduation had not been happy for the girl. It had been a time of soul-searching, and agony, and desperate sighing. Her friends were all getting married. At business college she had mastered typing and Gregg Shorthand and simple bookkeeping while half her mind bewailed woman's plight and wrestled with her problem: Sam. Why, Prudence asked herself a thousand times, did she hesitate?

People the town over said that Prudence and Sam were made for each other. Her mother had even hinted at how discomforting it was at the DAR, the way the ladies inquired about "Prudence and Sam – what a lovely couple. Haven't they been going together for *ages*?"

Oh, life! Oh, mystery! Prudence would throw down her shorthand pen and place her fists in her cheeks and her blue eyes would stare blankly out the window at Main Street. Should she marry Sam? Even though she felt no skip of the heart when he came through the door? Even though she resented his physical advances and had never allowed him to kiss her – passionately? He *was* acceptable, save for that silly mustache which, she vowed, would come off within twenty-four hours after marriage. As mother Snowden said, she who waits for the perfect man waits forever in vain! (Except for Daddy Snowden – but he was, after all, one in a million!)

When no new swains appeared in Elm Grove and all the other eligibles had either married or left town for Detroit, Prudence made her decision. She would be brave, and philosophical, and hold her head high, and marry Sam. "Who knows," she told herself over and over again, "maybe I *do* love him after all. Have I ever been in love? (*No.*) Then how can I know what love is like? And mother will be happy and so will all the ladies at the DAR and the Congregational Church."

But she had not had the opportunity to tell Sam. To further confuse the poor girl, a new family had moved to Elm Grove. The father was a manufacturer of brake drums, was a friend of Sam's father, and – here was the rub – there was a daughter. Was there a daughter! Her name was Kathrine, aged nineteen just like Prudence, one year of women's seminary out of the way, dark-haired, dark-eyed, big-bosomed and peek-a-booish about it. For the first time in her life Prudence had a competitor for Sam. True, she found Sam a dull boorish young man who smelled of axle grease and unwashed male-with-a-mustache, but he was, after all, Elm Grove's remaining eligible man.

"Do I want to end up an old maid like Aunt Madeline?" the girl asked herself. Maybe and maybe not. But something more, something of the primitive female crept into fair Prudence's psyche. She saw, and she knew. At the Fourth of July picnic Sam had almost dropped a dish of strawberry ice cream down Kathrine's blouse – for looking at those peek-a-boos. And oh! They *were* bigger, far bigger, than Prudence's two treasures.

Prudence may have questioned her love for Sam, but she was not going to let a big bosomed brazen newcomer snatch him away. Desperation led to drastic action. (Possibly she was more jealous of Kathrine's torso than she was afraid of losing Sam.) Whatever the explanation, Prudence drew $9.95 from her small savings still housed in a toy Liberty Bell bank, and mailed an order to Sears, Roebuck and Company. Nervously she awaited delivery, determined to seize the package without her mother knowing of its arrival. Good fortune was with Prudence, in a manner of speaking, and on the day before the family was to leave for their Yellowstone Park holiday, she received the mysterious parcel, 'wrapped in plain paper'.

Prudence tiptoed to her room, that warm afternoon, with goose-pimples rising on her smooth young arms and chills running up and down her back. Never before had she felt so – so wicked! When she closed and locked the door to her room, that tingling sensation heightened, as one feels when all alone with the doors closed, and the mind is filled with anticipation of something illegal, or even immoral. Lovely Prudence, late that August afternoon, gently laid the package on her boudoir table. There!

She propped herself on the bench in front of the mirror. Prim and slim and five feet six, she examined her evil blue eyes. At least they looked that way to her. Then she examined her image and contemplated herself, and the box, and the locked door. She heard the sounds of horses clopping by and wagon wheels crunching on the gravel street outside her window. As she surveyed herself, she paid particular attention to her bust, which she found too small under the starched white blouse. She bit her lower lip lightly, paused in her movements, then impetuously reached for the package. Hastily she untied it, making as little noise as possible. Then the wrapper was off. There lay the cardboard container labeled: DR SAMUEL'S PATENT BUST DEVELOPER COMPLETE WITH ONE POUND OF PERFUMED EXPANSION CREAM.

The girl visibly shuddered as her fingers tore open the box to expose this most modern discovery of the cosmetologist's art. She frowned as she gazed at the 'instrument', picked it up gingerly, and then set it down on the boudoir while she read the instructions.

"First," it read, "in privacy of boudoir, expose bosom and apply Expansion Cream with finger tips. Massage vigorously, coating bust well. Now grasp Bust Developer in right hand. Slap head directly over left bust. With left hand, draw out handle and push in – in and out again. After a few minutes, repeat procedure with right bust. Such a combination of pressure, plus Expansion Cream, *if used diligently* upon rising in the morning and retiring at night, is *guaranteed* to expand the bust an inch in one week, and up to three inches in the first month."

"Oooooooooooo," Prudence cooed. "Just what I need." Carefully she examined again the Bust Developer, which looked like what it really was – a plumber's helper attached to a bicycle pump. Tingling with anticipation, Prudence first scanned the broad outdoors from her second-story window, where the rays of the late afternoon sun cast long shadows from the elms. Impulsively her hands darted to the buttons of her blouse. Off it came, and, as she watched her actions in the mirror, down came the straps and her chemise. She observed her ivory-smooth, exposed self from the narrow little wasp waist up, especially noting her small but delicately, perfectly shaped breasts.

She broke a fingernail in her haste to open the can of Expansion Cream. Prudence dipped her fingers into it – a sickly greenish, like swamp moss, and the perfume reeked of cheapness, but never mind.

She applied the greasy mixture diligently to her left breast, not quite understanding the strange feelings the action elicited within her. *Something* happened. She felt wickeder than ever! Then, her left half all coated with the slimy green cream, she grabbed the Bust Developer according to directions. Smack! Now it was clapped over her left breast like a bulldog grabbing a bone. Prudence's eyes widened at the sensation. Then, slowly, experimentally, the girl grasped the handle and pulled it back. "Oooooooooooom," she cooed, feeling wicked beyond all saving.

Then in, then out. She could feel the suction. "An inch a week," she whispered as she pushed and pulled the handle. "An inch a week, an inch a week, an INCH A WEEK, an INCH TONIGHT. She worked that miscast bicycle pump until her left breast felt expanded to twice its usual size. "There," she finally gasped, breathless and joyful. "Now for the right one." She pulled the Developer to take it off.

It refused to budge.

Prudence stared at the ugly thing, the red rubber plumber's helper slapped over her left breast, the long shiny cylinder out from the Helper, the handle at the end. It began to look like some horrible beast that had bitten her and now wouldn't let go. She struck the cylinder. The Developer bounced up and down, but it would not let go. She pulled hard on the handle, but the pain was so sharp that she stopped.

It would not let go.

With her fingers she dug into the flesh around the red rubber cup, but the suction was too great. It would not let go.

Prudence's blue eyes widened with terror. Floods of tears dripped from her fair cheeks. Perspiration dotted her forehead. Her breath came in quick gasps as her whole body shook with fear. She gritted her teeth and grabbed the cylinder with both hands and pulled and pulled until she had a vision of herself looking like an African wench she had seen in a lantern-slide lecture at the church. Still, the Developer refused to relinquish its grip.

She stood up and tried jumping up and down. The Developer shook with her – but it would not let go. She fell on her back onto the bed, breathed out to make her chest small, pulled on the cylinder with all her might.

The Developer stuck fast.

Then, downstairs, the doorbell rang. She lay and listened in disbelief as Mother welcomed Sam. "Prudence," Mother called. "Sam's here."

"Yes, Mother. I'll be right down," she forced herself to say.

But the minutes went by. She could not remove the Developer. Horrified, she heard Mother say, "Sam, I'll go see what's keeping her," and then the sound of Mother coming upstairs.

In a flash Prudence experienced the humility, remorse, shame that was to be her cross to bear – evermore. Better, thought the girl, that only Mother knew – of her sins and the dark, depraved cravings of her wicked mind. All Prudence desired now was freedom from that – THING.

"Mother?" she asked in a weak, semi-hysterical voice. "Will you – please – come here a minute?"

"What is it, Prudence?"

Awkwardly, what with the Developer sticking out from her left breast, Prudence stepped to her door and, by turning sideways, was able to unlock it. She awaited Mother's coming as a Christian martyr about to be fed to the lions. Mrs. Snowden opened the door, cast one long, *long* look at her daughter, the Developer with its bulldog grip on Prudence's fair left breast, and then, before tearful Prudence could stop her, Emily Snowden let forth with a shriek such as no one who knew her had ever heard from her before.

"No, Mother," Prudence began, but it was too late.

Mother screamed again, stepping back into the hall. Worse. Sam had set down the flowers he had brought for Prudence and was bounding up the stairs. Right behind, flying in through the front door and running two stairs at a time behind him, was Philip shouting, "Emily. What's wrong?"

Prudence heard those sounds – like a herd of elephants – and she reacted as if the elephants were about to trample her to death. She screamed in unison with her mother, then thoughtfully reached to slam the door. But the Developer got in the way and sprung the door right back in her face. Father and Sam reached Emily, who was silent now, just pointing. Their eyes followed: there was Prudence, nude to the waist save for the ugly contraption called a Bust Developer, her hands covering her nude right breast. There stood she, exposed for ridicule of Father and Sam too. The humiliation of it all set Prudence to screaming well above her mother's scale of shrieks.

All of this was happening just as the Reverend Steele, pastor of the First Congregational Church, was climbing the steps of the front porch, his mission to wish the Snowdens a happy vacation. He heard the commotion and came bounding up the stairs just as Madeline, the maiden aunt, dashed upstairs from the kitchen. She was joined by Prudence's brother Rusty, who had been testing a Boy Scout hatchet he was taking along to Yellowstone. When Rusty gazed upon Prudence, one hand covering her right breast and the Developer stuck to the other, all the while screaming at the top of her voice, he darted downstairs and out the front door and down the street a block to Dr. Fisher's. That kindly old gentleman left his evening meal, grabbed his black doctor's bag and puffed alongside the redheaded boy. By the time the two arrived on the second floor of the big frame house at 3010 Fifth Street the local constable had arrived and the second floor hallway was filled with curious humanity, including several nosy neighbors. Judge Snowden was trying to calm down the spectators by shouting at them above the screaming. Maiden Aunt Madeline was trying to calm Emily. Anytime anyone approached Prudence, she screamed louder than ever. Whenever Sam moved in her direction she reacted like a maniac.

But Dr. Fisher was not to be deterred. He marched right through the crowd, takeover person that he was, entered Prudence's bedroom in spite of her protestations, and slammed the door behind him. "Huh," he grunted as quiet settled outside in the hall, even Emily ceasing her screams. "Now, young lady," they heard him say in his gruff, authoritarian but not unkind voice, "you are not having a baby and you've not been raped. Control yourself this instant or I'll have to slap your face!"

In the hall they heard the screams change to sobs as Prudence buried her face in her hands and her golden tresses fell over her shoulders.

"Now, now," soothed Dr. Fisher, gently touching the top of her head. "You know, Prudence, I brought you into this world. Don't be afraid. Sit down on the bed."

Prudence obeyed. "Kill me, Dr. Fisher," she pleaded between sobs. "Please kill me."

"Can't do that, Prudence," the Doctor replied, all the time eyeing the Bust Developer, the box, the instructions, smelling the Expansion Cream, making a face. "It's against the law." When he comprehended the whole thing, Dr. Fisher slapped his leg and guffawed. Which caused Prudence to lift her head from her hands, brush her hair back from her face and look with swollen, reddened eyes at the Doctor. He had seen her through chicken pox, measles, mumps, and puberty. Her body shook again. "Please," she pleaded weakly, "please remove it, and then put me to sleep – *forever.*"

The Doctor picked up the instruction booklet and then touched the Developer – gently. "Prudence," he asked, "why in Heaven's name would you want this thing. You don't need any developing."

"To take Sam's eyes from that – that – bosomy Kathrine, who Sam likes so much," she whispered.

"Bosh," retorted Dr. Fisher, tugging at the Developer, trying the handle, but only evincing winces of pain from the girl. "Prudence, you are prettier and cuter and smarter and lovelier than that Katherine, whoever she is, will ever be."

"*He* doesn't think so," she whimpered, pointing at the bedroom door. "And after this he'll – he'll – never speak to me again."

"He will, Prudence, if you want him to."

Prudence made no reply. Instinctively she knew that the Doctor knew – that she didn't really love Sam.

Exasperated with his failure to remove the Developer, Dr. Fisher motioned Prudence to stand behind the door as he opened it and asked for Rusty.

"Here I am," said the red-haired lad right below him, for Rusty had edged through the crowd to the door and was looking through the keyhole. Dr. Fisher looked down upon him, and saw the hatchet in Rusty's hand.

"Give the hatchet to me," he ordered, reaching for it.

The boy quickly swung his hand with the hatchet behind his back. "No. I go where the hatchet goes."

"Rusty," came Judge Snowden's authoritative voice. "Give the Doctor the hatchet."

"No."

"Rusty," Madeline commanded in her best school teacher's tone.

The boy spread his feet apart and molded a grim visage into his freckled face. "I go where the hatchet goes."

Dr. Fisher sighed. "Very well, Rusty. You may come in, too." Prudence shrieked again when she saw her brother entering the room.

This bothered Rusty not a bit. He pointed to the Developer. "What is that thing?" he asked.

"Never you mind," replied Doctor Fisher. "Prudence, kneel down by this chair and place the cylinder across the seat."

"Oh, a Bust Developer," commented the boy, picking up the box. "What's a bust?"

Dr. Fisher and Prudence ignored Rusty's question. The physician made sure Prudence and the Developer were positioned correctly. "Now, Rusty," he commanded, "hit the cylinder with your hatchet. Hit it with all your might."

"Okay. If you say so," Rusty replied, spitting into his palms, rubbing them together, then grasping the hatchet like a medieval executioner.

"One, two, THREEEEEEEE," the lad yelled. Down came the hatchet onto the metal cylinder. Metal sounded upon metal, then there was the 'pssssssssssssss' of escaping air. Plop! The Developer let go of Prudence's tender young left breast and clattered to the floor. Rusty's eyes grew wide. "Gosh, you're big up there," he said as Prudence clasped a hand over her freed appendage, albeit with a wince showing the pain.

Dear Dr. Fisher, a small-town general practitioner, gazed with the love of an aging patriarch at the distressed young girl beside him. He ordered Rusty out of the room, slammed the door, and then ordered Prudence to bed. He gave her a sedative and waited until she was asleep. Upon leaving the bedroom he found the upstairs hallway deserted, people, he mused, already having enough to keep tongues wagging into next year. Downstairs was Judge Philip Snowden, Emily his wife, and Madeline. Emily was squeezing a tear-sodden handkerchief; the maiden aunt sat prim and erect. Sam had retrieved his bouquet and left, as had the Parson, quoting pertinent Scripture on the way out. Rusty could be heard playing outside, in the gloaming.

Just what the Doctor said to the Judge, and Emily, and Madeline, is not known, but it had something to do with youth, and understanding, and had very little to do with the care of the bust.

### III

Prudence, standing to the side and a little behind her parents and Madeline on the railroad station platform at St. Paul, could hardly believe the terrible thing that had happened to her just yesterday afternoon. And, oh my! *Was* she glad she with her family left Elm Grove this morning. It didn't even bother her that Sam Ericson had failed to come down to the railroad station to see her off. In her heart, she knew it was over. She had lost Sam.

Now they were in St. Paul awaiting the Northern Pacific's Yellowstone Special. Prudence Mehitabel Snowden, nineteen going on twenty, humiliated and lonely and forlorn – and a little sore in a delicate place – stifled a sob. "I hope I *never* return to Elm Grove," she said to herself. "I am so miserable." Conversation came stilted and awkward with Daddy and Mother and Madeline. Would they ever forgive her? Truth was, they had forgiven her, but Prudence's feeling of guilt would not allow her to accept their absolution.

Just ahead of her on the platform, standing by the Judge, was Emily, Prudence's mother. She was feeling a little more rested now, but there had been all the arrangements before leaving Elm Grove, and Prudence's terrible shame – and then there was Rusty. Emily glanced down at the fruit of her womb, standing in front of the group, scanning the other passengers awaiting the conductor's "all aboard". Rusty was wearing high-topped shoes and black cotton stockings, which were badly twisted and wrinkled. Above them he was dressed in tan knickers and a coat to match; underneath the coat was a white blouse. She had also purchased him a straw hat, but she had not seen it for several hours. Because he did not like it, she surmised that he had probably left it on the Chicago train. If she asked him about it, she knew what he would say. "I forgot, Mother." "I forgot," she mused. Those were Rusty's favorite words these days, always said with the devil dancing in his brown eyes. Emily sighed. Prudence and Rusty: would she ever get her children raised successfully?

Then Emily looked up at her husband Philip by her side. He was, she reflected, still handsome even though he had to watch his diet. True, Philip was no longer the slim young man she had married, his hair was graying at the temples below his straw hat, and he smoked those smelly cigars. But his fine features, his sparkling blue eyes, his disarming smile, and his – Emily hesitated even though her thoughts were all to herself – disarmingly affectionate ways with her made her love him just as much or more than when they had first married.

After all, Emily reflected, Philip was not the only one who had lost a youthful physique. She no longer sported quite the figure she had at twenty-one. Her hips were fuller, nor was her waist as waspish as it had once been. But worst of all, what with raising two children, and church activities and the Parent Teachers Association, she had recently discovered herself accepting the coming of middle age as if it represented the end of physical and sexual joy. One night a week or two ago, when Philip had shown interest which she, tired from some church affair, could not reciprocate, she had said, "Oh, Philip. Physical love is for the young!"

Philip was both hurt and shocked. "I don't feel that old," he had grumbled.

"Shhhhhhhh, Prudence is in her room."

"Hell, Emily. You're only forty and I'm just forty-five. What—"

"Please, Philip."

Philip had turned away from her, and eventually slept. But Emily had laid awake unhappy. How, she asked herself, could she have said such a thing? Treated her Philip so? She was glad they were vacationing soon. She needed a change.

Her reflections were cut short by overhearing Rusty's conversation with Madeline. The boy was pointing to an old switch engine across the yards. "Why," he asked her for the third time, "do they call that smokestack a Jenny Lind?"

"For the same reason," Madeline replied curtly, "that they call the old headlight a Cyclops. They just do."

Emily waited, amused, to see if Madeline's reply would satisfy Rusty. All the while the sun was setting and the lights of St. Paul were coming on. Finally, down the tracks, came the Yellowstone Special, its bright black engine emitting steam and conveying power just barely suppressed. It squealed to a stop ahead of the concourse. The Pullman Palace cars, windows cleaned and sparkling, seats inside dimly flooded by the yellow overhead lights, awaited occupants. Black porters hustled up and down the aisles. Unhappy Prudence gazed blankly at the Pullman in front of her, the General Mead. A porter stood by the car steps while luggage was piled to the side. Still the crowd awaited the 'All Aboard'.

"I'll bet I know why it's called a Jenny Lind," Rusty piped up. "Because it's big at the top, just like Jenny Lind."

"Hush, Rusty," said Madeline. "You don't even know who Jenny Lind was."

"She was a girl. I know that. And *all* girls are big at the top," Rusty added authoritatively. "Sis's is *huge—*"

Madeline's gloved hand swatted Rusty across the mouth. Prudence, within hearing distance, turned crimson while great tears welled in her blue eyes.

Philip, who had overheard the exchange, removed his cigar. "Rusty," he said to Emily, "needs a bit of the Old West."

"Or his mouth washed out with soap."

But Rusty's young mind had already left that subject and was geared to something else. "Know what I'm going to get in Yellowstone, Dad? I'm going to get the biggest elk antlers in the USA."

"What for, son?"

"For our clubhouse, that's what for."

"What if the elk doesn't want to give up the antlers?"

"I've got a secret weapon in my luggage. Don't worry, Dad. I'll get my antlers. I promised the fellers I would." Rusty folded his arms convincingly, confidently. "I'm going to get 'em, all right. Just you wait and see."

"And I'll bet he does," Emily agreed. "I feel sorry for the elk population of Yellowstone Park."

From down the concourse they heard sounds of someone running, and a voice full of English long a's.

"I'm heauh. I'm heauh. You may staht the train now. I'm heauh."

Philip removed his cigar from his mouth. "So that's what's been holding us up," he commented, sizing up the running figure as it came closer. It became a young man wearing a black bowler, gray English tweed suit with knickerbocker trousers, black shoes, and gray spats. The young man carried an umbrella. He was at least six feet tall, under thirty years of age, Philip guessed – perhaps not much over twenty-five – and when the wind tilted back the bowler, it revealed a fine growth of dark hair. The young Englishman's features were finely chiseled and his complexion, though flushed from exertion, was clear.

"Ahhhh, the General Mead," he gasped. "Heah it is. Well, let us be aboard." The young man climbed the steps as the porter bowed to him. "Howdy, Lord Billner. We was afraid you wouldn't make it."

"Never mind, Willie. I'll make it. I always make it. Have to look after the ranch, you know. Haying season's coming on."

"Yes, suh. Oh, suh, your luggage is already aboard. You have berth 10A."

"Thank you, Willie," replied the young Englishman as he disappeared into the vestibule. Just then the conductor shouted, "All Aboard" and passengers lined up to present their tickets and enter the car. When Philip's turn came, he asked, "Why the preferential treatment for this Lord What's-his-name?"

The conductor punched their tickets. "Just a young man with connections, I guess."

"Harrumph."

Emily, Madeline, and Philip may have observed the young man and his Very Important Person treatment with disgust, but Prudence, who had also watched it all, displayed a different emotion. The young man had looked so – so clean cut, so handsome, so – civilized. Her misery momentarily departed. She began dreaming of that handsome young man, hoping to get a chance to meet him.

With Rusty leading the way down the aisle of the General Mead, the Snowden family searched for their berths – 16 for Rusty, 17 for Prudence, 18 for Emily and Philip, and 19 for Madeline. Rusty sat nearest the window, of course, with Prudence beside him by the aisle. Philip gave Emily the window seat. Madeline had to sit alone in seat 19. She sat primly, apprehensively, awaiting a stranger to occupy seat number 20, next to her. But no one came. Soon the luggage was stored, other passengers entered the car – a plump middle-aged overweight man, obviously a "drummer"; a well-dressed family with two little girls and a baby; a shy young couple, probably honeymooners; and finally (as the Snowdens soon learned), a portly stentorian-voiced Congressman from Louisiana, albeit with a friendly, intelligent face, and his plump and fortyish wife named Dolly. The latter couple would subsequently invite themselves to accompany the Snowdens around the Park.

Missing was the young Englishman. Apparently he had walked through the car and out the back door. Prudence wondered what could have happened to him.

From outside they heard the conductor's last muffled call, "Aboard", and the first metallic jerks of Northern Pacific's Yellowstone Special signified the beginning of the journey to America's Wonderland. A "butcher" – the name given to hawkers on trains – came through selling magazines, candies, fruit and sandwiches. Prudence bought Rusty an apple to keep him busy and quiet. Soon the outskirts of St. Paul were whizzing by at twenty-five miles an hour.

"Oh, Emily," sighed Philip, removing his straw hat, dropping his head back upon the seat and closing his eyes. "How I need this vacation."

Emily turned from the window and cast a warm glance at Philip. She placed a hand on his. "I know how hard you've worked for the children and me," she said quietly. "I'm so happy that we are all together. Until the train started, I was afraid a telegram might catch up with you calling you back to the office."

Philip tilted his head toward her and opened his eyes. "You know, Emily," he said, "we've been too busy. Too shamefully busy for each other." With her hand still resting on his, he moved his own hand over so that it rested on her skirt, where she felt a little squeeze on her thigh. "Yes, Philip, I know," she replied quietly.

They heard the throaty toot of the whistle up ahead. As the August day gave way to night on the northern prairie, and the conductor came through to check tickets, the dark, flat farmlands of Minnesota faded to black nothingness outside the windows. Yellowstone lay ahead two nights and a long day. Yellowstone!

Prudence noticed that Rusty had gone to sleep. She awaited another glimpse of the young Englishman who had so mysteriously disappeared. But he failed to appear, and later she noticed that his berth was unoccupied when they retired for the night.

Madeline Snowden sat straight as a ramrod in seat number 19. Without it registering on her mind, she had watched the last golden rays of the sun give way to dusk; now she stared into the black nothingness outside the window. The change did not bolster her spirits. The fact was, Madeline Snowden was in a blue funk. Prudence's misery, she thought, was nothing compared to hers. The difference was that through the years she had learned to hide her feelings well, while Prudence's were written all over her young face.

Madeline breathed deeply, and sighed, and let herself collapse. Her whole straight-as-a-ramrod spinster school teacher thin-lipped self slipped down into the corner of the seat nearest the window. Beneath the little veil that fell from her hat the hard lines of age thirty relaxed, and her eyes – the hard, dark eyes that could sight a peashooter hidden up a dirty sleeve from thirty paces – closed momentarily. When they reopened they were soft and misty, gazing vacantly into the black morass outside.

"I shouldn't feel this way," she soliloquized bitterly. "I've had two month's rest from school, had a job at the Carnegie Library that enabled me to pay my own fare to Yellowstone. And school doesn't start for another three weeks." Madeline, who was a three-quarter size woman with figure dimensions identical to what they had been a decade ago, nevertheless bit her lips and nodded her aristocratic head back and forth to fight back the tears. She found spinsterhood a hard trail to follow.

"I'm really lucky," she argued to herself. The wheels below the car clickety-clacked, and, she repeated, "I'm really lucky, I'm really lucky, I'm really lucky" in cadence. Then the train sped up after passing through a town and she tried saying "lucky, lucky, lucky" until the wheels sped too fast. She placed a small gloved fist to her mouth and bit her knuckles through the leather to stifle a sob. She breathed deeply again, her prim little figure shook briefly, and then she regained her composure.

"I *am* lucky," she told herself again, this time with more reassurance. After all, her dear brother Philip had saved her from all the terrible shame illegitimacy would have brought her and her parents, had paid for her residence and confinement at a home for unwed mothers in Chicago, and had even arranged, and paid her way, to Normal School. True, by her sophomore year Emily was substantially working her way through college, but whenever she was short of funds, Philip was as close as a telegram. And it was Philip, dear Philip, who had helped her land the English teacher's position at Elm Grove High, and had even invited her to board at his and Emily's house.

"Madeline," Philip informed her in Emily's presence when she moved in with them, "your past is hereby forgotten. It will never be mentioned, never hinted at, never be remembered. It is erased."

And it had worked out that way. The Snowden home under Emily's supervision was a haven of love, relaxation, and comfort. And Elm Grove accepted the prim and correct little three-quarter-size spinster, who in spite of recurrent "ain'ts" and "don'ts" from her former students, was an immediate success.

What bothered Madeline was the destruction of all her dreams, the ever-recurring necessity of reconstructing her life as a spinster school teacher. Truth was, she had become so standoffish that men did not approach her. Sometimes she became so embittered that she buried her head in her pillow in her bedroom – her lone place of privacy, such as it was – and stifled the sobs that shook her frame. Then she pulled herself together, bathed, dusted her person with lavender talc, stepped into that 1909 version of the Iron Maiden, the woman's corset; slipped into a brown or black high-necked dress, buttoned her black shoes, fixed every last brown hair in her head and, standing primly erect, entered the world, hiding from everyone the truth of her past.

When the Snowdens – Philip, Emily, Prudence, Rusty, and Madeline – returned from the diner the bunks had been made. Madeline was relieved to be the first to crawl into the cozy bed and let the clickety-clack of the rails put her, finally, to sleep.

By the next afternoon the Snowdens were showing signs of relaxation and boredom. They had passed the great bonanza wheat farms of the Red River Valley and were chugging across the prairies of Minnesota, North Dakota and Montana. The large towns – Moorhead, Fargo, Jamestown, Bismarck, Glendive, Miles City – and small ones too numerous to mention, all looked alike with their drab false fronts facing a main street that sometimes paralleled the tracks, and sometimes headed due north at right angles. Men sporting Stetsons, flannel shirts, denim trousers, and heavy boots lounged on the station platforms. It was consistently drab. Philip dozed while Emily read a book. Prudence toyed with magazines, keeping one eye alert for any signs of the young Englishman. He had slept in his berth, she knew, because she saw the porter taking linens from it that morning. But the young man was not to be seen. Rusty swatted flies, asked about dinner, walked up and down the aisle, and pestered everyone with ridiculous questions.

Eventually the sun lowered on the western horizon and a white-coated black boy came through the cars announcing dinner. The Snowdens dined, lounged, and retired as soon as the berths were made. Tomorrow they would be in the Park.

## Chapter Two

# The First Day

## I

Emily hardly noticed the sign hanging from the railroad station:

LIVINGSTON, MONTANA

ELEVATION: 4,490 FEET          POPULATION: 5,359

The town was in a glorious setting, especially appreciated after the miles and miles of prairies they had crossed. The mountains were in bluish hues. Above them was the enormous Montana sky. Not far off the Yellowstone River ran placidly through the town. An impression of excessive fertility permeated the land, as becomes the flora during the high-altitude, short growing season.

Livingston's civilized face – if one could call it that – was of false fronts, dance halls, saloons, and tough-looking characters, both male and female. Prudence, Emily, and Madeline instinctively clustered close to Philip; only Rusty took in the scene with gusto. He was fascinated by the drovers, hitching up whinnying horses and braying mules, all accompanied by the most majestic swearing Rusty had ever heard. Bearded miners tromped across wooden sidewalks in heavy, dirty boots and shabby clothes. Small wonder that Rusty was inclined to stray while the family waited on the station platform, along with many others, for the narrow-gauge Park Branch train to steam up, load up, and carry the tourists to Wonderland.

Prudence by now had regained much of her zest for life. Some of the bloom had returned to her cheeks, for it was clear that the Bust Developer would never be discussed; it was a non-event. She regretted that the young Englishman had never shown his face, but, she observed, there were other handsome young men. Now her eyes were fixed on one particular two-story structure, badly needing a coat of paint. An old wooden sign stuck out above the swinging doors: The Bucket of Blood. Her attention had first been drawn to it by the brassy notes of a new song, 'Pony Boy', which wafted over the air from the entrance, even though it was just eleven o'clock in the morning. She readily identified the establishment as a saloon, but her innocence prompted consternation about what was on the second floor. None of the windows had lawyers', doctors', or dentists' signs. Nor did anything say it was a hotel. What was it?

Suddenly loud noises came from the second story, then a scream, then unladylike oaths from a female voice. Glass tinkled. A hairbrush crashed through a window pane as the shade shot up and flapped round and round, on its roller. A coarse male voice pleaded between the female expletives:

Female: "You stinkin', lecherous..."

Male: "Rosie – I'm a-goin', Rosie – don't throw that pitcher!"

Another crash. What was once white crockery flew through the broken window onto the wooden walk below, where it shattered. Sounds followed: a slamming door, shrieks fading into the depths of the building, a crescendo of noises from the back of the first-floor saloon, the stomping of booted feet, the notes of 'Pony Boy', the doors swinging open – fast – and the appearance of a grizzled, gray-haired man. He wore heavy woolen trousers, a faded blue flannel shirt, a sheepskin coat – hardly necessary in August – and a stained old campaign hat pushed airily to the back of his head. He also possessed a straggly beard.

He was six or eight feet beyond the doors, across the wooden walk and into the street when the saloon doors swung open again. Straddling the doorway was a mass of female utilitarianism – of the most fundamental kind. She must have weighed 175 pounds stripped, and nearly stripped she was. Half of her peroxide-blond hair fell down her back and half down her face – a face with a red, sensuous mouth, a prominent nose with flaring nostrils, pinched eyebrows, and wrinkles coming through a thick coating of powder and rouge. Rayon bloomers and a corset of which too much was demanded made up most of the rest of her. This was Rosie O'Toole, madam and bouncer as well as owner-manager of The Bucket of Blood.

It happened so quickly! Emily grabbed Rusty and turned his face away – again and again. The judge nearly swallowed his cigar.

Madeline, who had raised her parasol for protection from the bright sun, lowered it in front of her eyes. Prudence's jaw dropped, and her shapely mouth opened wide. So did her eyes. She stared, raised a hand to her mouth, and stared on.

It was all over in a few seconds. Madam Rosie, oblivious of the waiting trainload of people, delivered final expletives. A girl inside the saloon handed her an old carpetbag, which she sent sailing over the poor fellow's head, almost to the station platform.

"Awwwwww, Rosie," the cowed man began, turning to her, but when Madam raised her bare arm, strong as the Arm and Hammer trademark, he ceased his supplications. With a futile, "Thank ye for me bag, Rosie," he walked to it, picked it up, and continued to the station. Rosie disappeared into The Bucket of Blood. 'Pony Boy's' strains were beginning all over again.

"Mother," Rusty began. "Did you see *that—*"

"Hush, Rusty," Emily whispered, covering his mouth with her gloved hands.

Madeline raised her parasol again and looked composed and demure as if nothing had happened – but was there a trace of a smile on her face? Prudence dropped her hand and cast her eyes downward. Others on the platform coughed nervously, blushed, or commented to their spouses in hushed tones. Only Philip, standing beside his prim wife, seemed upset. He wanted to laugh, he wanted to roar, but he knew he shouldn't. His body shook and he began to chuckle. "Philip. Philip!" fussed Emily. "Control yourself."

Judge Snowden did his best.

They heard the whistle. Far down the tracks came the narrow-gauge train that was to take them from Livingston to Gardiner, at the Park entrance. Passengers, between one and two hundred of them, became active, picking up or otherwise shepherding their luggage and their loved ones. The grizzled recipient of Rosie's wrath emerged from the waiting room, ticket in one hand, carpetbag in the other. Looking at his ticket and not checking where he was going, he ran into Philip's back, hitting him so hard that the cigar popped out of the Judge's mouth onto the platform. Philip whirled around in wrath, but the mountaineer held up his hands to calm him down. "Beg pardon, Colonel," he said politely, bowing low and sweeping his campaign hat like a cavalier. "Hezekiah Hotchkiss at your service, sir." He reached inside his dirty sheepskin coat and drew forth a piece of hard paper. "My card, sir," he added, handing it to Philip.

Philip, flustered, read the card: "Hezekiah Hotchkiss: Stage Driver: Yellowstone Park Company."

"Be mighty obliged if you asked for me to be your coachman for the Park tour, Colonel." Hezekiah noticed Philip's disapproving analysis of his person. "Er – don't mind these clothes, sir. I've been up at Emigrant – that's a little town near here – looking over some of my mining property. I'm well-dressed when I'm on duty, ye can bet. When ye get to Mammoth Hot Springs, sir, just tell the clerk that I'm to be your coachman."

"Yes. Yes, well, possibly," Philip began. Then he felt a gentle kick from Emily. He recalled that Hezekiah had just emerged from The Bucket of Blood. Hezekiah sensed the silent interchange between husband and wife. "I got several things in my favor, General. More than twenty years in the Park. I know of geysers and hot springs and wonders that none of the tourists 'cept mine ever see, and – " his eyes narrowed and he looked Philip straight in the eyes, " – and the ability to obtain certain, er, commodities not ordinarily found in the Park. You know," he added, lowering his voice, "the Park is dry. Yes, sir. Nary a drop of *joie de vivre* sold there, 'cept in the hotel dining rooms. No saloons."

The Park Line train had puffed up to the station and the conductor shouted his "All Aboard". Tourists gripped their luggage more tightly and held onto their protesting progeny with grim determination.

"We'll – consider it," Philip replied, moving towards the train.

"Thank you, sir," replied Hezekiah.

Rusty had been looking up at the grizzled character, whom he instinctively liked. "Say, mister, why did your wife kick you out?" he asked. Emily uttered a hasty "Hush."

"And why didn't she have more clothes on?" shouted the lad before that gloved hand, which he was becoming well acquainted with, clamped over his mouth again. Emily sighed, looking to Philip for support. "This wild country," she said. "You saw! And so did Rusty. And Prudence. I declare, Philip, if there was a train bound for home, I'd climb aboard it right now!"

"Now, now, Emily," Philip reassured her as he dropped his new cigar to the platform and stomped on it. "Yellowstone won't be like this. It's a beautiful morning and the scenery is magnificent. Let's enjoy ourselves."

Emily raised an eyebrow and looked devilishly at her husband. With Rosie O'Toole in mind, she asked: "What kind of scenery are you referring to, sir?" As she took the first step into the car she let out a little shriek and her hand darted to a just-pinched hip. She whirled around and looked into the oh-so-innocent face of her husband. "*Philip!*" she whispered.

"Eh? What dear?"

A Mona Lisa smile appeared on Emily's face. She guessed she was not angry. She noticed his clear blue eyes and the trace of a twinkle. "I'll get even with you later, Judge Philip Snowden," she warned. She felt the support of his hands on her waist as he helped her climb the steps. The message spouse to spouse was clear.

Theirs was the last car, and save for the Snowdens, it was vacant. Madeline and Prudence chose to sit on one side, Emily and Philip across the aisle, and Rusty, without permission, sauntered to the rear platform. The conductor had shouted his last "All Aboard" and the train had started when, from the distance, Prudence heard, "Wait. I say, wait theuh. Wait for me!"

"Hey, Prudence," yelled Rusty. "Look at that man trying to catch the train. It's that Englishman we saw in St. Paul."

Prudence's heart skipped a beat. 'The handsome young Englishman,' she thought. 'The one who never showed his face after St. Paul.' Impetuously she hurried to the back of the car. Framed in the doorway, running along the tracks as fast as his legs could carry him, was the same Lord Billner who had kept the train waiting earlier. He was wearing the same tweed suit, black bowler (now askew on his head – it would have fallen off if one hand hadn't held it there), and black shiny shoes with gray spats. With his other hand he was swinging a Gladstone bag.

"Here comes the bag," he shouted. With a great sweep of his arm he threw it so that it flew over the railing onto the platform and would have struck Prudence had she not stepped aside. It landed with a plop and burst open, spilling out extra shirts, drawers, a velvet dressing gown, a deck of cards, a half-empty fifth of White Horse Scotch whiskey which rolled glug-glug-glug to Prudence's toes, and a French postcard.

"Now give me a hand heauh," the running figure shouted between breaths. Now close enough to the platform, he leaped for the railing, grasped it firmly, squirmed around to the side steps, then slipped. Prudence was there offering him a helping hand. In desperation he grabbed it with his one free hand, regained his balance, struggled up the stairs and sprawled spread-eagled safe, halfway on the platform, halfway on the steps. He released his hold on Prudence's hand. She leaned over to pick up his bowler, which was rolling to the other side of the platform. The young man raised up on his elbows and breathed a sigh of relief. His line of vision embraced Prudence's well turned ankle; as he raised his eyes he observed a tight hobble skirt which covered a most curvaceous derriere.

Rusty emerged from the doorway holding the bottle of White Horse. "You hurt, mister?" he asked. "Maybe a slug of booze will help you."

"Rusty," scolded Prudence, handing the hat to the young man who was getting up now, and brushing his clothing.

He ignored Rusty as he looked at the girl who had helped him onto the car. "My special thanks to you, Miss – Miss –"

"Prudence Snowden," replied the girl. Then words left her as she appraised the young man standing in front of her. She could not help herself. This young Englishman, the very one who had nearly missed the train in St. Paul, was the handsomest man she had ever seen. His soft dark hair, high forehead, straight strong nose, clear ruddy cheeks, and firm chin gave him an aristocratic appearance that was most uncommon among the swains of Elm Grove. His eyes danced with life. They had already caught her own sky-blue counterparts. The two gazed, bewitched, into each other's eyes. Prudence's heart skipped some beats. So handsome!

As for Lord Billner's impression of this blond beauty – when he gazed into her eyes the Devil met its nemesis. All hell-raising would cease if he could but have this beautiful creature by his side. Soft golden tresses underneath that huge vintage 1909 millinery, complexion smooth as new fallen snow, pert little nose, puckered lips succulent as ripe cherries, white, even, sparkling teeth exposed when she smiled, and the cutest little form—

Rusty pulled on the gentleman's coat. "Hey, you want some hooch?"

"Oh – er – no thank you, my boy," he replied absent-mindedly, still looking at Prudence. "Your name again, Miss?"

Prudence broke her trance, lowered her eyes and blushed. "Prudence Snowden, sir," she repeated. "And yours?"

The young man bowed low, nearly losing his balance. "Billner is the name. Stephen L. Billner. Around heauh, I'm known as Lord Billner." He swept his hand toward the doorway. "Shall we enter the cah?"

In the middle of the aisle was Rusty repacking the Gladstone. He held up a pair of red flannel drawers. "Gese. You wear these in summer?"

"Rusty!"

"Ohhhhhhh, sis."

"Your brother?" Prudence's affirmative nod led Lord Billner to take a quarter from a pocket. "Here's a quarter, young man. Be sure you pack everything carefully. Be sure to cushion the spirits."

"Yes, sir."

"And now, Miss Snowden," said the Englishman while offering her his arm, "shall we choose a seat and sit down?" Flustered, feeling the eyes of Mother, Father, and Madeline Snowden upon her like guests turning to appraise a bride walking down the aisle, Prudence nevertheless gave her arm to Lord Billner. The two strode with great dignity to a seat conveniently behind and out of hearing distance of the rest of the family – save for Rusty. He was fascinated by a French post card. It had some cancan girls kicking and showing their unmentionables. He contemplated borrowing it for a few days.

Lord Billner graciously offered Prudence the window seat. She sat down gracefully but kept her back straight and her shoulders back so that Lord Billner could imagine her wasp waist and the swelling of her young bosom. Not knowing what to say, she directed her eyes out the window. There was the panorama of the mountains and Paradise Valley, and the Yellowstone River flowing between hayfields freshly mowed. Even the air inside the coach smelled of the new-mown hay. Occasionally a ranch building passed across her line of vision, and cattle and horses grazed. Prudence's heart was beating fast: one fist kept crushing and uncrushing a small, lightly perfumed handkerchief. She felt she should say something, but what? Finally she turned to the young man and blurted, "Aren't you the same person that –" but at the very instant he turned to her and blurted, "I say, where are you from?" Their eyes met again, and they both laughed.

"You speak," said Prudence.

"No. Ladies first."

"Didn't you – just barely make the train at St. Paul?"

"Why, ah, yes. Yes."

"Do you make a habit of catching trains – just barely?"

"Not usually."

"You did catch it, though, didn't you? At St. Paul. The train?"

"Oh, yes. Oh, my, yes. Better that I hadn't, I venture."

"Then – where were you all the way from St. Paul to Livingston? We saw you enter the car and then you just disappeared."

"Well, I was, ahh, in conference, shall we say? In a cah up front."

Prudence's blue eyes opened wide. "What kind of conference? Are you a diplomat? Or a railroad president? I noticed that they kept the train waiting for you at St. Paul."

"Me, a diplomat?" Lord Billner threw back his head and laughed. He slapped his knees. "That's good. That's rare. Oh, deauh, no. My fathah would have liked that. But – such a life is not for me."

"Oh," Prudence replied softly. She looked down in her lap at the crushed handkerchief. She pouted.

"If you must know, Miss Snowden," Lord Billner added hastily, noticing that he had humiliated her, "my conference was with three sporting acquaintances in the baggage cah. Our business was stud poker. And as usual, I was reminded that I am a poor gambler. I lost all my remittance, save for a small sum I always keep for emergencies. My, my. I do wish I had missed the train at St. Paul. But then," he paused and then said softly, "I wouldn't have met you."

Prudence pretended not to hear. "You mean," she exclaimed, "you *gambled* for two nights and a day?"

"Oh, I climbed into my bunk for a few hours each night," he explained, "but I got up and went back to – er – work very early each morning. We had our meals brought to us."

A tingle signaling danger and adventure crept up Prudence's back. A worldly young Englishman who plays cards for two days and nights at a time!

Just then Lord Billner leaned across her and scanned the scene outside. "We should be passing my ranch in a few minutes," he said.

"Your ranch?" Prudence asked, surprised. "You own a ranch in this beautiful country?"

He nodded affirmatively. "You like this country?" he queried. "I do too. So wild and yet so serene." He breathed deeply as if relishing the fresh mountain air, but what he really savored was the faint perfume exuding from the lovely female.

"You *really* own a ranch?"

"Oh, yes. The Double Bar B. A nice spread of several thousand acres. It has good water and lots of good hay land. A hundred acres less than it originally had, but it's still a good spread."

"What happened to the hundred acres?" asked Prudence.

"I lost them in a horse race," he replied. "What a horse race!"

"You didn't bet your land on a horse race!" said Prudence with profound disapproval. "How terrible!"

The young man nodded his head in pseudo-mortification.

"Afraid so, Miss Snowden. It was the silliest of all horse races. It was sundown, we were through haying, we started for the ranch house and next thing you know we were neck and neck and going faster and faster. 'Bet you the meadow I can beat you,' my friend said. Of course I accepted the challenge and there we were galloping fast as we could. It must have been a funny sight."

"Why so funny?"

"Why, you see, Miss Prudence – may I call you Miss Prudence? – the horses were still hitched to the hay rakes. I can hear the clatter of those old machines even now. Bang onto the ground, scrape, scrape, scrape, then up, then down, bang, bang! You should have seen the hay rakes when we finished. Completely wrecked. Completely!"

Prudence turned to Lord Billner with anger written all over her face. "That was a terrible thing to do. Inexcusable. Both of you should have been ashamed of yourselves." Like lightning the thought flitted through her mind that possibly Lord Billner was not such a catch after all. "I hope your father punished you severely for doing such a foolish thing."

"My fathah," Lord Billner leaned back and laughed – but it sounded to Prudence like a forced laugh. "My fathah couldn't have caahed less. Just so long as I stay out of England, he caahes not."

"Your father doesn't care?"

"Oh, yes, I suppose so. He sends me a remittance every three months. It is plenty to live on. My only obligations are to stay out of

England and collect my quarterly remittance at the Livingston Post Office. If I return to England, he cuts me off; if I fail to pick up my remittance at the Livingston Post Office every three months, then I am considered either dead or self-supporting. Either way I will be cut off. Jolly interesting set-up."

Prudence was puzzled, so puzzled that her stress at meeting this handsome stranger had disappeared. In Prudence's steel-trap mind she had decided that he *was* worth saving, and she could be the savior of this handsome lost soul. To marry him and reform him and for him to love her dearly all the rest of the days of her life had already entered Prudence's plans, like a daydream, only here he was, real flesh and blood, next to her, real, real, *real*.

"You mean, if you return to England, or if you fail to pick up your remittance at the post office—?"

"Just – poof!" Lord Billner snapped his fingers. "Fathah cuts me off like that, and leaves me in this cruel world to fend for myself." He feigned a shudder. "Of course, I would still have the ranch."

"But—"

"Look over theauh," he interrupted. "See that little white frame house nestled among the cottonwoods? That's the Double Bar B ranch house. There's the corral, and the brook running down from the mountains."

Lord Billner relaxed in his seat as the ranch house passed by. He found himself speaking so matter-of-factly to this lovely mid-western American girl – and she was so charming – and so pretty! Within minutes he knew her age, her home town, her schooling, and all about her father and mother, who were sitting up ahead casting so many glances in his direction. He knew that Madeline was the maiden aunt. He already knew Rusty. He was gratified to discover that Prudence's favorite subject in school had been English literature, that she liked to ride horseback, and, most important, that she was unattached. He liked her smile, her eyes, her rippling laughter. As for Prudence – Elm Grove, Sam Ericson, and Bust Developers were forgotten.

The reaction of Prudence's next of kin was something else. Emily expressed, concern. "Do you approve of Prudence so boldly striking up an acquaintance with that young stranger who nearly missed the train – twice?" she asked Philip.

Philip was rather amused, hardly concerned. "It *was* rather bold, I suppose, for Prudence to help him aboard," Philip conceded. "I presume you would have preferred, my dear, to have let him miss the train? Fall on a steel rail and die of a concussion?"

"No. I suppose not. But – " words failed her. "Anyway," Emily finally said, "he is a handsome young man. He doesn't look – bad."

"He's an Englishman," Rusty interrupted, sticking his head between his parents from the seat behind them. "He drinks booze and gambles and likes pretty girls."

Philip turned, scowling. "How do you know all that, Rusty?"

"Easy. There was a bottle in the bag, and it was half empty, so he drinks. There was a deck of cards, so he gambles. And there was—"

"Yes. Go on."

"Nothin'."

"Then how do you know he likes pretty girls?"

Rusty patted the French post card in his back pocket. He mustn't mention that. "Because he's talking to Prudence."

Emily darted a glance to the back of the car where Prudence and Lord Billner were sitting, engrossed in conversation. "Look at her laughing, Philip. (But don't let them see you looking.) What do you think they're talking about? I hope he's a gentleman."

"He's a Lord," said Rusty. "An English Lord, whatever that is. He owns a ranch. And he gets a remittance from England. Dad, what a remittance?"

"Hmmmmmmmmmmm. So that's it," mused Philip. "A British remittance man. I wonder what he did to get himself sent away."

"Something bad?" Emily asked, timidly.

"Perhaps. Or maybe just a second son who couldn't make it into the clergy or the armed forces. Such young men from aristocratic British families are often sent out into the world to live out their lives on remittances from home."

Emily cast another quick, evaluatory glance at the young man. She again reflected upon his good looks. "Don't be alarmed, Emily. This is just a little summer flirtation. Prudence won't be out of our sight until we return to Elm Grove," the judge assured her.

"I hope you are right, dear."

"I am."

The journey from Livingston up the Yellowstone Valley to Gardiner, a small settlement whose main street is also the northern Park boundary, was barely two hours. For Prudence they were the happiest and fastest two hours since she had left Elm Grove.

"So you are holidaying the Pahk," Lord Billner commented as he gazed, apparently, across Prudence and out the window – but was really taking in the scenery closer at hand. "Ah, Wonderland, they call it. Where the realities of hell approach the surface of Terra Firma."

"Hmm?"

"How does Milton's Archangel describe it? 'Farewell, happy fields, where joy forever dwells. Hail, horrors! Hail, infernal world...'"

"Heavens, Lord Billner. Is Yellowstone full of such horrors?"

"And fire and brimstone and superheated waters, they tell me, straight from there." He pointed downward.

"They tell you?" she asked. "Haven't you seen Yellowstone?"

"Why – ah – as a matter of fact – no. I've been at the ranch for three years now, but I've never been to the Pahk. And – I've been thinking. That is why I didn't have the train stop near my ranch. Do you know what, Miss Prudence? I have decided that right now is the time for me to tour the Pahk." (If the truth were known, he had been so absorbed with Prudence that he had forgotten to pull the cord and stop the train. But why tell her that?)

"With us?" asked Rusty, who had sauntered down the aisle towards them, encouraged to do so by his mother.

"In the same coach with us?" Prudence blurted out – excitedly. She put a gloved hand to her mouth. Such talk was bold and unladylike, she realized too late. Thank goodness neither Mother nor Madeline had heard her.

"Why, yes," Lord Billner replied, the idea jelling in his mind. "In the same coach with you fine people. Let me see now. My remittance does not have to be picked up until the twentieth at the latest, and today is the tenth. I can make it back to Livingston with time to spare."

"Won't they just hold the remittance for you?" asked Prudence. "Besides, today is not the tenth, it's the—"

"For ten days, yes. Then they will return it marked 'Unclaimed', and then I receive no more remittance. I should have to live off the earnings of the ranch." Lord Billner shuddered. "Horrible thought. But enough of that. This will be fun."

"I'll say, Mr. Lord Billner," Rusty exclaimed. "I've got a secret weapon and I'm going to use it to get some elk antlers. You want to help me?" Rusty did not wait for an answer, but ran up the aisle. "Hey, Dad. Lord Billner's going with us through the Park."

Emily glanced at Philip. "Just a little summer flirtation?"

"Now, now, Emily," replied Philip, contemplating the problems confronting parents with a beautiful virgin-on-the-verge daughter. "Let her have a little romantic fling. She won't be out of our sight and it will help her forget about the Bust Developer."

She sighed. "Well, he *is* clean-cut and young and aristocratic," she commented. "But gambling, and that liquor bottle – he must be awfully – worldly-wise."

"Then he'll have sense enough not to get fresh with our daughter," Philip growled.

The train slowed down for the Gardiner station.

## II

Prudence thought she had never seen so many happy, expectant people in her life. Most of the tourists, like the Snowdens, had spent a minimum of two nights and a day on a train. Now they were at Gardiner, Montana, about to leave the taste of smoke and cinders, and the greasy grime that covered their faces, and work off that stuffy, lethargic feeling in the solar plexus. Spirits had risen perceptibly. The Congressman from Louisiana, Talmadge Beauregard Griffin, had introduced himself to Philip – whom he called the Judge – along with that Southern Solon's syrupy-speaking, well-padded wife Dolly. She smelled heavily of gardenia toilet water and – *could it be?* – bourbon.

"Ah say, suh, this heah is beautiful country, ain't it, though, suh?"

Philip – the Judge – removed his cigar from his mouth, cleared his throat, and agreed, in reward for which the Congressman from Louisiana began talking politics, Louisiana politics, concerning which Philip did not give a damn. Still, the Congressman was a diversion for the Judge. After two nights and a long day with his family, Philip was quite willing to stride up and down the platform with the Honorable Member of Congress. As they chatted, the Judge admired Electric Peak, looming to the southwest; and he tried to get the stiffness out of his legs. Emily he had left with Dolly, the Congressman's wife, which, he reflected, was probably not a very nice thing for him to have done.

Up and down the station concourse was conversation and activity as luggage was unloaded and claimed, and people moved to the side of the station opposite the tracks. A wave of excitement swept over the crowd. "Here they come!" someone shouted. People strained their eyes down the road to observe a cloud of dust and, coming into sight, seven, eight, nine, ten of the biggest tally-ho coaches most of them had ever seen. As they approached, a gasp of admiration surged through the crowd, for each of the yellow vehicles was drawn by three teams of matched horses – great Belgian Percherons and Clydesdales. High on the driver's seat of each tally-ho was a coachman wearing a long white linen duster, a campaign hat, and hands covered with whip-leather gloves holding the reins.

The great coaches clattered to the station entrance. Prudence noticed that the coachmen all sat the same way, on the right side of the seat, not facing straight ahead but at right angles. She heard someone say that such was their normal position, because the drivers kept one foot at all times on the brake pedal. It was located to the right and at the foot of the driver's seat. "Now, now, Mother," she overheard a husband reassuring his wife, "these drivers have taken an oath never to desert their post while a passenger is in the coach, no matter what calamity might befall them." In a tourist brochure Prudence had read that the vehicles held thirty-six passengers, and were used primarily from the station at Gardiner to the great National Hotel at Mammoth Hot Springs. The distance was barely five miles up the Gardner River Canyon.

The crowd divided into groups, each of which assembled by a tally-ho. Men were busy fetching their Excursion tickets. The Snowdens were in the group by the second coach from the front, because Talmadge Beauregard Griffin had been warned in advance of the dust, so that sometimes the last coaches advanced in such a cloud that the passengers could not see, let alone enjoy, the scenery. Just as they were about the climb aboard, Emily asked, "Where's Rusty?"

Where *was* Rusty? The Judge searched the men's room: the Congressman, who with his lady had attached themselves to the Snowden party for no apparent reason, called his name into the empty railroad cars; and Madeline called Rusty up and down the street. No sign.

"Never you mind, sugar, we'll find that naughty little boy of yours," Dolly Talmadge consoled Emily.

The minutes ticked away. Coaches two, three, four, five, six, and seven, filled with laughing, singing, happy humanity, clattered down the road towards Yellowstone; coaches eight and nine were filling fast.

"Have you seen Rusty?" asked Philip of Lord Billner when he emerged from the ticket office with his Excursion tickets. "We can't find him."

Lord Billner scowled a few seconds, then snapped his fingers. "He asked me what was over there," he said, pointing, "and I told him it is the Yellowstone River. I'll bet he's down there."

Indeed, down there he was. Philip's tongue-lashing was lost as the boy pointed to the big trout he saw in a quiet pool. The worst of it was, Lord Billner, Congressman Griffin, and Judge Snowden were suddenly little boys. They asked to see the fish, and Rusty pointed to them. All were fishermen, and all vowed to do some fishing in the Park.

"Hey," said Philip suddenly, "we better get back. The coaches are leaving!" The three men-cum-boys hastened back with Rusty, who was unchastised as his elders contemplated the big trout they would catch in the Park.

Waiting for the stragglers was the last tally-ho. Three women stood patiently by the coach door. Philip caught Emily's sigh of relief when she saw her redheaded son sauntering along with the three men. Prudence sighed too – at the sight of Lord Billner.

Rusty asked of the coachman, "Can I ride up there with you?"

'Sure, laddie. Come on up."

"Oh, no. Don't let him," pleaded Emily, placing a hand on Philip's sleeve as he joined her.

"Oh, Emily, he'll be all right."

"Way up there? What if he falls?"

"You'll hold on tight, won't you, Rusty?"

"Hold on like a bulldog, Dad."

"All right, then. Up you go," said Philip as he swung Rusty up to the driver's seat.

Philip and Emily boarded, then Congressman Griffin and Dolly, and then Prudence, helped gallantly by Lord Billner into the very back seat, where he quickly seated himself beside her. Madeline sat primly alone on another of the wide seats. Then the grizzled veteran first seen leaving The Bucket of Blood, Hezekiah Hotchkiss, appeared from nowhere. He exchanged salutations with the driver and then climbed into still another seat. Philip was about to reach out and swing the door shut when a horse and buggy came dashing up to the station. Out jumped a tall, slim, athletic man, thirty to thirty-five years old, dressed in the uniform of a United States Cavalry officer. "Wait, driver," the soldier shouted in a low, authoritative voice.

"Yes, sir, Captain," replied the coachman who had been about to whip the horses into action.

Madeline had watched the horse and buggy drive up, observed as the passenger paid the hack driver, noted as the – Captain, was he? – fetched a heavy black valise from the buggy and with confident, manly strides approached the tally-ho. Out of the corners of her eyes she watched him appraise the occupants. She gasped and her heart skipped a beat, for the cavalryman entered the tally-ho and seated himself beside her. Why, thought Madeline, with all those empty seats, had he decided to sit next to her?

But then, she thought, what difference does it make? 'He's probably married and has five children,' she told herself as she placed her parasol on the floor, folded her gloved hands in her lap and, breathing deeply, aimed her eyes straight ahead – into the wrinkles of Congressman Griffin's red neck. That in straightening up and breathing deeply she had accentuated her wasp waist and her small but exquisitely molded bosom did not cross her mind – *or did it?*

Meanwhile the coachman yelled a lusty "Giddap" and the heavy coach lurched down the road.

The Captain, whose six feet and more placed him head and shoulders above her, tilted his broad-rimmed campaign hat back on his head, brought forth a fresh white handkerchief and patted his brow – a medium high forehead, Madeline had noticed, slightly wrinkled. This much of him she had caught in a quick glimpse. Now she just *had* to look straight ahead. How dull was Congressman Griffin's red neck!

But if Miss Madeline Snowden, English teacher at Elm Grove, Michigan, felt obligated to look only ahead, the Captain felt no such restraint. Even as he patted his forehead and tightened his boots, he kept his eyes angled so that quick flicks of them surveyed the lady by his side When he examined his boots he noticed her small, black-buttoned walking shoes, her slim ankles showing just a wee bit below her hobble skirt, which was, he observed, tight. It hugged her legs underneath the close-fitting, stylish travel coat she was wearing. He contemplated said appendages and decided that could one see them – her legs – they would still be firm, slim, and smooth. As he tucked in his shirt, which had ballooned a bit in his hurried transfer, he noticed her starched white blouse and the curve of the coat above the waist. The curve hinted at rather haughty and sublime feminine charms there. When he sized up her total profile he paused longer than he should have, so impressed was he with the Dresden-doll lines, the clean-cut parts.

He estimated her age at no more than thirty, decided she was unmarried, probably a school teacher, but still, most attractive. Madeline, aware of the Captain's lingering eyes, began to blush inside her veil; her brown eyes blinked, and she thought she was going to sneeze. Quick as a wink the gentleman-soldier offered her his white handkerchief, but she stifled the sneeze.

"Oh, thank you, sir. I'll not need it," said Madeline, holding her own scented handkerchief to her nose, smiling demurely and relieved to be through with analyzing Congressman Griffin's red neck. "It *is* rather dusty, isn't it?"

The Captain smiled, folded his handkerchief and placed it neatly in a side pocket. "Yes, it is. But I've seen it much worse, Mrs. - Mrs.—"

"I'm Madeline Snowden," replied the school teacher.

The Captain removed his wide-brimmed hat, revealing a shock of sandy, close-cropped hair. "Pleased to meet you, Mrs. Snowden."

Madeline caught that one quickly. "Miss Snowden," she replied. "I'm traveling with my brother's family, Judge Snowden, his wife, his son, who is up with the coachman, and his daughter Prudence - she's sitting back of us with the young Englishman."

The Captain surveyed the passengers, picking out Madeline's relatives. She was aware that his arm had swung around the back of the seat behind her shoulders when he turned to appraise Prudence and Lord Billner. "That's the daughter back there, I presume," he said. "She's just a child, isn't she?"

"Yes," Madeline replied, relieved. "She certainly is. Just a child."

He straightened out again, but Madeline noticed that his arm remained around the back of her seat. She did not mind. In fact, she hoped Prudence noticed it.

"And what, may I ask, is your name?"

"My name is Freeman W. Taylor, Captain, US Second Cavalry, stationed at Fort Yellowstone." He paused, then added, "Just call me Captain."

"Do you know Yellowstone well?"

"Yes," he replied casualty. "I guess I could say that. I've been stationed at Fort Yellowstone four years now."

"Do you live in the Park?"

"Of course. I'm stationed at headquarters right at Mammoth, but in the course of duty I've been to all four corners of the Reservation. Why, Miss Snowden, I could show you some wonders that not fifty white men have seen. The Park is all Wonderland, all fabulous and beautiful—"

"Does your family live with you? Through the winters, I mean." Madeline hoped her question was not too obvious, too forward.

Captain Freeman Taylor smiled. His teeth shown white and even beneath his well kept mustache. "No, no family," he replied simply. "I am an Army Captain, West Point Class of 1901. Too busy with my career for marriage, I guess. I am a soldier, a bachelor, and a gentleman, in that order."

"Mmm," Madeline mused to herself, her spirits lifted. It was then that she felt his fingers lightly gripping her shoulder. Her natural reaction was to bristle, but those fingers felt so nice that she relaxed almost immediately. The Captain leaned close to her face and pointed with the fingers of his free hand. "We'll be passing under the Roosevelt Memorial Arch in just a minute," he said. "And then we'll follow along the foothills for a short distance until we reach the Gardner River. We'll follow it along its banks for a mile or two."

Some distance ahead Madeline could just make out the last of the other tally-hos. She could see that the road was leading into a gloomy canyon amidst ever higher mountains. She thought of a Victrola record they had back home: 'In the Hall of the Mountain King'.

"I know you'll be amused at me, Captain," she said. "This is all old shoe to you. But I'm thrilled." She shivered slightly. "I've always dreamed of a visit to Yellowstone, and I can hardly believe that my dreams are coming true." She felt the Captain's fingers gently squeeze her shoulder, for reassurance, of course; and his right leg, which just – happened to brush her left leg as he readjusted his position. Madeline, her heart thumping, pretended not to notice. "Will you point out some more landmarks to me?" she asked.

She was well aware that this handsome Captain had been appraising her. As for the Captain, he was nearly mesmerized by the most delicate scent of Yardley's Lavender. Here was a spinster with real flesh and blood! Pink, healthy complexion and white teeth and lovely brown hair and a three-quarter-size figure that was simply exquisite. Now just why in tarnation, he was wondering, hadn't she ever married? What, he asked himself, is the flaw in her personality? Why has she trod the dreary path of Old Maidism?

Wrapped in these thoughts, Captain Taylor failed to reply to Madeline's question, so she smiled and raised an eyebrow as she looked at him, gazing contemplatively at her as he was. She repeated: "Captain, won't you point out some of the landmarks? Look, old Hezekiah's pointing out something to the Judge."

Now it was the Captain's turn to blush. He immediately began his travelogue. "Look up there," he said, "and you'll see a herd of antelope. See them?"

As she leaned toward the window the tally-ho jolted over a rut and she lost her balance. One arm came down on the Captain's shoulder and the other landed on his upper thigh, which she inadvertently squeezed. Her face grazed his smooth shaven cheek. She detected the faint odor of saddle soap and leather, while he enjoyed the fragrance of Yardley's Lavender. Before she could express apologies he was holding one of her arms and pointing with it. How pleasantly close he was!

"Antelope? Oh, yes. I see them, Why, Captain, they – they're playing tag. Look at them bounding after each other."

"Interesting beasts," he commented. "Playful, with springs on all four legs. Look. They've seen something. See them bound away." They disappeared out of sight over a knoll.

"Why did they all bound at once?"

"They got a signal."

"What kind of a signal?"

"One of them flicked her tail. I mean *his* tail."

"Oh?"

"Yes. They have cute little white tails that' cause great attention when they are wiggled." The Captain paused, about to say something, changed his mind, reddened, smiled, looked out the window.

"Oh," Madeline replied simply. "It's sort of an animal semaphore system, isn't it?" She straightened in her seat and placed her hands in her lap.

The Captain decided to change the subject. The tally-ho rounded a curve and followed the road along the base of the canyon, the river on one side, the mountains rising on the other. He pointed out the Army's firing range and a few minutes later showed Madeline Eagle's Nest Rock, a tall stone column on top of which perched an eagle's nest, which had been occupied for as long as anyone could remember.

The canyon narrowed. Now the river's roar was louder than the clatter of hooves and the grating of the wheels. And Madeline, dear Madeline, was happy. The Captain was a talkative, pleasant fellow, wasn't he? And a bachelor! Now why on earth, she asked herself, would so eligible a man, so – so *masculine* a man – not be married? What, she wondered, was the personality flaw that had kept him in the ranks of lonely bachelorhood? Whatever it was, at the moment Madeline did not care. She was content in the knowledge that he was unmarried, and beside her in the coach.

The driver shouted commands to the great matched grays. The tally-ho turned abruptly, crossed a bridge, and ran some distance along the other side of the canyon, working up to the crossing of a rocky, narrow ravine. Madeline may have been the first passenger to see the trouble coming. The Captain had just told her about some hot springs flowing out of the side of a hill, and she was scanning the terrain ahead searching for them when she noticed the hind quarters of a black horse, the rest of it standing behind a huge boulder. It startled her, because a horse hardly belonged where there were just stones, Spanish bayonet, and prickly pear cactus. Hardly had her thoughts formed than the horse moved ahead and she spied a tall, gaunt horseman swing his mount out from the boulder into the middle of the road ahead. He faced the tally-ho with a six-shooter pointed directly at the coachman. He wore a black hat and a black mask that covered all but his eyes and forehead, and fell below his neck.

"Halt," commanded the figure in a strange, crackling voice.

"Whoaaaaaaaa," said the driver, pulling on the reins. "What the hell—!"

"Holdup!" shouted Rusty, riding shotgun with the coachman. "Holdup!"

The two lead horses whinnied as the coach halted so fast that the passengers were slammed against the seats in front of them.

Prudence screamed and clutched at her companion.

"Great jumping Jehosephat," exclaimed Philip.

"What in the name of the Great Horned Spoon—" began Hezekiah Hotchkiss, his jaws momentarily canceling a great spit of tobacco juice.

"My God," Madeline gasped quietly, gripping the Captain's arm.

"No funny business," said the highwayman. He calmly dismounted and stepped to a forty-five degree angle in front and to the side of the coach – a position, the Captain noted, from which he could see all the passengers and still keep an eye on the coachman and Rusty. "Open the doors and get out. All of you. QUICK!" he ordered.

The coachman lowered his arms. The robber's pistol raised like lightning and a single shot sent the driver's campaign hat sailing through the air. "I don't mean you," said the bandit. "You and the kid stay up there and *keep your hands up!*" The driver complied, his arms maintaining a slight upward turn, while Rusty's stretched heavenward, straight up. "Yes, s-s-s-sir," Emily heard Rusty say with more meekness than was usual with him.

No one moved.

"I said GET OUT," shouted the masked man. Quickly he ran to the coach and opened the doors, reached in and grabbed Congressman Talmadge Beauregard Griffin by his coat lapel and pulled that illustrious statesman out of the coach and sprawling into the gravel. Leaving him to pick himself up as best he could, the highwayman lithely sprang back to his original stance. "Now get out, all of you, or do I have to pull you out?"

Dolly Griffin scrambled out amidst screams and Southern hysteria, helping her disheveled husband to his feet. "You'll not get away with this, heauh?" protested the Honorable T. Beauregard, "Ahm a United States Congressman, and ah'll see that you are hoss-whipped before you are incarcerated, you – you—"

"Shut up!" commanded the thief. He leveled his Colt .45 at the Southerner, by now standing as straight as his paunchiness would allow, his thinning white hair disheveled, his white suit dusty and soiled – and nary another word from him.

Emily and Philip gingerly stepped down; Hezekiah squinted at the highwayman, then stepped out squirting a stream of tobacco juice in the direction of the holdup man. The Captain, after whispering to Madeline to do everything she was told to do, climbed down and then helped the little school teacher to the ground. Finally Lord Billner jumped down, reached up, grabbed Prudence by her slim waist and lifted her down. The bandit's eyes narrowed as he watched the procedure.

What Prudence saw, as they lined up alongside the tally-ho, was a man at least six feet tall, heavily built, dressed in miner's boots, heavy gray woolen trousers tucked into the boot tops, a blue denim shirt beneath a khaki sheepskin which was unbuttoned, and a strange black mask – strange because it covered not only the man's face, save for his forehead and eyes, but hung loosely, at least to his breastbone. On his head, pulled low, was a dirty black Stetson. His hands were gloved. In his right one was the six-shooter, held steadily, as if he was used to staging holdups. The bandit surveyed them all, but his eyes stopped when they reached Prudence. Briefly their eyes met, and a feeling of stark terror raced through her. Never had she seen such piercing, evil eyes. They seemed to – undress her!

"That's better," commented the clipped voice. "Now, gentlemen, hand me your watches, any other jewelry you have, and your wallets. Remember, no monkey business." He waved his pistol menacingly.

Philip pulled his watch from his vest and released it from the chain. "That watch belonged to my father," he commented bitterly. "He gave it to me just before he died."

"He won't miss it," said the bandit, holding out an open black bag that he had fetched from behind a nearby bush. "Let's have your wallet, too." Philip obediently reached into his breast pocket, came forth with the item, and tossed it in the bag.

From Emily the thief took a cameo that Philip had given her on their fifteenth wedding anniversary. The highwayman then nodded toward her rings, but she had difficulty removing them. After a few moments the thief said, "Hmmph. Pretty small diamonds, aren't they?" and he passed her by. Philip swallowed hard, his pride hurt.

Now the highwayman came to plump, bejeweled Mrs. Talmadge Beauregard Griffin. "Lady," he said as she too strained to remove her rings, "those are nice big diamonds. Worth a lot – but probably not as much as your husband says they are."

Dolly Griffin tugged at her rings.

"Lady," said the bandit, exasperated, aiming the pistol directly at her hands. "I'll give you thirty seconds to remove those two diamond rings, and if they ain't off by then, I'm a-goin' to shoot two fingers off your pudgy left hand. One, two—"

Amidst tears, lamentations, and scraped joints the two sparklers were removed.

"And now you, Congressman," said the bandit contemptuously, "let's start with your diamond stick pin."

Talmadge Beauregard Griffin grumbled while, with shaking hands, he removed the stick pin, followed by his watch and his wallet. "I'm a Congressman, suh. A Congressman," he insisted. The robber was not impressed. "Too bad," he replied. "Then you don't have nobody you can write to, do you?"

Next in line was Captain Taylor. "And now, Captain," continued the robber, "if you will kindly reach into the coach and fetch your black valise—"

The Captain bristled. "You will not get away with this."

"I hate military men," the highwayman hissed, seemingly sucking in air. "And especially shavetail Captains. Now, get the valise." He moved his six-shooter menacingly.

"You get it," replied Captain Freeman boldly.

The bandit's Colt .45 flipped in his hand, his arm shot up and the pistol whipped across the Captain's left temple, drawing blood as he fell to the ground. "I said *get the valise*, Captain!"

Madeline screamed. Instantly she was kneeling by the officer, who sat up, dazed and bleeding. Placing her arms around his shoulders, she turned to the masked man. "You beast!" she shrieked.

"Shut up!" commanded the outlaw. He waved the gun at Lord Billner. "You. Fetch the valise."

Lord Billner hesitated. "Do it," ordered the Captain from his sitting position.

The Englishman reached inside the tally-ho and pulled out the black valise.

"Throw it to the side of the road."

Lord Billner did as he was told.

"Your watch and wallet."

Silently, the young man tossed them into the bag.

Now the highwayman was in front of Prudence. His eyes, half closed, gazed straight at the frightened girl. She edged closer to Lord Billner "No rings. No pins," observed the robber. "I guess I'll just have to take you!"

Just then a gust of wind blew by, fluttering the mask. Prudence saw why it was placed so low. In the small of the man's throat was a silver oval with a hole in the middle, just smaller than a dime. The desperado was breathing through it!

Prudence's mouth opened in awe and the bandit knew what she had seen. He shut the bag with the loot in it and chucked it under his right arm, lifted the Captain's black valise and chucked it beneath the bag, all the time holding the pistol. Then with his left hand he grabbed Prudence's wrist, holding it in a vicelike grip. "I'm taking this little lady with the golden tresses," he announced.

"No, no!" screamed Prudence.

Philip and Lord Billner stepped forward to bar his action but the robber waved his pistol at them, "Stay where you are. I've killed before and I can kill again. Don't – tempt – me." The highwayman edged toward his horse, the terror-stricken girl forced to walk alongside him. "No, no," Prudence whimpered. "Mother. Daddy!"

From the driver's seat came Rusty's shout "Someone's coming!"

This, as nothing else had done, upset the highwayman. He paused, then released the girl, who lost her balance and fell to the ground. "Get back in the coach," hissed the man. "Fast!"

Madeline helped the bleeding Captain in, Lord Billner ran to Prudence and carried her, sobbing, to the coach. The others scrambled in as best they could. "Git," shouted the highwayman, "and don't look back." He fired his pistol twice into the air. The horses reared, then ran. The tally-ho shot off like a cannon ball. And the man with the black horse disappeared as they rounded a curve.

## III

It was rather nice being the center of attention, Rusty thought, as he leaned against a wooden pillar that helped support the long verandah of the great National Hotel at Mammoth Hot Springs. He stuck out his tongue as far as it would go and licked the top of a strawberry ice cream cone – his third within the last half hour. People called him a hero, and ladies with great hats who smelled of powder and perfume patted him on the head. One particular bejeweled old dowager had actually said "nice doggy", then caught herself, blushed behind her fan, and given him a quarter. All because he had shouted, "Someone's comin" and frightened the bandit into giving up Prudence, but the truth was, it hadn't been what the Captain called "presence of mind" at all. Rusty really *had* thought someone was coming.

Some of the excitement had died down and routine was being reestablished. As became guests in 1909, at vacation hotels, in mid-afternoon, they were napping upstairs in the bedrooms. That was where Rusty had left his mother, and Prudence and Emily. The bedrooms, he had barely noted, were plain and drab. Muslin covered the walls. From the center of the ceilings hung a single light cord ending with a small electric light. Equally dim lighting in the hall led to the "retreats", as restrooms were called at that time. Although Philip had reserved three rooms, only two were available, with promise of a rollaway in his and Emily's room "for the little boy". Rusty's tongue curled upward to snatch a drop of strawberry ice cream from the tip of his nose. He was too young to have caught the significance of the conversation at the front desk:

"Move the rollaway into the young ladies' room," Philip ordered.

"Oh, no, dear," Emily protested. "Have it delivered to our room."

Philip frowned. He turned to Emily to argue, but, seeing her pale white face, recalling the ordeal they had just been through, he changed his mind. "Very well, dear," he replied. "The rollaway to our room, please." Frustrated by two nights in a Pullman berth, the first night both of them too tired, the second night Emily just too nervous to "do it" on a moving train, Philip was – in a mood. And now this, a frightened wife and an eleven year old boy. Oh, well, he sighed, what is another night's frustration? Besides, Rusty, once asleep, was dead to the world. Philip's face brightened. Perhaps...

Afternoon, checked into their rooms, exhausted, Emily lay down on the cool sheets to rest. So did Prudence and Madeline in the room next door. Philip and Rusty had gone downstairs "so that the ladies could rest". While Rusty basked in his notoriety, Philip saw to the business of telegraphing for more money and absorbing such gossip as he could gather, leaving Rusty to the verandah, praise, and strawberry ice cream cones.

Rusty relived in his mind everything that had transpired. Why hadn't he yelled sooner? Why didn't he carry a concealed Derringer with which to kill the robber? Deadeye Dick of Deadwood, his Dime Novel hero, would have done it. And wasn't Madeline brave, calling the bandit a beast? And hadn't she been nice, cradling the Captain's head in her lap and patting his bleeding temple with her handkerchief? Strange, though. When soldiers came to escort the Captain to Fort Yellowstone (those big stone buildings east and at right angles to the hotel) the Captain had seemed almost resentful. Did he like his head being in Madeline's lap? Some things, for eleven year old boys, just didn't add up.

Rusty slapped at a mosquito. A fat old man snored noisily in a wicker rocking chair. Nearby, the hotel grounds were vacant. Beyond them to the southwest were the steaming white and varicolored Mammoth Hot Springs. Rusty leaned on the railing and squinted into the bright afternoon sun, gazing at the phenomenon. He was not aware of his sister's presence until she spoke to him from behind.

"Let's climb to them, Rusty."

The freckle-faced lad turned in surprise at her kind tone and at what she had suggested. Their usual stance was somewhere between a standoff and a hot war, but the events of two hours ago had led them to realize their value to each other – a temporary situation, to be sure.

"I thought you were resting."

Prudence scanned the verandah, saw nothing approximating her age of the opposite sex, particularly failed to spot Lord Billner, sighed, leaned on the railing, and viewed the hot springs terraces. "Oh, I'm not tired," she said. "The last thing I want to do is lie still and think of that horrible bandit. And Madeline really is tired, and I felt I was keeping her awake—"

"You were brave, sis."

She sniffed and reached for the handkerchief that was deposited down the front of her white, loose-fitting blouse, so stylish that year. She had just put it on, along with the olive green skirt and comfortable, though fashionable, walking shoes Mother had insisted she buy. She was ready to see the sights, was Miss Prudence Mehitabel Snowden. "Rusty," she suggested, "won't you go up to the terraces with me?"

The boy did not have to be asked twice. Prudence had taken along two guidebooks, the *Haynes Guide* and an older one, *Henderson's Guide*. They indicated where the trail began and what to see as they strolled along. And so the two set out, freckle-faced boy and slim young lady, up the trail past the entrance to McCartney's Cave and the Liberty Cap (a defunct cone whose shape bothered Prudence for reasons she only vaguely understood).

"Looks like a big thumb, doesn't it?"

"Yessssss," she replied hesitantly.

They went on, Prudence reading the guidebooks as they walked. Soon they were climbing Terrace Mountain, passing Cleopatra's Terrace, and then running along the Narrow Gauge Terrace. Prudence paused to read: "Boiling water is seen through a narrow fissure that extends through this, and all other horizontal terraces. Near the eastern end the boiling water pours through a bed of sulfur and arsenic, making a noise like sleepers on a night train and is called The Chamber of Snorers." Prudence laughed as she read further: "It is amusing to hear the lady visitors tell which of these melodious tones resemble her husband's night song." She listened and nodded. One sound was just like Daddy's.

She was interrupted by Rusty, who was perched on a ledge by a bubbling spring. "Rusty—!" she began.

Her unexpected reaction caused the boy to lose his balance. He waved his arms wildly and fell hard, fortunately onto a dried up terrace.

"Owoooooooo," the boy groaned, reaching for his right ankle. "I've twisted it."

Prudence hurried over and knelt beside him. "Are you hurt, Rusty?" she asked. "Not *you*, Rusty. Come on. I'll help you to your feet."

With her aid he stood up and hobbled about. "I must've sprained it," he moaned.

"Oh, come on. Walk ten steps and you'll feel good as new."

Rusty hobbled ten steps, turned to his sister and whined, "I ain't either good as new. It still hurts. I'm goin' back."

Prudence could not believe Rusty was really *that* hurt. She suspected that he was tired of seeing the hot springs. She looked longingly on up the trail. "We're almost to the top of the terraces, Rusty," she argued. "There are all kinds of new sights." She looked at one of the guidebooks. "There are the Teller Mountain Terraces, the Orange Geyser Cone, and the Twin Cones and on the other side is Bath Lake." She particularly wanted to see Bath Lake because of what the guidebooks said: "It is the favorite bath tub for up to three hundred bathers at a time... It is to be regretted that both sexes cannot share this delightful bath. Ladies cannot even see it, for in pleasant weather large numbers of nude male bathers occupy it exclusively."

It piqued Prudence's imagination, for indeed, her hormones were very active. Yes, she did want to see Bath Lake. And it was so quiet this mid-week mid-afternoon. No one was about, not even any men, and so surely no one was bathing there now. She just wanted to see it.

"You go on, sis," said Rusty, grabbing a stick to use as a cane. "But I'm goin' back to the hotel."

The girl was undecided. She looked first at Rusty, then far down the terraces to the hotel, then the other way towards new adventures. "Are you sure you can make it, Rusty? I'll just explore a little more." "Sure, sis. See ya." She watched him hobble down the trail. Before he was out of sight he had cast off his cane and was walking quite normally. Then Prudence set her firm little jaw westward and tramped rapidly on, beginning to perspire as she headed toward Bath Lake. Birds twittered and a beautiful doe bounded in front of her. Then, amidst fragrant cedars and pines, backed up on the far side by a stony, tree-covered hillock and mountains rising beyond, lay the most inviting body of water Prudence had ever seen. Water bubbled up from springs on the far side, and little wavelets slapped at the shore. "Come in," they beckoned, "and cavort and be refreshed." Nor was there a soul about. It was quiet, calm, warm, and sunny; aromatic pine needles and cedars hinted of wild, healthy nature.

The girl quietly rounded Bath Lake to the far side with the trees and the hillock. She stepped to the shore, knelt and tested the tepid water. She stood up. "I wish I were a man," Prudence said out loud. "How good a bath would feel." For it had been cindery-sooty days and nights on a train, and a dusty drive from Gardiner, and the stress of the holdup, all without her body being bathed. And of course the ladies' bathroom at the hotel was busy with several women awaiting their turns.

The girl's eyes suddenly gleamed. Here were trees and big boulders. She could take off her shoes and long cotton stockings and, if she lifted her skirt high, she could at least have the pleasure of wading. Wouldn't the water feel good? She looked around her. All was still save for the chirping of birds. "I'll do it," she announced to herself, sitting on a rock. Off came the dusty walking shoes and stockings. She placed each stocking carefully in a shoe and set them neatly behind the rock upon which she was sitting. Looking and listening once again, and hearing nothing, the girl stepped into the water. As she lifted her skirt she knew her cotton drawers were showing, but then, no one was there to see.

The water felt sublime. She waded in over her knees, then paused. No soldier on guard duty ever scanned the terrain more carefully than did Prudence, but she heard nothing human, saw nothing human. And she felt that tingling relief of tired feet in clear, warm water, with sand squeezing between her toes. Then – for what else was there to do? – she waded back to the rock and with a sigh sat down and reached for her shoes and stockings.

With a stocking held in mid-air the girl stopped. "Why can't I take a bath?" she asked aloud. "Women get just as dirty as men. Dirtier, maybe." She looked all about, she listened. "Nobody is here. Just two minutes to plunge all the way in and rub off the dirt and grime of three days, and then out to this rock and into my clothes – *just two minutes...*"

The blue-eyed girl's breath came fast. "Could I? Would I dare?" She looked again, then took her shoes and stockings and climbed behind a big boulder. "Just two minutes is all. Cleanliness is next to Godliness and I can be clean in two minutes."

The sailor middy blouse slipped over her head in a jiffy, taking with it the little handkerchief. Quickly she unbuttoned the hobble skirt and stepped from it and then she pulled off her petticoat. Now she was down to an eyelet-cotton vest and the white cotton drawers that extended from waist to knees. The drawers were fresh as the afternoon, pure white and new, and she had hated putting them on over her body-in-need-of-a-bath. Again she stood still, like a wild little animal that drinks, listens, drinks, and listens. She peered over the boulder at the Lake. Dare she go all the way? Maybe – take off the vest but keep the drawers on? But if she did, the drawers would be all wet and imagine walking all the way back with wet drawers? Carry them home wet? How could she hide them? She'd left her purse at the hotel.

Oh, the Lake was so still and inviting...

Off came the vest. She sucked in air as a passing breeze caressed feminine parts not usually exposed to outside air. She did pause to examine the fading black and blue streak on her left breast, a reminder of the Bust Developer. Now Prudence stepped from her bower and stood at water's edge – again listening and looking around – placed thumbs on waist and quickly divested herself of the drawers; she placed them between two small boulders near the shore. Then, blind to her own beauty, her pert young breasts, flat tummy, firm, smooth legs, and other parts of interest – quietly, she plunged in.

And it felt – wonderful. The girl tried to keep her hair above water as she cavorted. She used her hands as a wash cloth to rub down and remove the dust and cinders and greasy coating of travel. Then she began swimming. Two minutes became five which became ten. When she first heard the sound of horses hooves she was in the middle of the Lake. She swam back fast as possible, forgetting her hair, then ran buck (or doe!) naked toward her dressing bower. By the time she had reached it she could hear the husky sounds of singing men.

Hidden now, she knelt catching her breath as the voices and hoofbeats came closer until, peeking through the branches of a small cedar, she saw a troop of soldiers appear on the far shore. Then, to her horror, they halted and dismounted.

Terrified, Prudence nevertheless realized that the first thing to do was to get herself dressed. She reached for her clothes and – Heavens – her drawers! There they lay, apart from her other clothes, down by the shore between two big stones – lay there very white and incongruous amidst the works of nature. For all she could do with them, they might as well have been a thousand miles away; she wished they were a thousand miles away! She put a fist to her mouth to stifle a cry. It was some moments before she realized that she still had a petticoat, vest, blouse, skirt, stockings and shoes to put on. Keeping herself hidden, she was soon dressed – *sans* drawers. Prudence leaned back against a boulder, relieved that she was at least presentable. Now, if only the men would leave, for her only way back was around the Lake, where they would see her, and past their horses to the trail.

Instead of fading voices and hoofbeats, she heard sounds of splashing water. She gasped. Were they swimming? Panic at the thought of being discovered nearly overwhelmed the girl as the voices commingled with sounds of splashing water and horseplay. Where were they, she wondered, vis-à-vis her drawers?

Courageously Prudence risked peeking out from the cedar branches. Her eyes grew large and some innocence fell away from them, never to return. For she was feasting her eyes upon a score of lusty men, some of them still disrobing on shore, some knee deep in water, some waist deep, some swimming – but every one in the buff.

"Prudence! Prudence!" her conscience spoke to her, but feminine curiosity shooed it away. What she was observing was far more interesting than that picture book of Ancient Greece she had seen at Elm Grove's Carnegie Library. Then one particularly well-built young man, who had swam closer to her side of the Lake than the others, stood up, turned around and faced in her direction. The girl lost all fears and blushed instead. It was Lord Billner! In spite of herself

Prudence took his measure, and she thought him the handsomest of the lot, by far: broad shoulders tapering down to slim hips, muscular legs, a cat-litheness about him, just enough hair on his chest to make him look athletic rather than revolting. He was the most statuesque man there. And the soldiers seemed to accept him as one of their own as they tossed a rubber ball about in some kind of game.

Prudence could not take her eyes away from what was for her a sinful spectacle. Finally a sergeant, or someone in command, announced something about the time and to a man, though with a few protests, all scrambled out and after drying themselves as best they could with the sun's rays and their own hands, all dressed. This included Lord Billner, although he was no American soldier. She watched him step into his BVDs, his white shirt and his tight trousers, pull the braces over his shoulders, do the necessary buttoning, sit down and put on his socks and shoes. Soon the men were mounting their horses and trotting off.

Prudence sighed as she waited and listened to the fading hoofbeats. Silence again came over the Lake. She jumped up like a young fawn, darted around the Lake, reached the trail, and made her way to the terraces, nodding her head back and forth to dry her hair. In the rarefied air most of the dampness was soon gone. Seeing some tourists coming towards her, she slowed to a walk and appeared to all the world, she hoped, as just another tourist. Halfway down the trail, just as she remembered that she had left her drawers back at the Lake, she met Mother and Dad slowly sauntering up the terraces.

"Prudence! There you are," said Emily. "You shouldn't have left Rusty. Where have you been?" Her mother's gaze caused Prudence to cast her eyes to the ground, blushing for all the things she had done and seen.

"Just seeing the sights, Mother," she replied in as normal a tone as she could muster. ('And what sights I've seen,' she thought to herself.) She blushed even more.

"Rusty's all alone at the hotel," added Philip. "Why don't you go back and keep him company. Or out of mischief." No word of Rusty's sprained ankle.

"I will, Daddy."

"And don't go straying off with that young Englishman, Prudence," added Emily.

"Oh, no, Mother. He isn't there. He's..." she faltered. "I've got to get back to Rusty," she announced, and was past them, almost jogging down the trail.

Actually Lord Billner was closer to everyone than Prudence could have imagined. When the soldiers turned their mounts towards Fort Yellowstone, Stephen Billner, after riding with them for a few minutes, took leave and returned to Bath Lake on his rented horse. Wanting to do some more exploring, he followed an old trail, which is why he missed seeing Prudence as she made her way homeward. In leisurely fashion he rode around Bath Lake, intending to climb above it to see if there were any more hot springs, then perhaps to ride south to the road leading from Mammoth to Swan Lake Flats. It was while rounding the lake that his eyes caught sight of the incongruous white cloth between the rocks. Curious, he dismounted to investigate and make sure they were what they appeared to be – crisp, clean, women's drawers. Examining the narrow, sandy shoreline he discovered footprints, women's footprints, small and dainty, so recently made that water had not yet oozed into them. Further investigation revealed a little hiding place behind a boulder where one could dress and undress. Then his eyes spied on a low cedar bush a little wisp of cloth – a woman's handkerchief. Lord Billner picked it up, smelled it and broke into a smile. "By Jove," he said out loud. "She's a spunky little creature." For the perfume was unmistakable. Miss Prudence Snowden used it. He frowned. Or was he fantasizing? Perhaps this was just too much of a coincidence. Surely others used that perfume. And the drawers: they had to belong to the same lady, but was that lady Prudence? He folded them carefully, unbuttoned his shirt and slipped them inside for safe keeping. He surveyed the scene, even noticing how someone could have spied from behind a cedar tree and not be seen. "Why," he surmised, "that pretty creature must have taken a swim, been surprised by the soldiers, hidden from them – from *us* – in this bower while we swam." Surely she had peeked, and seen the soldiers – and himself! He remounted and continued his leisurely explorations. "The little scamp," he mused. "The lovely little scamp." Somehow he was convinced that it had to have been Prudence Mehitabel Snowden.

He reached the road and passed through Silver Gate, Rustic Falls, and through Kingman Pass into Swan Lake Flats. There he was surprised to see a horseman galloping down the road, leaving a trail of dust behind him. A lone horseman on a black steed who reined in his mount, looked back, and then galloped on.

It was indeed the man with the silver disk in his throat. After the holdup he had entered the pines and followed the ridges until he emerged on the heights overlooking Mammoth Hot Springs. There he had dismounted and, using a pair of powerful German binoculars stolen in a previous caper, he had surveyed the scene: the hotel, the post office, the Weather Bureau, Haynes Picture Shop, and Fort Yellowstone. He was relieved to note that there was no unusual activity there. Then, into his field of vision, appeared a young woman and a boy. He recognized them immediately – and followed them with his glasses – and rode to another lookout and watched them again – and eventually secured his horse and hiked through the timber to an eminence above Bath Lake. There, binoculars glued to his eyes, he observed with rising lust as milady bathed in the nude. For a man with two murders and a vicious rape on his record, the opportunity was just too good to pass up. He was making plans when the soldiers appeared, forcing him to abandon his scheme. "I'll have her yet," he muttered as he remounted, made his way to the road, and galloped off. Even the normal sound of his breathing was sinister through the silver disk, a result of a desperate operation in his youth to save his life from diphtheria. "But meanwhile, I better get down into the Park. They must be searching for me all over the northern section."

## IV

The National Hotel at Mammoth Hot Springs was a four-story wooden structure with a 440-foot-long verandah; the building was sixty feet wide and could host eight hundred guests at a time. A creaking fire-trap of a building, replete with bad plumbing, it was nevertheless wired for electricity when it opened in 1883. It did not have a bar, known as a saloon in those days, but liquor was legally available to guests in the dining rooms. The National Hotel also boasted a ballroom with a resident band playing the popular tunes of pre-ragtime to an ever-changing clientele. Whether or not the guests really were "the right people", they were upper-middle-class Americans. When, back in 1909, they met there from all over the nation, with a few foreign tourists thrown in, with the five-day tour of the Park ahead of them, the atmosphere was friendly, relaxed, and mellow. It also smelled heavily of Havana cigars and the perfume of refined, stylishly dressed ladies. It was the "best of all possible worlds" in that ballroom at the National Hotel in the summer of 1909.

Visitors were not aware that they were led through a fixed daily ritual. First, from the long verandah, they observed the precise formations of retreat carried out by the Cavalry. This climaxed with the lowering of Old Glory and the firing of the Sunset gun. Then they entered the dining room where a good American dinner was served. From there they strolled into the ballroom. Among the guests that August evening were the Snowdens.

Philip was wearing a heavy Scotch tweed suit with knickerbockers. He was, as usual, smoking that offensive Havana cigar. Emily, still nervous from the hold-up, was attired in a stylish white lace dress with a narrow skirt, slit midway up her calves, and a form-fitting top that ended with an embroidered choker that set off her kind, intelligent face like a cameo. Her soft, dark hair was coiffured in great, upswept masses, and a graceful fan in her right hand swept away the stuffy air. The dress had been the subject of some indecision on her part. Although she was pushing forty, she still possessed a school girl's form – well, perhaps a slightly plump schoolgirl's form. She had shifted from attire of youthful boldness to matronly modesty and back again. Madeline had finally tilted the scales for her in favor of the youthful dress. From the way Philip held her hand, Emily reflected that perhaps she wasn't as old as she thought, and perhaps Madeline was right after all about opting for the more fashionable outfit. Frankly, it *was* nice knowing that men were casting admiring glances at her.

"Oh, my deah," gushed bosomy Dolly Griffin, whom Emily spied too late to escape from her and her husband. "How can you look so lovely after that terrible incident this afternoon?"

"By Gad, suh," added the Congressman, speaking to Philip as well, "if this was Louisiana we'd have had a posse of sheriffs and a hundred bloodhounds after the culprit, and he'd be hangin' from a magnolia in the moonlight."

"You don't mean you'd lynch him, Congressman?" Philip asked, expressing shock.

"Not exactly, suh," replied T. Beauregard. "We'd try him first and then hang him."

"Hi, Dad," Rusty cut in, tugging at Philip's coat. "What can I do?" The boy surveyed the ocean of adults dancing or standing and conversing.

"Why don't you go out onto the verandah, Rusty. See a deer, maybe, or perhaps a bear. Or an elk! Or saunter over to the General Store. Here, son. Take this quarter and buy a souvenir." And the boy was gone.

Prudence and Madeline meanwhile stood demurely by Philip and Emily, looking contented although they were not. Each one was searching the crowd, each for a very special face.

Madeline's heart was the first to skip a beat. There he was, resplendent in a Cavalry officer's dress uniform. Shiny black shoes, gray trousers with a gold stripe down each side, royal blue coat, brass buttons, and a Sam Brown belt around his waist accentuating his V-shaped, manly form. She noticed the high collar with the gold US on it and the crossed sabers, the hat held so-so-correct, under his arm. She saw the white bandage over his left temple, the sandy, short-cropped hair, the penetrating dark eyes, the flaming white teeth. Madeline thought she had never seen so handsome a man in her life, so muscular, slim, wiry, and brash. Even the white bandage added to his good looks.

He spied her just as she saw him, and as his face lit up in recognition he started toward her. Madeline barely had time to check herself over. Everything she wore was the most feminine she could find among her small store of vacationer's apparel: the tight corset, crisp cotton vest and drawers and crinoline petticoat (*two* of them) beneath the off-white linen suit. It set off her dark brown hair and olive-brown face with the perky nose. Little sea-shell earrings and a jeweled white comb in her hair, and a white fan with a Japanese scene painted on it, completed her dress. As he strode toward her, the Captain whistled once, long, and low. This Madeline Snowden – she was *special*.

"Good evening, Captain Taylor," she said softly, gazing into his handsome face and diverting her eyes to the white bandage. "I see they dressed your wound. Is your head still aching?"

The Captain gingerly touched the dressing, and winced. "It began to hurt when you peremptorily turned me over to the soldiers," he said, a twinkle in his eyes. "And the surgeon may have attended

Harvard Medical School, but he can't duplicate a woman's gentle touch, nor can a pillow equal a woman's soft—"

"Captain," she whispered, knowing that Philip and Emily and Prudence were close by. She hid her face with the fan and lowered her head as she blushed. True, she *had* rested his head on her bosom.

The band struck up a waltz. Before the Captain had even finished asking her for a dance, he had swept Madeline onto the dance floor. Philip and Emily, Prudence, and the Griffins had barely heard his brief "Good evening". Then Philip and Emily waltzed off. This left The Honorable Talmadge Beauregard Griffin to appraise his plump and fortyish wife, compare her with the willowy nineteen-year-old, contemplate asking the young lady for a dance, see Dolly staring at him, think better of it, and, on the theory that actions speak louder than words, swing his wife off and out of sight of Miss Temptation. Dolly, having won her way without saying a word, danced with rare zest. T. Beauregard Griffin soon forgot all about Prudence. That Southern Belle of his could still interest him with her feminine charm.

Prudence retreated to the wall, by far the prettiest flower there. Yet she did not feel particularly sad. She had experienced enough adventures for one day, she reflected, as she scanned the couples dancing by. She did get something of a start, however, when one couple whirled by and the back of the lady's skirt flared up, exposing the beginning of drawers. Should she be asked to dance, Prudence thought, she should be careful, for while she was crinoline-petticoated, she was quite drawerless.

Only one piece of luggage was allowed for the five-day tour, so their clothing was restricted. Prudence had taken just two pairs of drawers. One was lost at Bath Lake, and the other, with a batch of the family's dirty clothing, had gone that afternoon to a hotel laundry with promise of delivery before the coaches left the next day. The girl rubbed her derriere ever so slightly against the wall. Truth was, the cool crinoline against her young hips felt so – so – alluring.

Then she heard his cultured English voice. "Pahdon me, Miss Snowden."

"Oh," fluttering her eyes, "I didn't see you."

"Is this dance taken?" Obviously it was not.

"Yes," she replied joyously, "with you." Away they whirled, Prudence forgetting about her unmentionables, so smooth a dancer was Lord Billner.

# V

Meanwhile, Rusty had traipsed to Henderson's General Store. There he had purchased as a souvenir a Chinese backscratcher made in Hong Kong with the words YELLOWSTONE NATIONAL PARK burned into the handle. With the nickel he had left he had become the owner of five huge candy jawbreakers. The licorice one he had placed in his mouth; the rest he held in a small paper bag. Scuffing gravel along the path, the lad had begun a desultory walk back to the hotel when he heard a familiar voice speaking to someone off to the side.

"I'm sure I know who the varmint is," the gruff-voiced man was saying, "and if I'm right, we've got a matter of long standing to get settled, him and me." The man spat. "I hope they catch the s.o.b."

"Where do ya' think he'll hide out?" asked the other.

"Huh. Down in the Tetons, of course. If they don't catch him before he leaves the Park, they'll never catch him. Not for this robbery, at least."

The throaty-voiced man was, for sure, Hezekiah Hotchkiss. The boy recognized the sound, turned off the path and walked toward the two men. "Hi, Mr. Hotchkiss," Rusty said cheerfully as both men ceased conversing and turned to the intruder. At first Hezekiah's face, bathed in the moonlight, had shown irritation, but when he saw who it was, his grizzled features mellowed. "Why, look who's here," he said to his companion, "Rusty Snowden, the hero of the holdup." Hezekiah placed a hand gently on the boy's shoulder. "This is the laddie that scared the bandit away."

Rusty looked up at the teamster. "I'll bet the bandit'll be sorry if you ever catch up with him, won't he, Mr. Hotchkiss?"

"That's for certain, laddie, that's for certain."

Hezekiah's friend took leave. Rusty accompanied the coachman down a path leading to the coach house and stables. "Are you going to be our driver, Mr. Hotchkiss?"

"You want me to be?"

"If you'll let me ride up with you shotgun style," replied Rusty eagerly. Hezekiah glanced down at the freckle-faced boy who was looking up at him so enviously. A glimmer of his wasted youth, a pang of sadness at his own failure to procreate, crossed the mountaineer's eyes. He reached down and scratched the boy's tousled red hair. "I reckon it might be arranged," he answered thoughtfully. "Who else do you want in your coach?"

"Oh, Dad and Mother, Prudence and Madeline, Lord Billner and the Captain. And maybe that Congressman and his wife."

Hezekiah held up a hand. "Hold on there, young feller. I better write down the names. Let's go down to the coach house where I have pencil and paper."

"Right with you, Mr. Hezekiah."

They strolled past the hotel some distance until a long, narrow building loomed in the moonlight. Hezekiah gained entrance into the dimly lit building because all the attendants knew him. Down they walked in front of coach after coach, waiting there, mute and inert, while their means of mobility munched hay and oats down at the stables. All the coaches were identical, yellow and brown and open at the sides. The cabs were supported on long, leather straps called thoroughbraces, which gave them a comfortable, softened ride almost like being on a ship at sea.

"These are Yellowstone coaches, laddie," said Hezekiah. "They're really Concords, just like the Deadwood Stages, only the Park Company ordered them without sides, so people could view the scenery."

"What if it rains?" asked the boy.

"They have leather curtains," explained Hezekiah, pointing to the rolls at the top of each side of the coach. He abruptly halted in front of one of the vehicles. "Here we are, laddie," he said. "Here's the *Shoshone Belle* – my coach, and the best of the lot."

Although it looked to Rusty like the others, the boy did not question the coachman's statement. He watched as Hezekiah reached up to the driver's seat and produced an old carpetbag, which tinkled as he lowered it – very carefully.

"Tell you what, laddie. Why don't you go on down to the end of the coach house and look at the big tally-hos lined up there? Go on, now."

Rusty had no desire to see tally-hos because he had ridden on one earlier in the day, but the persistent note in the old man's voice verged on an order; Rusty complied. The mountaineer waited until the boy was well toward the end of the row. Then he unclasped the bag, removed a covering of clothing, and drew out ten one-pint bottles of liquor: Old Crow, White Horse, Old Quaker Rye, and a bourbon called Green River. Then he reached up and unrolled one of the four rain curtains, bedded a couple of bottles in it, then rolled it back up and tied it. True, it was somewhat bulkier than before, but no one could notice. He went through this procedure with all four curtains and was just completing his task when Rusty showed up again.

"What you doin', Mr. Hezekiah?" the boy asked.

"Just adjustin' the curtains, young feller," he replied, "and fetchin' somethin' to write on." Out of the nearly empty bag he pulled an old pocket notebook and a stubby pencil. He proceeded to sit down on the floor with his back against a front wheel, licked the pencil point, and began making his list. He grumbled about including the Captain, but reflected that probably Captain Taylor was staying at Fort Yellowstone and would not he going on into the Park as a passenger. He muttered something about including Congressman Griffin and his wife, but then he stopped.

"Thunderation. If I don't include them I might get that preacher and his wife who asked me about the tour at the hotel. We'll settle for your Congressman, Rusty."

Hezekiah closed the notebook and groaned audibly as he stood up. "Best turn in this passenger list or not get your people," he said. "Let's be going back to the hotel, young 'un."

Rut Rusty hesitated. "Mr. Hotchkiss?"

"What is it, laddie?"

"Mr. Hezekiah Hotchkiss, I have – well, I have a big favor to ask you."

"What kind of favor. Speak up, lad."

"It's about some elk antlers."

"Elk antlers?"

"Yes. See, Mr. Hezekiah, a bunch of us guys back home – we've got a club called the Elklets. That's 'cause some of the dads are big Elks –"

"Elks, eh? The Benevolent and Protective Order of Elks. Their demand for elks' teeth almost extinguished the elk from Jackson Hole. They made watch fobs out of the molars." Hezekiah took long strides as they left the coach house, angered at the thought of such waste.

"But Mr., Hezekiah," Rusty pleaded, trotting along beside him like a puppy, "I don't want an elk's tooth, I – we – our club wants his antlers."

The mountaineer halted abruptly and looked down at the boy.

"I have a secret weapon to make the elk come to me," said Rusty, "but once he's there, how do I get his antlers?"

Hezekiah threw back his head and laughed. When he got control of himself he said, "Laddie, you don't need a live elk. The live ones are reluctant to give up their antlers. You need a dead one – one that starved to death last winter or froze or fell in a gully and broke a leg. Why, I know where there's a magnificent set of antlers."

"Would you help me get them?" asked the boy excitedly. "I have to get them kind of secret-like. Mother wouldn't want me out alone looking for them."

"Why, shore, Rusty. Tell you what. We'll head out from Canyon Lodge in two or three days and I'll take you to the most beautiful elk antlers you've ever seen."

"Oh, boy!"

They were approaching the hotel. "Now you run along and get to bed, young feller. We start at seven in the morning. And I need to get this passenger list to the agent so he can book your people on the *Shoshone Belle*."

They arrived at the verandah. "Yes, sir, Mr. Hezekiah," said Rusty excitedly. "Good night."

"Sleep well, Rusty," Hezekiah replied with kindness in his voice.

## VI

Rusty watched the figures on the dance floor for a few minutes, finished his second jawbreaker, yawned just as his father saw him, and soon found himself, as per Philip's orders, tromping upstairs, keys to bedroom in hand.

Philip ardently hoped his young son would sleep the sleep of the dead. Inactivity had left unspent energy in Judge Philip Snowden. Being constantly close to Emily, whom he dearly loved, had brought out strong desires. Emily was dancing divinely. She smelled of powder and perfume, that faint fragrance that bespoke refinement. Her face was radiant. Her eyes sparkled as if to say, "You are everything to me, Philip. And isn't this fun? And can't it go on forever?"

Some additional zest had been added to their enjoyment by the Louisiana Congressman and his lady. Dolly had suggested they exchange dancing partners. Philip had found her rather shockingly forward, while her husband's tactics on the dance floor had prompted Emily to confide that she "never wanted to be left alone with *him*."

Now it was after nine thirty and they had to rise, be dressed, packed, and breakfasted by seven the next morning. It would be an exciting day of geysers, hot springs, and wild animals. They should retire early.

But more than that – much more than that – Philip wanted Emily. And her glances, squeezes of his hand, her way of leaning on him as they waited for the next dance, indicated that she wanted him. "Oh, Rusty," Philip muttered to himself, "get up there and climb into that bed and sleep the sleep of the blessed." Then to Emily he said, "One more dance, dear?"

## VII

Captain Freeman Taylor complained that his head was throbbing, the air being so close in the ballroom and his left temple so sensitive. "Couldn't we step outside for a little fresh air?"

Madeline smiled puckishly. "Why, Captain, I thought it was the lady who always felt faint."

"Oh, come now, Madeline." (She was no longer "Miss Snowden" but she enjoyed calling him Captain.) "You know my head isn't really throbbing. Let's just get away from the crowd."

"I've noticed the number of ladies that flirt with you," she replied. "It *is* quite a crowd, isn't it?"

"Now you're teasing," he said. Holding one of her gloved hands firmly, he led her out onto the verandah, taking, she noticed, every opportunity to guide her by placing his other hand on her waist. She had a strong presentiment that the Captain would like to swat her, gently, lower down. "I could have many a young Miss for a dancing partner," he ventured gallantly, "but I have chosen you."

Madeline stepped to the railing and gazed off at the hot springs, white and steaming, bathed in the light of a full moon. Her eyes were limpid and silvery. "And why do you choose me, Captain?"

"Why, because..." and then he paused.

"Because?" she queried.

"Because you are intelligent, lovely, self-contained, and gentle as Florence Nightingale," he said softly, tapping his left temple. "And a good dancer."

"And I'm thirty."

"That confession alone makes you different. You admit it." He looked compassionately down at the winsome woman beside him.

"And you accept it," he continued. "And you still love life, and in your eyes I see a tinge of devilment, which intrigues me very much. For instance..." he paused.

"Yes?"

"'For instance – if I were to suggest that I show you McCartney's Cave tonight, right now, I think you would accept."

"Wouldn't it be dark?"

"Oh, yes. And gloomy, too. And a little scary. But it is beautiful, and I know where there is a lantern."

"I'm – not dressed for it, am I?"

"We wouldn't go far. There's a place near the entrance where the moonbeams splash down into the cavern, and the stalactites sparkle in the moonlight like a maharaja's treasure. Come on, Madeline." He grasped a hand and pulled gently. She held back, uncertain, then moved slowly with him, and by the time he had directed her down the verandah steps she had fought her do's and don't's, and the don't's had lost.

"It's out here in the big field between the hotel and Fort Yellowstone, Madeline," he explained, leading her along. As sounds from the hotel diminished and the mountain silence overtook them, he said softly, "Isn't Yellowstone beautiful in the moonlight?" He released her hand and placed his arm around her waist, snugly. She resisted the temptation to place an arm around him, too, and instead looked up at the moon. "It is beautiful, Captain."

They strode in silence until they reached a small log cabin with a sign on the door that read: McCARTNEY'S CAVE – Admission: 50 cents. Captain Taylor ignored the sign, opened the door with a key he drew from his pocket, picked up a lantern convenient to the door (but did not light it), then led Madeline through the cabin and out a rear door into a fenced enclosure in the center of which was a gaping hole in the ground. A crude wooden ladder showed a top rung or two, plus two upright posts sticking a couple of feet out of the hole, like the antennae of some huge subterranean insect.

"That's it, Madeline," he whispered, for no good reason. "We'll go down the ladder into the cave before I light the lantern. If someone saw the light they might come snooping. We wouldn't want that, would we?" He paused. "I'll go down first and light the lantern and then you come down."

Madeline stared down into the gaping hole, and at the ladder, and she shivered. She glanced toward the hotel, with its bright lights. But even as incoherent thoughts were racing through her mind, the Captain disappeared. In a few moments a glow of soft yellow light appeared and, peering down, she saw Captain Taylor perhaps twenty feet below, holding high the lantern, looking up at her. "Come on down, Madeline," he whispered. "Everything is fine."

It had been many a year since Madeline had stepped down a ladder. Not quite sure of the procedure, she gingerly turned around, leaned over to place a foot in a too-high rung. A second step placed her in a more normal stance; she was relieved that, methodically, she was descending. She was also quite aware of her tight slit skirt and of the Captain watching her. She hoped she did not appear too broad in the back. As for Captain Freeman Taylor, he pursed his lips. 'Fetching. Absolutely fetching,' he thought.

Then his hands were firmly around her waist. "Oh! Oh, you frightened me, Captain."

"You are safely down, Madeline," he announced quietly," and you may turn around. I'll hold you." She knew she had reached terra firma, but only her toes touched because he was holding her so tightly. Slowly she swung around, face to face with him, his lips barely two inches from hers. Their eyes met. She felt the warmth of his lips upon hers – softly, at first, but his masculinity was overpowering and she reciprocated the increasing pressure, lips to lips. Finally she released her grip on the ladder and wrapped her arms around his shoulders. His arms enveloped her back, her feet completely left the ground. For long moments she clung to him, her whole body supported by his strong arms. Then slowly, ever so slowly, he let her slide down until her toes touched earth once again, and their lips broke away and she buried her head on his chest.

It had been twelve years since Madeline had been kissed like that. She had closed her mind and her personality and her social life to sex, had buried herself in her studies and her career as an English teacher. In all those years she had met nothing to tempt her along romantic lines. The country bumpkins, factory workers, and storekeepers of Elm Grove she had passed by and they, assuming her spinsterhood, had rarely so much as approached her. But now – was it the altitude, the change from Elm Grove, Yellowstone? – she yearned for the dashing Captain who was holding her in his arms. Her eyes were closed and she wished time would stop. She could feel him nuzzling her mass of soft, brown hair. Finally she broke away. "Can we sit down somewhere, Captain?" she said. She glanced around and from the moonbeams and the lantern made out, dimly, several crude wooden benches along the earthen wall. Silently they walked to one, and sat down. "Where," she asked, "are those stala – stala—"

"Stalactites," he said, his first words since kissing her. "Can't you see them sparkling over there? Here. Let me swing the lantern. Now watch them sparkle."

"But I thought you said they sparkled in the moonlight."

"So I did," he said softly, lifting the lantern to his face and blowing it out.

"Oh, no!"

"It's all right, Madeline," he said reassuringly. "Here I am." She felt his hands on her arms and she grabbed at them. He laughed and sat down. "We'll have to wait for our eyes to become accustomed to the dark," he added.

She shuddered. "Captain, it's chilly down here. And I'm a little scared. Perhaps we should go."

He gathered her in his arms and almost before she knew it she was sitting on his lap and they were kissing again. She was no longer chilly and she no longer shivered, but when one of the Captain's hands started up her leg, from the slit of her skirt, she quickly stopped him.

"Oh, come now, Mary Anne."

"No, Captain. In the first place, I am not Mary Anne. In the second place, I will not be one of your conquests."

"Oh, my Gawd. Did I say Mary Anne? I'm sorry, Madeline." He moved to kiss her again, but Madeline's hand slipped between his lips and hers. From the dim yellow moonlight that bathed the cave beneath the entrance, he could make out the wetness in her eyes. She was, he realized, fighting back tears.

"We better get back, Captain," she said, barely above a whisper. "I've already made a fool of myself. I know you are angry with me, because I led you on. I'm sorry." She started to get up, but he held her tightly in his lap. "It's just – oh, the moon, I suppose, the place, dancing with you. The fact that –" she fought back a sob, pressed her lips close together – "that I am just another lonely, frustrated school teacher." She broke free, ran to the ladder and started up.

"Madeline. Wait."

Before she reached the third rung his hands were around her waist. "I said wait, Madeline," he repeated in an officer's authoritative tone.

"Please let go, Captain. There are many ways to seduce a woman. Please do not try any more of them with me."

"On my honor as an officer in the United States Army I will not attempt anything, Miss Snowden," he said. "But you come back down here."

She hesitated. His hands clamped her waist like a vice. "Very well, Captain," she replied, realizing that she had no choice.

She stepped back down, turned to him with her back leaning against the ladder and the full light of the moon above her, facing up to him defiantly. "Yes, Captain. What is it?"

She was so beautiful standing there, her face bathed in the soft moonlight, tears falling down her cheeks, that he forgot what he was going to say. He released her and walked around the room, composing his thoughts. He stumbled over the lantern. The racket echoed through the pitch black chambers. "Oh, blast it," he said, giving it a kick.

Madeline's eyes softened. She felt that she knew him so well – it was hard to believe that she was just another of his conquests. What did he want to say to her? To show that she trusted him, she walked back to the bench and sat down.

He stood directly in front of her. As she gazed into his face she had to stifle a laugh. His countenance reminded her of a school boy caught with a peashooter, and totally unprepared to offer an excuse. "Sit down, Captain," she ordered, patting the bench beside her.

He obeyed, but was tense, and allowed a separation between them.

"Oh, Madeline," he began, "there have been Mary Annes and Bettys and Barbaras and Connies and Nancys and the like. I'm a thirty-one year old bachelor with a good career and pretty natural desires. But – damnit – you *are* different, Madeline."

"You needn't swear," she said softly. "How am I different, Captain?" She turned to him and looked straight in his eyes.

"Different? Oh, yes. For one thing, you appear rather worldly for a spinster school teacher. I think you have a past – some great sorrow, some heartbreaking experience. It forged your character, made a finer woman of you – a woman of substance. Lovely and adorable you are, Madeline, but you are of tougher fiber than most women. That's why I say you are different."

Perceptibly Madeline's temperament changed. She straightened up stiffly; a hardness came into her face that disturbed the Captain. She had lived with her secret for twelve years and she could live with it a hundred more. How dare he suggest that "she had a past". She bristled. "Perhaps," she said icily, her nostrils dilating, "perhaps you have some secrets in your past too, Captain."

He shrugged his shoulders. "Yes," he replied. "Not involving women, though. I've never got a girl in trouble – at least, not to my knowledge." He noticed Madeline blanch. "But – I do harbor a troubling secret. You'd laugh if I told you. But by Jove, it bothers me! And because I can't keep my mouth shut, it's going to interfere with my career."

"Interfere with your career, Captain?"

"Yes. If my secret was out the Colonel would have me transferred to the swamps of Louisiana or the icy wastes of Alaska."

"My goodness. Don't you like the Army?"

"I love the Army. The Army's my life. After all, I'm a West Pointer. Stood well in my class, too. To be a Captain at thirty-one is doing well these days."

"Congratulations."

"Oh, yes, Madeline. In this day and age, with no Indians left to fight, no trails to keep open, no battles to be fought, about the only way to be promoted is to have your superiors die. And believe me, Miss Snowden, *old soldiers never die.*"

She laughed in a relaxed way that gave him hope that he had not lost this intriguing, beautiful woman. "Come on, Captain. What is your secret?"

Captain Freeman W. Taylor, US Second Cavalry, frowned with indecision. He foolishly looked about him to make sure no one was eavesdropping. "Well," he began, "it's – it's sort of a two-sided thing, Madeline. You won't tell, will you? You won't laugh at me? Because no one else, and certainly no other woman, knows my secret."

She rested a hand on his shoulder and squeezed. "Of course not. Heavens! Who would I tell?"

He stood up abruptly, clasped his hands behind his back and began pacing back and forth through the moonbeams. "Madeline," he began, "I – Oh, damnit – *I hate horses!*"

"What?"

"That's right. I, Captain Freeman W. Taylor, Second US Cavalry, West Point Class of 1901, *hate horses*! I hate their smell. I hate their ways. On purpose, they'll step on your feet, bite your arms, buck you off, kick you to Kingdom Come. They'll break out of a pasture and you'll waste a whole day searching for them. Madam, the horse is not, repeat, NOT a friend of man. Until the horse is obsolete, man will never advance. The horse is the greatest deterrent to progress in the world today. Every horse should be – should be—"

"Retired?" suggested an amused Madeline.

"Yes. Put 'em to pasture and let 'em play tag. Sell 'em to animal rendering plants. Make dog food out of 'em. But *get them out of the Army*! The Captain's voice boomed down through the cave chambers. He pounded a fist into the palm of his hand. "Get 'em out of Old Army or by Gawd we'll never win another war!"

"Captain! Control yourself."

"Miss Snowden, let me ask you. Have you ever ridden in a buggy pulled by a bloated horse in alfalfa time? Oh-h-h!" Captain Taylor raise his arms in horror. "There's a reason for the dashboard on the buggy, you know!"

"Watch what you are saying, Captain. I may be worldly-wise but I am a lady. Restrain yourself. You've made your point." Truth was, it was all Madeline could do to prevent laughing out loud.

He sat down again beside her, still distraught. "There's more, Madeline," he continued, looking straight into her kind face. "Swear you'll never tell."

She promised. He breathed deeply, then continued.

"Madeline, I have suffered the absolute, ultimate humility at the hands of a horse."

*"Hands* of a horse?"

"Hands. Hooves. Hell! There I was in review before President Roosevelt and General Leonard Wood. Teddy had even pointed me out to the General, had spoken highly of my leadership qualities. And what happened? Do you know what happened, Miss Snowden?"

She shook her head, frightened.

"The saddle girth loosened. In front of President Roosevelt and General Wood my saddle slipped. I fell to the ground!"

"Oh, Captain. How horrible!" exclaimed Madeline, suppressing her laughter.

"The damned nag was responsible," he explained. "It kept air in its lungs when I adjusted the girth and then at the crucial moment emptied them. There I was, literally sliding into oblivion. If you'd stripped me naked and placed me in front of a punch bowl at a White House reception I wouldn't have been more mortified."

A picture of Captain Freeman under such circumstances overcame Madeline; she laughed out loud.

The Captain was so worked up he ignored her. He placed his elbows on his knees and hid his face in his hands. "And here am I, a Captain of Cavalry wasting my life on *horses*."

Madeline gained control of herself but she was at a loss for what to say.

Now Captain Taylor stood up ramrod straight and beat a fist into the palm of his hand with a resounding sock. "And, by Gadfry, the horse will go. Because there's another side to my secret, Madeline." He turned to her. "The internal combustion engine. That's what will put the nags to pasture – make glue out of every one of 'em: Palomino glue, Cowpony glue, Quarterhorse glue, Percheron glue, Tennessee Walking Horse glue, Appaloosa glue, Clydsdale glue; Indian pony glue and Cayuse glue and gelding glue and sorrel glue and pinto glue and stud glue and mare glue and nag glue and mule glue..."

He sat down stiffly again, holding a hand to his bandaged temple which, Madeline concluded, was beginning to throb, 'and no wonder,' she thought.

"Well, then, Captain, you should—"

"Automobiles," he blurted out. "They just need gasoline and a little oil, Madeline. No oats or hay, No epizooti –" he noticed the puzzlement on her face "– that's horse influenza," he explained. "And when you want an automobile, you just turn the ignition and crank it up."

"That *is* convenient."

"They don't stray, either. Or bite or buck or kick – well, 'cept the crank, once in a while." He turned to Madeline. Then he almost roared: "*What we need, Miss Snowden, is mechanized cavalry!*"

She started to say something, but he placed a hand to her lips. "Just think," he began. "Guns carried on trucks, armor-protected troop carriers – the possibilities are beyond our wildest imagination."

"I agree, Captain."

"Why, there could be air cavalry with aeroplanes. For observation, you know."

Madeline clapped her hands enthusiastically. "That's the future. Mechanized cavalry. And you, Captain Freeman W. Taylor, will be on the ground floor of the transformation. Your future will be assured. You will be a General – a wonderful General!"

"Ah, yes, my dear Madeline. Except for one thing. Just one little thing."

"And what is that?"

Captain Taylor rose, stepped to the ladder, and peered up at the entrance. He scanned the passageways of the cavern. Then he returned to the bench, placed a foot on it, looked straight into Madeline's eyes and said: "It's the Colonel in command here at Fort Yellowstone, Madeline. Colonel 'Saddle-Pants' Peavey. He hates automobiles like I hate horses. He is an anti-automobilist."

Madeline placed a gloved hand to her mouth. "An anti-automobilist! How – horrible!"

"Oh, my dear, you don't know the half of it," he half-whispered to her. "He's – what does Sigmund Freud call it? – *psychotic* on the subject. For example – because it was heavy, the bandit thought my valise contained the payroll. It is really filled with back issues of *Automobile Age*! If Colonel Peavey knew that, he'd bust me right down to Second Lieutenant."

"That's terrible," commented Madeline. "Why doesn't he come into the Twentieth Century?"

"Saddle-Pants? Ha! His whole career's been with the Cavalry. He can't visualize Old Army without horses."

"Never mind, Captain," encouraged Madeline, rising and walking towards the ladder. "You cannot stop progress. You keep up the fight. You'll win out, I just know you will. And the day will come when the automobile will be in Yellowstone. And there will be motorized cavalry, and you", tapping him on the shoulder, "will be a General."

"Just think," mused the Captain while holding the ladder for her, "a day when people can drive from all over the nation in their own motor cars to see the Park."

"You know, Captain, automobiles interest me. When I worked at the Carnegie Library this summer I read everything I could about them."

She climbed to the top and held out a hand to help the Captain up. They walked back to the hotel so absorbed in conversation that they did not even hold hands.

"Why, just think," said Madeline, "the roads will be filled with Peerlesses and Thomases and Aerocars and Maxwells and Ramblers—"

"And," he added, "Cadillacs and Jewells and Studebakers, Singers, Hupmobiles, McIntires, Franklins – air-cooled Franklins, Models D, G, K, and R, and the new Franklin Torpedo – not to mention Buicks, Reos, and Oldsmobiles."

"In touring bodies, surrey bodies, limousines, landolets, and single rumble-seat bodies—"

"But I'll bet you don't know these," interrupted the Captain. 'Fully equipped with Bosch Magnetic High Tension Single Ignition Systems."

"Oh, ho, Captain. With Exide Batteries and Pennsylvania Pneumatic Safety-treads, and safety carbide lamps and gleaming windshields—"

"But wait, Madeline. We've forgotten the most important car of all."

"Of course," she said. "The Ford."

"Right. The Ford for the masses and a luxury car you missed. The Pierce-Arrow for the privileged."

"Have faith, Captain," Madeline said excitedly. "You just wait. It will come about – in due time. And soon. And won't it be fun?"

They halted at the verandah steps. Captain Freeman paused, looked around him, and said, "Why, you little vixen."

Madeline looked innocently into his finely chiseled features, her eyes wide and sparkling. "What do you mean?"

He hesitated. He liked this woman more than any of the many he had known. Surely she knew how she had diverted him from matters of the flesh. "Oh," he replied inconsequentially, "nothing. I do hope I see you again. You carried me away with engines and automobiles and" he lowered his voice "my hatred of horses. I'll bet I bored you silly."

"Oh, no, Captain," she replied sweetly. "It is all most interesting. I told you I was fascinated with automobiles." She climbed the first two steps to the verandah.

Again he said, "Madeline, I want to see you again. May I?"

"Of course, Captain," she replied. Then she bent close to his ear, being on a level with him because she had taken two steps up. "But, Captain," she whispered, "I thought you wanted to seduce me tonight!" She brushed his bandage with her lips, then broke away. Before he composed his thoughts, she was across the verandah and halfway through the lobby, too late for him to catch up with her.

## VIII

Just as she had fantasized, Prudence found Lord Billner a superb dancer; he thought she was the smoothest dancing partner he had ever had, but – something bothered him. Strange! Why did he feel that *she* was mentally undressing *him*? Women were supposed to have feelings like that sometimes, but men, never. Then he thought of what this innocent girl must have seen at Bath Lake. Oh, come now; it was probably not her.

Even as he whirled her around the dance floor, as her lovely golden tresses became disheveled, and he was hardly aware of more than a thin wisp of humanity in his arms, so light on her feet was she, he still harbored that feeling. He searched out those big blue eyes, but each time he caught their glances they seemed to go click-click, blinked, and that knowing look disappeared, making way for sky-blue innocence.

Had she seen him? 'I have to be wrong,' he thought. 'Too much of a coincidence. It can't be.' Then he got a whiff of that faint fragrance of Prudence's perfume, the same fragrance of the handkerchief he had found at Bath Lake.

Just as he had thought: and if this was true, then she had seen him. In spite of himself, Lord Billner blushed. "How did I act?" he asked himself. "Did she just see me nude or did I do something to make me super-embarrassed?" Try as he would, he could not put the subject out of his mind. It bothered him. Fine physical specimen that he was, he well realized how ludicrous, awkward, and unaesthetic the male nude is – at least to the mind of normal males. "Oh, my Gawd," he said aloud.

"What?" asked the girl, her lips parting in a smile. "Did you say something, Stephen?"

"No. Prudence... What did you do this afternoon?"

He felt her body stiffen. There was a pause. "Well, I went up on the terraces and – and..." she hesitated. "And saw the hot springs."

They danced some more. Then she asked, "What did you do?"

"I rented a horse and went sightseeing up on the terraces. Strange we didn't meet."

"There were lots of people around."

"After a while I joined some soldiers and went up to Bath Lake and took a bath."

Prudence's heart skipped a beat. She paused before replying – too long, he thought. "Well," she began hesitantly, "I got rid of soot and cinders too. But of course, I bathed at the hotel."

"Of course," he replied dryly.

The dance ended. They stood on the dance floor, neither of them talking. Lord Billner kept asking himself, 'Was it Prudence?' and she kept thinking, 'He couldn't possibly suspect – could he?' Both wanted to be at their courting best, but both flunked the proficiency test. Prudence even stifled a yawn. Time dragged.

"Say," Lord Billner suggested, "I hear they post the passenger lists for the coaches in the lobby. Let's make sure we're on the same coach."

A small crowd was gathered around a bulletin board with more than twenty coaches listed by name and coachman, and the passengers for each in a column below each coach name.

"There we are, Prudence," said Lord Billner. "The *Shoshone Belle*. We're in Hezekiah Hotchkiss's rig."

"That terrible old man!"

"He's all right. Not too old, either. Just a mountaineer. And look, Prudence. Besides your family and me, there's the Congressman and his wife."

"And look," added Prudence. "Captain Taylor's on our coach. I can hardly wait to tell Madeline. She denies it, but I know she likes him."

"I wonder," remarked Lord Billner as they strolled to the Haynes Picture Shop to look at souvenirs, "why is the Captain coming along?"

"Probably to protect us," Prudence replied, stifling another yawn. Then Lord Billner yawned. Then they yawned together. "Prudence, we're tired," he said to her as if they had been married for years. "Let's retire early. We'll be together tomorrow and it should be great fun."

The girl could not deny her fatigue. When they returned to the lobby, they simply held hands and said good night. Stephen had run into three English tourists and wanted to speak to them, so Prudence started up the stairs alone. "Oh, by the way, Prudence," he said.

She turned. "Yes, Stephen."

"You dropped your handkerchief." He handed it up to her.

"Oh, thank you, sir."

Not until she reached her room did it strike her like a bolt of lightning: she was holding *two* handkerchiefs! One she had taken with her to the dance. The other? The other one? It couldn't be – had she left it at Bath Lake?

Prudence thought about it as she undressed, thankful that Madeline wasn't back. Her spinster aunt might make it embarrassing if she noticed that she wasn't traipsing around in her drawers like she usually did. She quickly changed into a long cotton nightie, took care of necessary ablutions "down the hall", switched out the light, and lay in bed. "The handkerchief," she mused. "Where oh where did I lose the handkerchief?" She concluded, not entirely to her satisfaction, that she had dropped it somewhere along the terraces.

The moon shone through the windows and the flimsy curtains rustled as a light, cool breeze sweetened the room. The young girl stretched sensuously, her body tingling as it made its place amidst the fresh, crisp sheets. She placed her hands behind her head and stared at the ceiling, breathed deeply and sighed. She was back again at Bath Lake, and all her thoughts were on Lord Billner. The nude soldiers faded into mist, but the young Englishman's lithe, athletic body, standing thigh deep in water, tossing a ball to the others, came through in her thoughts as if she were still watching. She sighed again and moved one hand across the other side of the bed, sliding her palm back and forth. 'Gosh but I wish he were here,' she thought. 'To be loved by someone like him.'

She thought of him again at Bath Lake. She ran her hands over her young body as if the hands belonged to Lord Billner. 'I wish he'd seen me bathing' she thought.

There was the sound of a key being inserted in the door and Madeline entered. She switched on the light, saw Prudence in bed, and hastily switched it off again.

"It's all right, Madeline. I'm awake," said the girl.

"I can undress in the dark," Madeline replied. Prudence watched her figure moving about, stepping to the closet, emerging in a white nightgown and robe. What surprised Prudence was Madeline's humming of tunes. This was not like her maiden aunt at all. Madeline returned from down-the-hall and lay down beside Prudence in the double bed. Both lay on their backs.

"Captain Taylor is very handsome," said Prudence.

Madeline's body was instantly taut; she was on guard, "Oh, yes. He's pleasant company."

"He sure made a beeline for you in the ballroom. He almost forgot to pay his respects to Mother and Daddy and the Congressman and his wife 'cause he wanted to dance with you so."

"Oh, Prudence. Hush. He's just an acquaintance."

For moments they lay in silence, two lovely women side by side, their heads framed like paintings on the white pillows.

"Madeline. Madeline. How do you know when you're in love?"

Madeline turned on her side toward the wall, with her arms hugging the pillow as if it were a man – a particular man. But her eyes were wide open.

"Why? How should I know?"

Prudence sighed. "Is it maybe a languorous, delicious feeling?"

Without realizing what she was doing, Madeline sighed too. "Maybe," she replied simply.

Then she frowned. What was this? Madeline Snowden, thirty-year-old spinster sighing like a lovesick girl of nineteen! Watch it, girl, she said to herself. Was Captain Taylor and the vacation and the high altitude and Yellowstone robbing her of her better judgment? She didn't even know for sure that she'd see him again, even though he had asked to. She conjured up all the problems caused by love, from heartbreak to pregnancy; she warned herself of the difficulties in keeping a love affair under control. Perhaps the Captain was just toying with her like a cat with a mouse. Maybe his "campaign" lasted just five days, the duration of the Park tour. Perhaps he waged a dozen "campaigns" every summer, each lasting five days. Then, whether in victory or defeat, the jilted girls left the Park. To Madeline, yearning for husband, home, and family, such callousness on the part of a man, such flippant playing with a sensitive soul, seemed the height of cruelty. It was, she thought, the whole, eternal dilemma of womanhood. "Maybe it is, as you say, a tender, delicious feeling. Then again, Prudence, maybe it is a bitter sweetness. Let's get some sleep."

"By the way," said Prudence, ignoring Madeline's suggestion, "did you know that Captain Taylor's going to be on the coach with us tomorrow?"

Madeline's eyes opened wide. "He *is!*" she blurted out, happiness and surprise in her voice. Quickly, restoring her composure, she said matter of factly, "That's interesting. Now let's get some sleep."

Prudence was beginning the slow, heavy breathing of a sleeping young girl. Madeline was wide awake, tossing and turning, even weeping some tears because she knew it was all so silly, she having fantasies about the Captain loving her. But then her thoughts switched from the bitter to the sweet, to his kisses, his strong arms around her, and above all, his apparent enjoyment in talking with her. Madeline too passed into deep slumber.

## IX

Somewhere between nine thirty and ten o'clock Philip and Emily left the ballroom. Emily's face was flushed. When their eyes met, or when they held hands, there was a conveyance that lovers have known since Adam and Eve. She was aware of Philip's eagerness as they climbed the stairs, his steady pressure on her elbow, keeping her moving a little faster than she desired. As he opened the bedroom door he held a finger to his lips. Emily understood. They tiptoed inside, found Rusty sound asleep in the rollaway, and proceeded to prepare for bed as quietly as possible without turning on the light. Down-the-hall was quickly taken care of. In no time at all they were side by side between the sheets. Emily shuddered at the sudden coolness, brought her body close to his, and they both lay on their backs staring at the ceiling.

"A little chilly, dear?" he whispered, placing an arm around her shoulders.

"Not really. Just cool. Just thinking of all the excitement today. Was it really just this morning that we were held up?"

"Let's not think about it, Emily."

"I wasn't really afraid," she said, stretching. "Not as long as you were beside me, Philip dear." She turned on her side toward him, one of her legs came up over his, he felt a hand stroking his hair as her lips came so close that they touched his as she spoke. Her breath smelled sweet, of Colgate toothpaste. "You are my hero, sir. My lord and my protector. I love you, Philip." Emily kissed him hard, then their mouths opened for even more intimacy. Philip's hand ruffled her nightgown upward and she raised her hips to help it on its way. He caressed her cool, bare hips. The day is about to end, he thought, just as he had wanted the past two days to end. "Gad, but Emily is woman with a capital W when she's in the mood."

Their pending coupling was abruptly interrupted. From the rollaway came a muffled cry, a gurgle, coughing, a tumultuous movement of bedclothes and the squeaking of springs.

"Rusty's choking!" cried Emily, throwing off the covers and starting for the bed as her gown fell back to her ankles. "Rusty. Are you all right?"

More gurgling and jouncing of the bed.

Philip by now had risen and snapped on the light. There was Rusty, his eyes glazing, face livid purple, pointing at his mouth.

"He's suffocating!" Emily screamed again. "Something's stuck in his throat!"

Philip grabbed his son's ankles, lifted him upside down and slapped his back. One hard whack between the shoulder blades sent an enormous jawbreaker shooting out of his mouth onto the floor. Immediately Rusty got relief. "I'm okay. Put me down, Dad," he gasped.

"Oh, Rusty," said Emily, hugging the lad, brushing his red hair from his face as he sat on the edge of the bed and rocking him back and forth.

Philip scowled, examining the sticky jawbreaker he had retrieved from the floor. "Rusty," he asked sternly, "how could you be so stupid? Going to bed with a jawbreaker in your mouth."

"Oh, Philip. He's just a child," Emily defended, bristling. Then to Rusty, "Are you all right now, dear? You could have died."

"Yes, Mother. I guess. Can I sleep with you and Dad tonight?"

Fortunately neither saw the look on Philip's face, "Of course, dear."

Philip sighed, started to say something, but thought better of it. Emily tried to catch his eye, to let him know that she was sorry, but he purposely avoided her. She and Rusty climbed into the big bed and Philip made do with the rollaway. He switched off the light.

For nearly an hour Emily and Rusty talked, until the boy calmed down and dozed off into deep slumber. Emily contemplated joining Philip on the rollaway, but a light snoring sound told her that he was asleep too. Emily smiled. There's always tomorrow night, she thought. And then she too fell asleep.

## Chapter Three
# The Second Day

### I

Old timers said that Yellowstone has two seasons, nine months of winter and three months of cold weather. Others said the seasons consisted of winter and the Fourth of July. Hezekiah Hotchkiss arose from his bunk just as the summer sun was flooding the hot springs terraces with vivid red. He stretched in his long-handled cotton underwear, shivered, slapped his legs to get the blood circulating, cast a quick glance about, saw that his fellow drivers were still asleep, and darted a hand underneath his mattress. Out came a slim pint of Green River bourbon which he quickly unstoppered, sniffed, then lifted to his lips. He tilted back his grizzled head and took one, two, three big swigs.

"Whewwwww," he whispered. He stoppered the bottle, gave it an affectionate pat, and deposited it back under the mattress. Quietly he drew on heavy old gray woolen trousers, a blue denim shirt, sat down on his bunk and pulled on dusty, shapeless boots. From a peg on the wall he grabbed his white linen duster and slipped it on. Then he reached for his wide-brimmed campaign hat and planted it squarely on his head without the aid of a mirror. Finally, from his battered carpetbag he fetched a pair of fine, soft, tight-fitting Berlin whip gloves which he carefully pulled over his hands. He shivered again in the morning cold, tossed his bedclothes into place and stepped gingerly out of the bunkhouse into the crisp morning air.

He paused, dug for his treasured pocket watch and cursed when he realized it had been stolen. He squinted at the sun which was changing from a red fireball to a silver medallion, glanced at the terraces, and figured it must be five o'clock. He was just about right.

He heard voices in the bunkhouse. This spurred him to business, for Hezekiah was up early for a reason: first coachmen got the best horses and tack. Now he was at the stables, choosing his horses – four matched grays would do – and he had the stableboys up in a jiffy, rubbing their hips where Hezekiah's boots had helped get them started. The horses were led down the row of Yellowstone coaches until they came to the one named *Shoshone Belle*. Hezekiah stood beside the coach.

"This is the one. Hitch 'em up good, now," he ordered as he chocked the front wheels. With a crude jack he trussed up one wheel of the vehicle. Dexterously he released the linchpin, removed the wheel, daubed the axle with a brush dipped in a bucket of axle grease, then reset the wheel and the linchpin. He repeated the process with each wheel. Then he examined the thoroughbraces; with a whisk broom he swept out the black, horsehair upholstery, and the floor. He then checked the singletrees and the harness, which the stable boys had just hitched up. He growled at the two pimply-faced "barn dogs" (as they were called). "Ye let any other driver come close to this coach-and-four, and ye'll feel my boots, ye hear?"

They heard.

Hezekiah grunted and trudged through the big carriage house doorway. He squinted at the sun again, noticed how bright the day had become, and then headed for the employees' mess. He planned to eat and be back soon. He had a full load of "packagers" – another name for the "couponers" who had purchased the five-day tour – and he didn't want them to have to eat everyone else's dust. So – he'd best eat and get back early.

That explains why the Snowden party found itself the happy occupants of coach number four, one of the more than twenty-five coaches that would be starting off on the tour that morning. The entire verandah was crowded with tourists most of whom were still searching for their coaches, but Prudence had learned of her party's assignment to the *Shoshone Belle* the night before and they were waiting for the coach when it clattered up to the verandah. Philip and Emily, Madeline and Prudence, Congressman Talmadge Beauregard Griffin and his wife Dolly were seated in the coach, awaiting only Lord Billner and, Madeline so hoped, Captain Taylor. Rusty was with Hezekiah.

The four ladies were wearing white linen dusters that came down to their calves; their enormous hats served as excellent anchors for the massive veiling that was pulled down over their faces. They had heard tales of the terrible, gritty dust that rose in great clouds along the Yellowstone roads in spite of Army Engineer attempts to keep it down with huge, horse-drawn water sprinklers.

Then Lord Billner arrived. Out of the corner of her eyes Prudence spied him trotting down the verandah towards the *Shoshone Belle*. He was wearing a brown corduroy sporting outfit, shoes, long stockings, knickers, a plaid cotton shirt, many-pocketed coat and a soft corduroy hat. "I'm heauh," he said to Hezekiah, placing his Gladstone bag in the coach's boot and then determinably climbing in, seating himself beside Prudence in the middle seat; Madeline sat in the back seat with the Congressman and his wife, while Philip and Emily occupied the front seat.

The verandah slowly emptied as people climbed into their vehicles. There was less commotion, less shouting. Finally the liveried doorman standing beside the lead coach gave a signal, coachmen issued commands to their teams, whips whooshed through the air. Just as Hezekiah issued his "giddyap" a cavalry officer with a small white bandage on his left temple came running across the field from the direction of Fort Yellowstone. "Stop, Hezekiah," he commanded.

"Whoa-a-a-a," responded the coachman, pulling back on the reins.

The Captain opened the door, caught sight of the heavily veiled Madeline in the rear seat with the Congressman and his wife, and hesitated. How could he sit with Madeline?

From the back seat came Cupid's voice with a Southern drawl. "Talmadge," said Dolly, "why don't I sit up with Philip and Emily, and why don't you enjoy the sights with Rusty and Hezekiah up on the driver's seat. You know how bored we'll get, sitting back here."

"I say – what's that? Uh, why, we sho-all will, Dolly," he replied. With a wink from the Congressman to the Captain the change was made. Captain Taylor was now in the back seat with the heavily veiled but very happy Madeline, Lord Billner and Prudence were in the seat ahead, and in the front seat Dolly, Emily, and Philip. The Honorable M.C. from Louisiana seated himself authoritatively on the left side of the driver's seat, with Rusty in the middle and Hezekiah on the right. Just as Hezekiah yelled "giddyap", Congressman Griffin shouted down to Captain Taylor. "You know, Captain, I'm a member of the

Armed Services Committee. I want to talk to you sometime about Army matters."

"Any time," replied Captain Taylor.

Dolly wiggled her plump self and got settled into her seat. "He'll be much happier up there, really he will," she assured Emily. "He'll light up his cigar and be making a political speech every time we stop for more than five minutes, or anywhere there are more than two people within hearing distance. Talmadge loves to talk to constituents."

"He may get a little lonely around here," commented Philip. "Not too many Louisianians here."

"Why, Talmadge'll make rebels out of all you damyankees," Dolly replied. "Especially out of you, Philip. Last night Talmadge told me he'd make a Democrat out of you before we get to Old Faithful."

Philip puffed heavily on his cigar, so much so that Emily waved the smoke away from her face. "Talmadge," he commented dryly, "may be a little overambitious. But let him try. Let him try."

Meanwhile, in the back seat, a flustered but excited Madeline sat primly, gloved hands in her lap. The Captain finished his good mornings and apologies for being late, ending with a soft "and especially, good morning to you, Miss Snowden."

"I didn't expect to see you again, Captain," Madeline lied. "You can add to the enjoyment of our journey," she added, "by pointing out places and things we would miss." She watched as his left hand slid lightly across his lap to her own. When he clasped her right hand and squeezed, she squeezed back. Indeed. The Captain was glad to see her, and she him.

The *Shoshone Belle* did a 180 degree turn and started up the road to the south-southwest. The route passed a fenced buffalo pasture, then skirted Mammoth Hot Springs but did not stop, since the guests were expected to have observed the phenomena during their brief stay at the hotel. They would pass Rustic Falls and Silver Gate – a narrow pass through the canyon in which the road was built out from the cliffs – before emerging onto a mountain plateau called Swan Lake Flats.

The Captain spent the time informing Madeline of Yellowstone's history. He told her about Philetus Norris, the first really active Superintendent, who built the first roads; of Interior Department mismanagement that resulted in the Army policing the Reservation even though Interior still administered the Park; of the road system constructed by the Army Engineers. Madeline felt increasingly at ease with her traveling companion, the Captain was so close, so friendly, so talkative.

Ahead of them sat Prudence and Lord Billner, very close together, Madeline thought, though she and the Captain were hardly at opposite ends of *their* seat. It was a rather early departure for Lord Billner. His cheeks showed the results of a rushed shave, with little red streaks and white dust where a styptic pencil had been applied to stop the bleeding. Shaving before one is wide awake, with a straight-edged razor, can be dangerous, as he discovered. But he smelled nice, of Pinaud aftershave, and his teeth had been brushed and were white and even, his breath sweet with the odor of peppermint flavored toothpaste.

Prudence squirmed. Lord Billner had yawned a dozen times if he had yawned once. He was not talking, he was not full of life; he was not fun. She knew nothing of the long hours he had sat up talking with a trio of Englishmen the night before, nor their killing of a fifth of Hague and Hague. She squirmed again. The upholstery on all Yellowstone Concords consisted of horsehair stuffing because it was vermin and mouse proof. But when horsehair worked up through the covering, it stuck up like thin, taught wire. Not one but several hairs had made their way through Prudence's clothing to her sensitive derriere. She made a face, squirmed again, and then, noticing Lord Billner's not very wide open eyes upon her, flashed him a smile from within her face's veil prison.

"You're awfully quiet this morning," she commented.

"Aren't I, though," he replied, stifling another yawn.

Prudence puckered her lips. What kind of an answer was that? He'd thrown the conversational ball right back at her. Now another darned old horsehair was bothering her. She squirmed again, raised her head aristocratically and gazed out upon the scenery. Suddenly she frowned. She turned to him and said in an accusing tone, almost like a wife demanding an explanation for her husband's late arrival from lodge meeting, "How long did you talk to those Englishmen last night?"

"I guess it was about three o'clock when we broke up."

"Three o'clock!" the girl repeated. "And you knew we were leaving at seven? Lord Billner, you should be ashamed. You must take better care of yourself."

'My Gawd,' thought Lord Billner dreamily, 'she's talking to me as if she's my wife.' His tired face showed amusement. 'But I kind of like it,' he reflected. To her he said simply, "I know."

Ahead of them sat Dolly Griffin, Emily, and Philip. Dolly discovered that she could lean her head out of the open coach and talk to her beloved Talmadge. This she did until she lost her grip and nearly fell out of the coach. After that she stayed inside a little more. Philip was chomping an unlit cigar and flipping pages of the *Haynes Guide*. Emily was concerned about something else.

"Philip."

"Yes, dear."

"I hate to be a prude, but – I wish we were sitting in back and Prudence and Lord Billner were in front of us. I just don't like her back there with him alone."

Philip removed his cigar and half turned to appraise the occupants in the seats behind. By this time Prudence was pouting, her exciting Englishman having turned into a tired boor. She had removed her body two full feet from him, partly because she was angry with him, partly to get off of the horsehairs. She was, Philip observed, sightseeing while Lord Billner was dozing. In the rear seat were Captain Taylor and Madeline, and their situation, Philip surmised, was something else again. The Captain and Madeline were sitting very close, he was leaning across her pointing to something, and Madeline looked as happy as he had ever seen her. Nothing to worry about, though, Philip surmised. That is what he told Emily.

"I hope you are right, Philip. Prudence is so naive, so innocent."

"I know," replied Philip with mental reservations. He thought of the Bust Developer incident, of the "shotgun marriages" that took place every year in Elm Grove. True, Prudence had never been really serious with a boy, but she had several friends who had full term babies just seven or eight months after hasty marriages. Prudence, the Judge concluded, knew a thing or two about life. At least by hearsay.

Hezekiah stopped briefly at Rustic Falls and the rock formations beyond called the Hoodoos. By the time they entered Swan Lake Flats they were a thousand feet above the National Hotel and two thousand feet above Gardiner. They did not tarry long, however, what with

more than twenty Concords behind them followed by people in private
carriages and buggies and finally camping families – sagebrushers, as
the innkeepers called them derogatorily, since they did not stay at the
hotels but camped in the sagebrush.

New mountain beauty opened before their eyes. Hezekiah pointed
out Electric Peak, second highest point in the Park, the Gallatin Range
to the west of them, and Gardner's Hole, "One of them thar places,"
Hezekiah informed his passengers, "whar the Mountain Men used to
hang out, y'ars ago."

"You ever hole up there?" asked the Congressman.

"Naw. All those doin's were before my time."

"Oh, I'll bet you had some fun in your time," taunted Dolly from
her seat below.

"Didn't say I hadn't."

"I know what they say about you old frontiersmen and pretty
Indian maidens," she went on. "Tell us, Hezekiah, have you ever
been married to a squaw?"

Hezekiah removed his pipe from his mouth. "Matter of fact, I was
married once, sorta, to a Shoshone gal. A pretty Shoshone Belle.
That's where the coach's name comes from."

"Are you," queried Dolly hesitantly, "still married to her?"

"Naw," replied Hezekiah, pulling out a tin of Sir Walter Raleigh.
"I sent her to roam."

"To Rome? To Rome, Italy?" asked the Louisiana matron.

"Nope," said Hezekiah matter-of-factly, "to roam on the prairie."

Congressman Griffin roared, Philip laughed and Mrs. Griffin
sniffed and ended the conversation.

The coach clattered slowly south down Swan Lake Flats. Suddenly
Rusty cried, "There's a moose!"

The coachman ahead had also seen it and stopped. Prudence
opened the door to get out and walk toward the great beast with its
huge hatrack of antlers above its head and its bell-shaped appendage
hanging from its neck.

"I wouldn't, Miss," warned Hezekiah, spitting to the side.

"Why not?" asked the girl.

"Moose, they're unpredictable, that's why. You get too close to
that moose, he may just take a turn for you and you'd end up strewn
across his hatrack."

"But he looks harmless," argued the girl.

"Yep," growled Hezekiah, "but it's that time of y'ar when he's getting in rut. And then watch out! Giddyap," he snarled, snapping the whip at the grays.

Prudence sat back, her feelings hurt. Everything was going wrong. Lord Billner was asleep and old Hezekiah wouldn't let her photograph a harmless looking old moose. Behind her Madeline and the Captain were conversing and laughing. Up ahead Mother and Dad were talking with Dolly and all three were conversing with the Congressman in the driver's seat. She could even hear old Hezekiah and Rusty talking.

Fortunately the brief stop jolted Lord Billner awake. He shook his head a couple times and realized that his drowsiness was at an end. Yes, there was that beautiful girl sitting beside him. She was pouting. 'How pretty she is when she pouts,' he thought. He'd better make up for lost time.

"Beautiful day," he commented.

"That mean old man," she said. "The time of year when he's likely to be in rut," she mimicked.

Lord Billner chuckled.

"What's so funny, sir?"

"Nothing. Oh, nothing really, Prudence. Just laughing at old Hezekiah. Moose in rut. That's rich. The old boy doesn't mince words, does he? Even if there are ladies present."

"The joke seems to be especially on me," she said. "Dare I ask – what does it mean – 'a moose in rut'?"

Her companion chuckled some more. "You mean, you don't know?"

"Well – I suppose it means he's hungry."

Lord Billner laughed again. "Yes," he replied with mock seriousness. "In a manner of speaking, that's what it means. The moose is hungry."

They rode on for a while in silence, but it was very obvious to Lord Billner that wheels were whirling in Prudence's head. "You mean," she finally began, looking straight at him with those innocent blue eyes blinking, "you mean moose only get hungry at certain times of the year?"

She awaited his reply. Now he was puzzled. How could he explain it and still be a gentleman? "You see, Prudence – there are different kinds of hunger." The young English gentleman was not sure whether to shock this beautiful picture of innocence with truth or protect her from the facts of life.

"Different kind of hunger? What *are* you saying?"

"Well – er – there's hunger for sweets, and hunger for good, solid, food, or maybe for something sour."

The coach ambled on. After long minutes, she said, "That doesn't make sense, that a moose goes into rut for something sweet, solid, or sour. He'd always be in rut for those things. Stephen, what are you hiding from me?"

The remittance man sighed. Her big, innocent blue eyes were searching his face – for a moment he thought they were almost *too* innocent. 'Who's pulling who's leg?' he thought. Or were those blue eyes accusing him of not being honest with her? Lord Billner reached over and took Prudence's gloved hands and said, "Yes, Prudence, there is more. But I'm not sure you should know." He was amazed at the sexual charge those words gave him.

"Mercy," Prudence burst out. "After all, Lord Billner – I mean, Stephen – I *am* nineteen. I can't be protected all my life. Now, Stephen, you tell me, you tell me everything, you tell me the complete and unvarnished truth, or I won't speak to you again on this whole trip."

"Now, Prudence—"

"Is it – does it concern" – she wet her lips – "s-e-x?" she whispered.

Lord Billner feigned shock. He gasped. He turned his head and scanned the scenery on his side of the coach, and smothered a smirk. But he held her hands, and squeezed gently.

"Does it?" she whispered again. Exasperated by his continued silence, she blurted aloud, "It does, doesn't it?" She broke a hand free and put it to her lips. Mother and Dad had turned to her. "Nothing. Nothing," she said to them, and they turned away.

Finally, regaining his composure, Lord Billner turned to her. "Yes," he said quietly.

"Ohhhhhhhhhh, I knew it," gasped the girl. "Who'd have thought such things of an innocent looking moose?"

"Just proves you can't even trust a hatrack."

Prudence giggled. 'So if the moose is in rut, he's – he's—"

"Anxious."

"Ohhhhhhhhh."

"See Prudence," began Lord Billner, trying to elevate the conversation to an educational level, "moose, elk, buffalo, and other wild animals – well – they are only – *anxious* – at a certain time of the year. When that time comes around, they are very unpredictable. So we should steer clear of them."

"They wouldn't do anything horrible to *me*, would they?"

"Oh, heavens no. They are just grouchy and unpredictable."

"Whewwww," she replied, relaxing. "I was afraid – imagine being – oh. Oh. I just never knew that."

"That's the way it is in the world of nature," said Lord Billner. "Now let's talk about something else."

A long silence followed, which made Lord Billner uneasy. Those wheels were spinning around in Prudence's head. 'What,' he thought, 'is going to come from that pretty mouth of hers next?' Then it came, right out of the blue.

"Are men like that?"

"Oh, Prudence. Goodness, no. Men are civilized creatures."

"You mean, men are never in rut."

Lord Billner withdrew his hands from hers, pulled a white handkerchief from his pocket and wiped perspiration from his brow. She was quiet again, but she wasn't watching the scenery. He saw her lips moving, almost imperceptibly. Then her mouth closed tightly and she turned her head slowly to him. "That," she said, "doesn't make sense either."

"What doesn't make sense either?"

"That men are never in rut. Don't you mean, sir, on the contrary, that men are *always* in rut?" Her voice was accusing.

"Now, Prudence—"

"That's it," she said, her mind clearly made up. "Men are always in rut. And moose are nicer than men because they're only – hungry – one season of the year. So girl mooses can go all over the forest alone and be in no – danger – except in one season. I like that."

"But, oh, Prudence," said Lord Billner sarcastically, "that season!"

"Hmmph. I knew it was a good moose," she replied.

Lord Billner sighed. "OK, Prudence. I am a lecherous, hungry man. In rut all year 'round. Go back to your old moose."

She laughed and patted his shoulder. "No," she said. "I think I'd still prefer a lecherous young man to a moose at any time of the year."

"A man like me?"

"Mm. Maybe. But I like men who are awake in the morning. Are you always sleepy in the morning? Such a boor?"

"Oh, my, yes. And I'm terribly lecherous, too. And hungry. I'm at the ruttiest age, too. Madam. Are you sure you don't prefer the moose?"

"I'm sure," Prudence replied warmly, and they both laughed. "I know you are far handsomer than a moose," she added. Lord Billner had a fleeting glimpse of himself in Bath Lake with Prudence observing him from a hidden bower. He was relieved when they left Swan Lake Flats and stopped at the Apollinaris Spring, where the water tasted like soda pop, and he could change the subject.

## II

Rusty Snowden was in boy's heaven. The high point of his eleven years had arrived. For five days he would ride shotgun up in the driver's seat with Hezekiah, and sometimes with Congressman Griffin, too. Clothed in black shoes, black stockings, brown corduroy knickers that always hung down over his knees, unclasped; a tan flannel shirt, and his carrot-topped head sometimes covered with a wide-brimmed straw hat his mother had purchased for him at Mammoth, the boy sat as satisfied as a grand monarch surveying his realm from the castle tower.

"What ye got in that package yer holdin' onto, laddie?" asked Hezekiah.

"This?" The boy examined a long, narrow something, amateurishly wrapped in brown paper. "This is my secret weapon. I'll use it to call an elk, when the time comes."

"And what you gonna do," Hezekiah asked further, "when the elk comes to ye?"

"Then I'll get my antlers."

Hezekiah and the Congressman laughed and the mountaineer patted the boy's shoulders. "Heck, laddie, we won't need any secret weapon for that. I told ye last night that I'd get you some prime antlers in a day or two."

"Oh," replied the boy, shrugging his shoulders. "Anyway, I'm still gonna hang onto my secret weapon."

"You do that."

"But what is it, this secret weapon of yours?" asked Congressman Griffin, highly amused.

"It's a secret," Rusty told him, grasping the package tightly.

"Come on, now, sonny. Why don't you-all tell us how it works?" suggested the Congressman.

Rusty thought for a while and then said, "you know about the Pied Piper of Hamlin?"

"Yep," answered Hezekiah. "He's the feller that got rid of the rats."

"That's right, Mr. Hezekiah. With a flute. I've got something better than that. You should hear it. It makes a high squeal just like animals might. Real, wild animals. It sounds real weird."

"And that's your weapon, son?" asked the Congressman.

"Yes, sir. I'll work it and the elk comes in, and then Mr. Hezekiah hits him and takes away his antlers. You can't take away an elk's antlers if you don't have the elk, can you?"

"Can't argue with that," both men agreed, exchanging winks. They let him keep his weapon, knowing they could bring up the subject again whenever conversation lagged.

"See up ahead there," said Hezekiah loud enough for all to hear. He was pointing to a dark cliff jutting into the valley, with the road hacked out of its west side. "That's Obsidian Cliff, a mountain of glass."

"Real glass?" asked Rusty.

"Real, black, natural glass, young feller. First seen by old Jim Bridger, a mountain man. May his soul rest in peace."

"Ahhhhhh, that ain't glass," taunted Rusty.

"Oh, but it is," said Hezekiah. "Jim Bridger was out here a-huntin', and he saw this elk, and he raised his rifle and shot at it, and nothin' happened. That old elk just kept right on grazin'."

"Why?"

"Now, just be patient. Old Jim, he advanced real stealthy-like up to twenty-five yards of that elk, and took keerful aim again, got the elk right in his sights, and crack! He pulled the trigger. And that thar elk just kept right on grazin'."

"Why didn't it drop dead?"

"Why, ol' Jim, he didn't know either. So he slammed his rifle to the ground and ran toward the elk to wring its blarsted neck. An' you know what?" Hezekiah removed his pipe, spat, and replaced the corn cob in his mouth. "He ran right smack dab into a glass wall and fell down with blood oozin' from his nose. He'd run into a mountain of glass, he had. And the elk, it was grazin' on the other side."

"Awwwwwwww."

"So Jim, he clumb *over* the glass wall to get that elk."

"And did he get him?"

"Nope. Because ya see, laddie," and Hezekiah winked at the Congressman, "that thar glass wall was magnified. "The elk ol' Jim thought was just twenty-five yards away was really twenty-five miles away!"

Hezekiah paused and spat again. Rusty, his mouth open in dismay, gazed up at the mountaineer. "Hy'ar, giddyap!" yelled Hezekiah, and the horses moved a little faster.

The boy was silent for a few moments. They paused briefly to pick up some of the obsidian shards. Then Rusty blurted, "I think old Jim Bridger was a liar."

"You get up in that seat, young feller," ordered Hezekiah angrily, "and no more contradictin' yer elders or I'll make you ride down in the coach."

Rusty quieted perceptibly, the others returned to their seats, and the journey continued.

### III

The Snowden vehicle – and all the other coaches along the way – continued southward along the road to the geysers. After Swan Lake Flats they had started climbing, while the scenery, which had been of swamps, with beaver dams and ponds and moose meadows, became heavily timbered with lodgepole pine.

Captain Taylor reached for his watch, swore softly as he remembered that it had been stolen, then gazed at the sun. "We're doing pretty well," he surmised. "I judge that it is about ten o'clock and it is about eight miles to Norris Geyser Basin where we have lunch."

"Then?" Madeline prodded him.

"Then we explore the sights around the Norris Geyser Basin, then ride on up to the Fountain Hotel where we spend the night. That's in the Lower Geyser Basin, another twenty miles farther on. I expect we'll all be ready for a rest by then."

Madeline agreed, waving a mosquito from her veil. "But it is all very beautiful," she added good-naturedly. He failed to respond. She glanced at him, frowning slightly. "Captain, you didn't hear a word I said. When we've talked – and we've talked a lot – I've felt, some of the time, that your mind is elsewhere. As a matter of fact, why are you making this trip? Is it to protect us?"

"Perhaps."

"Do you think the bandit is still in the neighborhood? Do you think he will strike again?"

"Maybe."

"Oh, Captain Taylor, tell me. Who could I tell military secrets to?"

The two cast long looks at each other. He smiled, a calm, relaxed smile, revealing, she thought, his true personality. "First I'm doing some detective work, then some escort work, Madeline. Under orders."

"The bandit?"

"Yes,. the bandit, although he's probably down in the Tetons by now."

"And what else?"

"I'm after an automobile. Remember what I told you last night about Colonel Saddle-Pants Peavey? Well, he's in a dither over a Pierce-Arrow."

"An automobile – in Yellowstone!" she gasped. "Horrors!"

"You think it's funny, and I think it's funny, but Saddle-Pants sees no humor in it. No humor in it at all. To hear him talk, this is the worst crisis facing the Army since Custer was massacred at the Little Big Horn."

"Tell me more, Captain."

"It seems this beer baron from Peoria, Fritz Buschmeister, came huffing and puffing in his monster of a car to the South Entrance a couple of days ago. He demanded his constitutional rights to drive through the Park to the North Entrance. When they refused to allow his Goodyear Tires to ruffle the furrows of Yellowstone's virgin roads – er, pardon my metaphors – he protested. He got on the telephone and told Saddle-Pants a thing or two. It seems he has connections. He threatened to get old Saddle-Pants transferred and – well – even old Saddle-Pants weakened, a little."

"A little?"

"Yes. The car is going through the Park to the North Entrance."

"Wonderful!" exclaimed Madeline, clapping her hands. "An automobile finally going through the Park."

"Going through the Park loaded on an oversize freight wagon drawn by mules, with a huge tarpaulin covering the machinery so that it won't scare the horses. And that's not all. Colonel Peavey directed the wheels be taken off and placed on a second wagon."

"Oh, how ridiculous"

"And I, Madeline, am under orders to meet the 'automobile wagons', as Saddle-Pants calls them, and escort them through the Park to the North Entrance."

Madeline laughed. "You, Captain? You, who love automobiles?"

"It's not funny, dear lady. Saddle-Pants said he'd bust me to buck private if the Goodyears ever touched Yellowstone's good earth. He doesn't trust Fritz Buschmeister. Seems this fellow goes around the country establishing firsts – first car up Pike's Peak, first car in Estes Park, first car in Jackson, Wyoming, first car over Togwotee Pass. He's been establishing firsts for years. Saddle-Pants suspects that the first Buschmeister wants most of all is, first automobile through Yellowstone National Park. So you see, I've got to make sure the wheels stay on one wagon and the car on the other, both covered with tarps."

"My poor Captain," Madeline sympathized with mock pity.

"If I fail," said Captain Taylor – and he made as if to slit his throat. "But there's still more to my trip."

"More?"

He nodded, then pointed toward the front of the coach, and up. "Hezekiah Hotchkiss," he said quietly. "That old mountaineer has been on the narrow line between legitimacy and illegitimacy in this Park for twenty years. We think he has connections inside the Reservation with bootleggers, poachers, and perhaps even gold miners."

"Gold miners. In Yellowstone?"

"Shhhhhhh, Madeline. Yes, Gold miners. There's plenty of gold here, but of course we don't advertise it. And poachers, especially in the far corners of the Park. But what we're suspicious of right now about old Hotchkiss is bootlegging. We think he brings liquor to Company employees who then sell it to tourists."

Madeline looked up towards the front of the coach. "Old Hezekiah? I don't think he'd do wrong. He just talks tough."

"Think of the company he keeps," reminded the Captain.

She recalled the near-naked madam who threw him out of the Bucket of Blood. Madeline suppressed a smile. "Are you referring to Rosie?"

"Right. He knows the shady people, the seamy characters." Captain Taylor dug out his pipe and filled it, struck a match and produced a cloud of fragrant smoke. "They say," he continued, "that Hezekiah has a claim to Rosie. That long years ago when they were both young she said she'd marry him if he gave her $5,000. He struck it rich in a gold mine, came galloping into town and gave Rosie the $5,000 cash. She accepted the money, so the story goes, but reneged on fulfilling her part of the bargain. Preferred a life of sin, I guess."

"That's terrible."

"So old Hezekiah returns every so often to – er – collect his interest and plead to Rosie to give up being a madam and make good her part of the bargain."

"We're comin' to Roaring Mountain," announced Hezekiah as if in answer to the crescendoing roar heard ahead of them. He hardly gave them a minute to observe the steam vents before he announced that it was "just four more miles to lunch" and "let's be sure and get there before the other coaches arrive." This was sufficient encouragement to send the passengers scrambling back into the coach. Even the horses sensed the impending rest period, for they voluntarily stepped up their pace.

The Captain continued: "Bootlegging is our immediate concern," he said, "but there are other possibilities involving Hezekiah. We know there are squatters in the Park, men who live here all year round, hidden in deep canyons or in thick timber. And we suspect old Hezekiah may know a few of them. He's been known to disappear from the coachmen's barracks for a day or two. Nobody knows where he's been."

"It's hard to believe anyone could escape the surveillance of the United States Cavalry, though."

"This is a big Park, Madeline," Captain Taylor reminded her, "fifty-five by sixty-five miles big, the size of Delaware and Rhode Island put together. Plenty of people get lost in those states."

They rode on in silence, talked out after five hours. Even the sight of a mother bear and her two cubs failed to perk them up. It was a relief for all when Hezekiah drove up to a peppermint-striped tent where a man in a white coat came out to greet them.

"I'm Larry, the Irishman," he announced, "begorry, I'm proud to make yer acquaintance. Ladies' retreats to the right, men's to the left, and good vittles awaitin' yer return."

A few minutes later they entered the long tent, with its board floor and wooden walls extending up four feet, and long rows of picnic tables filling the interior. Within a few more minutes the tent was filled with talkative humanity from the other coaches, while others, late comers, awaited their turn. Lunch consisted of thick bread, beef stew, and coffee, tea, or milk. It was not an elaborate spread, but everyone was hungry. The Snowdens, like everyone else, bolted their food with gusto.

## IV

Hezekiah, eating at the Mulligan Dump (as the employees' mess was called) inquired of the coachmen about the possible sighting of a tall man on a black horse, with a silver disk with a hole in the middle attached to his throat, probably the result of a doctor saving his life when he had diphtheria. "If ye see him, ye won't fergit him," said Hezekiah. "He looks like the Devil's lackey – mean, dirty, and evil." He recounted the story of the holdup, recalling every last detail even to the way the highwayman had tried to snatch Prudence. "Everyone figures he high-tailed it for the Tetons," Hezekiah told those present, "and at first I thought so, but now I think he's still in the Park. I think he's shadowin' the *Shoshone Belle*. Just feel it in my bones."

"Say," volunteered a burly teamster at the other end of the table. "I think maybe I saw him. I was at Old Faithful last night when a couple of horses broke out of the corral and I had to go lookin' for them. Got down toward some meadows and in a deep growth of timber was this lone horseman. I wouldn't have seen him 'cept his horse whinnied, and when I looked man and rider blended so well in the timber that I almost passed them by. He was muzzlin' his horse, so I figured if he didn't want to see nobody, then I'd not bother to see him."

Hezekiah slapped a hand on the pine-board table. "That's him," he said. "That's him. He's stickin' around for some reason. You men all keep an eye out for him. Believe me, I'm goin' to."

Another coachman cut in. 'Yep, Hezekiah. Can't have anyone buttin' in on your side business." He winked at the others. "People are gettin' right thirsty down in the Park."

Hezekiah pretended not to hear, left the table and returned to the *Shoshone Belle*. No one heard, but he was mumbling something about "that damned Captain being along." He found his passengers already seated in the coach, eager to go to the geysers. Instantly he changed his mood, becoming the hearty coachman once again.

"We'll be at the geysers in just a few minutes, folks," he announced. "Ye can all get out and take the trail through the basin. Takes about a half hour."

First they spied the steam vents, then they smelled a faint, sulfurous rotten-egg odor, and then they heard the Black Growler steam vent which was close by the road. Near it the *Shoshone Belle* swung into a parking space; the passengers got out and started down the trail that more or less circumvented the Basin. Rusty led the way with Philip and Emily following, instructing the boy not to stray nor get too far ahead of them, not to step there, not to get too close to that spring, and "Rusty, don't you dare throw gravel in that pool!" It was Rusty, Rusty, Rusty.

Behind Philip and Emily came Congressman Griffin and Dolly, she with a frilly parasol for protection from the sun, he walking along portly as a statesman should be, with a cherry wood cane tapping on the soil or, at other places, on the wooden walk. Then, lagging, came Captain Taylor and Madeline. Where were Prudence and Lord Billner?

They had lagged behind, and the others had been too excited to notice. "I say there, Hezekiah, this *Haynes Guide* tells us there is a geyser and some hot springs on the other side of the road. Where's the trail?"

The mountaineer removed his stubby pipe from his mouth and grinned, for all the world loves lovers, and he rather enjoyed aiding cupid. "Right over there," he pointed, "but ye'll have to move fast to make the circle afore the others return."

"We'll hurry," said Prudence as the two skipped down the trail and out of sight. Hezekiah relit his pipe. "Hmmph," he grunted, "I'll bet they slow to a walk as soon as they're out of sight."

They did more than that. Ever since Lord Billner had roused from his nap it had been thigh against thigh and squeezing of hands and conversation bubbling from their lips. Now, as the pines enveloped them, Lord Billner halted. He leaned against a tree and pulled Prudence to him.

"Lord Billner – Stephen – please!" – but this was as far as she got. His strong arms encircled her narrow waist and held her to him, and his lips met hers through her veil. Slowly Prudence's arms encircled Lord Billner's shoulders. She broke free just long enough to lift the veil. Then she succumbed again, only this time with more emotion: she wrapped her arms around him as tightly as her muscles would allow. Only when they heard sounds of people approaching did they break away. Slowly they swung down the trail, arms around each other's waists, not even noticing the Steamboat geyser as it erupted.

"Prudence," began Lord Billner. "You are the sweetest, loveliest, girl I have ever known," he began.

She glanced at him appraisingly. "I like you too, Stephen. Even though you are obviously in rut."

They strolled on, made a turn in the trail and again – no humans being about – took time for another long, lingering kiss. This time Stephen's hands drifted down to the small of Prudence's back and even to her upper hips. The lovers broke and strolled some more.

"But I know so little about you," said Prudence. "Why are you here? Do you have brothers and sisters? Who are your parents? What do you really do for a living? What is your future?"

"I suspect," he replied, "I am what you Americans call, just an ordinary guy."

"But you aren't, Stephen. Daddy told me. And you told me you are a British remittance man, whatever that is."

"And that is bad, is it? Did your father say it is bad?"

"I – I don't believe Daddy thought it was very good. Stephen, just what is a remittance man?"

Lord Billner scowled. He let go of her, picked up a twig and played with it with his hands, breaking it into bits. They walked along in silence. "Did I say something wrong, Stephen? I didn't mean to, but – you know, I don't let just anybody kiss me – like you just kissed me. Gosh. I've *never* let anyone kiss me like that!"

It struck Lord Billner that the kissing was not all on his part, but he simply said, "It's all right, Prudence. It's all right."

"But it isn't, Stephen. All of a sudden you're angry with me."

He stopped short, swung around in front of her, held her by the shoulders and looked into her face. "I think you should have it straight, Prudence. Yes, I am a remittance man. I'm – a rotter. I am forbidden to return to England."

"No! No! It's not true!" protested Prudence. "Stephen, you are not a rotter. I know you're not. You're too good to be a rotter. I don't believe it. Why, Stephen. What could you have done?"

They resumed their stroll, Stephen placing his arm lightly around Prudence's waist; Prudence reciprocated.

"You see, Prudence," Lord Billner began explaining, "England has changed so in the last fifty years. It used to be that a second son, which is what I am, who could never inherit his father's estate, could join His Majesty's Army or Navy, perhaps become a barrister or a clergyman, or join the Foreign Service. But times have changed. Now one has to take Civil Service examinations, one has to compete with progeny of the middle class, and some of us second sons discover that our blue blood has run thin. When we compete, we lose."

"But not you, Stephen. You could pass any old exam."

"As a matter of fact, Prudence, I never took any examinations. After Oxford I studied for His Majesty's Foreign Service, when—"

"When—"

"When – uh – something happened and I came here instead."

"When what happened, Stephen?"

"That, I choose not to tell you, Prudence."

She looked up at him. "And why not?" she asked.

"It is a private matter involving only my older brother Percival, my fathah, and myself."

"But they are thousands of miles away. I'll probably never meet them. I don't understand why you won't tell me."

"I know all that."

"And you still won't tell me?"

"I – don't think so."

"Then please do not expect to kiss me again." The coach was in sight, everyone was aboard waiting for them, and Prudence ran to it,

Lord Billner several paces behind. Once aboard, she sat so straight in her corner of the seat, that all noticed. Emily was glad. There were four more days to go. A little spat could cool things down.

## V

From the Norris Geyser Basin the road lead southerly through tall pines toward the Lower Geyser Basin, overlooking which was the massive Fountain Hotel. There they would spend the night. Hezekiah kept the horses at a brisk trot, hoping to arrive before sunset. In addition, the sun had disappeared behind great thunderheads and a cool wind had sprung up, and the fresh odor of rain was in the air.

"Giddyap," Hezekiah commanded, wielding his whip.

"Oh, pshaw," said the Captain to the passengers, "he can't beat the rain. Why doesn't he let the poor horses make their own speed?"

Suddenly rain came pelting out of the heavens, hail mixed with it. "Ohhhhhhhh, we're getting soaked," protested Dolly Griffin. In the driver's seat the Congressman, hunched over with an arm around Rusty, pleaded with Hezekiah to stop so he and Rusty could climb into the coach out of the rain.

"Hezekiah. I say, *Mister* Hotchkiss. You-all heauh me? Stop this coach so we can get under the roof and let down the rain curtains. Everybody's getting wet!"

"Giddyap," yelled Hezekiah, and the horses trotted faster.

Rusty held on for dear life. "Faster! Faster!" the boy yelled.

"Giddyap, hyar." The mountaineer snapped his whip and the coach fairly flew up the canyon. And the rain came down in torrents.

"Hotchkiss!" from inside the coach ordered Captain Taylor in his strong officer's voice. "You hear me, Hotchkiss? Stop this coach at once or I'll have you ousted from the Park permanently. You hear me, Hotchkiss? I'll have you fired and expelled *permanently*. Now *stop this coach!*"

A long silence followed, and then the passengers heard a long, drawn-out "whoaaaaaaaaaaaaa". The horses slowed to a stop and the coach stood still, as rain and hail staccatoed off the roof and the rain blew in through the open sides, soaking the passengers.

"That's better. Now help me unroll the rain curtains," ordered the Captain as he gallantly stepped into the rain and hail and began untying them one by one.

"But Captain, sir," Hezekiah pleaded from the coachmen's seat, "this is just a little afternoon shower. Ain't no need to put down the rain curtains."

"This is a violent thunderstorm and you know it, Hotchkiss. I can't understand you."

Hezekiah watched with miserable fascination as Captain Taylor untied the first knot. Before their eyes it happened: down rolled the curtain and onto the ground clinked two bottles of Old Crow. One smashed on a rock and the fragrant, orange-brown liquid spread over the gravel. The other landed in dirt and remained intact.

"Well, I'll be..." said Captain Taylor, surprised.

"Why," said Hezekiah, jumping down from his seat in violation of regulations, "who would have done that?"

"Yes," replied the Captain, eyeing the mountaineer, "who could have done that?"

Hezekiah looked at the sky. "Oh, well, the rain's ending. Let's roll the curtain back up and be on our way. There's a hot meal awaiting us at the Fountain Hotel."

"The meal can wait," said the Captain, picking up the good bottle. "Let's unroll the other curtains too. But be more careful this time, shall we? Here, Congressman," he said, handing him the bottle. "Hold Exhibit "A" for us, will you please?"

Captain Taylor, ignoring the pouring rain, carefully untied and unrolled each of the other curtains, from which he obtained eight more pints: one of Green River, four of White Horse, and three of Old Quaker Rye. Congressman Griffin had fetched his satchel into which he carefully placed the bottles.

"Hotchkiss," said the Captain sternly, "I am hereby arresting you on charges of smuggling liquor into the Reservation. You will continue to Fountain Hotel where I shall turn you over to the sergeant stationed there. I'll have you up before Judge Meldrum, the United States Commissioner at Mammoth, and you will be expelled from the Park, permanently. Now let's get moving, and no funny business. We are all wet and tired."

"But, sir—" protested Hezekiah more meekly than the passengers had ever heard him speak.

"Save your excuses," replied the Captain, climbing back into the *Shoshone Belle*. Poor Hezekiah, his shoulders wet and drooping, climbed back to his seat and uttered a disconsolate "Giddyap" and flapped the reins. He was so quiet that all four horses turned their heads to him to see what was wrong. The coach started off at a snail's pace, and so it continued even as the storm blew over and a late afternoon sun brought welcome warmth. The curtains were rolled back up.

Bottles tinkled in the Congressman's satchel as the coach jolted along. The Honorable Talmadge Beauregard Griffin considered liberating one of them so the others would have more room, and, he reasoned illogically, therefore would be less likely to crack, but he quickly realized that was ridiculous. Then there was the problem of Captain Taylor, West Point Class of '01. He was probably above reproach – incorruptible and thorough. That meant that he had counted the bottles and would raise an uproar if one of them came up missing.

"They sound so musical, don't they, Talmadge," commented Dolly.

"Don't they, now."

The *Shoshone Belle* approached Gibbon Falls. When everyone got out to look at them Dolly pulled her husband aside. "Talmadge," she asked, "what's going to happen to all those good bottles?"

"Don't rightly know," he replied.

"Remember that long weekend at your fraternity at L.S.U.?" Dolly giggled like a school girl. "Remember the bottles, Talmadge? And how I'd never tasted it before – or anything?"

The Congressman puffed on his cheroot, then removed it as a whimsical smile spread over his fleshy face. "Ho, ho, ho. Do I remember, my dear. Do I remember?"

"We could do it all over tonight at the hotel, Talmadge, if we could acquire a bottle or two." She giggled like a young bride.

"I'll think of something, my dear. Just leave it to me," he said, casting a knowing wink at her. "After all, you don't become a Louisiana Congressman without using your head a little. That Captain has such integrity! But, hey, Dolly: What is integrity against a Louisianian, eh?"

"You'll succeed, Talmadge. I just know you will. See you later." She hustled back into the *Shoshone Belle* while he climbed back up with Rusty and Hezekiah. Then a thought struck him. He asked Hezekiah to wait while he handed Rusty, over Rusty's protests, down to ride in the coach with Prudence and Lord Billner. Truth was, Congressman Griffin wanted a private conversation with Hezekiah.

"Warmer down there for the lad," he said. "Don't want Rusty to catch pneumonia, what with his wet clothes and all."

Two hours later they arrived at the Fountain Hotel overlooking the Lower Geyser Basin. It was another big, rambling wooden hulk, drably painted a dull gray. Hezekiah guided the *Shoshone Belle* into the porte-cochère, gave his resounding "whoaa-a-a" and sat disconsolately puffing his pipe as bellboys fetched the luggage and the passengers climbed down. As they started into the lobby, Congressman Griffin grabbed Captain Taylor's arm.

"Could I have a few words with you, Captain?"

Captain Taylor was impatient, for he had to get to a telephone, talk with the sergeant in charge of the small contingent stationed there, and place Hezekiah in proper hands. He was also making plans for dinner with Madeline.

"Yes, sir," he replied militarily.

"Couldn't you allow Mr. Hotchkiss to complete the trip with us? After all, Captain, we'll end up back at Mammoth Hot Springs, and that's where the United States Commissioner's office is located, isn't it?"

"But Congressman Griffin, this man is—"

"Awww, come on, Captain. What the hell. He's a nice old codger. An old Indian fighter."

Dolly Griffin cut in, "Please don't be harsh with him," she said in her most syrupy way.

"Nice old man!" exclaimed the Captain. "Why, Mrs. Griffin, that old buzzard knows more about poaching, bootlegging, illegal fishing, and illicit mining in this Park than anyone else alive. He's been around here since the 1880s, all the time walking the narrow line between legality and illegality." The Captain paused to catch his breath. "My duty, sir, is to turn him over to the proper officials and have him permanently expelled from the Reservation."

Dolly bristled. She turned to her husband. "Talmadge," she asked, "what is the Military Affairs Committee going to think about Army officers who browbeat old Indian fighters and deny them a way of making a living?"

"War veteran, too," her husband added. "Nez Perce War of '77."

Captain Freeman W. Taylor, US Second Cavalry, West Point of '01, blanched. Like army officers from time immemorial, he was feeling the pinch of politics. Uncertain of what to say, Madeline, who had overheard the conversation, broke the impasse. "Oh, Captain, I think the Griffins have a fine idea. Let Mr. Hotchkiss continue to guide us through the Park and we'll settle affairs when we get back to Mammoth Hot Springs. No harm will be done." She tugged at his coat. "Come on, Freeman," she pleaded quietly, becoming very personal, "let's go into the hotel."

"Well stated, Miss Snowden," said Congressman Griffin, bowing to her. "The little lady is right, Captain. You hang onto her. She'll have you a Major before you know it. By the way, what is your complete name, suh? Captain Freeman W. Taylor, Second US Cavalry? Got to remember that, young man. Yes, suh. We should have a talk. We like to see good soldiers advanced in the Service, you know."

Captain Taylor would like to have punched the Congressman's bulbous red nose, but again Madeline tugged at his coat. "Come on, Captain," she urged. He began walking away with her. "Remember, Freeman, discretion is the better part of valor."

Once away from the Congressman and his wife, the Captain began again. "Madeline, don't you understand? Hezekiah is smuggling liquor into the Park in direct violation of regulations."

"And," she reminded him, "Congressman Talmadge Beauregard Griffin is a member of the Armed Services Committee of the United States House of Representatives. Captain," she said boldly, "let's face it. Like it or not, you've been checkmated. And remember, it is a compromise. Hezekiah will get his just deserts once we are back at Mammoth."

"Well, at least I can confiscate the whiskey. That's the evidence." He turned around and began walking in long, swift steps back toward the porte-cochère. Madeline ran after him as fast as her hobble skirt would let her. "Captain, no."

"Why not?" he asked, not slowing his pace.

"Oh, Captain, don't you see? The Congressman and his wife want the whiskey!"

"What?" Captain Taylor stopped short.

"Of course. They don't care anything about old Hezekiah. They want the whiskey. We'll probably be pouring them into the coach tomorrow morning."

"But, damnit, Madeline, that's my evidence. Without it old Hotchkiss'll go free."

"I know, but..." she replied, pleading for understanding.

The military man paused, then started for the entrance again. "No, by gadfrey. I've got to get that evidence." He swung open the screen door and marched under the porte-cochère, then stopped. The *Shoshone Belle* was gone. All passengers and their luggage had been removed. "Damn, Madeline. You know old Hezekiah will get rid of the evidence."

"What do you think the Congressman was talking about with Hezekiah?" she asked, then answered, "I'd guess they arranged for the Honorable Talmadge Beauregard Griffin, M.C., to take custody of the satchel." Slowly they turned back into the lobby. "It would be kind of silly, would it not, to be denied promotion because of a thirsty Congressman?"

He looked puzzled. "What do you mean by that?"

They strolled across the lobby. "See," said Madeline, motioning her head. Indeed, Congressman Griffin, carrying the small satchel, and his wife were climbing the stairs, with a bellboy carrying their big suitcase.

"Recognize the satchel?" asked Madeline.

Captain Taylor impetuously started for them, but Madeline restrained him. She laughed. "I think it's funny, Captain. And you'd best think so too." Her eyes sparkled with warmth.

Captain Freeman Taylor turned to this winsome little school teacher with a new look in his eyes. "You win, Madeline. You win," he said.

## VI

Captain Taylor left Madeline in the lobby, promising to meet her in the Fountain dining room at six thirty. She went to her room where she found Prudence already dressing for dinner. On down the hall a door or two, Philip was pleased to discover that Rusty had been given a separate room. Maybe, he thought, the holiday would really be complete tonight. Meanwhile Emily sat on the bed, testing the springs. "It seems to be comfortable, dear," she commented. "Let's not stay for the dance tonight." Philip understood, and was glad.

There was a knock on the door, followed by Prudence's cheery voice. "May I come in?"

Philip opened the door for his comely daughter who, eyes sparkling, entered the room clad in a beige linen hobble skirt with jacket to match, and her big, feathery hat above her stylishly coiffured golden curls. In her right hand she toyed with the handle of a frilly parasol. "I just want you to know that I'm meeting Stephen in the lobby and we're going to see the paint pots."

"That's your alternate skirt," said Emily. "You'll get it dirty, Prudence. Remember, you just took two skirts."

"Oh, I'll be careful. The guidebook says the trails are well kept and clearly marked, and anyway, the whole distance is hardly more than a city block from the hotel."

Philip scowled. "Stephen?" he asked. "Who's Stephen?" As if he didn't know.

"Oh, Daddy. You know. Lord Billner. Stephen's his first name."

Philip, sitting on the bed, noisily unwrapped a cigar. He bit off an end, took it from his mouth and threw the stub in a wastebasket. Noisily he opened a matchbox, scratched a match into flame, and lit his cigar. "Stephen, huh?"

"Oh," said Emily hesitantly. "I guess it will be all right. We're dining at six thirty. Be sure and be back by then. And keep your clothes clean."

"Oh, easily," the girl replied, meaning both time and clothes.

Then Madeline knocked and entered. She wore a sedate brown hobble skirt and jacket to match, her dark hair was likewise nicely coiffured and topped by a big hat, and she too held a parasol. "Just wanted to tell you," she announced, "that I'm dining with Captain Taylor tonight. So – I won't be dining with you."

"Oh, then, Mother and Daddy," Prudence piped up, "can Stephen eat with us? I want you to meet him – formally. He's smart and well educated. I just know you will like him. Since Madeline won't be with us…"

She considered their exchange of glances as an approval. The two women, one nineteen and the other thirty, both radiant in hope of love, strolled down the dark hall to the stairs. Inside the bedroom all was quiet until Rusty charged in without knocking, and threw himself across the bed.

"Hey. Your bed's softer than mine," he complained. "And mine's just a little cot."

"You'll be safe and sound, Rusty," his father assured him.

"Yep. I'll be fine. Say, Mother, have you seen my bag of jawbreakers? I can't find it."

Nor did he that night – but one of them turned up later.

## VII

Prudence and Madeline stepped aristocratically down the long, curved stairway to the rustic lobby. They were aware of eyes upon them, for the massive room was filled with dozens of those great American inventions for hyperactive nationals – rocking chairs – and they were all occupied. Dowagers, remembering their lost youth, cast admiring glances at the two young women. Several fat, successful businessmen appraised their beauty, then sighed, while one or two lecherous old goats harbored carnal thoughts until, upon closer scrutiny, the clothes, faces, and demeanor of the two women pronounced them unmistakably genteel, churchgoing, and "nice". If anyone had designs, they were shattered when the splendidly uniformed Captain and the handsome young Englishman in tweeds strode across the lobby to the staircase and greeted the young women. All that was left for the rocking chair rockers were reminiscences.

"First, I want to see the Fountain Paint Pots," Prudence instructed Lord Billner, "and then the Celestine Pool and the Fountain Geyser. We should hurry because Mother and Daddy have invited us to dine with them at six thirty. Come on. Let's go."

"Shouldn't we wait for them?" he asked as Prudence started through the lobby, leaving the Captain and Madeline behind.

"Oh, no, silly. They're going to have dinner alone. They don't want us around."

"Nor we them," he added. "Let's be on our way."

They followed the trail to where the hot mud of clay, quartz, and opal bubbled and puckered and burst like bubble gum out of a boy's mouth. They strolled around the Celestine Pool, then reached the Fountain geyser just as it played fifty feet high. Trouble was, people were about. Lord Billner had soothed Prudence's feelings about refusing to tell her why he had become a remittance man. Now he was anxious to get away from crowds and kiss her again – and the way she held his arm he was sure she would not resist. But people were everywhere, so they talked. And as six thirty approached, they reappeared at the hotel.

"It will help, Stephen, if you will be your absolute most gentlemanly best at dinner."

Lord Billner bowed low before her. "In the name of His Majesty King Edward VII, I promise."

Meanwhile Captain Taylor and Madeline were strolling along a different trail, for he had surprised her by suggesting a private walk before dinner. Being an old Yellowstone hand, and not bashful about admitting it, he had escorted Madeline along the wagon road that led to Firehole Lake and the hot lakes. He knew a dim trail to an unlisted spring, he told her, and that spring, when reflecting the sunset, was more beautiful than anything in the Basin.

Madeline was thrilled, for she yearned to be alone with him again. And it felt nice, his hand at her waist, guiding her through a bower of pines and then, just as he said, to a dim trail leading through a grassy sward. When they no longer heard voices the Captain slowed and tugged at her arm. She broke away and started running. "Come on, Captain, let's get on to the spring. We haven't much time." As she ran the Captain, momentarily grumpy, set out after her. Seeing this, Madeline laughed and ran faster, heading for some woods and a big downed log where they could sit down. She darted around a big tree and almost kicked over a coffee pot hanging over a small campfire. She halted, surprised, as the figure who had been sitting in the shadows rose not three feet from where she stood. He had gray, matted hair, piercing eyes, and in his throat a silver disk with a hole in the middle through which he breathed with a sickly whistle. She put her fist to her mouth and screamed as the Captain's voice came through the stillness: "Madeline. Madeline! Where are you?"

The figure, dressed in dark clothing, was diverted by Captain Taylor's voice. Quickly he took a step forward and pushed Madeline hard, so hard that she lost her balance and fell back crashing through some young pines. She ended on the flat of her back. The man turned and ran, leaping over logs and boulders, to a horse tied in the shadows. The sound of faded clomping ensured that the culprit had left the scene.

Captain Taylor was more concerned with Madeline. "Are you hurt, Madeline? Are you hurt?" he asked as he tenderly lifted the small figure into his arms, off her feet, and held her there.

She buried her head in his chest. "I guess – I'm all right – Captain," she replied, regaining her composure. "That man – he's the same man—"

"I know," replied Captain Taylor, looking in the direction the horseman had fled.

"You can put me down now, Captain," said Madeline, looking up at him.

He looked into her face, pale and beautiful in the lengthening shadows, her long, brown hair disheveled and hanging from the back of her head, her hat still on the ground. She seemed so light, such a mere wisp of life. So – beautiful. Their eyes met as the Captain slowly let her slide down the length of his body, and her arms clutched his shoulders, and before her feet touched ground she was being kissed. Madeline held tight and gave him back his kiss with passion-interest to spare. Then their lips broke away, he let her feet touch the ground, and once again she buried her head in his chest. He continued to hold her tightly and nuzzled her hair. "Madeline. Madeline," he whispered.

She broke away completely. Her hands went to her hair. "We'd better get back, Captain," she said simply.

He picked up her hat and held it as she completed fixing her hair. While he watched she tucked in her shirtwaist, which had come out in the fracas, and finally twisted her skirt back to its right position. She knew the Captain was watching her with tender interest, but she cared not. "There," she said finally, "do I look all right now?" She placed her hat on her head and ran a six-inch-long hat pin through it.

"Adorable. Absolutely adorable, Madeline," he said as they started back to the trail. Then a thought struck him. "I should go back and see if the bandit left anything there. Then I have to report the incident to the soldier station." He looked down at her. "As soon as we get to the main trail, can you make your way back to the hotel alone? There is no danger now."

She was disappointed but courageously assured him she could. "Will we not have dinner together?" she asked.

"I'll make it, Madeline. I promise. So that you won't be alone, why don't we eat with your people? I'll join you."

And so they separated.

## VIII

"Do join us, Madeline," urged Philip. "We'll leave an extra place for the Captain. It's family style and there's no sense in your waiting alone for his arrival."

They were assembled in the lobby at the dining room entrance, Philip and Emily, Prudence and the tweedy-dressed Lord Billner, his black hair brushed immaculately; Rusty, in a Sunday School suit "when it warn't even Sunday"; and now Madeline, too. She had described the incident, but not as if it was anything terrible. Nevertheless, Emily had ordered Prudence and Rusty not to stray from the hotel.

They entered the drafty, rustic dining room with walls, they had read, plastered with mud-pot mud. It also boasted linen tablecloths, crystal dinnerware and shining silverware. Vittles included a big platter of roast beef, a tureen of string beans, a gravy boat brimming with dark, brown gravy; another tureen of mashed potatoes, and a pitcher of milk. Coffee was served to those wanting it. Beside each plate was a big wedge of apple pie.

"Shouldn't we have Grace, Daddy?" asked Prudence just as Philip was about to place his first forkful of food in his mouth. Embarrassed, he put down his fork and agreed.

"I'll say it," volunteered Lord Billner, "if you don't mind an Episcopal prayer."

All bowed their heads. In clear, humble tones, with a sincerity and dignity they had not noticed before, the remittance man gave thanks:

"Give us grateful hearts, Our Father, for all thy mercies, and make us mindful of the needs of others; through Jesus Christ, Our Lord. Amen."

Lord Billner's thanksgiving helped create happiness and contentment among the Snowdens. Prudence beamed as she saw Mother and Daddy look at Lord Billner approvingly.

Halfway through the meal the Captain made his appearance, storming in at his brusque military best, bowing low to Madeline, apologizing for his tardiness, and producing an old sack. "Guess what's in here?" he asked.

"Antlers?" suggested Rusty.

"No antlers, Rusty. But watches, rings, a diamond stick pin, a cameo pin, and wallets with the money and cards still in them. I found them in this sack at the bandit's camp."

"Our watches! And our wallets!" exclaimed Philip. "Emily's cameo?"

"Yup," replied the Captain, opening the sack. He proceeded to hand out the recovered valuables. "Here's your watch, Judge – and is this your wallet? And Stephen, I believe this is your watch and wallet. Here's your cameo, Mrs. Snowden. I've already retrieved my own.

When I see them, I'll return Congressman Griffin's watch, wallet, stick pin, and his wife's diamond rings. And - oh, yes, this last watch belongs to Hezekiah."

"I'd rather the sack contained antlers," said Rusty.

Captain Taylor took his seat beside Madeline, whose eyes sparkled and, thought Emily, whose face simply glowed; she had never observed such happiness in Madeline before.

"No sign of your satchel, Captain? The one containing past issues of *Automobile Age*?" Madeline whispered to the cavalryman.

The Captain nodded. "I'm afraid those are behind the boulder where he held us up. Like to have seen his face when he discovered magazines instead of the payroll," he said quietly.

"Well," said Prudence, not to be left out of the table talk, "Stephen and I saw lots of wonders on our walk, didn't we, Stephen? We saw all kinds of phallic symbols."

Lord Billner choked on his beef. Philip swallowed too large a lump and reached for the water glass; he coughed. Madeline, who knew her Latin and Greek but doubted Prudence's knowledge, blushed. Captain Taylor snorted.

"You saw - what?" asked Emily, who did not know the meaning of the word.

"Phallic symbols, Mother. Stephen says they are all over Yellowstone."

Emily frowned, confused. "Like what?" she asked, puzzled and a little suspicious.

'Like - like - as Stephen says, Cupid's Cave and the Grand Canyon and Old Faithful and the Spouter and the Liberty Cap down at Mammoth and that Devil's Slide we saw just before we entered the Park." The girl frowned. "But Stephen," she asked, turning to him, "you never did tell me. What exactly *is* a phallic symbol?"

Lord Billner, embarrassed and realizing that he was losing all the goodwill his saying of Grace had earned him, cleared his throat and prayed for quick thoughts. The faces of Prudence and her mother indicated ignorance of the word; of Philip and Captain, condemnation; of Madeline, embarrassment; and of Rusty, nothing at all. Lord Billner whispered a fast, silent prayer. How could he explain away this faux pas?

"Miss Prudence," he began, suave as a diplomat, realizing all eyes were upon him, "you misunderstood me. I said a *phalanx* of geysers – a whole army of them."

She caught his eye, the gentle nod of his head. "Oh. So that's what you meant. A phalanx of them," she said. There was a pause, and agonizingly, Lord Billner knew she was thinking. As with the rutting animals, he could almost hear the wheels whirling in her head. He dreaded what she might say next. "But why," she asked, "did you add that it could give a maiden ideas? What kind of ideas, Stephen?"

Madeline decided the subject had advanced far enough. "Philip," she broke in, changing the subject, "I hope you and Emily will take a walk to the geysers tonight. They should be a beautiful sight in the moonlight. There'll be a lot of people there, so no danger."

"And what am I supposed to do?" asked Rusty impolitely, his mouth full of meat and potatoes.

"You could attend the lecture," Emily suggested, "a magic lantern show accompanied by a Ranger's description of Yellowstone in winter."

"Can I buy some candy too?"

"Yes, with the nickel I've given you for sitting quietly up in the driver's seat during the storm this afternoon."

"Okay," said the boy. "I'll go."

Dinner ended. The Snowden party strolled into the lobby. Lamps had been lit, but talk was subdued, befitting the time of day. Prudence excused herself. Lord Billner said he was going to look up a couple of Englishmen who, he was told, were in the army stationed at the Lower Geyser Basin; he promised Prudence he would not stay with them too long. Captain Taylor took leave because he also had business at the soldier station. He told Madeline he would meet her next day and continue on with the *Shoshone Belle*, but if his orders were changed he would let her know. So Prudence and Madeline returned to their room, Rusty promised to stay in the lobby for the magic lantern show, and Emily and Philip left for the geysers. In due time they had observed most of what was to be seen within walking distance. Emily hooked her arm in Philip's as they strolled back to the lighted hotel.

"Tell me again," she asked, "how do geysers work?"

"Well – er – there's a source of energy that forces out the water."

"I know that, Philip. But where does the energy come from?"

"Deep down in the earth. Magma, they call it."

"But if it is deep down, how does it get up here?"

"Steam, my dear. It rises as steam."

"Oh."

"Yes. That's it."

She hummed a little tune for a while. "Then why isn't it just a steam jet, like the Black growler we saw at Norris, or the Buryl spring?"

"Because there's water. Steam forces the water out."

"What happens when it runs out of water?"

"Then it's – it's latent for a while. Until more ground water comes in, it gets heated—"

"But why does it push out all at once? Why not a continuous geyser?"

"Then it wouldn't be a geyser. It would be a hot spring."

"Oh."

They strolled on.

"Philip?"

"What is it, Emily?"

"Philip," she repeated, lowering her head so that all he saw of her was her enormous hat with all its feathers. "Am I wicked – or why is it that I seem to see – suggestions – yes, suggestions – in so many things here?"

Philip chuckled. "Phallic symbols, you mean? I didn't think you knew the definition, dear." Philip smiled. "That young Englishman sure did some fast thinking, didn't he. A *phalanx* of geysers. Huh!"

"What? Philip. You mean phallic symbols are – are—"

"Just symbols of – our private parts – mostly male, but not always, dear."

Emily's jaw set hard. "I'm not going to let Prudence out of our sight with that evil young man," she announced.

"Oh, come now, Emily. Prudence is nineteen. She's a product of Elm Grove society, and we have our scandals and she's heard them. She's learned a new word, that's all. I find it amusing. And if Stephen is evil, dear – what can you say about yourself and the question you just put to me?"

Emily did not answer for a while. Finally, a smile appeared on her kind face. "Well, Philip. It is true, isn't it? Geysers getting motivated and all stirred up and then erupting."

"We're both wicked, Emily. I've thought of it. And I've thought of the beautiful Grand Canyon, too. And Cupid's Cave."

"Philip!" She tightened her grip on his arm.

"Yes, dear."

"I hope Rusty doesn't buy any more jawbreakers, and I hope he doesn't get frightened alone in that room, and I hope he gets to sleep early."

"So do I," replied Philip, squeezing Emily's arm.

They were almost at the hotel. Stars had appeared in the clear sky and an exhilarating breeze had sprung up. It was about then that they heard both human and non-human sounds.

"What is all that commotion, Philip?"

"I don't know, Emily. It's coming from the hotel, whatever it is. Sounds like the Elm Grove brass band playing 'The Stars and stripes Forever'. And lots of voices."

In the gloaming they made out fifteen or twenty Yellowstone coaches occupying the driveway and portico at the hotel. Strange people began to appear – men in outlandish turbans and fez hats and satin sashes, women in harem gowns. The clink of bottles was heard. On the verandah a barber shop quartet sang 'Down by the Old Mill Stream'. From the lobby a brass band was now playing another Sousa march. Philip and Emily could hardly enter because of the milling humanity.

"Howdy, friend," welcomed an inebriated, fat little man with a flushed face and a bulbous nose. On his bald head was a too-small fire engine red fez, from the top of which dangled a gold tassel that swung over his face and tickled his nose. He sneezed.

"Who the – What the devil is going on here?" Philip asked.

"Ah, ah," nodded the little man, rocking back and forth on his heels and nearly losing his balance as he waved a pudgy finger in Philip's face. "Let's watch our temper, old man!"

"Who are you, anyway?"

The little man's visage turned serious, he stood up straight, though still rocking slightly, and at attention. "We, sir, and madam," he announced, "are the Concatenated Order of the Antelope. Hic."

"The Con – Concat—"

"The Concatenated Order of the Antelope, sir. On our way to the International Convention of the Concantenated Order of the An-An—"

"Antelope."

"Thank you, sir. Concantenated Order of the An – An – Antelope, in Seattle, Washington. By special train from Chicago, sir, with a tour of the Park thrown in."

"Good Lord," exclaimed Philip. "How many of you are there?"

"Two hundred and seventeen strong, sir."

"Where are they putting you up? I thought the hotel was full."

Philip and Emily heard a "Daddy. Oh, Daddy." Prudence and Madeline came struggling through the mob of happy Antelopes. "They've evicted us from our rooms!" Prudence exclaimed.

"They've what?"

Madeline confirmed the news. "They were polite about it all," she said, "but even as we protested, the bellboys were closing our luggage and carrying it off."

"There was nothing we could do," Prudence added, "but follow them. We've been moved into one wing of the attic. It's a great big room with about twenty cots, like a dormitory. And that's where all the ladies have to sleep."

"Like a hospital ward," Madeline added, "only not as clean."

"And no partitions, or *anything*," protested Prudence. "When I carried in my luggage some old lady just sat over on the next bed and stared at me. I was mortified."

"By gadfrey, we'll see about this," Philip stormed, planting his cigar between his teeth, damning the Antelopes and casting his face in the direction of the front desk. "Emily, you and the girls go out on the verandah while I get this straightened out."

"Wait, Daddy," Prudence said before he had taken two steps. "There's more."

"More?"

"Yes, Daddy. You and Mother have been ejected too!"

"What?"

"Mother has the bed next to Madeline."

"She what?"

"And you and Rusty have been put in the big room on the other side of the building."

Philip was flabbergasted. "But how? And why?"

"To make room for these horrible people," sniffed Prudence. "I wish Stephen were here." Fearfully she surveyed the teeming lobby, Antelopes cavorting everywhere, blowing noise-makers, drinking, singing, telling off-color jokes. "I'm almost afraid to walk back to the stairs," Prudence added. "I've been touched and," rubbing her backside, "pinched. Oh, it's ghastly!"

Madeline, rubbing her own slim hips, smiled at Emily. "They're a bit wild, all right," she commented. Emily opened her mouth in shock.

I know what we'll do," Philip announced. "We'll get Congressman Griffin to come to our aid. The Hotel Company won't dare cross him. I'm going upstairs to the Congressman's room and explain the situation to him."

"Be careful, dear," pleaded Emily.

Philip stomped ahead, plowing through a Persian riot of tassels, fezzes, and women in fantastic harem costumes. He ignored all their good humor and growled so that he would have had a fight or two had he stopped moving. He climbed the stairs two at a time and tramped down the hall toward where his and Emily's room had been; just across the hall, he knew, was the Congressman's. As he made his way he was aware of a concentration of humanity ahead; about every five seconds a roar of laughter filled the air. It was not until he was almost there that Philip realized the sounds emanated from an open doorway – the entrance to Congressman Griffin's room. Philip caught a quick glance inside before boisterous humanity blocked his view. His hopes sank with what he saw.

For Congressman Talmadge Beauregard Griffin and his lady were holding court. There stood the honored Solon, minus his coat, his vest unbuttoned, his white shirt bulging out on either side of his big red galluses, his black string tie untied, collar open, sleeves rolled halfway up to his elbows – there he was, dispensing White Horse and Old Crow and Old Quaker from bottles Philip had seen before. Half reclining on the bed was the bejeweled Dolly, a long, expensive satin gown being wasted on her pudgy form, the front unbuttoned enough to show her throat and the upper half of her large breasts and the top of a lacy black corset. She held a glass in her hand and was about to imbibe when she caught sight of Philip, who had pushed his way into the room. "Judge Snowden," she said, propping herself up. "Now our party is complete. Come over here and sit by me, Judge. Talmadge, pour the Judge a good drink. Make it White Horse and ginger ale. Only the best for our coach companion. And very little ginger ale, Talmadge. Philip has to catch up with us, you know." She winked at him. Then she patted the bed. "Come over and sit down by me," she urged.

"White Horse and ginger ale comin' right up," the Congressman-bartender announced. "Glad you could make it, Judge. These here are Louisiana Antelopes. And some from Atlanta and Chicago and – hell – I dunno. Best damned people in the world, I tell ya. Put some life into this five day funeral procession around the Park."

Before Philip had gathered his thoughts he had been steered to Dolly and found himself seated beside the semi-reclining lady with a glass in his hand. Hardly was he seated before he was aware of a satined leg rubbing his. He turned to Dolly and found himself facing a bosom whose exposure had rather increased in the last ten seconds.

"Isn't it fun, Judge," she said, sipping her drink, "to be wild and wicked once in a while?"

Philip, for nothing better to do, took a deep swig of his drink. It warmed him and it was, he had to admit, good whiskey. "Uh, huh," he replied.

"You know, Judge," Dolly went on, snuggling closer and catching his free hand, "it isn't easy being a Congressman's wife. From Louisiana."

"No. I don't suppose—"

"You can't let up a minute, Judge. If the ladies of the First Baptist Church could see Talmadge and me now—"

"They'd church you, I'll wager."

She smiled sardonically. "First," she said, "they'd turn *green* with envy. *Then* they'd church us. Here, Talmadge, refill my glass." When her hand was free it came down on Philip's upper thigh. 'Oh, My Gawd, what have I got myself into?' Philip thought.

"Sorry about them hotel people kicking you out of your rooms, Judge," said the Congressman as he mixed Dolly's drink, "but the Chief Eminent Buck of the Antelopes and his wife needed a room, so I intervened and it turned out to be yours. And then their Eminent Archon and his wife and his kid needed rooms, so I gave them the Snowden girl's and Rusty's. I knew you wouldn't mind. You know, Judge, its politics," he went on, waving the bottle as if it was a flag, "a Congressman has to look after his constituents, and the Chief Eminent Buck is from my district in Louisiana. No hard feelings are there, old man? Here, have another drink."

"No, thanks," Philip replied, standing up. "I have to rejoin my party."

"Stick around, Judge. Dolly and I are being initiated as honorary members of the Antelopes at ten o'clock. Wait and see it."

"Thanks anyway," replied Philip.

"Don't go away angry, Judge," said Dolly, still holding his hand and looking up at him. When he looked at her this time Philip aimed to focus on Dolly Griffin's face. The way she was squirming in that corset who knows what he might see? "Good evening," he said again. She released his hand, and, with several more "good evening's" Philip was out of the room, into the hall, and walking rapidly back to the stairway. He heard strains of "For He's a Jolly Good Fellow" until concatenated cat-calls in the lobby overwhelmed his auditory powers. Downstairs, he made his way to the front desk to lodge a strong protest with the manager, but so sorry, the manager was not in.

Dejected and benumbed, Philip made his way onto the verandah where he found his women folk in a corner. The moon cast a soft light across Emily, who was seated in a rocker; Prudence and Madeline were perched on a nearby railing.

"No luck, ladies," said Philip with resignation. "I'm afraid we sleep like soldiers in barracks tonight."

"If we sleep at all," sighed Prudence. "Listen to those people singing."

Philip listened, recognized the ditty, and said strongly, "No, Prudence, don't listen to it."

"So there you are!" came a boy's voice out of the darkness. "Gee, I'm glad I found you. The magic lantern show was canceled when all these people came into the lobby, so I went upstairs and found somebody else in my room, so I went to ask Congressman Griffin what to do and two women were in there comparing corsets and—"

"Horrors!" exclaimed Emily. "There weren't any men around."

"Only about a dozen. They said you'd been there, Dad."

"I left," said Philip icily, "before anything like that happened."

"Well, anyway," said Rusty, "there ain't goin' to be no—"

"Rusty! Isn't going to be any," corrected Madeline.

"—magic lantern show," Rusty finished.

The family conversed a while. Philip, dejected, held Emily's hand. No loving tonight. She understood. Close to him, she whispered, "There's always tomorrow night, dear. Remember that I love you."

Finally Philip flipped the dead stub of a cigar onto the grounds. "Let's all turn in," he suggested. "There's not much more we can do here tonight."

And so the Snowdens headed for bed, the women to one side of the attic, Philip and Rusty to the other.

# Chapter Four
# The Third Day

## I

Philip Snowden greeted the morning sun as he had rarely welcomed it in his life. As a boy he, along with an entire generation, had risen by dawn's early light, or even before, to do the chores. He had shivered as he dressed in the cold, slipped into that old sheepskin coat, lighted the dirty, smelly lantern with its flickering flame and headed out to the barn. That old red barn! The aroma of hay and oats and horse manure and cow chips, and old Bess in her stall, giving off sufficient heat to warm the stall, munching away on her cud all night long – chomp, chomp, chomp: he recalled it all with bittersweet nostalgia.

Philip relived all phases of the procedure, including how nice Bess's udder felt to his cold hands. He also remembered her halitosis – whewwwww! – and he relived the time a rat fell off a rafter onto Bess's back and how she kicked over the pail.

Philip Snowden yawned, marveling at how a man lying in darkness while sleep deserts him can relive his life. He turned to one side and observed Rusty, sound asleep. What a fine, normal kid he was!

He turned his head the other way. There, still fast asleep, was Lord Stephen Billner. When Philip and Rusty came in last night they found Lord Billner in bed reading a book. The young man explained that because of his late ticket purchase he had to accept a cot in the attic, whether or not there were Antelopes around. Such was not the case with the male vacationers who subsequently came stumbling in, cursing the Yellowstone Park Company, the Department of the Interior, the United States Army, President Taft, and some, the Concatenated Order of the Antelopes. Several times Philip had dozed off when another tourist entered and flicked on the lights. "I'd like to

have a nickel for every time someone yelled 'turn off the goddamn lights'," he mused. And then there was the professor searching for bats.

Restless and wide awake, Philip lay on his stomach and set his chin on a palm, his elbow on the bed, and contemplated the sleeping young Englishman. Not really a bad fellow, he thought, saying Grace so sincerely at the table, as if he yearned for a family life being denied him. Philip frowned thoughtfully. Last night the young man had struck him as being lonely and lost, reading that book, all alone in the cavernous attic. Asleep now, his face looked clear, wrinkle-free, and innocent; he looked boyish. "Strange, the questions he asked last night," Philip mused. "What's life like in Elm Grove?" And, "Do you like it there?" and "What fine people are the American middle class." Philip studied Lord Billner's face in the dawn's early light. "Are you really interested, in an honorable way, in Prudence?" he wondered. "And if so, how do Emily and I feel about it? What kind of a son-in-law would you be?"

Philip reached under his coat, which he had folded and used as a pillow (the hotel company having run out of them), and found his watch: 5.35. The sun had appeared. "Hell," he grumbled, sitting up in the chill air and swatting a mosquito. He fished in his suitcase for his razor, shaving mug, comb, toothpaste and brush. Stiffly he got out of the cot and quietly stumbled down the aisle, through the doorway to the men's room. At least he'd be washed and shaved before the barrage began.

As he shaved (with cold water, the hotel having slipped on that account also) he thought of that brazen Dolly Griffin and compared her adversely with his puritanical, yet loving, Emily – and smiled at the little bit of the devil Emily had in her. Poor girl. She was finding the trip a bit difficult, he feared – the near-naked hussy at The Bucket of Blood, the hold-up, Rusty nearly suffocating on a jawbreaker, and now this. He thought of that plaintiff look last night that said "Please don't leave me," and her reminder that there would be another night. Good thing Madeline and Prudence were with her. In her eyes Emily had told him all – how she loved him, needed him, and would miss him.

Shaved, teeth brushed, hair combed, clothes on, Philip was still grumpy as he made his way downstairs to the coffee shop. A young college girl waitress was unlocking the door for business. Just as he entered as the first customer, he heard the staccato sound of boots behind him. "Good morning, Judge Snowden. How are you?"

Philip turned to find the Captain standing behind him, militarily immaculate, hat under arm. "Sure could stand a cup of coffee, sir. How about you?"

"Let's," replied Philip, "though I'm in a sour mood and probably not very good company. Put up in a damned barracks last night. Might as well be in the Army."

"I didn't sleep too well myself," countered Captain Taylor. "When I returned the Griffin's watch and jewels he inveigled me into a drink and a conversation." The Captain frowned. "I talked too much. If he spreads my lecture on why we should have automobiles in the Park and why the Army should become mechanized, my career will end, pronto."

"I judge him to be smarter than we give him credit to be," assured Philip. "I think he'll keep his mouth shut." Philip decided not to divulge his own experience with the colorful M.C. – and his lady.

The two men were soon seated and were quickly given hot, fresh brewed coffee. It bolstered their spirits. Philip explained the Snowden's expulsion from their rooms. "I couldn't sleep. That's why I'm up so early. Are you always up at this hour, Captain?"

"Usually," said Captain Taylor. "We're kept busy. You'd be surprised at what goes on this Park." In no time he had discussed the bandit, and his belief that Hezekiah had a score to settle with him. "He might lead us to him," Captain Taylor observed. And then he told Philip about his assignment to escort the Pierce-Arrow through the Park. This struck Philip as a hilarious situation, what with the Captain divulging his love of motor cars. "Captain," he said, "I feel better already."

Captain Taylor started to say something, then paused. "Now let me ask you something," he said finally.

"Certainly, Captain, what is it?"

Captain Taylor hesitated. No longer did he appear the self-confident army officer of a few minutes before. "Mr. Snowden – Philip – Judge – sir – I – tell me something about your sister."

"Madeline? Why do you want to know?" Philip replied defensively. He was naturally protective of Madeline. His sister's one tragic mistake loomed large when people asked about her.

The Captain sensed the hostility immediately. "Allow me to make myself clear, Mr. Snowden," he began. "I am a bachelor, a graduate of West Point, and a Captain in the Second Cavalry. I strive to be an officer and a gentleman. My friendship with Madeline has become rather – special."

"Madeline is a fine woman," said Philip. "She teaches English at Elm Grove High."

"Thank you, sir," Captain Taylor replied. But Philip Snowden's manner, the way he bristled, confirmed the Captain's suspicion. He was hiding something – something – about Madeline. Divorce? Insanity? What? He contemplated another question, but the ladies appeared at the doorway, and the subject was dropped.

## II

While the Snowdens breakfasted (Rusty having come in a few minutes later with Lord Billner, the two sitting at their own table with Rusty bursting with pride at being treated like a real grown-up) Captain Taylor excused himself to wind up affairs at the Army camp. Outside the hotel Hezekiah Hotchkiss fussed around the *Shoshone Belle*. He had greased the wheels, swept the floor, wiped dust off the seats, and made sure the horses, at the stables, were well fed and watered. He looked older, did Hezekiah Hotchkiss. He was in a peck of trouble, and he knew it.

The Captain had nevertheless returned his watch, along with a strong reprimand. He had also questioned the coachman about the bandit, bootlegging, poaching, trapping, and prospecting. The Captain sure was suspicious, observed Hezekiah. Well, he thought, maybe he had a right to be.

For Hezekiah was sure he knew who the bandit was. He knew that he was still lurking around the Park roads. He was convinced – felt it in his bones – that beautiful Miss Prudence was in danger. He knew how the highwayman had once almost been lynched at Miles City for an alleged rape of a merchant's daughter. "Too bad they didn't succeed," he growled.

Hezekiah yawned, and stretched, and yearned for the hair of the dog (a stout swig of whiskey to get one started in the morning). Lacking it, he cursed the luck that brought on the storm yesterday, and the loss of his bootlegged liquor. In lieu of the hair of the dog, cursing seemed to make him feel better. He ambled over to the stable where he gave orders to the "barn dogs" to hitch up the teams. "Good thing we only go to Old Faithful today," he reflected, "I don't think I could make it much farther." His back ached from an old accident.

In due time the *Shoshone Belle* was at the head of the caravan, ready to take on its passengers at the porte-cochère. Hezekiah lit his pipe as Rusty emerged from the lobby, waved to the mountaineer, and climbed up, with the coachman's help, and sat beside him. The boy tried to start conversation, but the old gentleman simply sat in his seat and ignored him. Hezekiah removed his pipe and spat. One of the horses let wind; the coachman growled. The lad sat straight beside him, silent.

Philip, Emily, and Madeline appeared next, Madeline humming a tune as she climbed into the back seat, alone, but confident that Captain Taylor would be along soon. Emily was glad the night was over. Some of the Antelopes had charged through the women's quarters at 2.30 AM awakening everyone. Women screamed and disrupted the sleep of the few who had lapsed into the arms of Morpheus. Philip countered that story by telling how a college professor had clicked on the lights sometime after midnight, waving a big net around, looking for bats. When it was demanded that he quit and douse the lights, he responded by delivering a lecture on the importance of bats – until someone hit him on the temple with a well-aimed shoe. "He left," Philip said dryly, "without any bats."

Next appeared Prudence and Lord Billner, Prudence in her olive green hobble skirt and a little sailor blouse.

"Oh, dear," muttered Emily. "I was afraid Prudence would choose to wear that sailor blouse."

"What's wrong with it?" asked Philip.

"Oh, Philip. You have eyes. It's so revealing. When Prudence leans over—"

"Oh, Emily," Philip chuckled.

"Philip," she insisted, "it is not a laughing matter. She's been seeing that young man for more than three days now. Sitting close to him in the coach. Viewing geysers with him. Dancing with him. It – it's – oh, Philip. You know. Prudence is so young."

"She's nineteen, Emily," replied Philip, lighting his cigar. "And young Billner isn't a bad sort. I got rather well acquainted with him last night."

Regardless of her fears, Emily gave them both a big smile when they entered the coach.

"Today is one of the big days," Lord Billner informed Prudence. "We see the Middle and the Upper Geyser Basins. The guide book says there are seventy geysers in the Upper Basin alone, and hot springs too numerous to mention."

People swarmed along the driveway now, finding their coaches and climbing aboard. Most were in a mood combined of disgust and pleasure – disgust with their treatment by the hotel company and pleasure at finally being on their way. "To hell with the Antelopes," someone shouted. "Are they coming too?" another asked, and still another replied, "Nope. Not until noon. They're all upstairs sleeping off a drunk." And still another: "Are they going to steal our rooms at Old Faithful?" and a reply, "Yep. But then they go to Canyon and back to Mammoth while we go to Lake and then to Canyon and then back to Mammoth. We'll only be bothered with 'em tonight."

"Emily," Philip commented, "you and I are not going to be separated again. We're staying together tonight even if we have to camp out in the woods."

"I hope so, dear – that we can be together. Last night was simply horrible."

"We'll see, by gadfrey. First thing when we reach Old Faithful, I'll check in and when we get to our room we'll bolt the door."

Now Captain Taylor arrived. He was in excellent spirits. "The Pierce-Arrow left West Thumb this morning in two Studebaker wagons pulled by teams of strong Missouri mules. I'll meet Fritz Buschmeister at Lake and escort him and his inert automobile out the North Entrance." He looked out the side and up at the dejected Hezekiah, slouched in his seat, pipe clamped in his mouth. "Let's be on our way. Hotchkiss."

Hezekiah removed his pipe. "Can't."

"Why not? The coaches are loaded and you're front man today. Let's be on our way. We'll be ahead of the dust."

"Yer fergittin' the Congressman and his lady, ain't you, Captain?"

Hezekiah was right. Their spaces were vacant. Behind the *Shoshone Belle* more than a score of coaches waited. Shouts began to emanate from behind the *Shoshone Belle*. Men looked at their watches. The doorman came up: "Hotchkiss, you can't keep twenty-seven coaches waiting for you. Either get moving or get out of the way."

"I'm waitin' for Congressman Griffin and his lady," replied Hezekiah, not moving the reins an inch.

This silenced the doorman, but pressure continued to build. Drivers began yelling at Hezekiah, who just gritted his pipe and sat still as a statue. Finally Captain Taylor intervened. "I guess you'd best let them pass, Hezekiah," he said reluctantly. "Even a Congressman has just so much authority. People will be protesting to headquarters pretty soon if we don't let the others go on ahead."

"As you say, Captain," growled the mountaineer, kicking off the brake. "Heauh," he yelled, as the horses jumped to life, pulling the coach out from the porte-cochère down the driveway and off to one side. Dejectedly, the Snowden party watched as twenty-seven Yellowstone coaches passed them by and disappeared up the road; only a thick dust cloud was left.

For long minutes there was silence. Then two figures appeared at the lobby doors. They paused, looking for their coach and glancing at the stairs and wondering if they could safely descend to the driveway. One was Congressman Talmadge Beauregard Griffin. He was wearing a wrinkled, out-of-place flannel ice-cream suit, white shirt, neck open, black tie hanging untied around his neck, black high-topped shoes, untied, straw Panama hat tilted back from his forehead.

His lady – Dolly *sans* makeup – wore a long, black travel dress with a wasp waist bulging (like a pregnant wasp, Emily thought), gray-blond hair hanging disheveled under a hat full of red and purple feathers. Their suitcase, with pieces of clothing sticking out, evidence of hasty packing, was carried by a black porter. The Congressman was holding his personal satchel.

"I say, theuh," shouted the Congressman in a deep, whiskey-cracked voice, "is that you. Hotchkiss? And the Snowdens? Well come on over here and get Dolly and me. By gadfrey, you-all better not have gone without us. I'll have the Company up before the Committee, by the Eternal. We've taken about all we can from the Park Company."

'What the hell's he complaining about?' thought Philip.

As Hezekiah, with the finesse of an old hand with horses, guided the teams across the road and then backed the coach into position under the porte-cochère, a fussy little man in a herring-bone suit, with a flower in his lapel, came dashing out of the lobby and launched into a vigorous discussion with the hungover Solon. By his gestures it was clear that the little man was busy humiliating himself in behalf of the Yellowstone Park Company.

"Who's that?" the Judge asked no one in particular.

"The manager," Captain Taylor replied. "A typical sycophant. Toadying for the Company. Whatever the trouble, I can assure you that the manager couldn't care less, except that this is a Congressman complaining. They, like all high officials, always receive the VIP treatment. All others—"

"We know," chirped Madeline. "The cot last night. Captain! Honestly, I felt bumps where I didn't know I had feelings."

"Let's hope they treat you better tonight," he replied. "But Madeline, you don't look a bit worse for wear." He squeezed her gloved hand.

While the Congressman was haranguing the manager Philip got an idea. "Say," he said, turning to the others, "let's give the Honorable M.C. and his lady the silent treatment. We'll answer them with a simple yes or no, but other than that, no conversation. Quiet now. Here they come."

Whatever the trouble, which involved a telegram to Washington D.C. that, because the telegrapher was just part-time, would not be sent for several more hours, the matter was soon settled. The Congressman climbed up on the driver's seat and Dolly in beside Emily. The coach started through dust still not settled from twenty-seven other coaches drawn by one hundred and eight horses. Nor was it long before the Louisianians noticed the icy atmosphere. By the time Dolly was pulling down her veil to protect her face from the dust, even she understood the extent of their sin.

"Talmadge," she called up to him, "why are we at the tail-end of the coaches? Why aren't we up in front, like we were yesterday?"

"Hush, woman," he answered gruffly. "You know damned good and well why we're at the tail-end."

"I do not."

Exasperated, he glanced down at his wife who looked her morning-after worst. "It's because I couldn't get you out of bed. And once out you couldn't find your damned corset. And so we made everyone wait and we're being given the silent treatment and I've got a splitting headache and shut up."

"You know how I misplaced my corset. And who, might I ask, suggested—"

"Hush, woman. We're not alone on this coach."

"Now, you listen to me, Talmadge Beauregard Griffin. Don't you dare blame me for everything that's happened. I – oh –" she placed a hand to her forehead, "my head is throbbing."

Silence followed. Only the crunching of the wheels on gravel and the creaking of the coach's thoroughbraces disrupted the mountain stillness. Congressman Griffin finally reached back for his satchel, which was behind him on the roof. From it he removed a bottle and a collapsible cup. In spite of the impression this might make on the red-haired lad sitting by him, he poured a strong drink for himself, which he finished in two gulps, then poured another and carefully handed it down to Dolly, saying "Hell, Dolly, let's face it. Neither of us is as young as we once were and now we're payin' for it. Here. Have this hair of the dog. It'll make you feel better."

"Oh, Talmadge! What will our friends think?"

"They've already made up their minds. You gonna take this cup or do I have to drink it?"

She accepted the offer, reaching for it carefully and quickly disposing of the liquid in fear of losing a drop. The rest of the party saw all and said nothing. The gregarious Congressman and his wife were lonelier than ever. Not even Rusty, not even Hezekiah would talk to the gentleman and his wife from Louisiana – although Hezekiah would have loved a cup of the liquor. But, he reflected, he was in enough trouble already.

The dust was intolerable. "The Park is big, appropriations small, and there just aren't enough water sprinklers," explained the Captain as he wiped dust from his face. The fine particles made the eyes water, the nose run, the lips crack, and the skin greasy and gritty. Everyone was happy to arrive at the Middle Geyser Basin to stretch and walk a short tour. The strain of the punishment being meted out to the Griffins was being felt by the executioners.

Captain Taylor guided Madeline around the Basin in reverse order, so that they would avoid most of the tourists. They visited the lovely Turquoise Pool, Opal Pool, and the Grand Prismatic Spring. At the Turquoise Pool the wind subsided and the two gazed in awe at its indescribable beauty, while at the Grand Prismatic Spring the rising steam showed a coat of many colors to add to the beauty of the deep, hot, clear water in the pool.

"Madeline," he began in a serious tone as they strolled along the path, "Madeline, do you know that you are a lovely, unusual woman?"

She twirled her parasol. "Oh?" she replied as they approached the crater of the old Excelsior, or Sheridan Geyser. "Tell me more, Captain."

"Freeman, Madeline. Please call me Freeman. I couldn't get you off my mind last night, Madeline. I wanted to rejoin you so, after my duties were completed, but when I got back to the hotel you and the Snowdens had already retired."

"I'm sorry, Freeman. Had I have known, I'd have waited for you."

They strolled on. "Madeline," he began.

"Yes, Freeman."

"Let's have dinner tonight – alone."

"Alone? How do we work that, Captain?"

"Simple. We reach Old Faithful early, you know. I'll get a picnic dinner from the hotel kitchen, rent a horse and buggy, and we'll go to a place I know of. Please say you'll do it."

"Do what?"

"Why, come on a picnic with me. I hardly want to go by myself."

The two peered into the seething, boiling cauldron of the blown-out geyser. Alone, in this wilderness, with the Captain? Just by accepting, she realized, she was placing her integrity in jeopardy. And yet – of the men she had known, this one came closest to her ideal. She hated herself for fantasizing the wonderful possibilities of marriage and a life with him: it just couldn't be, and she was going to be so let down when the fantasy ended! When she turned to him she still had not made up her mind, but the boyish, hopeful look on his face changed her mind. In spite of herself she said, "All right, Captain Freeman W. Taylor. I'd love to."

As they slowly headed back to the *Shoshone Belle* they passed Prudence and Lord Billner going the other way. Prudence twirled her parasol as they stepped along. She sneezed. "Oh, that dust!" she protested. "I feel so dirty. My face – in spite of the veil – and my eyes, my lips, my clothing!" She pinched two fingers to the front of her middy blouse and shook it. Lord Billner caught an exciting glimpse. "It's getting all over me. I hope I can take a bath tonight," she said boldly.

"Me, too," he said, picturing Prudence in her bath.

Just as she had a fleeting glimpse of Lord Billner at Bath Lake. She breathed deeply and sighed, but, sphinx-like, looked down into the Turquoise Pool.

Meanwhile the Congressman and his wife remained in the coach complaining of the dust, headaches, and the Yellowstone National Park in general. Mrs. Griffin asked her husband for water, describing an insatiable thirst. Hezekiah volunteered to obtain some good, cold water for them. Rusty – who saw little use in viewing more bad-smelling pools of hot water – climbed down and followed the coachman along a trail leading through deep woods.

"Now," said the boy firmly, "when do I get my antlers?"

"Rusty," Hezekiah answered gruffly, "you stop pesterin' me about them antlers, or by gadfrey, I won't get 'em for you."

"Gosh, Mr. Hezekiah, I'm sorry. Only I promised the fellers back home..."

They arrived at a cool, fresh water spring. The coachman filled the army canteen with the sparkling clear water. Then Hezekiah sat down on a log to rest, removing his campaign hat and wiping dampened dust and perspiration from his face with a red bandanna handkerchief. Rusty sat beside him, placing in his lap his secret weapon, clumsily wrapped in brown paper.

"You bring your secret weapon all the way out here?"

"Of course. I can't leave it around for just anybody to steal, Mr. Hezekiah. Besides," added the boy, looking around, "I thought we might get our antlers here."

The mountaineer studied the lad, reached over and messed his tousled red hair, and said, "Rusty, just what is this hyar secret weapon of yours?"

Rusty looked around again and, satisfied that no one else was about, patted the package. "Would you like to see it, Mr. Hezekiah?"

"Shore would. If you've got the time." He addressed Rusty as if he was an adult.

"You won't tell anybody, will you?"

"On my honor as an old mountaineer."

The boy carefully untied the cord and unwrapped the brown paper wrapper. "It's sort of funny-lookin'," he commented as he unfolded the last of the paper. "There it is."

'What – in – tarnation?"

"It makes noise," Rusty explained. "Lots of noise. A high pitched noise. See, I hold it like this and pull out the handle, then push it in as hard as I can. It's real hard because there's a dent in it where I hit it with my hatchet." Rusty pushed with all his might and from the rubber hemisphere at the other end came a monstrous, primitive, high-pitched whistle.

"Good Gawd," exclaimed Hezekiah. "It sounds just like a bull buffalo or maybe an elk in rut."

"Huh?"

"Yes, Rusty. Like the mating call – the sound of some big animal calling his wife."

The boy handed his secret weapon to Hezekiah, who examined it carefully.

"What is the dern thing?" he asked.

"You've got to keep it a secret, Mr. Hezekiah, or I'll be in real trouble. Promise?"

"I promise."

"See, it ain't really mine. It's my sister's."

"Hmmmmmmmm. What's she do with it?" asked Hezekiah, his curiosity aroused.

"It's her bust developer."

"Her *what*?"

"That's what Mother and Daddy call it. See, she takes this rubber thing and puts it over one of her busts..."

"Her busts? Oh, you mean her teets," said Hezekiah, thinking out loud and envisioning something funny.

"Tits. That's what I've always called 'em, too. Same thing a cow has only a gal has 'em in a different place and not so many. Grown-ups call them busts, though. Anyway, she puts this rubber thing over each one and pushes and pulls the handle and it's s'posed to make 'em big."

"Ho, ho, ho," roared Hezekiah, throwing back his head. "What'll they think of next?"

"Sis didn't think it very funny when it got stuck on her. Neither did Mother and Daddy. And see this opening? I had to take my hatchet and hit the – the –"

"Cylinder?"

"Yes. The cylinder. I had to hit it hard enough to make a little hole to let the air out of it and free Prudence. See where it's dented? That's why it makes all the noise. At least, I think that's why it makes all the noise. I don't think it made any noise until I hit it with my hatchet."

Hezekiah continued examining the strange contraption. "Mind if I work it, laddie?" he asked, sounding like a boy again.

"Go ahead, Mr. Hezekiah. Push it real hard and fast."

Hezekiah held the instrument correctly and pushed the plunger with all his might. A sound more hideous than before emitted from the Developer. "Danged if it ain't some kind of secret weapon, Rusty," he said. "Now wrap it up and keep it hidden. And I'll tell you what, laddie. If you ever get in trouble within hearin' distance of old Hezekiah Hotchkiss, why you just blow this hyar secret weapon, lad, and I'll come a-runnin'."

"Sure will, Mr. Hezekiah," replied Rusty, happy at the coachman's enthusiasm. "And you won't tell anybody, will you? They all think my hatchet is in the package. If sis knew I had her Bust Developer she'd—"

Hezekiah touched the boy's arm, his other went to his mouth in a sign of silence. "What was that?" he asked. They heard a sound so similar to the secret weapon that they faced each other in surprise. All of a sudden through the woods crashed the biggest bull buffalo Hezekiah, let alone Rusty, had ever seen. There it stood, appraising them from hardly twelve feet away, its shaggy head lowered, its beady little eyes trying to fathom the absence of another bull buffalo. At the back of its long, narrowing torso its little scorpion tail twitched.

"Time we get back to the coach," Hezekiah said with studied calmness. "Don't move fast, laddie. Just walk along beside me, slowly. That old bull don't look too happy." They sidled down the trail while the buffalo stood there snorting and pawing the earth. Pretty soon they were out of its sight. "Whaw," sighed Hezekiah. "I'm glad to get away from him. I don't savvy buffaloes in rut."

They reached the *Shoshone Belle* and presented the grateful Griffins with the canteen of cool water. Prudence and Lord Billner arrived, their circle of the geyser basin completed. The others were already there.

"Guess what you missed," Prudence said excitedly. "Stephen and I heard this weird noise up in the woods and then we saw a huge buffalo cross the road and head into the timber, and then a few minutes later another one came along going in the same direction. And did they make a racket!"

"Two of 'em?" asked Hezekiah, glancing at Rusty. "Two of 'em?" Hezekiah uttered a low whistle. He grabbed the reins and released the brakes. "There's about to be a knock-down no-bones-spared combat between two buffalo bulls," he said. "Hyaah," he shouted to the horses. "We best be on our way, pronto." The horses, pulling the *Shoshone Belle*, trotted toward the Upper Geyser Basin leaving a trail of dust behind them.

## III

It was approaching two o'clock when the *Shoshone Belle*, after crunching through more choking quantities of dust, drove up to the porte-cochère at Old Faithful Inn. No one was in good spirits, for the drive had been a hot, dusty ordeal, and the night before had hardly been one of good sleep. Lunch was overdue. The Congressman and his wife, feeling punished for their activities, got off first and trudged into the lobby.

"You wait here," said Philip to his party. "Before we have lunch I'm going to exact a promise from the manager that we will have private rooms."

"Don't be too belligerent, dear," said Emily, casting a glance around the area. "Where else would we go?"

"By gadfrey," stormed Philip, "we'll not stay here unless we have private rooms. We'll rent a carriage and go on to Lake if necessary." He clenched his fists, gritted his cigar, and marched up the steps.

Emily hoped he would calm down. She was tired and a bit nauseated from the ride; she did not want a scene. Philip meanwhile marched straight up to the front desk and pounded the bell. When no one appeared in fifteen seconds, he rang it again. A tall, scrawny college boy appeared wearing thick tortoise-shell glasses.

"Name's Snowden. Philip Snowden," said the Michigan lawyer brusquely. "Party of five: myself and Mrs. Snowden, Miss Prudence

Snowden, Miss Madeline Snowden, and a child, Rusty Snowden, aged eleven. We have reservations. For three rooms."

The clerk peered at some kind of register before him. "Ah, yes."

"Do we get our rooms?"

"Yes, sir. We'll put you up, sir."

Philip caught something in the clerk's tone of voice that he did not like. "Three rooms?"

"Frankly, sir, we're a bit crowded now. Middle of the season, you know. And a convention tour stopping here tonight."

"Point, point, point, young man. Do we get our rooms?"

"Yes, sir. We guarantee accommodations. However, we are not obligated to give tour-trippers individual rooms. I'm afraid you and your son will have to pair up with some other gentlemen, and your wife and—"

"Damn!" Philip roared. "I've paid my money and I demand separate rooms. Where's the manager? I want to see the manager!"

"Please sir," said the young clerk, raising his hand and looking around with annoyance.

"The manager!" demanded Philip.

"He's not here," replied the clerk. "This is his day off."

Philip was speechless. He reverted back a few thousand years and began growling like an animal. "I see the Congressman and his lady are accommodated," he said, pointing to them as they registered with another clerk.

Philip's clerk surveyed the lobby, removed his glasses and began polishing them with his handkerchief. "Can you beat it, sir?" he commented. "That old cuss and his wife have one of the nicest rooms, complete with a vase of fresh wild flowers, and they are paying exactly the same as you. We were alerted to their coming. Let's face it, sir. He is a Congressman. You are not." Philip growled some more, his cigar jumping from one corner of his mouth to the other.

"You should have seen what happened when the Secretary of the Interior was here," the clerk went on in a low voice. "Catherine the Great's trip through Russia was nothing compared to the way the Company pulled the wool over the Secretary's eyes." The clerk looked with sympathy at Philip. "I'm a student at Michigan State, sir. I'd rate you above the 'Honorable' Congressman any day. But sir, I'm not the Yellowstone Park Company. There is nothing I can do." Then his face lit up. "But I do have a suggestion, sir."

"Shoot."

"Why don't you spend the night at the Wylie Way?"

"The Wylie – what?"

"The Wylie Way. Surely you've seen their camps. They house people just like the Park Company does, only cheaper. In tent camps, you know. Semi-permanent tent camps."

"Tell me more, young fellow."

"The tents consist of wooden floors and wooden walls about four feet up the sides. Above that, candy striped canvas walls continue up to a peaked canvas roof."

"Could they accommodate us?" asked Philip.

"I think so, Mr. Snowden. They have both one and two bed tents. They could put you and the missus and the boy in one, and the two ladies in the other."

"Where do the guests dine?"

"They have a nice dining hall, sir. And after the evening meal, dancing and a lecture around the campfire, and popcorn and singing – they have all kinds of fun. Matter of fact, they make a lot of the well-heeled jealous, they have such good times. The Park Company has been trying to get them kicked out of the Park for years. Let me phone and see if they have any vacancies."

Philip gave the young man permission, and there was room. So, after bidding adieu to Lord Billner, who would remain at old Faithful, and the Captain, who would spend the night at the soldier station – or so he said – Philip had Hezekiah drive his family up the road to a pine-fringed meadow. There, nestling among the pines, were thirty to forty squarish tent houses and one long tent house that held offices and the dining-recreational facilities. The red and white striped canvas added a festive aura to the scene.

As the *Shoshone Belle* drove up, the horses whinnied and reared; it took all of Hezekiah's horsemanship to restrain them. The cause of their panic became apparent as a black bear with a streak of gray fur up the middle of his head came charging out from between two tents and ran into the timber. Close behind him were a half dozen young men throwing stones and pine cones at bruin, shouting obscenities. When the bear had disappeared two of its pursuers came to the *Shoshone Belle* and took the Snowden's luggage.

"Sorry for the commotion, folks," explained the young man who turned out to be the clerk. "We've had a lot of trouble with old Tom."

"Tom?" queried Philip as his family huddled close by, a bit fearful of the bear. "That's a funny name for a bear."

"Not for this one," replied the clerk. "We call him Tom because of his curiosity. Curiosity killed the cat, you know. Well, it may kill this bear."

"How's that?"

"He used to hang around a road camp," the clerk continued. "He was curious about the machinery. The road workers got tired of him, so they took a rancid slab of bacon, inserted a dynamite cap in it, placed it in a stealable position by a road scraper, and waited. Tom saw the slab, inspected it, grabbed it and ran into the woods with it."

"Yes."

"Then there was this loud boom! No one saw any more of Tom until about a week ago. Now he's back, with a streak of gray hair right over the middle of his thick skull. But curious as ever. Know where we just found him? Peeking down into the ladies' bath house from his perch on a branch above it."

"Well," commented Philip, laughing, "that's a lot more interesting than rancid bacon."

The clerk showed them to their tent, which turned out to be very comfortable. Emily was so delighted with it that she just sat down in the rocking chair, and smelled the canvas and observed the clean floor with the thin cotton rug, the wash stand with the big white porcelain pitcher and basin; the big, inviting double bed with the heavy blankets neatly folded, the little army cot in the corner for Rusty. Canvas and wood separated them from the other bedroom, which was reached by a Lilliputian hallway, and Emily noticed that the bed in the girls' room was across from the separating wall. Subconsciously all this registered with her, and she concluded that, though they must be quiet about it, she and Philip could "get together" this night. She hummed a little tune, she was so happy.

## IV

After a late lunch the family strolled to Old Faithful and watched it erupt not once but twice. At the Haynes Picture Shop they purchased post cards and souvenirs made in Japan. Prudence and Madeline took their soap, wash cloths, and towels to the ladies' bath house. A long line of dusty women awaited its use. Madeline, aware and excited by the pending picnic with the Captain, was determined to await her turn, but Prudence impatiently returned to the tent and tried to clean herself with a basin of cold water. She washed her face, neck, and upper chest, but the rest of her, and her hair, remained unpleasantly gritty. Madeline returned humming a tune and smelling of Yardley's lavender. It was still just mid-afternoon. The young women enjoyed the leisure, lounging in their canvas-topped bedroom until evening approached.

"Are you going to see your young Englishman?" asked Madeline from a wicker chair.

Prudence lay on her back across the bed, looking up at the canvas. "Is your Captain coming?" she countered.

"Yes, I think so," Madeline replied. "He and I are going..." she hesitated, deciding quickly that she did not want to say picnic. "He's getting a horse and buggy and he's going to show me – some – more hot springs," she lied. "He's – bringing something for us to eat."

The younger girl failed to catch the hesitation. "This place is exciting," said Prudence, changing the subject. "Just think, Madeline. Maybe just a mile under us there's red hot superheated rock. All that pent-up pressure down there."

A mischievous gleam appeared in Madeline's eyes. "That's not the pent-up pressure I'm worried about," she replied, rising from the chair and leaning over the low washstand, surveying her image in the twelve by sixteen inch wavy mirror. Her soft brown hair was piled up stylishly. She slapped her big, feathery hat on top of it and darted a six-inch hat pin through it all. Then she straightened up and analyzed critically the reflection of her body from waist to neck. She was wearing her brown hobble skirt and a frilly white blouse with long sleeves and cuffs. It buttoned up the back and was demurely high-necked, framing her fine-featured face. She placed her hands on her hips, smoothed the skirt and tucked in the blouse at a place or two. She was not disappointed. She possessed a genuine wasp waist when wasp waists were stylish, her derriere was curvaceous enough under the tight skirt to make a man want to slap it, and there was a fullness in the frilly blouse that gave assurance of a body still quite capable of the baby-bearing process.

The younger girl had risen from the bed and was sitting in the rocking chair. She watched Madeline's preparations, at first without comment. A loose board squeaked as she rocked. Prudence had been too preoccupied with her own affair to pay much attention to

Madeline, but now, all of a sudden, she was making up for lost time. It occurred to her that Madeline was still a woman who might like the company of a man. Was this attractive person standing in front of her the spinster English teacher at Elm Grove High? Prudence rocked on, appraising her maiden aunt. Now Madeline was pinching her cheeks to bring blood to them and give them a rosy tint. Next she was opening a jar of Vaseline and curling her eyelashes, making them fluttery.

"What'd you say," asked Prudence, "about 'pent-up pressure'?"

"Oh – nothing. Just thinking out loud."

Prudence rocked more rapidly, the squeak becoming annoying. "Know what?" she ventured. "I think Captain Taylor likes you. I think he likes you very much." She rocked still faster. "And I think you like him."

Outside they heard a horse and buggy and the Captain's voice, "Whoa-a-a-a-a."

"That's him," said Madeline excitedly. "Quick, where's my coat?" She found it, the same olive green material as her skirt, and hastily put it on. She glanced quickly once again in the mirror. "Do I look all right?" she asked Prudence, woman to woman.

"Devastating," replied the girl, feeling sort of old. Intuitively the two looked at each other; as Madeline walked out she paused, leaned over Prudence in the rocking chair and kissed her niece on the cheek. "Good luck, Aunt Madeline," Prudence whispered. Then the little school teacher from Elm Grove was gone. Prudence waited until the clatter of wheels had ceased, then walked to the porch just as the buggy disappeared around a curve. For the first time ever, she felt compassion and sisterliness for her maiden aunt, and she wished her a happy evening.

For Madeline the evening started well. The Captain was dressed in a fresh khaki uniform, his Sam Brown belt shining from recent polishing, his face smooth-shaven, save for his mustache. He even smelled nice, of saddle soap and tanned leather, enough even in the open buggy to set Madeline's heart beating faster. After he helped her to the seat she slyly slipped more to the center, so that when the Captain climbed in he had to sit perforce closer to her, each of their bodies touching the other. As the black, open buggy, pulled by a trotting bay horse, clattered down the dirt road from Old Faithful Inn, Madeline hooked an arm through his and held her hat with the other.

She raised her aristocratic head to the breeze, soaked in the beauty of the waning afternoon, and the tall lodgepole pines, the steam puffs here and there, the occasional carriages filled with sightseers, or pedestrians out for an early evening stroll. She breathed deeply of the pines, a little of the sulfur from the hot springs, and the tang of leather and saddle soap that came from the Captain. She forced away ten years of spinsterhood and school teaching, and loneliness and sadness, and she grasped the happiness – ecstatic happiness – of these right-now moments. Was this the mousy little English teacher at Elm Grove High, Madeline Snowden, out for a picnic with a handsome bachelor Captain, and unchaperoned at that?

"We're in for a feast tonight, m'lady," said the Captain, breaking her reverie. "I've got porterhouse steaks for us."

"Already fried?" she asked, laughing.

"No," he replied. "Of course not. We're going to fry them."

"Where?"

"You'll see," he answered as he guided the horse around another curve and started it briskly down a quiet, little-used road. Grass grew high between the barely discernible tracks.

"I hope it isn't far, Captain," said Madeline. "I mean – they'll be expecting me back at a reasonable time."

Captain Taylor reached for his watch. "It's just about five now. What time should you be back?"

"By the time the dance is over. Or the campfire talk. Ten o'clock?"

Her escort relaxed and broke out in a smile. He placed a free arm around Madeline's shoulders which, she decided, was much cozier than hooking arms. "That'll be fine, just fine. We'll have you home by ten o'clock – the horse, the buggy, and I."

Oh, the way he said it, and his arm around her shoulders, and the smile on his face! For a fleeting moment she saw in him a well-scrubbed Simon Legree. That *was* a smile, wasn't it? Not a leer? Her heart beat faster. If he tried to seduce her, what was she going to do? She knew well enough what she *should* do. But – she glanced at him again, his handsome, strong face, his manly chest under the uniform, the hidden strength in those legs – could she resist? That primitive desire, that secret yearning that affected her whole body from a tautness in her legs and loins to faster breathing and a pounding heart, *that* was what worried Madeline Snowden, the English teacher. She was so unsure of herself. Yes, she wanted this handsome man to sweep her into his arms and carry her to a bower and be Adam to her. But no! She must not be Eve to him! For a few moments she even wished she had rejected his invitation.

Apparently Captain Freeman sensed some of what was whirling around in Madeline's mind; he said no more. Instead he hummed some old soldier's song which Madeline thought he'd best not sing the words to, and so the buggy clattered down the dim two tracks for another ten or fifteen minutes. They spied a moose and two elk, but the Captain did not care to stop.

The two dim tracks led them up a hillside and into a grove of white-barked aspen. Just when they were deepest into the woods the cavalryman wheeled the horse and buggy off to the left of the two tracks and around a huge, granite boulder. Here he halted, the horse turning its head to him as if asking, "Haven't you made a mistake?" Madeline also looked around, for although the aspens were lovely, still it was an ordinary place, hardly warranting a stop.

"Here's where we get out and walk," said the Captain, jumping down and holding his arms to Madeline. She place her hands on his shoulders and was relieved when his strong arms embraced her just long enough to place her gently standing on the ground. It was getting chilly now, the shadows were longer, and night was creeping on. This, right here and now, she knew, was not the place for love.

Captain Taylor tethered the horse to a nearby aspen and reached behind the buggy seat for the picnic basket.

"Where to now?" she asked.

"Just follow me, Madeline," said her escort. He started through the grassy sward, swinging the basket, and assumed that the lady was behind him. And she was, rather running to keep up. She could make out no sign of a trail, nor was she aware, after five minutes of fast walking, of the cabin, until they were abruptly upon it.

"Here it is, Madeline," he said, waving at the tiny log hovel, with its sod roof broken by a chimney at one end, square window with four panes in front, and a weather-beaten door with a big, rusted padlock securing it.

"Why – I never even saw it!" Madeline exclaimed. She appraised the rustic cottage. "Does an evil witch live here?" she asked. "Or elves and leprechauns? This reminds me of fairy tales from my childhood."

"No witches, no elves, no leprechauns," Captain Taylor replied. "They don't know it exists – and neither do many people."

"Why is it here?"

Captain Taylor did not immediately reply. He tinkered with the padlock; there was a distinct click and the lock was released. He swung open the door, which creaked eerily on rusty hinges. "Ladies first," he said, standing aside and waving to Madeline to enter. Then he picked up the basket and followed her in.

The last rays of the setting sun cast light through the single window and a long shaft of sunlight, shining through the west-facing doorway, shed enough luminescence for her to make out the interior. First, she noticed, it smelled musty, but not unpleasantly so, and the air inside was warm. The floor was of dried, hard-beaten earth. The far wall was almost all fireplace, and above the mantle were two crossed snowshoes. Set on the mantle was an ordinary kerosene lamp. In the middle of the small, single room was a round, rustic table, barely a yard in diameter, with two crude kitchen chairs set to it. On the windowless wall was a built-in bunk, about three-fourths the width of an ordinary double bed. Beneath the window was a long bench. And on the front wall, the one with the doorway, were two wooden pegs, but nothing hanging on them. The only ornamentation was a picture, torn from a magazine, of a Gibson girl; it had been punched into a nail in the wall.

"Like it?" asked the Captain, casting his eyes around the little room. "This, Madeline, is a Snowshoe Cabin," he explained. "There are several of them throughout the Park. Hidden cabins where game wardens and soldiers on patrol take refuge in winter."

"But – it's so hidden."

"That's the idea, Madeline," the Captain went on as he walked two steps to the bench below the window. He lifted up the bench top; beneath it lay a deep, tin-lined storage space, partitioned and full of the necessities for survival. "There's everything here to last a man for a couple of weeks, he added. "All kinds of canned goods. Here, take these string beans, and here are some canned Irish potatoes." She took them as he handed them to her and placed them on the table.

"And here's the most vital implement of all, a can opener. And two tin plates, two cups, two knives, two forks, two spoons, two saucepans, one frying pan, one coffee pot," he continued, keeping her busy receiving the utensils and placing them on the table. "Some salt and pepper, matches, and over in this part of the chest, separated by a partition, are blankets to sleep with." He reached over and flipped up a heavy Hudson's Bay blanket, tossing it to the bunk.

Madeline scarcely noticed. She clapped her hands with joy. "I still say it's like a fairy tale," she exclaimed. "Are you sure," she asked again, "there aren't elves and leprechauns around, or maybe a wicked witch?"

"Nope," responded her escort. "I'm hungry. Aren't you? Let's get to work. I'll fetch some firewood while you open the cans and prepare the steaks." He grabbed an ax from behind the door and pointed to the picnic basket, indicating where she would find the perishables. "I'll just take a couple minutes," he said, and was gone.

Madeline stood still for a few happy moments, then delved into the basket. She found the steaks, as the Captain said she would, plus an onion – and then she heard a tinkle, lifted a linen napkin and exposed a bottle of French champagne, plus two crystal cocktail glasses glistening incongruously in the sylvan light. The sound of the Captain's ax roused her from her reverie, and she set to work. She was thrilled and excited. When had she last had champagne?

The victuals, which also included two carefully wrapped slices of chocolate cake, were all nestled in what she realized was a crisp, red and white checkered tablecloth. She forgot all apprehensions as the feminine desire to please conquered her, heart and soul. In a whit she had the checkered tablecloth over the rough-hewn table; she found two candles and placed them in wooden blocks kept for the purpose, set them in the center and lit them. With the two tin plates and the flatware she fixed two place settings. She was preparing the steaks for frying when her escort returned with an armful of wood.

"Splendid, Madeline," he said, carrying the wood to the fireplace. "Now, open the cans of potatoes and string beans. By the time you've poured them into the saucepans, I'll have a fire blazing away here." He set about his task like an old hand. Indeed, barely had Madeline poured the vegetables into the pans than shadows from the firelight were dancing on the log walls. She handed him the tin pans and watched as he attached them carefully to hooks over the fire. Then she handed him the heavy, black, cast iron frying pan. He placed in it the fat she had cut from the steaks and set it over the fire. While the fat sizzled and covered the pan, she sliced the onion and after first rubbing the steaks with it, added salt and pepper, and handed them to him, one held in the fingers of each hand. He set the steaks to frying. The aroma of pine pitch, string beans, steak and onions tantalized their hunger.

Captain Taylor stood up from where he had been kneeling at the fireplace and stood by Madeline. "It's getting warm in here now," he said, unclasping his Sam Brown belt and unbuttoning his jacket. "Take off your coat and for heaven's sakes, Madeline, remove that hat!"

She laughed, a laugh that rippled. He didn't think he had ever heard such a melodious sound, and he watched as she gracefully reached up and pulled out the long hat pin and removed the mass of bird feathers that women considered stylish in 1909.

"Now your coat," he said as he laid her hat on top of the bench, along with his own jacket and belt. Again she laughed as she removed the form-fitting apparel that came down over her blouse and skirt, midway down her calves. The frilly, high-necked blouse in the firelight revealed the gentle swelling of her breasts, her graceful swan's neck, her soft brown hair piled so stylishly upward.

"There," she announced, turning to him, eyes dancing and teeth shining. "Now, Freeman, let's eat."

For just a moment Captain Freeman Taylor lost his tongue. 'My God,' he thought. 'Here is perfection. There's not a flaw in her face, nothing but an expression of kindness and sweetness. And her eyes! They smile!'

"Freeman," she repeated. Did she sense the impression she had made?

He considered embracing her there and then, but she parried his thoughts. "Let's have some champagne."

This broke his chain of thought. In a jiffy she had the two champagne glasses on the table while he tackled the bottle. At the fireplace she knelt and turned the steaks and stirred the vegetables. She had just finished when she heard the pop of a bottle. She held the glasses before him, one in each hand, as he poured the bubbling liquid.

"Where did you get it?" she asked as he poured. "From Hezekiah?"

"Hardly. Hezekiah and his friends don't have the sophistication for champagne. Let us just say, sometimes it pays to be a man of authority. The bartender at the Old Faithful dining hall was most obliging."

"And those steaks came from an old friend in the kitchen, I suppose? And the chocolate cake?"

"Correct."

Now the glasses were filled. He set the bottle on the table. She handed him his glass. They lifted them high, watching the bubbles rising in the light amber fluid, highlighted by the firelight. "Here's to us, Madeline," pronounced the Captain, tinkling his glass with hers but showing a sober, thoughtful countenance.

"To us, Freeman," she said simply. Then she looked into his eyes and added, "What does it mean, Freeman?"

"Maybe – more than we dare believe," he replied.

"The steaks," she said suddenly, turning to the fireplace. "They look done. And the vegetables are beginning to boil. Bring the plates, Captain, quickly."

He handed them to her. As they knelt before the fire she gingerly lifted each sizzling porterhouse onto a plate and scooped up some onions for each of them. "If we both eat onions, we won't notice it," he remarked with a chuckle. The Captain then ladled out the string beans and potatoes. From the basket she had already obtained a wedge of butter which was added, a little to the steaks and more to the potatoes, as they sat down across from each other, the candles and the firelight illuminating their movements. The Captain again filled the champagne glasses.

It was the most enjoyable meal either of them had ever experienced, and one neither of them would ever forget. He told her about his boyhood, about West Point, and then he got onto his dislike of horses and his faith in the internal combustion engine. She talked about the joys, as well as the frustrations, of teaching English to small-town Michigan boys and girls. By the time the steaks were consumed, and only scraps of string beans and potatoes left on the plates, he had recounted his life story and they had consumed the bottle of champagne. Madeline felt a little giddy, but happier, and more uninhibited, than she had since she was a girl. The Captain's complexion turned ruddy.

"Hey," he said, "we forgot to put on the coffee. And we've got chocolate cake, too."

"Not now, Freeman," Madeline said, breathing deeply. "I'm so stuffed that I'm about to burst out of my corset. Let's put the coffee on and we'll have it with the cake after a while."

"Got to fetch some water for it, though," he replied. "I'll go to the spring for a bucketful. You wait here."

In a jiffy he was out the door. Madeline began humming a tune as she scraped the plates. When the Captain returned she had everything stacked in a small dishpan. He filled a kettle with water for the dishes, and the coffee pot, and placed both over the fire. She stood by, watching him, and then he was finished, brushed his hands on his trousers, and stood up beside her. She felt his arm around her waist. Not tightly – just – right. She leaned her head on his shoulder. "Oh, Freeman. It was a good meal," she said.

She felt him nuzzling her hair. His other arm swept around in front, and he faced her. "Madeline," he whispered. He leaned down to meet her lips. Softly at first, then, as he felt her arms wrapping around his shoulders, harder. He felt her fingers clawing at his back. Captain Taylor swept her off her feet and held her in a carrying position. She broke from his lips and buried her head in his shoulder saying "Freeman. Oh, Freeman." He glanced at the bunk and silently cursed himself for having failed to spread out the Hudson's Bay blanket. He set her down and released her as he stepped to the bunk to spread it. "Help me, Madeline. So we can lie down and watch the fire."

She stood, light-headed and undecided, watching him in his clumsy man's way trying to spread the blanket. Then the champagne took over. "Here, let me do it," she said, deftly spreading the heavy cover while he went to the bench and returned with two pillows – *sans* pillow slips. She took them from him, fluffed them, and placed them at the head of the bunk, side by side. "There. That's how a woman would do it, Captain."

"Perfect. Just perfect," he said, coming up behind her and wrapping his arms around her waist. She felt his cheek on her face, and looked up sidewise and there were his lips and they kissed again, and his hands moved slowly, up and down from her waist. Then he said, "Why are we standing?"

"Oh, I'm afraid I'll get my clothes wrinkled," she replied.

"Then take them off," he whispered. "There's no one within ten miles of here. You couldn't be safer if you were on the moon." He began unbuttoning her blouse, which fastened at the back. She stood still, letting him. "There," she heard him say in a barely audible tone, "now just take it off." She did as he ordered, then realized that he had deftly slipped the straps of her petticoat down her arms. Again, she complied without speaking. It was she who continued, pulling the straps off her arms. Now her corset was exposed. She felt him tugging at the laces. "You said you were about to burst," he commented. "My Gawd, Madeline. How can you breathe in anything like this?"

Before she could answer she felt relief; she knew he had untied the knot, and heard the whir each time a string passed through an eyelet. Then she knew the corset was open. She felt it part at the back, and she leaned back against him as both his hands came around under the loosened bodice and gently enveloped her bare breasts.

Madeline almost swooned. She shrugged her shoulders and threw out her arms so that the corset, with a little wiggling, and help from the Captain, slid off and fell to the dirt floor. Slowly he turned her, nude to the waist, to face him. He kissed her with tender intensity, lifted her off the floor and carried her to the bunk. There, carefully, he laid her down. He kissed her neck as his hands groped for the buttons to her skirt. He grew flustered and impatient as he failed at first to find them; then exasperated when he found them but could not unbutton them with all due speed. Nor was she helping him. This had not crossed his mind, when he felt her arms leaving his back, felt the flat of her hands on his chest, realized that she was trying to push him away. "Wait," she pleaded.

He ceased kissing her, ceased unbuttoning the skirt. Puzzled, he leaned on an elbow to look at her face. "What?" he asked gruffly.

She did not want to face him; if she had to face him she was sure she would surrender. Freed from his embrace, Madeline turned over on her stomach, stuffed a pillow under her bosom, and then laid her chin in her hands, looking at the fire. Her eyes were misty, but he did not see them. "Let's watch the fire for a while, Captain," she said. He noted that she did not call him Freeman.

Captain Taylor did not move. He was undecided. Why the wait? Why not pull off that skirt with its fifty buttons right now? But her face, profiled in the firelight, her smooth, unblemished back tapering down to a tiny waist where the skirt began, softened him if it did not check his desire. She looked so small, lying there beside him, so fragile, so exquisite. He knew he had the strength to do with her whatever he wished, that she was entirely in his grasp – and that if he did abuse her, he would hate himself to the day he died. He was, after all, an officer and a gentleman. And this Madeline – she was different from all the others.

He did not pretend to understand what had led her to ask him to stop, for that was women for you. He grabbed the other pillow and stuffed it under his chest and placed his chin in his hands and lay down just as she was doing, staring into the fire. Hers was the next move.

He waited. The fire crackled. The coffee pot began to steam. He glanced at Madeline and saw that she had now laid her head down. It was turned to the side; she was looking straight at him. She reminded him of a small, beautiful child. So he smiled back at her, and placed a hand on her bare back. Gently he ran it up and down her spine. He was careful to stop at her waist.

"Freeman," she said quietly.

"What, Madeline?"

"You've told me all about your life. Your boyhood, your days at West Point, your career in the Cavalry, and your love of motor cars."

He laughed, for his passion had receded and he accepted that he was not going to have his way with her. "I must be an egotistical fellow."

She did not smile back at him. Instead she said softly, "What do you know about me?"

"About you? Why – why—"

"That's it. You only know that I am a thirty year old spinster, that I teach English in Elm Grove, Michigan, and that I am part of Philip Snowden's family."

"Well, now—"

"Please, Captain. Let me continue. You have asked me nothing about my childhood, my education, or – or—"

"That's because I am so enthralled by your personality, Madeline. And your beauty. Your exquisite beauty." His hand glided up and down her bare back.

"Or because I'm just another conquest."

"That is not true."

"Then," she asked, her eyes misting so that she turned from him and gazed into the fire, "haven't you wondered why I am a spinster? Why I have never married?"

He quit stroking her back. "Yes," he replied. "I have wondered. I was so curious that I asked your brother, and an icy chill developed immediately."

This startled Madeline. For long moments she stared into the fire. He saw tears falling from her cheeks. "What have I done?" he asked himself silently. Then, aloud, he said, "Since Philip would not give me an answer, perhaps you will. Madeline, how does it happen that you have never married?"

Both gazed into the fire, the Captain awaiting an answer, the woman considering what she should say. "Are you going to tell me?" he asked softly.

A shudder rippled down her back. He started to place an arm around her, but thought better of it. Intuitively, he knew she was going to tell him. And he knew that whatever it was, it was a struggle for her to talk about it.

"Very well, Captain. I'll tell you. And it is a simple story, and I am not alone. What happened to me has happened to many others."

"Oh?"

"When I was seventeen I fell in love, and I became pregnant, and the boy reneged, and my brother, who was already a lawyer, placed me in a home for unwed mothers in Chicago. There I gave birth to a baby daughter who was put up for adoption when she was two weeks old." Madeline sobbed as she spoke. Her voice was rising. "And I was expected to come back into society as if nothing had happened. Do you hear me, Captain?" she cried, turning onto her back and facing him, exposing her breasts as her hands and arms lay flung out over her head toward the fire. "As if nothing had happened! As if I was still Madeline Snowden, maiden of age seventeen!"

"Madeline, I—"

"And so Philip sent me to Normal School, and I obtained a degree, and he got a job for me in Elm Grove and there I have lived ever since. And people feel sorry for this little spinster English teacher – poor, mousy, frustrated little school marm."

She turned over and flung her face into the pillow. Her bare shoulders heaved with sobs.

"All right, Madeline," the Captain said gently.

Abruptly she sat up and swung her legs over the side of the bunk. She was oblivious to her nakedness; she sniffled and accepted a clean handkerchief from him. "I'm sorry I led you on, Captain," she sobbed, reaching for her corset. "You are so kind, so much fun to talk to. And I wanted you to make love to me so much that – I had decided to give myself to you – but when you started on my skirt – oh, it was a memory, Captain, of thirteen years ago when an impetuous boy fussed with my skirt – and the terrible outcome of it all for me." Now she had slipped the corset on and placed her back to him, implying that he, sitting up in the bunk, was to lace her up. Businesslike, he began to do so. "But there are others involved," she went on. "The Snowdens. Prudence and Emily and Philip. Rusty. I can't be the subject of another scandal. I can't take the risk of pregnancy, Captain, because of them." He finished the lacing and she walked to the bench, at the same time placing her petticoat straps over her shoulders. She picked up her blouse and put it on. "You hate me," she said, losing control and beginning to sob, at the same time backing up to him to button her blouse. "Don't deny it. I know you do."

"Dammit, Madeline. I don't either," he replied loudly as he completed buttoning her blouse. "Here. Let's have some coffee." Frustrated and shocked, he could think of nothing else to say.

"You can find another girl down at Mammoth," she said.

He did not reply, instead pouring the steaming coffee in two cups and sitting down at the table. She put on her coat and sat in the other chair, and stirred the coffee in the tin cup, loudly. The chocolate cake remained unwrapped. Her sobs were coming less and less often, but occasionally he still heard them begin, ripple through her like a dozen little hiccups, and then stop.

"It's all right, Madeline," he said quietly, sipping his coffee.

"Thank you, Captain," she said simply.

And then, with almost no words between them, they cleaned the cabin, smothered the fire, blew out the candles; she put on her hat, then she held the picnic basket as he padlocked the door, then followed him down the sward to the buggy. The stars were out and the fresh air was invigorating, but she felt the chill. As they rode back to the Wylie Way, she did not try to sit close, nor link her arm with his. Captain Taylor was quiet, apparently in deep thought. She was sure that he was leaving her life forever, and she could not remember when she had felt so miserable. Terrible waves of doubt passed over her. Had her resistance cost her the love of a fine man? Would a really good man have tried to do what the Captain had wanted to do to her? And her own frustration! How she desired him! How she still wanted him! Why had she stopped him? Why had she let him unclothe her to the waist? What in the world is the world all about? She was glad it was dark when they clattered up to the Wylie Way. No one was around, for the dance and campfire festivities were all going on, and the Snowdens, thank God, were busy being tourists. Madeline started to climb down from the seat, but the Captain was quickly there to help her, his hands on her waist, lowering her quickly to the ground. He made no attempt to hold her tight or kiss her.

Together they walked to the canvas doorway. Then she turned to him. She wanted to plead with him, to express her apology for the shabby treatment, for she knew she had held out high hopes and then smashed them, but all she was able to say was, "Good night, Captain."

Captain Freeman W. Taylor removed his hat and stood looking down at her. She was so beautiful in the starlight, he thought. But words refused to come to him. "Good night, Madeline," he said curtly, turned on his heels, slapped his hat on his head, walked rapidly down the path, jumped into the buggy and whipped the horse to a fast trot. Madeline's eyes filled with tears again as she fled into her tented room, threw herself on the bed and sobbed like a broken-hearted school girl.

## V

When Madeline and the Captain had left the tent at the Wylie Way, Prudence returned to the rocking chair and for some time rocked back and forth over the squeaky board while her clear young face puckered into a look of extreme discontent. Finally she arose and stomped to the mirror, so single-minded and decisive that the rocker slithered back a foot and remained rocking for another minute. She stood erect, smoothed out her stylish brown wasp-waist skirt, tucked in her middy blouse and eyed her form. She noticed stray wisps of golden hair, so she undid the pins and fetched brush and comb and discovered snarls which she brushed out; them she reset her hair again. "Darn," the girl complained, "it's so dirty." Then she examined what at first looked like a blemish on her left cheek, and was relieved to discover it also was just dirt. She felt an itch on her left thigh, and scratched it. She felt dusty and dirty all over.

Then she heard a merry whistle and the sounds of someone walking up the path. Her heart skipped a beat, for she knew it was him – and she so wanted it to be.

"I say, anyone home?"

"Yes. Come in."

She heard a flimsy screen door swing open, then shut, and then he was there, standing in the entrance to the girls' bedroom. Lord Billner was wearing heavy shoes, puttees, those same corduroy knickers, but an incongruous white shirt, a brown tie, and the same corduroy coat and hat that he had been wearing since Mammoth. He removed his hat and smiled at her, his white teeth showing from his well-shaped mouth.

"So this is the Wylie Way," he commented, scanning the striped canvas and the boards and the cheap rug and the furniture, but his eyes soon came back to the golden girl who stood in front of him.

"It's hardly Old Faithful Inn, but at least our family is together," replied Prudence.

"I think it's great," he responded. "At least there's no Order of the Antelopes to disturb you."

"I know," she said. "Daddy and Mother can sleep together tonight, and Madeline and I won't have to undress in front of doting old dowagers."

"Let's take a walk before dinner," he said, changing the subject. "Hot springs and geysers are all over the place. I've been talking with Hezekiah and he's told me about some springs most people don't see. Come on, Prudence. Just leave a note for your parents that you've gone for a walk with me."

Prudence was more pleased than she wanted Lord Billner to know. She scribbled her note in haste and grabbed her hat and smashed that feathery monstrosity onto her pretty head and in no time they were on their way.

They strolled to Old Faithful geyser, then followed a path up Geyser Hill and observed the Infant geyser, the Butterfly spring, the Giantess geyser, the Teakettle spring, the Sponge geyser, the Lion geyser and its nearby spouter, the Lioness. At one beautiful pool Prudence sighed. "All that hot water and no place to take a bath. I feel so dusty."

"So do I," replied her swain as they strolled on down the path. "They tell me a Chinese laundryman once made good use of these pools."

"A Chinese?"

"Yes. He found himself a little spring, pitched his tent over it, and had a perfect place to boil his laundry."

"How inventive."

"He made out fine until one day a carton of soap fell into the pool. Suddenly the spring became agitated, churning and rushing and jumping up, and then, lo and behold a geyser erupted and laundry, tent, and supplies went up fifty feet in the air. The Chinaman is still running."

Prudence laughed and barely noticed when Lord Billner guided her off the main path onto a wisp of a trail that led into some pines. Shadows were getting longer now. They paused once or twice to catch their breath and wipe perspiration from their faces.

"Why are we here, Stephen?" she asked, aware that they were no longer on the main trail, that no one else was to be seen.

"You'll see," he said mysteriously as they continued. It was still and quiet as they picked their way along the dim path amidst the darkening woods. Suddenly they reached Lord Billner's planned destination.

"There," he announced with an air of success. "Just as Hezekiah said."

Prudence looked down upon a spring perhaps ten feet in circumference whose wavelets lapped at a shallow shore. A single boulder, extending about six inches above the water, almost bisected the pool. Lord Billner stooped and tested the water, then stood up and dried his hand. "It's warm," he said, "but not too warm."

Prudence looked up at him quizzically. "Not too warm for what?" she asked.

"A bath," he replied simply. "Hezekiah told me about it. Seems that he used to come up here to take a bath."

She looked into his face with renewed interest. "Oh."

An awkward silence followed. "Ahhh. We are hot and sweaty and dusty, aren't we, Prudence? From those long miles in the coach. Along that dusty road."

"Hmm?"

"I mean – well – don't you like being clean?"

"Of course I like being clean."

"Well, Prudence – no one knows about this place but Hezekiah. I mean – we could take a bath and—"

"We? Lord Stephen Billner. How dare you!"

"Yes, *we*," he replied firmly, certain that the best defense is a good offense. "Don't be angry..."

"Stephen," she said, her eyes flashing, "you – you remind me of little boys who draw things on the sidewalk asking little girls to come into the barn."

"My goodness," he replied impulsively, "do they do that in America too?"

Now Prudence was gazing at the pool, clear and blue, the little wavelets lapping the shore, seeming to invite her in. "But I never went along," the girl added absentmindedly. "I told Mother and did those boys get a whipping."

"Well, just an idea," he said flatly. "I guess we better go back."

"Wait," said Prudence, hesitating. She scanned all 360 degrees of the terrain. "I didn't – say no."

Lord Billner's heart jumped with anticipation, but he strived not to appear too anxious. "See," he said, "I'll turn my back and you can – disrobe – and come and sit in the water on this side of the boulder and then you look the other way and I'll undress and get in on the other side. We won't see each other, but we'll both have a bath and get clean without – without—"

"Seeing each other," she said, completing his sentence. She recollected that she had already seen *him* – and would like to steal another look.

Again Prudence scanned the terrain – the pines, the faint artery of a trail, the deepening twilight. "My hair is so dirty. If I could just dip it in that nice warm water and rub it good, it would be cleaned, because it is all just dust. Do you – really – think we'd be safe?"

"Oh, yes, Prudence. It's safe."

"The water isn't too hot?"

"A little warm. I think it will feel wonderful."

The violent mental wrestling match being waged with her conscience ended. "Of course, if Mother and Daddy ever found out, they'd never let you see me again," she said.

"How would they find out?"

"I don't know," she replied thoughtfully. He saw her hand go to her middy blouse. "You'll – not look – Stephen. You promise you won't look."

"Cross my heart," he said, his heart beating so fast that he wasn't sure whether he crossed it or not.

"Then walk over to that big pine and cover your head against it like you are playing hide and seek."

Lord Billner dashed rapidly to the big pine and gladly hid his head. Prudence darted behind another tree and began disrobing, so excited and thrilled that she shook. Hat, shoes, stockings, skirt, middy blouse, petticoat, cotton vest – all came off quickly, leaving the girl nude save for her white drawers. She unpinned her hair and let it fall in ripples to her shoulders. At first she paused, thumbs along waistband, thinking she would keep them on but then she remembered that she was already short one pair. She began pulling them down, paused once again, then quickly removed them. It was cool; goose flesh crept up and down her body.

"You're still not looking," she called.

"Not looking," he replied. "I promised."

She scampered out of the trees like a forest nymph and slowly submerged herself in the warm water on her side of the boulder. Finally she was in up to her neck. "Ooooooooooooo, Stephen," Prudence cooed. "It's wonderful. So warm, so – ooooooooooooooooo – wonderful. Come on in." While she waited she dipped her golden tresses into the water and scrubbed them clean.

If Prudence had been nervously excited over her daring, Lord Billner was verging on sheer apoplexy. So eager was he to disrobe that he pulled his cravat the wrong way and gagged. When kneeling to untie his shoes he lost balance and fell on two dry limbs that snapped loudly as he fell on his seat. He pulled off his trousers so fast that the buttonholes in the fly would never be the same. He never could remember how he divested himself of his BVDs. But somehow the task was accomplished and in a jiffy he was cavorting toward the pool. And she, curious as to his progress, turned her head just in time to see close up what she had glimpsed from a distance at Bath Lake. The girl blushed at seeing Adam *sans* fig leaf. She turned her head away without Lord Billner having noticed as a strange thrill ran through her luxuriating body. She thought, 'Some of the girls in Elm Grove said naked men are ugly – but I don't think so. They're so – so – masculine.'

"Isn't it delightful?" she said to him when he was finally engulfed on his side of the pool.

"Wonderful."

Prudence sat up slightly and slavered her body. In the gloaming Lord Billner could see her shiny, wet shoulders and the soft, symmetrical lines of her breasts. "Mmm," the girl sighed, looking to him, noticing his broad shoulders as he too sat up a little straighter. "I wish we could stay here for hours rather than minutes," she added as their eyes locked upon each other. He placed his elbow on the top of the stone barrier and turned his body towards her. His free arm came over the boulder and touched her body below an armpit, caressing a full young breast. She turned to him; her free arm embraced his shoulders; both tightened their grips and were about to kiss when she protested with an "Ouch."

"Wh-What?" he asked.

She sat up and removed his hand from her breast. "You hurt me," she protested.

"How?"

The girl slid back into the water, up to her neck again. "It's a long story, Stephen. And a humiliating one."

"Tell me, Prudence," he coaxed her. "Tell me."

"It's better now, but it was so sore I could hardly touch it."

"What's better now?"

She raised herself to a half sitting position, so that the décolletage of the water revealed as much of her bust as a low cut gown. "Tell me, Stephen," she said quietly, "do you think they are too small?" She cupped her breasts in her hands but only revealed the upper forty-five percent above the water.

Lord Billner looked and gulped. "Oh, my goodness. They're lovely. Prudence. Just right."

She slid down in the water again, up to her neck, much to his disappointment.

"I'm glad you think so, Stephen," she continued quietly. "See, I thought they were too small, so I bought a Bust Developer from Sears, Roebuck to make them bigger. And it got stuck on this one, and it wouldn't come off. Oh, Stephen, it was awful!"

"Good Lord," replied Lord Billner, roaring with laughter. "Prudence, I say, my dear, you are the most interesting female I've ever known. Getting a bust developer stuck on one of your pretties. Ho, ho, ho!"

Prudence puckered her lips and began to pout. Lord Billner quit laughing and became deadly serious. "That must be why I love you so much," he said quietly.

"What – did you say?" asked the girl, turning on her side to him and forgetting her pout.

"Why I love you so much, Prudence." He too turned on his side, their eyes met once again. He reached his free arm over the stone and held her back while one of her arms went to him; this time their lips met over the stone barrier. The kiss was so heavenly that neither thought anything of the shuddering of the earth and the far off sounds of rocks striking rocks. To them, it was the kiss. It was the earth-shattering revelation of love. But when like a flash all the water disappeared from the pool with a loud, sucking gluck, leaving their bodies exposed to the cool evening air – more naked that Adam and Eve – they were aroused from their bliss. They looked – no water! They lay in the gloaming surveying each other's nakedness.

"Hello, Eve," he said. "What's happened?"

"Hello, Adam," she replied. "Where'd the water go?"

The earth shook again. Suddenly boiling, steaming hot water gushed back into the pool. It churned and splashed. Prudence gave a little scream as the boiling liquid touched her toes. Both jumped up and scampered up the bank as the hot spring churned into a geyser twenty feet high. They watched it, fascinated, did Adam and Eve, locked for safety in each other's arms, oblivious of their nudity.

"I'm scared, Stephen," cried Prudence at last. "I'm scared. Maybe it's God telling us to be good and wait 'til we're married."

"No, Prudence," he reassured her. "It's just a little earthquake. They say these tremors are quite common in Yellowstone. And when they occur, the hot springs and geysers go crazy."

"Are you sure?" she asked.

"Oh, yes. But I think we better get dressed," he said decisively, aware of the fear in Prudence's eyes.

Suddenly Prudence was aware of their nudity. "Oh, my goodness," she gasped, trying to hide herself with her hands. "We better. I'm already dried off and I'm shiv-v-vering."

He started for his clothes and she for hers; then Lord Billner stopped. "Oh, Prudence," he called, "don't get dressed yet. I've something for you." He ran for his clothes, reached into a big pocket in his corduroy coat, and returned to her with the item. By now she had taken refuge behind a tree. "Here," he said, unabashedly oblivious of his own nudity, a twinkle in his eyes. "Your drawers. The ones you left at Bath Lake. Freshly laundered."

Prudence gasped. "You – you know!" she gasped. "Oh, you—"

"Ah, ahh," he said, placing a finger to his lips. "I love you, Prudence. Remember?"

For moments she was silent. She reached from behind the tree, snatched the drawers, and quickly put them on. "You better get dressed too," she said. Just then an aftershock rocked the earth, sent the trees swaying, and the geyser shot twice as high. Lord Billner ran to his clothes. "I'll be right with you, Prudence," he yelled.

Prudence was flustered. So Lord Billner did know that it was she who had been hiding behind the boulder at Bath Lake. As she put on her petticoat, the hobble skirt, the cotton eyelet vest, the middy blouse; sat down and put on her stockings and shoes, she tried to sort out that knowledge, and figure how she was supposed to respond. She folded her other drawers slowly, wondering how to carry them. Then she flounced her blond tresses, already nearly dry, took the hairpins she had laid carefully on a flat stone, and to the best of her ability arranged her hair as before, topping it with her big hat. Without a mirror she had done a pretty good job. She also made sure her middy was tucked in and the skirt correctly positioned. She walked out from behind the tree toward the spouting geyser with all the dignity that became a proper young lady from Elm Grove. There he was, waiting for her, fully attired. "We better get back, dear," he said, taking her arm. She looked up at him. It was the first time he had called her 'dear', and she liked it.

As they swung down the trail, arms around each other's waists, she handed him her other drawers. "Perhaps you can hide these in your pocket for me," she suggested, "and if you wish, you may wash them and give them to me another day." They laughed as he stuffed them into a pocket.

At one point coming down the trail they had an overview of the Upper Geyser Basin. They paused, astonished. By the light of the rising moon they surveyed a steaming, hissing, field broken by spouting geysers. It looked as if every geyser and hot spring and mud pot had erupted.

"Are those your phalanx – or is it phallic – symbols, sir?" she asked.

Lord Billner smiled, recalling his embarrassment the other night at dinner. "Don't know, Prudence. But I'm sure of one thing. They're not as frustrated as I am."

She stopped walking and turned to him, looking up into his strong features. She placed her arms around his neck and pushed her body onto his. She felt his strong arms encircling her back. "Tell me," she whispered, her lips touching his, "what did you mean by that?"

"Don't you know?" he asked, kissing her passionately.

She nodded even as they kissed. When they broke, she laid her head on his chest, and she asked, "are you in rut, Stephen? Like the elk and moose and buffalo?"

"I guess."

"Tell me," she coaxed. "Tell me what you said to me when we were in the pool."

"I said that I love you, Prudence," he replied softly. "Is it ridiculous for me to love you?"

"Oh, no," she moaned, clutching him tighter and pushing her body into his with all her might. "Because – I love you, too, Stephen. Ever since the day you were late for the train at St. Paul."

"But I suppose it's all impossible," he said as they started down the trail once more. "Your father would never approve of me as a husband. Nor your mother let you stay in Paradise Valley through the long Montana winters."

"They might," she countered. "After all, I'm nineteen. Most of the girls in my graduating class are already married. Babies and all. And I'm still a—"

"You mean, you'd marry me and stay in the Valley with me? Marry me in just a few days?" he blurted, hope rising in his voice.

"Maybe, Stephen. Would you want me?"

"Want you? Oh, Prudence. You are the sweetest, loveliest, most delightful, prettiest, most divine—"

"But you'd have to ask Daddy."

Lord Billner stopped in his tracks. He frowned. "Your father? Yes, stop and think of it, of course I should ask him for your hand. I'll ask him tonight."

"Or tomorrow, Stephen," she countered. "Let me build up Daddy and Mother to it first. I'll let you know when."

By now they had reached the main path. People were about. Kerosene lanterns of the Wylie Way flickered in the distance. What was surprising was that no one seemed upset by the earthquake. Soldiers and concessionaire personnel all reassured tourists, telling them that such tremors were common. For the scientist giving a lecture on Yellowstone's geology at the Wylie Way campfire, the event was his opportunity to drive home his point about the instability of the area and comment on the unusual activity among the thermal phenomena.

When Prudence and Lord Billner reached the campfire the speaker had just ended his lecture. The fragrant odor of popcorn was in the air, and a Wylie Way leader was about to lead the guests in songs. The young couple joined in, singing 'There's a Long, Long Trail A-Winding' and 'In the Gloaming'. Lord Billner fetched them popcorn. No two lovers were ever happier.

But of course it had to end. Emily had spotted them and when a song ended, she hastened over immediately. "Where," she demanded, eyeing Prudence's hair, which, having been put up without a mirror, was slightly disheveled, even a little damp at the ends, "have you two children been?"

"Oh, Mother," Prudence retorted, "we're not children. Stephen and I have been out seeing the geysers. I left you a note."

"I know. But since five o'clock?" she asked in disbelief. "You've eaten, I suppose."

The two exchanged hurried glances as Lord Billner gulped down some popcorn. "I - took some food with us," he lied.

"Yes, Mother. We had something to eat," the girl added as her stomach rumbled and she realized she was hungry. At least the popcorn helped. One cannot live by love alone.

Emily dilated her Yankee nostrils and breathed deeply, as if she smelled a lie. "Prudence," she said sharply, "I think it's time for you to say good night to Lord Billner."

"Oh, now, Emily," Philip cut in, having joined them after visiting the tobacco stand. But Emily was persistent. "Young lady, you be at the tent in fifteen minutes," she ordered.

"Yes, Mother," Prudence replied meekly, lowering her eyes submissively as she and Lord Billner walked away.

"My goodness, Prudence. Your mother seems angry with you."
"She suspects something," Prudence replied. "I think Mother knows we are in love. It frightens her."

"I guess this is hardly the time to ask your father for your hand," Lord Billner stated.

"Hardly, Stephen. But don't worry. Tomorrow is another day. I know Daddy and his moods." As they approached the tent-cabin, Lord Billner pulled Prudence off into the shadowy woods. He placed his arms around her, and kissed her. She felt his strength, and she wanted him. "Don't worry, dear Stephen," she murmured. "We'll be married."

Thus did they depart. Lord Billner made his way back to Old Faithful Inn a new man, full of ambition and new plans, while Prudence tiptoed first to the ladies' tent, then to the bedroom. She was surprised to find Madeline already in bed, bundled down beneath the heavy blankets and apparently asleep. Prudence blew out the lamp which Madeline had left burning for her and, for the second time in as many hours, disrobed. She was clean now, and her body felt warm in spite of the cool air. She slipped her nightie over her head and let it ripple over her breasts, tummy, hips, thighs, knees, and calves. She shook her long, golden hair and brushed it vigorously, delighting in how soft and thick and clean it was. Then she climbed into her side of the bed and lay on her back with her hands behind her head, and dreamed of her lover. In no time at all, she was asleep.

Madeline was glad, for she had only feigned sleep and she felt miserable; above all she had not wanted her niece to see her face, which was red from tears. It had also been difficult keeping that one position in the bed until Prudence dozed off.

## VI

Philip and Emily were late getting back to their tent because they had lost Rusty. He wasn't at the recreation hall, he wasn't at the campfire, he just wasn't. It was really her concern over Rusty's whereabouts that had led Emily to be so irritable with Prudence, and she felt guilty for having spoken to her daughter that way. She was still irritable until she and Philip found Rusty at the stables quietly listening to the tall tales of the stage drivers. Hezekiah was his patron.

It was not until they had sent the boy trotting down the path with orders to go to bed at once that Emily's demeanor changed. Philip was relieved to find that his wife was in an amorous mood. She ought to be, he thought. Two nights cramped in a Pullman berth where she was afraid of a train wreck at the wrong time, one night with Rusty's jawbreaker, one night separated by the Concatenated Order of the Antelope, and now, tonight. 'If Emily is a live, breathing woman and wife,' he thought, 'she should be ready tonight.'

Emily slowed their pace. Philip felt her leaning on his shoulder. The faint odor of lavender cologne aroused him. He looked down at his lovely wife.

"Yes, Emily."

"Did you notice Prudence and that young Englishman?"

"Yep."

"Do you think they're in love?"

"Sort of looks that way. Maybe it's just an infatuation."

"Do you approve?"

Philip removed his cigar from his mouth. "I'm not sure, Emily." They walked on.

"Philip."

"Yes, Emily."

"I heard one of the Antelopes telling a risqué joke in the Fountain Hotel lobby."

"Oh?" If Philip lacked enthusiasm, it was because he knew Emily's idea of funny jokes. Most of them were very hard to laugh at.

"This one is different, dear," she said. "It was told to a slightly overhung group of lodge brothers."

"Really," he replied with rising interest.

"I just overheard it, Philip. I mean, I didn't mean to hear it, but they were close by and—"

"Of course, dear. That's understandable."

"It's – it's – *risqué.*"

"Really?" again. "You tell a risqué joke, my dear? I don't believe it."

"Do you think I shouldn't tell it? Even to you? Will you think less of me if I tell you?" Clearly, Emily was uneasy and undecided, yet, Philip suspected, she was feeling a little wicked.

"Oh, Emily, dear," he reassured her, placing his hand at the small of her back. "Come on. You can tell me."

"If you won't condemn me," she began. "It seems an Englishman – not Lord Billner, for heaven's sakes! – got lost up here in the woods. Finally he came to a road and there stood a horse and buggy. And he could see that there was someone in it. So he knocked on the side of the buggy and said, 'I say, old chap. How far is Old Faithful Inn?'"

Emily tittered, and held Philip's arm with both hands. "And a voice came back from the buggy, 'None of your darn business!'"

Actually, Philip had first heard the joke in a somewhat different version at least twenty-five years before, but he did not want to disappoint his wife. He roared. He slapped his knees. And he quickened their pace back to the tent. At the entrance they were disappointed to find Rusty still up.

"I thought I saw a bear out there," he said, apprehensively pointing into the darkness.

His parents peered to where he pointed, but saw nothing. They rushed Rusty to bed in the cot, took care of their own ablutions, snuffed the lamp and stood by the double bed with the heavy blankets, where both disrobed. Philip contemplated the warm, cozy bed with his loving wife beside him; he thought she was thinking the same thoughts. Nightgowns finally on, they pulled down the covers and crawled in. Emily reached down and spread out the blankets, and then she snuggled up to Philip. She whispered something in his ear – something about Old Faithful. For moments, though, they lay silent. Was Rusty asleep? Yes. They could hear the boy's deep breathing. 'Thank God,' thought Philip.

He was a most happy man lying in the airy tent-cabin, the odor of pine needles and canvas and lavender all making a most heady atmosphere. And then there was the softness and warmth from a loving wife, cuddling next to him.

At long last! His hands wandered as he kissed her first softly, then passionately as she reciprocated. With the aid of two pairs of hands, both nightgowns were working upwards. Breathing was coming harder.

A pine branch above the tent snapped. A tenth of a second later the canvas ceiling ripped open and a dank, furry object landed heavily at the foot of the bed breaking the old frame. Like a thunderclap the headboard and footboard collapsed.

Emily screamed. In the darkness the unknown intruder roared, Rusty sat up and shouted. Madeline and Prudence sat up to see what was wrong. Prudence got up and headed for the bedroom doorway just as the beast lit out for freedom via that exit. The creature ran right between her legs and carried Prudence bear-back and backwards as her nightie split down the middle. Then there was a resounding "thump" as she fell off the unknown invader when it crashed through the screen door, not bothering to open it.

"What the hell. What the hell!" Philip shouted in the darkness as the three women continued screaming. It was Rusty, tugging at his father's nightgown, who brought order. "I told you I saw a bear," he yelled.

"Eh? So that's what it was," said Philip as help came running.

"Yes," said one of the attendants, holding high a lantern to examine the damage done to the canvas ceiling. "It was Tom the Curious Bear, all right. We've got to do something about him."

"He's never hurt anyone," added another employee. "But his curiosity plus his appetite get him into more trouble than any dozen other bears."

The men folks – Philip, Rusty, and the Wylie employees – tried to calm the women. Rusty reminded Prudence that her gown was ripped right down the middle from crotch to ankles even as the college boy employees, holding high their lanterns, followed the lad's pointed finger and drank in the view. Prudence reacted immediately, pulling her nightie together. And the family accepted Wylie's offer of transfer to another tent.

But once quiet and order were restored, and everyone was once more bedded down, Emily resisted Philip's advances. Not only was she fearful of another bear – the adrenaline stirred up by the event had been sufficient to interfere with everyone's sleep, even Rusty's. "We can't risk it, dear," she whispered. And she added, "How terrible it would have been, Philip, if we had been further along." So Philip listened to that phrase of rejection heard by husbands the world over: "Let's go to sleep, dear." But she did add, "Tomorrow night we'll be at Lake Hotel. I'll feel safer there."

'Damned building'll probably fall into the lake," he growled.

"What, dear?"

"Nothing, Emily. Good night."

And out in the woods a lonely, morose black bear with a streak of gray fur bisecting his head plodded along a narrow bear path. He was headed in the general direction of Canyon. In his animal mind, Tom, the Curious Bear, knew that he had better make tracks from Old

Faithful. They'd capture him and cart him off to the Lamar Valley where there were few tourists with ham sandwiches, olives, pickles, and half-consumed bottles of soft drinks. He'd have to dig for rodents and go berrying and break up old logs for grubs and otherwise fend for himself. Tom sniffed the air. Yep. He'd plod down to Canyon. No one would be looking for him there.

# Chapter Five
# The Fourth Day

### I

The temperaments of some of the *Shoshone Belles*'s occupants changed day by day. Leaving the Fountain Hotel with its cavorting Antelopes they had been surly, grumpy, and exhausted. Congressman Griffin and his wife had been hung over. Hezekiah was still brooding over being caught bootlegging, and even Rusty was quiet because he sensed that no one wanted to talk to him. Only the two young couples had remained happy.

Today, leaving Old Faithful, the mood was markedly different. In the driver's seat, as usual, was Hezekiah, cheerful in his usual grouchy way; next to him sat Rusty, talkative again; and finally sat the well-rested Congressman from Louisiana who greeted everyone as they were about to board the coach with a cheerful "Top of the mornin' to you-all." The silent treatment was over. Inside the coach were Philip and Emily, still rather quiet and beginning to wish for an end to their holiday. Then there was the buxom Dolly Griffin. She, too, was in better humor thanks to a sober, good night's sleep. Dolly's fleshy body was covered in a linen duster; she wore a huge hat that held up an enormous yardage of veiling, "To keep the dust out," she explained, adding that she was, "Sho-all glad to be seein' a lake today because ahmmm tired of seein', and smellin' just geysers and pine trees." In the middle seat sat Madeline, alone. Clothing-wise she looked lovely – slit skirt tightly belted and buttoned at her narrow waist; white, man-style blouse; formfitting jacket; and that huge hat atop her brown hair. But physically and mentally Madeline was a wreck. To cover up her feelings she sat primly, back straight as a ramrod, and thankful that a black veil was pulled over her face. She stared out of the coach at an angle, and moved so little that she could

have been a statue. She bit her lower lip over and over again to fight off the tears, though occasionally a salty renegade left a moist trail down her smooth face.

The Captain had failed to appear.

"Why, oh why," she asked herself, "must women be confronted with such decisions?" She had refused him. As a result, she assumed that she had lost him. But – to have given in? Would it have guaranteed his devotion? Or would he have left her, anyway?

The only consistently happy occupants were in the back seat. Lord Billner and Prudence were talking up a storm. Emily was relieved: as long as they talked they weren't pawing over each other, she concluded, wrongly.

"Hear you had a visitor last night," the Congressman talked down to Philip. "I presume you-all don't particularly like sleeping in a tent."

"The bear was no worse than the Antelopes, and their assorted friends," replied Philip.

"Didn't you find it rather barbaric, dear – sleeping in a tent?" queried Dolly of Emily.

"We found it fine," replied Philip for both of them. It hurt his pride that this tin-horn Solon had been able to use his political clout to gain a good room at Old Faithful Inn while he and his family were given a choice of dormitory-type rooms or a tent at the Wylie Way. His statement bore the mark of finality, and nothing more was said.

"I say," Lord Billner spoke up to Hezekiah, "what is our route to Yellowstone Lake?"

The coachman removed his pipe, spat, and leaned over and back into the coach. "Up the Firehole River, past Kepler Cascades, and on over the Continental Divide," he replied. "'Bout eighteen or twenty miles, I reckon."

And so the grays plodded on, slower than ever, it seemed to Madeline. The coach stopped to allow them to envy the beauty of the Cascades, where Emily noticed that Lord Billner and Prudence disappeared behind some trees and, she was certain, emerged with Prudence's face flushed and Lord Billner bearing a cat-who-just-ate-the-canary expression. She wished she could have heard their conversation when they got out at the Continental Divide. Perhaps it was just as well that she didn't. The Grand Tetons were in view to the south.

"The Grand Tetons," Prudence mused. "What a strange name. Tetons."

"It's French," Lord Billner informed her. "Named by French trappers and mountain men."

"Tetons. Tetons. Tet—" Prudence put a hand to her mouth and smothered a giggle.

"Yes, my dear. They say the French trappers named them for that, for obvious reasons," he explained as he gazed at them.

"My goodness," she said, grabbing one of his hands. "Who would ever think that lonesome trappers way out in the wilderness, and away from women, would ever think of naming mountains for such – things."

He smiled. "Maybe they were in rut. Seriously, Prudence, they do sort of remind you of—"

"No, they don't, Stephen Billner." She lowered her eyes. "And you should know," the girl added quietly. "They don't look like them at all. Besides, there are three of them."

"Prudence, I believe they were thinking of the she-wolf that suckled Romulus and Remus."

"No," the girl replied positively. "They were thinking of women. Stop and think of it, Stephen, men in the wilderness must not think of much else. Look at the names they've given to things: Tetons and Firehole River and Grand Canyon and erupting geysers and the Devil's Slide."

"Wait a minute, Prudence. I'm a man. Am I that bad?"

"You are different, sir," she said, swinging his hand with hers. "Only – not too different. I wish there was a boulder we could step behind."

"Me, too. That's the trouble with kissing. We always want more."

"And more and more," she cooed, brushing against his shoulder.

Suddenly Lord Billner felt the eyes of Philip and Emily upon them. He quickly changed the subject. "Prudence, when should I speak to your father?"

"Not yet, dear," she whispered as they strolled back to the *Shoshone Belle*. "Daddy's in a bad mood this morning, after the bear incident last night. I don't think he slept well. This is definitely not the time to approach him."

The coach plodded on. "Gee, Mr. Hezekiah. We've only got two more days after today and I haven't got my antlers yet. When do I get them?" asked Rusty.

"You just wait, young feller," replied the mountaineer. "We'll get them thar antlers down at Canyon. I'll take you to a place where you can take your pick. That's a promise, now, so let's hear no more of it."

"Okay," replied the boy. "But I ain't fergittin'."

"I know you ain't," said Hezekiah, rubbing the boy's hair. "I know you ain't fergettin'."

And so the coach plodded on. They observed the scenery and damned the dust until they came in sight of Yellowstone Lake and its West Thumb. The view lightened the boredom if it did not dispel it. Congressman Griffin asked Philip if his party was going to take the boat from the Thumb to Lake Hotel.

"What boat?" asked Philip.

"They don't encourage it, but it's an alternate way of going to Lake Hotel. We take the boat and Hezekiah comes down with the *Shoshone Belle*. It gives the horses a rest while we get away from the dust and the smell of these nags. It doesn't cost much. You-all come with Dolly and me."

By now they were approaching the facilities at the Thumb, which included a peppermint-striped dining tent from which issued the fragrance of beef and onions and coffee. When they got off the coach, Philip, whose party were all in favor of the boat ride, gave the necessary money to the Congressman who went to fetch the tickets, while the Snowdens and Dolly entered the tent.

Madeline searched the faces at the tables hopefully, but although there were a few soldiers about, there was no sign of Captain Taylor. How, she wondered, could a man appear to enjoy her company so much – enjoy her body so much! – talk to her so freely about his ambitions, say such nice things to her, and still discard her as if she was yesterday's newspaper?

What Madeline did not know was that the Captain had left a message at the Old Faithful soldier station to be delivered to a "Miss Madeline Snowden, Old Faithful." The enlisted man checked the register at Old Faithful Inn, failed to find Madeline's name, and peremptorily gave up. It did not cross his mind that she could have been registered at the Wylie Way. Buck privates are not paid to think.

The message read in part:

*Dear Madeline,*

*I have been ordered to Canyon immediately to intercept the two wagons loaded with the automobile. I am to escort said automobile out of the Park via the North Entrance.*

The note further explained that this constituted a change of plans, that the wagons had made better progress than expected, and that otherwise he would have continued to the Lake Hotel with the Snowden party and Madeline in particular. Captain Taylor ended his message with this sentence:

*I hope to catch you at Mammoth before you entrain for the East. I want to see you.*

*Love,*

*F.W. Taylor*
*Captain, 2d US Cavalry*

But Madeline had no way of knowing.

So not only Tom the Curious Bear had headed from Old Faithful to Canyon; so had a Cavalry officer who sat astride his mount, deeply absorbed in thought.

Hezekiah, free of his party and with plenty of time to drive the *Shoshone Belle* down to Lake, mingled with the employees. "Seen anything of a tall man with a breathin' hole in his throat?" he kept asking.

"You mean that bandit who robbed the tally-ho down at Mammoth?"

"Yep. That's who I'm lookin' fer."

"Nope. We ain't seen him. For a while it looked like the whole US Cavalry was after him, until that Peoria beer baron – what's his name? Fritz Buschmeister – came into camp t'other day with them two Studebaker wagons, all covered secret-like with tarpaulins."

"What was so odd about that?"

"That's what we all wondered. Up comes the Cavalry like a bunch of renegade Injuns and surrounds the wagons. Then stormin' off the driver's seat of the lead wagon comes this fat little man with a long, gray handlebar mustache and an enormous calabash pipe. He's wearin' a white duster, and a cap and goggles. And thunderation, was he mad! He cussed the lieutenant in charge in English, German, French, and a general combination."

"But what was in the wagons, pardner?" pressed Hezekiah.

"That's just it. Nobody knew. Troops escorted the wagons into the woods and established a cordon around them so nobody could see, and then the lieutenant he goes up to the tarps and, makin' sure all the soldiers are facin' out, he lifts them up and takes a long peek. Like he was undressin' his bride on his weddin' night."

"Damnit, man. I ain't got all day," Hezekiah stormed. "What was it?"

"An auto-mo-bile, that's what it was. A Pierce-Arrow auto-mo-bile. Shiny black and spankin' new. Purtiest thing you ever did see. Big, brass headlights, straw colored spokes in the wheels. Only the wheels and the top and the crank and the tool box and the cans of gasoline – they were all in t'other wagon. I know, 'cause one of the soldiers snuck a peek and told me."

"Jumpin' Jehosephat," exclaimed Hezekiah, nodding in disbelief and sitting down on some wooden steps. "An auto-mo-bile in the Park." He looked around. "Where is it now?"

"Left real quick this mornin'," was the reply. "Bound for Canyon where another troop will escort it out of the Park."

"Yep. We coach drivers' days are numbered," pitched in another.

"Don't give up hope," another piped up. "We ain't licked yet. Child and Haynes and the Wylies – all the big concessionaires – they ain't about to let au-tos in the Park. No, sirree. Not with their investment in five thousand horses and Lord knows how many Yellowstone coaches, buggies, and wagons."

"Hell, man," added another. "It'll be a long, cold day in July before they allow them contraptions to take over. Why, they've got the Interior Department and the US Army all arrayed with them against them au-tos. Nope. We ain't got nothin' to worry about."

"I ain't so sure," mumbled Hezekiah thoughtfully.

"Hah. Rumor says Colonel Saddle-Pants Peavey'll bust every mother's son of a soldier from Captain down if that Pierce-Arrow au-to ever moves an inch on its own power on a Park road."

"I hope yer right," muttered Hezekiah. "I've got to be goin' now. I'm dead-headin' down to Lake. My party's takin' the steamer." As he approached his rig he felt sadness for the horses and the *Shoshone Bell*. In his heart he knew their days were numbered.

"Bet you get there before them," said one of the drivers. "They've been havin' engine trouble on that boat."

## II

After hot springs, cold springs, mineral springs, geysers, fumaroles, mud pots, paint pots, pine trees, bears, buffalo, deer, antelope, elk, moose, and several cubic inches of Yellowstone dust, along with assorted flies – horse, blue bottle, house, deer, and buffalo – and diverse odors – sulfur, pine, and horse both internal and external – Yellowstone Lake looked heavenly to the *Shoshone Belle*'s passengers.

At the wharf the *Annie Laurie* did not look as splendid as a bride of Babylon, as the promotional brochure implied. Originally it had floated on a Wisconsin lake, had been dismantled, shipped across the prairies on the Northern Pacific to Livingston and the narrow gauge to Gardiner, and there loaded on wagons, brought to the Lake, and there reassembled. It had not profited from the process. Nor had a decade of service and ten harsh winters improved its appearance. But, as the slightly nervous passengers said to each other, the *Annie Laurie* was certified by the Coast Guard; therefore, it had to be safe. They were not aware of the date of that certification!

"I hope you are right about it being safe," Emily said apprehensively to Philip as they walked up the narrow gangplank. She eyed the once-white sides, paint scaling off, and the dirty decks, and she could hear the thump, thump, thump of an ancient piston slapping at something at the end of its stroke. "I hope it doesn't go too far out into the Lake," she said. (As if that mattered, since gentle Emily couldn't swim a stroke.) "Rusty, where are you? Stay close to me, young man," she ordered, placing a gloved hand on his arm and tightening it like a vise as he protested.

"Ohhhhhh, Mother!"

By the time the ship's whistle had blown, the gangplank been raised, the pistons had tripled their thump-thumps per minute, and the installations at West Thumb had begun to diminish, the Snowdens had split up. Philip and Emily found deck chairs and sat enjoying the scenery. Rusty had gone to the canteen. The Congressman and his lady were on the upper deck making the Captain's acquaintance. Madeline had strolled off to a railing and stood alone, trying to appear composed and happy while her heart thumped as out of kilter as the ship's pistons. Her misery was almost out of control. "Brace yourself, Madeline. This is nothing, nothing, nothing. Sheer fantasizing," she kept telling herself. Her composure would return, and then she would think of Captain Taylor again, and the intimacies of the evening before, and break down all over again.

And where were Prudence and Lord Billner? On the opposite side of the deck from her parents, of course, holding hands and standing so close together that some passengers took them for honeymooners; one middle-aged couple even hummed 'Here Comes the Bride' as they passed by the young lovers.

"I say, Prudence. How about asking your father now?"

"Oh, no, Stephen. I'm..." she breathed in and gritted her teeth. "Not – now. Wait. Let's enjoy the scenery. There's plenty of time."

"As you say, Prudence. But it has to be done, you know."

Philip reached for a match to light his cigar and caught his wife's eyes. Instinctively he knew that she had been looking not at the scenery but at him. Indeed, looking at him when he least expected it was one of her habits. He remembered how, when they were courting, they would have a long, long kiss as the horse pulled the buggy homeward – how more than once he had opened his eyes and there were Emily's big, blue eyes staring at him from less than an inch away. It was as if she was not participating in the passion of the kiss at all. Very disconcerting. And now she was looking at him with that same wide-eyed look, but not as close up.

"What is it, Emily?" he asked.

She reached for his hand. "Just thinking," she said, "how lucky I am to have you, Philip. And how mean I've been to you. I'm sorry."

"Mean? You haven't treated me mean. You've never treated me mean."

"Oh, yes, Philip. I've denied you."

"Oh, that. Well, Emily—"

"Tonight at Lake, dear. I promise. I'll be your wife all the way. We'll make up for lost time."

"When do we get there, anyway?" He blurted out, reaching for his watch. "Soon, I hope."

She laughed at his boyish impetuousness. "Philip," she said, "control yourself. Soon enough, dear."

"So there you are, you old Wolverine," came the voice of Congressman Talmadge Beauregard Griffin as he slapped Philip on the upper back so hard he lost his breath. "Get out of that deck chair and get your tackle and let's do some fishin'. This old redneck is the best bass fisherman in Louisiana, and I'm a-hankerin' to try my luck with trout. They say this Lake is full of 'em."

Almost before she was aware of it, Philip had left Emily and disappeared into the cabin and his chair had been occupied by the overdressed Dolly.

"What an exciting trip this is for you-all, isn't it?" she began, "with the maiden aunt being courted by a dashing Cavalry captain and your daughter falling head over heels for that handsome young Englishman. Why, I declare, every time I see them they look – guilty. Ahhhh, to be young and in love."

Emily sat up straight and bristled. "I'll have you know my Prudence is a well-raised, pure, innocent young girl, Mrs. Griffin. It is possible, you know, to be in love without being immoral."

"Possible, yes. Probable, oh, no, my dear. Let us not be naive." Dolly waved a mosquito away with her Japanese fan.

"I am not being naive, Mrs. Griffin. Prudence has done nothing wrong."

"Of course not, After all, it's natural."

"What's natural?"

"Why – it's natural. It."

"It's natural for young lovers to want to be together and talk and, perhaps, kiss. Pet a little. Yes, that's natural."

"That's all I'm saying, Emily dear. Just as two follows one and B follows A, hugs follow kisses and—"

"Yes," Emily agreed, "after marriage."

Dolly waved her Japanese fan before her face. "Ho, hum. I suppose so. If you say so, my dear. La-de-ah. But I wouldn't let them out of my sight after dark."

"Shall we change the subject, Mrs. Griffin?"

"Let's."

At the railing Philip and the Congressman were engaged in one subject that Republicans and Democrats, Damyankees and Rebels could converse about in friendship and common interest – fishing.

They had obtained rods and tackle from a rental concession on the boat, and were now casting their lines diligently.

But politics and Congressman Griffin were tied as close together as Siamese twins. Pretty soon he was telling stories about Louisiana campaigns, of ballots cast by citizens long dead, of corruption at Baton Rouge, of the corpse who cast the deciding vote for the lottery. Finally he ran out of stories – temporarily.

"Judge, don't you Wolverines have any tall stories to tell?"

Philip removed his cigar with his free hand and examined it. "Oh, I suppose so, Congressman. But we Wolverines tend to be – er – quieter about it. Frankly, there's a lot of finagling in Michigan but I can't visualize a corpse voting for a lottery."

So passed the afternoon, with the Congressman and Judge Snowden landing more fish in a few hours than they could hope to consume, and between bites, the Judge listening to Congressman Griffin's tall stories. The vessel's old steam engine thump-thumped along, Emily and Dolly chit-chatted until Emily was in torture fending off yawns, Madeline sat alone in a deck chair trying to read the American writer Winston Churchill's *Conistan*, and Prudence and Lord Billner talk-talk-talked. Rusty was with Philip and the Congressman.

"When, oh when, can I speak to your father, Prudence?"

"Not now. He's too busy catching fish and talking with that lecherous old rebel. When we get to Lake. Maybe after dinner."

The sun fell lower and lower, closer and closer to the fringe of the western mountains. In the gloaming, still several miles across the water, the twinkling lights of the big Lake Hotel appeared. A chilly, pre-autumn breeze came up. Philip and the Congressman, tired of fishing but boasting of their prowess, rejoined their wives. "We'll have 'em fried at the hotel for dinner," the Southerner announced. "A treat from your husbands, ladies, and some left over for the other guests. Bringing home the bacon, Yellowstone style."

The Honorable Talmadge Beauregard Griffin had been talking like the orator he was, in his stentorian voice, in order to be heard above the thump-thump-thumping of the steam engine. Suddenly the Congressman seemed to be shouting needlessly. The thumping had ceased. Heavy metal clattered on heavy metal. A steam cloud arose from the boiler room. An eerie silence encompassed the boat, which drifted silently, and slowly went dead in the water.

The passengers did not panic; there was no fire. The Captain hastily announced that there had been a temporary breakdown. The machinery, he assured them, would be repaired soon.

"Drat," uttered the Congressman. "I'm hungry. And Dolly is tired."

"And cold, Talmadge. I'm shivering."

"Oh, no," said Philip, nodding his head from side to side. "Emily, by gadfrey, we're snake-bit."

"The Captain says we'll be on our way soon."

"Want to bet?" replied her frustrated husband. "I'll bet we're stranded here for hours."

By nine o'clock it was dark, although in those northern climes a few streaks of light always linger, filling the heart with a melancholia difficult to explain but widely experienced. Prudence and Lord Billner felt it, standing at the railing, arms around each other, gazing off over the rippling waters, enjoying the chill breeze, watching the twinkling lights at the Lake Hotel. She leaned her head on his shoulder and he nuzzled her golden tresses.

But by ten o'clock the beauty had been obliterated by darkness. The chill breeze had turned downright cold. Congressman Talmadge Griffin's foghorn voice expressed his displeasure to one and all. "Captain, by the eternal, you'll hear of this. I'll report you to the Coast Guard. The US Navy will investigate you. Now you get this old tub to Lake by midnight or mark my words, suh, you'll be gone, gone, gone. Gone for good, I say. We American citizens deserve better treatment than this."

"Maybe," ventured Madeline, who had rejoined them, "the Captain will give the Congressman a first class cabin."

"Or a life preserver," Rusty chimed in. "Give him a life preserver to float to Lake."

It was nearly 1 AM when the steam engine started. Its thump-thump-thump was more like a thump-a-clank, thump-a-clank, thump-a-clank, and the vessel vibrated so badly that Philip thought leaks would spout in the hull. But the *Annie Laurie* moved, and an hour later the steamer and its tired, unhappy passengers disembarked. Fortunately there was plenty of room at the hotel. Philip and Emily were deposited in a comfortable suite with windows facing the lake, a doorway dividing them from Rusty's room. Across the hall was Madeline's and Prudence's room; Lord Billner occupied a room on another floor. They found their luggage already delivered, transported by Hezekiah in the *Shoshone Belle*.

They were the best accommodations of the trip. So dead tired were they all that they were asleep minutes after falling into bed. Emily snuggled up close to Philip, quite willing to be the loving wife as she had promised, even though she was equally tired. But she found Philip already sound asleep. She lay on her side and placed an arm across his chest, and she whispered in his ear "Good night, dearest Philip," kissed his cheek, and minutes later she, too, was asleep.

# Chapter Six

# The Fifth Day

## I

At six thirty sharp the bellboy knocked on their doors to announce breakfast and that the coaches were leaving at eight thirty. Prudence, asleep on her stomach, stretched, turned over on her back and hugged the pillow as if it was her lover – and promptly went back to sleep. Madeline was awake instantly, aware of her sadness, instantly conscious that her heart had stepped up its beating and that she was still miserable because of Captain Taylor's absence. Yet she was grateful for the trouble on the boat last night, for it had left her so exhausted that in spite of her sorrow she had slept. For having slept, she reflected, she could better combat the hurt. 'That's the key to facing life,' she thought, 'to keep going until you drop asleep. And then keep going until you drop asleep. And the next day, keep going again – until finally the hurt wears off.'

She sat up in bed, rubbed her face with her hands and stretched and sat on the edge and fiddled for her mules. 'And in two more days we'll be out of the Park and in two more to St. Paul and in one more to Elm Grove,' she thought. 'And I'll teach English until the day I die.' She broke into a sob. Her whole body shook as she tried to control her feelings. Then, afraid that Prudence might hear, she wrapped her robe around her body and left for the privacy of the women's lavatory.

Prudence's light sleep had indeed been disturbed by the unusual sounds of a woman sobbing, and she had opened her eyes just in time to catch Madeline leaving the room. It got her to thinking and in that way helped her wake up. She sat up in bed, brushed some golden tresses from her face, rested her chin on her knees and stared at the doorway.

It was because of Captain Taylor, she knew that for sure. The way he had looked at Madeline that evening at Old Faithful, and before that at Fountain, and even at Mammoth those four days ago – it was hard to believe that he would up and leave her. Then a smile appeared on her lips, like a rose a-blooming. For Prudence was in love, and young lovers are notoriously selfish and introspective. In her daydream reverie she saw Lord Billner, his dark hair, dazzling white teeth, firm chin, strong arms, manly chest. He was kissing her and she was blushing. Oh! It must work out. Daddy *must* approve of him! The rose that had bloomed so quickly, faded as in an Arctic blast. Today to Canyon, tomorrow back to Mammoth, and next day to the train and home to Elm Grove. Heavens! Lord Billner must simply, simply, must-must-must ask Daddy for her hand today! She leaped out of bed and reached for her cotton eyelet vest and white drawers. She divested herself of her gown and had her hands up and her blouse just dropping down over her shoulders when Madeline re-entered the room. The older woman, her composure regained, pretended not to see, but the magnificence of youth that was revealed in Prudence's young body plunged Madeline into despondency again. How, she thought, could she expect to compete at age thirty for the handsome Captain with such young females as Prudence all about the Park, working in the hotels, serving in the restaurants, single, unattached, and with flirtatious eyes?

"Madeline."

"Yes, Prudence."

"Would you – miss me – if I didn't come home with you?"

"What a strange thing to ask. Of course I'd miss you. We all would. Why do you ask?"

"What if I – oh, nothing."

"Nothing?"

"N – no. Let's get packed."

But the girl tarried. Madeline was packed and ready before Prudence, although now dressed, had even gone down-the-hall. The girl sat on the bed and stared at the floor. Her aunt sensed the presence of a distraught roommate. She sat down beside her niece. Prudence sniffled and blew her nose into a little handkerchief.

Always prior to this trip Madeline had looked upon Prudence as a child but now, in a wave of realization, the older woman looked upon her niece as a young woman – and an upset one. Perhaps it was the sight of the girl's body, making Madeline aware that Prudence was no longer a child – far from it – but a healthy young woman searching for fulfillment; or maybe it was the mature way Prudence had acted while her aunt had prepared for her meeting with Captain Taylor, back at the Wylie Camp at Old Faithful. Whatever the cause, when Madeline sat down beside Prudence this time, it was as woman to woman.

"You've fallen in love with him, haven't you, dear?"

The younger girl nodded and wiped tears from her eyes. "Oh, Aunt Madeline. I was so happy five minutes ago, and then I got to thinking, and I'm afraid I'm going to lose him. He is my knight errant. He's my prince on a white horse. He's my dream hero out of Sir Walter Scott and Rudyard Kipling. There's no one else like him in the whole wide world. Why, Madeline, all those bumpkins back in Elm Grove all put together couldn't equal the manliness in Stephen's little finger."

"Whew. You have it bad, don't you?"

"Real, real bad. I love him. Now I've said it. I love him I love him I love him. And he loves me. He says he does and I know he does. He loves me. And I love him."

"That's wonderful!" commented the older woman.

"Oh, Aunt Madeline. Would Daddy prevent me from marrying Stephen? Would Daddy refuse to let me get married right away? I don't think I can stand being away from him for months and months and months. What is there for me in Elm Grove, 'cept humiliation?" She lowered her eyes. "I'm afraid they'll never forget – you know. So – don't you think Daddy will let me stay here? Stephen would never leave me," she added, "like that horrible old Captain Taylor's left you."

Madeline straightened and again became prim Miss Snowden, English teacher. "Come, Prudence," she ordered, standing up, "get yourself ready. We're late for breakfast."

Simultaneously in their rooms across the hall Philip and Emily rose promptly upon the bellboy's knock. They might have tarried – after all, loving isn't restricted to when one goes to bed at night – but Rusty was already awake and standing in the doorway between the two rooms.

"I get my elk horns today," he announced.

"Your what?"

"My elk horns. Hezekiah's getting them for me."

188

"What's this about elk horns?" Philip asked Emily with a wink.

"You didn't know, dear? Rusty promised his club back home that he would bring them elk antlers for their clubhouse."

"Hmmph," grunted Philip, "I'll bet he's been hounding that old mountaineer since the first day we met him." Philip yawned as he rose from the bed. "The old mountaineer'll get the antlers just to be free of Rusty's nagging, or I miss my guess." He pulled on his trousers and slipped on his shoes. "Come on, Rusty. Let's go down to the men's room while your mother gets dressed."

In due time the Snowdens were dressed, packed, and ready for breakfast. Everything was cheerful in the big, sunny dining room of the Lake Hotel save for a number of bleary-eyed steamboat excursionists who were still squawking about "that damned boat". Lord Billner was waiting to greet them as they entered. Prudence was proud of the way he was dressed, in his brown corduroy suit with the incongruous white shirt and high collar and cravat. Emily and Philip both noticed the exchange of glances between the young couple. Of course Prudence and Lord Billner sat side by side, holding hands under the table. Occasionally when Lord Billner freed his hand it patted and smoothed the skirt covering the firm thighs whose warmth crept through to his hand, and brought a blush to Prudence's cheeks.

They were soon aware of the Honorable Talmadge Beauregard Griffin's presence, for his foghorn voice came across the lobby into the dining room before his physical presence was apparent. "Hoss whipped, suh," they heard him say, "anyone runnin' a steamer like that and riskin' the life and limb of his passengers should be hoss whipped and run out of this heauh Pahk, and suh, I assure you that when I return to Washington the Committee on Public Lands will hear of this." Finally his and Dolly's plump forms appeared in the doorway, where the host showed them to the nicest table in the room. It looked out upon the lake and was garnished with a vase of fresh wild flowers. Philip knew that this special treatment was not coincidental, and he fumed.

Suddenly the Congressman spied the Snowdens, who were halfway across the big room. "I say there, Judge," the M.C. shouted rudely.

"Oh, for heaven's sakes," mumbled Philip, trying to ignore him.

"You've got to reply," Emily said out of the corner of her mouth. "Everyone is looking at us."

"I suppose so." Then, "Good morning, Congressman Griffin."

"What say you and I get off the coach down in Hayden Valley and try our luck in the Yellowstone River? They say the fish there are as thick as pickaninnies around a watermelon."

"Let's talk about it on the coach, Congressman," Philip replied as quietly as possible.

"Nawwww. Got to make up our minds now. Have to make arrangements to be picked up by a later coach. Have to rent our fishing gear here. They've agreed to rent to me and my friends and return it to Lake on another coach."

"Oh, all right," replied Philip, hoping that would end the discussion that had been overheard by everyone in the room.

"Bet ya a mint julep I catch the first fish," shouted the Congressman.

"Oh, Philip," protested Emily quietly, "there must be three Methodist preachers in here dedicated to temperance, and I can feel them all staring at us."

"Ya here me, Judge. Ain't you a bettin' man?"

"Uh – er—"

"Don't you-all like mint juleps, Judge?"

Mercifully, Dolly intervened. She placed her hand over her husband's mouth, upsetting the vase of flowers. Some un-Methodist language followed, and from then on the two were quiet. The mess was quickly cleaned up and they were served their breakfast before many who had been waiting longer. In fact, the Griffins were leaving just as eggs and hot cakes were being served the Snowdens. Of course, the M.C. and his lady had to pause at the Snowden table on their way out to talk some more.

Mrs. Griffin, after exchanging pleasantries, turned to Madeline. "Don't give up on your Captain, dear," she said knowledgeably. "Talmadge heard that he got rush orders to go to Canyon and escort two wagons out of the Park. They are carrying of all things – an automobile! My, my. What the Army has come to. Used to chase Indians, and now it escorts automobiles. Isn't that ridiculous?"

Madeline's heart leaped, but she retained her composure. "Thank you," she replied icily, "but I haven't missed him."

"I know," replied Dolly in her most syrupy drawl, "but I just thought you'd like to know."

As the Congressman and his lady walked off, silence prevailed at the Snowden table. All knew that Madeline had been excited by the

Captain (although none realized just how deeply she felt about him) and so her icy reply stunned them. Eyebrows were raised, but nothing was said. Stephen broke the impasse by talking about fishing.

## II

Breakfast was over, the luggage packed and carried to the porte-cochère where coaches were lined up. Both horses and coachmen seemed lethargic after four days on the road. There was Hezekiah sitting up there in the bright morning sunshine, old campaign hat shading his eyes, gray handlebar mustache drooping to meet his beard, corn cob pipe in his mouth, dirty linen duster, shiny German whip-leather gloves, heavy old miner's boots. He was third from the front this morning, for which all the Snowden party thanked him.

"Hear ye had a little trouble last night," he commented. It brought nods of agreement.

"Well," drawled the coachman, "the horses are well rested, and it ain't a very far piece down to Canyon, and ye'll be able to rest there."

"Let the Judge and me off where the fishin' is best in Hayden Valley," ordered Congressman Griffin. "We've already made arrangements for a later coach to take us on in."

"I'll let ye off," replied Hezekiah, lighting his pipe.

If the horses were rested, as he said, no one would have guessed it from the slow pace they set as they left the Lake Hotel and started down the west side of the Yellowstone River towards the Grand Canyon. When, at about eleven o'clock, Hezekiah called a slow "whoaaaa" and the horses stopped on a dime and only their tails swishing flies indicated life, and he announced "Mud Volcano," no one bothered to climb out of the *Shoshone Belle*. He looked to his side and saw that the Congressman and even Rusty were dozing; then he leaned down and scanned his passengers. There was Dolly, hair disheveled under her veil, her head leaning back over the top of the seat as if she had a broken neck, her mouth open, snoring; and Philip and Emily asleep, her head on his shoulder and his chin resting on his chest, an unlit cigar about to fall from his mouth. In the next seat was Madeline, prim and awake with new hope. She held an index finger to her lips signifying Hezekiah not to awaken everyone. In the back seat Prudence and Lord Billner were asleep, or ostensibly so. One of his hands lay deeply embedded in her lap, one of her hands rested far up his thigh. Her head lay on his shoulder and his in her hair.

Hezekiah decided to forego regulations, which insisted that drivers stop at certain places regardless of conditions. Who would know? And so he said "giddyap" as quietly as possible and went on. When people began to rouse a few minutes later, and Prudence commented that they had missed the Mud Volcano, Hezekiah passed it off quickly: "Just another big paint pot," he said.

With talk renewed and everyone alert, the horses pulled the coach into Hayden Valley. There the passengers' spirits were lifted by the sight of several moose, an elk buck, and the quiet beauty of the swale. Philip and Congressman Griffin looked forward to fishing while others were contemplating the beauties, so often described to them, of the Grand Canyon of the Yellowstone.

"Over on your left," announced Hezekiah, "is Alum Creek."

"Why do they call it that?" Rusty asked.

"'Cause it tastes of alum, laddie. It puckers up yer mouth if you drink it."

"You mean like chokecherries?"

"That's right, young 'un."

"Terrible things have happened here," added the Congressman, winking at Hezekiah. "Can't ever let horses stop here to drink."

"Why not, Mr. Griffin?"

"Oh, terrible, terrible," cut in Hezekiah. "If the horses drank that water, laddie, they'd shrink to the size of Shetland ponies within five minutes."

"Awwwww."

"Now, you look here, young feller," said Hezekiah. "If you won't believe yer elders, why, I'm a-gonna' have to turn ye over my knee and beat some respect into you!"

"I know a better punishment than that," countered the Louisianian. "Don't give him any elk antlers."

"Mr. Congressman Griffin!"

"That's it," responded Hezekiah. "You don't believe what we tell ye, then ye don't get my help obtaining elk horns."

For a few minutes they rode on in silence. Then Rusty said, "Mr. Hezekiah, I wish you'd stop and drink that water. And you too, Mr. Congressman Griffin."

"Why's that, laddie," asked the M.C.

"Because if you would, then you'd be shrunk down to my size, and I'd beat the soup out of both of you, I would."

Talmadge Griffin felt the muscles in Rusty's arms and feigned fear. Hezekiah said, "Congressman, you and me better watch our p's and q's, I reckon."

The horses plodded on.

"Prudence," said Lord Billner suddenly, "why don't I go fishing too? Your father should be in a good mood while fishing. Then I'll ask him."

"Oh, Stephen. Do. Do it, please. Because there isn't much more time. And I don't want to go back to Elm Grove. I don't want to be separated from you." She paused. "But you don't have any fishing tackle."

"Oh, yes, I do," Lord Billner replied. I purchased an expensive rod and reel and tackle in St. Paul. It's packed away in my luggage and I can reach it easily." Then he directed his words to the front seat. "I say, Mr. Snowden. Would you mind if I joined you and the Congressman along the Yellowstone River? I've a new rod I've never tried."

"Glad to have you along, Stephen," Philip replied. The young Englishman would be a good balance to Talmadge Beauregard Griffin. Philip knew the Congressman would approve even without being asked.

Prudence grabbed Lord Billner's arm. "He called you Stephen," she whispered. "That's a good sign."

In due time the *Shoshone Belle* approached the halfway point through Hayden Valley. It is a long, meadow-like swale bounded on the east by the slow-running Yellowstone River. Hezekiah chose a spot close to the stream, brought the coach to a halt, and discharged the piscators and their tackle.

Before Lord Billner left his seat he whispered last minute plans to Prudence. "Sweetheart," he said, "I doubt if we're back for the evening meal. Meet me at Artist's Point. It's barely a mile from the Canyon Hotel. Say, at eight o'clock. I'll have news for you then."

"I hope it's good news, Stephen," Prudence replied, holding one of his hands deeply in her lap. "And please, please, Stephen, be real diplomatic. Use all your Englishman's skills. Don't take no for an answer. Because I love you, Stephen."

"Don't worry, dearest. I'll do my best," replied the remittance man, plunging his hand further into her lap and squeezing a thigh through her skirt. "I'll be as insistent as an English bulldog. Don't forget – eight o'clock, Artist's Point. Get Hezekiah to drive you there."

"Eight o'clock, dear," she whispered.

The three men stood by the coach fitting their rods together. "If we're not at Canyon by dinnertime, eat without us," Philip instructed Emily. She urged him to be careful, and not wade out too far into the stream, while Dolly Griffin gave her husband her own bit of advice: "Don't bother to bring the fish to me, Talmadge. And don't bolster yourself with any – er – spirits, until you are through fishing. I don't want a drowned Congressman to take back to Louisiana. Not in summertime."

"Have no worry, Dolly," he replied, at the same time winking at his two fellow anglers. "We will not imbibe hastily or foolishly. Have no fear."

"Coaches'll be along most all day through," Hezekiah informed them. "Good luck. Hyar! Giddyap!" His whip whooshed, the horses bolted ahead, and the coach was gone. Four women sat in it alone. Suddenly they missed their men. Conversation was stilted.

But in the driver's seat Rusty, who had been sulking because he was not invited to fish with the men, came to life. "Mr. Hezekiah," he pleaded, "when are we goin' to get my elk horns?"

"Don't you fret, young feller. I'm gonna get 'em fer ye."

"But when?"

"Tonight, maybe."

"Can I go with you?"

"Nawww. Your daddy'd want you in bed."

"He doesn't have to know."

Hezekiah glanced down at the carrot-topped lad, and they exchanged mischievous winks. "Course, it's only a half hour or so to the elk antlers."

"Please let me go."

"Yer pa'd have me expelled from the Park." 'As if I'm not expelled already,' he thought.

"I told you that Pa'd never know. There are lots of things he doesn't know," said Rusty boastfully.

"Why, Rusty. Ain't you a Peck's bad boy, now. Hyar, giddyap, now."

They rode on in silence. Then Hezekiah mumbled, "Course, if you was to happen down by the stables by seven o'clock, right after

194

dinner, I reckon we might get to the antlers and back afore the campfire lecture ends. Course, ye'd have to wait for me a spell in the dark. Ye could be safe in bed by the time your pa and ma check on you."

"Oh, boy!"

"Shhhhhhhh," whispered Hezekiah. He hunched over and let the coach go along at the dragging walk preferred by the horses, wondering why he should put up with this boy, take the risks with him. He shrugged his shoulders and bit his corncob pipe. "Guess I wish I'd had a son," he said to himself.

### III

After the Yellowstone River leaves the lake it heads northward toward the falls, a study in contrasting water moods. As it passes through Hayden Valley it is clear and smooth as glass, moving silently and slowly. It gives no indication of the turmoil ahead, save that the flow speeds, culminating in a plunge over the Upper Falls (109 feet) and the Lower Falls (308 feet). Then the river roars on down the floor of the deep, beautiful Grand Canyon.

Philip was provided with rubber fishing boots that came up to his crotch, while the Congressman pulled on heavy waders that came up almost to his armpits; Lord Billner had no fishing footwear, so he had to cast from the bank. When they were finally ready, Congressman Griffin held up his hand. "Wait," he said, "we need a bit of sustenance before we begin." From his canvas bag he pulled a bottle of Old Quaker Rye and uncorked it. "Let's all take a swig," he suggested, following his own suggestion by taking four big gulps. "Ahhhhh," he said at last, "good libations always improve the fishin'." But when he offered the bottle to Philip and Stephen, they both begged off. "I'll wait until we're through," said Philip, and Stephen agreed. "As you would have it, gentlemen," said the Honorable M.C., corking the bottle and placing it carefully in his bag. "If you want to catch fish, go where the fish are," he declared as he splashed into the river making enough noise to scare every trout from the lake to the falls. Lord Billner and Philip watched as the Congressman waded farther and farther into the stream. Finally Philip waded in, but with his hip boots could only advance a few feet into the water; Stephen remained on the bank.

"I think this river is deceptive," he told Philip. "Certainly the current is swifter in the middle where the Congressman is heading."

"He'd best be careful," added Philip. "He's probably used to sluggish Southern streams."

The two began fishing, Stephen stationing himself thirty or forty feet from Philip. Congressman Griffin, far into the river, was meanwhile casting his line with considerable finesse. Then Talmadge Beauregard Griffin hooked one – a big one. His reel went zing-g-g-g, the Honorable M.C. issued a Rebel yell, forgot where he was, took two steps forward and disappeared.

"Good God, where is he?" asked Philip.

The Congressman surfaced, an air bubble fortunately having filled a part of his waders. Then he began floating downstream. "Halp! Halp! Halp!" (Blub, cough.) "Halp!"

But how? Philip could not swim with his heavy fishing boots, and the current where the Congressman was floundering was so swift that a swimmer could not reach him anyway. "Halp me!" cried the Honorable M.C. "The falls! I'm headed for the falls! Dolly! Save me!"

"I'll try, sir. I'll try," shouted Lord Billner. With the finesse of a lifetime fly fisherman he cast his line sailing over the smooth waters, far, far out into the Yellowstone. It landed like a feather at the waist of the waders. "Now, hold on, sir," shouted Stephen as he yanked quickly, catching the hook on the rubber mass that engulfed Congressman Griffin up to his armpits. The M.C.'s forward progress slowed.

"Don't move, sir," Lord Billner yelled. "This is just a twenty pound line and I venture you weigh more than that. When I tell you, keep lying on your back as you are and start swimming toward me, just using your arms. Slowly Lord Billner worked the line until he had the Congressman headed for shore. "Swim with your arms, staying on your back, while I slowly pull the line," Stephen instructed. "Swim hard!"

The frightened Southern fisherman did as he was told, rotating his chubby arms as gently and steadily as he was capable of doing. Meanwhile Philip waded out as far as possible awaiting the desperate man's arrival. Steadily but slowly, the horizontal mass of man and fishing line approached him. It seemed like an eternity. The fishing line held. The time came: Philip swung out as far as he could reach, nabbed the Congressman's red galluses, and pulled him in just as Lord Billner's line snapped. Philip held on, the Congressman found his footing on the riverbed, and with Philip's and Stephen's aid, waded ashore sputtering and damning the Yankee stream.

Safe on the bank, the Congressman crumpled down. "Thank you, gentlemen. Thank you. My constituents thank you. My wife Dolly thanks you. Believe me, I could hear the roar of the falls below me. I swear it. Narrow escape. Terrible experience."

"Are you going to be all right, sir?" asked Stephen. "I'm afraid you lost your rod."

"Hell, yes, I'm goin' to be all right," replied the Congressman. "And the rod can take care of itself. I've had my fishin' for this year." He rose stiffly and squished over to his pack. "I'll be all right. Soon as I take off these waders with about fifty gallons of water in 'em. I'll just stretch out here in the grass and let the sun dry me out. Dolly'd never let me fergit it if she knew what happened. I can hear her now. 'Talmadge, think of your constituents. Think of Louisiana. Think of *me*!"

His two companions smiled while he divested himself of the waders and their water. Then he rustled in his pack. "Ahhhhh," he exclaimed as he drew forth the bottle of Old Quaker. "A nip, gentlemen?"

Neither Philip nor Lord Billner noticed the wishful look in each other's faces. Griffin's had been a very narrow escape, and after such an experience a little nip would have hit the spot. But Philip did not want the young man to know that he imbibed, and Lord Billner did not want his possible father-in-law to have any wrong ideas about him. They rejected the offer.

"Very well," replied the Congressman, almost too quickly, unstoppering the bottle. He stretched out with his head propped on his pack and took a big swig, and another. As the warmth inside and the sun outside began to take effect, he stoppered the bottle and said to it, "Me and thee, we are Friends, ain't we? We all..." and he slept, did Congressman Talmadge Beauregard Griffin.

Lord Billner and Philip Snowden took their gear and walked out of the Congressman's sight, then lay down on the grass and rolled over and over amid spasms of laughter. "He finally got his comeuppance," Philip roared. "Not even Stonewall Jackson could save him from the

Yellowstone." Then Philip got more serious. "You did a fine job, Stephen. Really kept your head and probably saved his life."

"Oh, 'twas nothing, sir." (Now, thought the remittance man, second son of *the* Lord Billner, descendant of a captain with the Black Prince, of a first mate with Sir Francis Drake and a favorite of Queen Elizabeth's, of a defender of Charles I, a Colonel under the Duke of Wellington – *now* is the time.) Lord Billner braced himself, wishing ardently for some of his family's backbone.

"Sister Mowden. I mean, Mr. Flowden. I mean, Sphillip – I—"

"What?" asked Philip, "are you talking about?"

"Sir?"

"What is it?" Philip was scowling. He knew the subject had changed from levity to gravity.

"Sir. Sir. I – I – I – love your daughter!" the young Englishman blurted out. "I want to marry Prudence."

Philip, who had just put a fresh cigar in his mouth, paused from striking a match on a stone. He cleared his throat and his visage became as serious as Lord Billner had ever seen it. "Eh? You want to what?"

"I have excellent breeding, sir. My pedigree is strictly blue-blooded."

"You want to marry Prudence?"

"An excellent education, sir. Fine public schools. Oxford."

"Marry Prudence?"

"And I own a splendid ranch in Paradise Valley between Livingston and the Pahk. I have cattle and irrigated acres, a ranch house and a wonderful hay crop this year and hay is fetching good prices—"

"Marry my little girl?"

"And I receive a remittance every quarter, sir, so even if everything else goes rot, sir, I could still support her."

"Hmm." Philip struck his match and lit his cigar, puffing a cloud of smoke.

"And I am in excellent health, sir." Lord Billner flexed his muscles.

Suddenly Philip Snowden snorted. "What the hell, Billner," he growled, "you've only known her four days."

"Four days and four nights, sir. Of bliss, sir."

"Four nights?"

Lord Billner blushed. "Four days, sir. But wonderful, wonderful, wonderful—"

"Hmmph," grunted Philip. "I'll say this much. You are no Shakespeare. Nor Shelley. Your blithe spirit got lost somewhere betwixt Billner Manor and here, eh? Wonderful, wonderful, wonderful. Great word, that. And tiresome."

"Ye – yes, sir. I think it probably didn't."

"What?"

"I mean – oh, sir, here I am making a perfect jackass of myself."

"They have jackasses in England?"

"I learned the word over here, sir. In England we simply say 'ass'."

"Same difference."

"But I do love your daughter, sir. My intentions are honorable. I—"

"Stephen," said Philip, pulling together his thoughts, "after all, you hardly know Prudence. As her father I can't consent to a marriage so soon. She should return to Elm Grove and both of you should think about it. I guess I'm not saying no, Stephen. I like you. But just four days, my boy. After all—"

"Well, sir, how long a wait? Today's August fourteenth. What if I traveled to Elm Grove September first? Would that be long enough?"

Philip removed his cigar and contemplated the dead serious young man. "In the first place, Stephen, today isn't the fourteenth. It's the twentieth."

Lord Stephen Billner's face blanched. He gulped. "Eh – what's that you say?" he demanded, clutching Philip's arm. Terror was in his voice and desperation written in his face. His eyes narrowed and turned hard as steel. "*What* date?" he demanded. "What date did you say this is?"

"Twentieth, Stephen. Twentieth of August. What's so strange about that?"

"It can't be," replied Lord Billner, staring blankly at the river. "Today has to be the fourteenth. The fourteenth of August."

"Sorry. Today, my boy, is August twentieth. Here in Yellowstone, at Billner Manor in England, in Louisiana, and in Elm Grove, Michigan." He paused. "You must have lost a week in St. Paul, or forgotten your dates while you gambled in the baggage car. Look. I bought a *Denver Post* this morning. It's two days late up here but still the date is August eighteenth." He pulled the paper from his sack and showed it to Lord Billner.

"My Gawd," gasped the young man, rising to his feet. "Oh, my Gawd!"

"What's wrong? What difference does it make?" Philip was about to ask him about his gambling, but Lord Billner did not give him a chance.

"My remittance, sir. It arrives in Livingston every three months, usually around the ninth or tenth. I have to claim it, you see. I have to claim it within ten days after its arrival, for right on the envelope it says 'If not Claimed Within Ten Days Return to Sender'. And then, sir, if it is not called for, and it is returned, *no more remittance*. That's the understanding I have with my fathah. If the remittance returns to England unclaimed, he ceases to send it. And I have to have that remittance to live. So you see, sir, I must get to the post office at Livingston before six o'clock tonight or I will lose my remittance. Then I'll have to support myself altogether."

"You like the word remittance about as much as the word wonderful," commented Philip.

"I must be in Livingston before six o'clock," announced Lord Billner.

"You can't make it there by six o'clock," Philip said, pulling his watch from his vest. "It's after eleven o'clock now and Livingston must be over a hundred miles away."

"I have to, sir," replied the desperate young man, already running to the road. "I've got to get to Livingston. Please tell Prudence I cannot see her tonight. Good-bye, Mr. Snowden. Remember to tell Prudence!"

"Get to a telephone," Philip shouted.

"Good idea. But I still haven't much time."

Philip watched Lord Billner run down the road and catch a passing horse and buggy. He noticed how, as soon as he was seated, the horse quickened its pace. Philip nodded his head in disbelief, and returned to a quiet few hours of fishing.

## IV

Canyon Hotel was an enormous Edwardian frame structure perched on the north side of the Grand Canyon not far from the Upper and Lower falls. Under its porte-cochère the *Shoshóne Belle* unloaded its passengers. The ladies arrived tired and irritable. They checked in, went to their rooms, and rested. Toward the forest were the stables; on down the road was the Wylie Way, and stationed to one side of the graveled artery was Troop K, 2nd US Cavalry, Captain Freeman W. Taylor commanding.

He was bothered and bored, was the Captain. He sat on a camp stool in front of an A tent and scanned the terrain. Over there among the lodgepole pines stood two Studebaker wagons, tarpaulins pulled tightly over them, only automobile axles showing from one; the other covered everything. The Captain philosophized about his fate. A man ahead of his time, that's what he was. A man of the future tied to the present. A believer in the impending adoption by the Army of the internal combustion engine, ordered to prevent its use in Yellowstone Park. A lover of automobiles he was (especially of that gorgeous Pierce-Arrow, winner of the year's Glidden Award for the most exacting cross-country race of the year). That car represented sheer perfection, he thought. It was poetry on wheels, and yet – here he was. In his hand he held Special Orders No. 1:

> *Proceed to Canyon, meet, control, and escort two Studebaker wagons containing one Pierce-Arrow Touring Motor Car, and parts thereof, to and through the Roosevelt Arch at the North Entrance of the Park. Under no circumstances is this vehicle to operate under its own power within the confines of the Reservation.*
>
> *J.S. Peavey*
> *Col., US 2nd Cavalry*

Captain Taylor threw a stone at a tree. Tomorrow morning at sunup the escort, led by him, would begin its task. Meanwhile he lived by the orders Col. Peavey had given him over the telephone. "*Do not let the wagons out of your sight.*" He had hurried to Canyon from Old Faithful without saying good-bye to Madeline Snowden. Ahhhhhh, Madeline: a vision of three-quarter size loveliness, her soft brown hair, flashing brown eyes, rippling laughter, firm, white, divinely shaped breasts. "Damn," he said aloud. "I hope I catch her tonight at the hotel."

His thoughts were interrupted by the spiral of smoke rising from a camp chair placed between the two wagons. Ahhh, yes. There was old

Fritz Buschmeister, smoking his calabash pipe vigorously. Look at him. Fat. Cheerful. Obedient – and sly as a fox. Just waiting. Biding his time. Waiting, waiting. Well, by gadfrey, he, Captain Freeman W. Taylor, would just let the old coot wait. By Jove, orders are orders, and the Pierce-Arrow stays on the wagons until it has been hauled out of the Park.

Anyway, it was nearly noon, time for chow. The Captain rose from the camp stool, stretched, yawned, and started for the mess tent. Suddenly a sagebrusher – the name given to independent campers – came running out of the forest. "Soldiers. Army. Call out the guard!" the camper yelled, running toward the mess tent where the personnel was congregated.

"What's wrong?"

"Sir. Colonel, Major, Captain, Private, sir—"

"Captain will do," replied Captain Freeman partly amused and partly angered at the prospect of being denied his lunch.

"A bear," the camper blurted out, pointing towards the forest from whence he had come. "A bear attacked our tent. Got everything: bacon, ham, sugar, flour. Our outing is ruined!"

'Oh, no,' thought the Captain. 'Now I have to go chasing after a thieving bear.' A far cry, he reflected, from galloping off to fight the Cheyenne and the Sioux to the tune of 'Gary Owen'. From Indians to bears. What humiliation.

"This is a terrible, terrible bear," the camper added. "It watched us from the woods when we went to bed last night. We could see its eyes reflected by our campfire. And it watched my wife go to the ladies' room this morning. It watched me when I stepped out in the woods to..." He paused. "It's a terrible bear. It has a gray streak running over the top of its head. You can't mistake it."

"Damn," groaned the Captain. "Not Tom the Curious Bear again! He's caused trouble at Lake and Thumb and more recently at Old Faithful. We're under orders to capture that bear and transport him to the Lamar Valley. And if he returns again, to kill him. You, Private Henry. And you and you and you. Grab some ropes. Grab that net. We've got to catch that bear. Call out the whole Troop." Captain Taylor turned again to the distraught camper. "Now, sir, if you will lead the way."

"Can't we have chow first, Captain?" pleaded a Private First Class.

"No. We'll have Tom the Curious tied up in a half hour. Then we can eat."

Amidst considerable grumbling the whole Troop infiltrated the woods towards the campground. Fritz Buschmeister, sitting relaxed in a canvas camp chair, puffed on his calabash and watched with interest. He looked at ease, with his linen duster open, his white cap tilted back with the goggles resting on his forehead. However, had anyone seen it, his body actions would have given him away. His left foot was working an imaginary clutch, his right foot the accelerator, and his hands were turning an imaginary steering wheel.

Tom the Curious Bear, fresh from Old Faithful, and hungry, had indeed raided a tent. He had entered without permission, no one being around at the moment to invite him in. He tasted some bacon and ham and some oranges and sugar. It had all tasted good – some of it peculiar – but good. Then he had spied a twenty-five pound sack of flour leaning against a chest. Upon touching it with his paws he had been fascinated at the soft thud it made. Little puffs of white smoke came out. Curious, Tom stood on his hind legs and picked up the sack as a human might lift a child. He walked thusly outside, where he propped the sack against a pine tree. Then he sat down just as a child might, his back legs straight out in front of him, as if he was about to play patty-cake. Then he stuck one of his long claws into the top of the flour sack and ran it all the way down, slitting it wide open. Flour spilled out. The Curious Bear scooped some up in his paws. He tasted it but did not like it – in fact, it tasted awful. Angered, Tom tossed the sack in the air as a child might toss a pillow. Not feathers but flour came spilling out in a white shower all over Tom and the surrounding ground. Amused, he rolled in it until the sack was empty. Then Tom heard voices: people! Looking more like a polar bear than a black one, he lunged for the brush in a nearby gulch. Tom listened to the shrieks of the women and the curses of the men, and he saw the head of household run off towards the facilities at Canyon. His animal instincts told him that he was in deep trouble. Not many minutes later he was sure of it: soldiers! He had heard them before.

For Captain Taylor and his Troop were infiltrating the woods, ropes tied for lasso use, some men with a big net, on the ready, searching for a black bear with a distinctive streak of gray across the top of his head. Tom the Curious did not wait to greet them. He plunged deeper into the brush, an apparition, a ghost of bears long departed. Soon he came to a pleasant widening of the gulch. There, lo and behold, grew a profusion of chokecherry bushes. Thousands and thousands of chokecherries had already ripened and dropped to the ground, fermenting in the warm late summer sun. Bees buzzed around them, but this did not bother Tom. Such morsels made a fine dessert after a five pound ham, bacon, oranges, sugar, and that awful flour. The whitened black bear plunged in, devouring large quantities of fermented berries along with assorted twigs and leaves and some plain dirt. Somehow other bears had missed this veil of succulence, and Tom gorged himself. When he heard sounds of humanity coming closer, he ran out of the gulch for the tall timber – and tripped on his own paws. He got up, weaving a little from side to side, the earth billowing in front of him like waves of an ocean. The trees swayed. He burped and plunged on. Tom the Curious Bear, a white ghost – save for streaks of chokecherry juice down his neck – was quite drunk! But not too inebriated to crawl among some boulders left by a prehistoric glacier, where his whitened coat blended with the quartz and granite. As he watched, still as death, two soldiers passed within a yard of him and went on.

Then Tom rose, fell, rose again, and ambled on. He spooked a black horse tied to a pine in the deepest timber. When it kicked and whinnied a tall man who whistled every time he breathed leaped up to muzzle his nervous steed. Tom plunged on until he came in sight of two inert wagons and a fat little human wearing a linen duster and a white cap with goggles, with a calabash pipe between his teeth. The little human was jumping around and peering under the tarpaulins at something strange, something that smelled of gas and oil, odors not common in Yellowstone. "Hic," went the bear, "hic, hic." Silently, save for his hics, Tom the Curious edged closer to get a better look. What was in those wagons, under the tarps, anyway?

Meanwhile Lord Stephen Billner had arrived at Canyon. He had reached the public telephone in the lobby, only to discover that a violent storm between Gardiner and Livingston had knocked out the line and it would not be repaired for at least twenty-four hours. If his mind had not been so focused on his remittance, he reflected later, he would have left a note at the front desk for Prudence. But so desperate was he that the thought never passed his mind. More frenzied than ever now, he inquired about renting a buggy, only to be told that it was top of the season and they were all out. Well, a good horse would be an even faster way to reach Livingston. No saddle horses were available either. "Why not see if you can borrow one from the Cavalry?" asked the livery clerk.

"Ask to see Captain Taylor. Sometimes in an emergency they'll let people borrow a horse."

"It's an emergency all right," Stephen replied, picturing himself in poverty without his $6,000 a year remittance. "If I can't claim a letter before it is returned to London – my Gawd, I'll have to go to work!" His last statement, which did not set well with the clerk, was given on the run, for Stephen knew this Captain Taylor and was already running down the road to the soldier station.

When he entered the encampment a few minutes later, he found it vacant, save for the cook, who swore an oath because Captain Taylor had ordered the whole Troop off, on foot, in search of a bear, just as chow was about to be served. For a few moments the desperate Second Son contemplated horse thievery, but weighing his remittance against a lynch mob or a Federal prison, he abandoned the idea. Besides, the cook was watching him closely and the horses were all in sight in the nearby corral.

"I'll wait," he announced, sitting down in a rickety camp chair, feeling miserable and dejected. He tried to convince himself that the Livingston postmaster would keep the letter another day or two. But persuasion came hard.

Then his eyes caught sight of the strange gyrations of the fat little man in the white linen duster, in the woods nearby.

"Who's he?" Stephen asked the cook, who had offered him some beef stew.

"Him? He's Fritz Buschmeister, the beer baron from Peoria. He's got a Pierce-Arrow automobile under those tarps."

"Oh?"

"Yep. Wanted to be the first man to drive an au-to through the Park. But Colonel Saddle-Pants Peavey, the Commanding Officer at Fort Yellowstone, he'd never allow it. Captain Taylor and K Troop are here to escort the au-to in those two wagons down to the North Entrance. Believe me, old Fritz is mad. He'd give his eye teeth to give the Cavalry the bounce and drive that Pierce-Arrow through the Park."

"Hmm," mused Lord Billner. He finished his stew and slammed the plate on the wooden table. "I – uh – think I'll amble over and take a look," he said. "I'm simply fascinated by automobiles. I do believe I've never seen a Pierce-Arrow."

"She's a beauty," the cook replied. "Got every new gadget known to the trade on her. But watch out. Old Fritz'll talk your leg off."

In no time at all Stephen had made the acquaintance of the little man. "They tell me they won't let you drive this beautiful machine through the Park?"

"Ach. Himmel. Zese people are so old-fashioned. Zey love horses out here. Horses zey love – I ask you simply – how could one love a horse when he can travel overland in a machine like zis?" He let Lord Billner look under the tarpaulins.

"I can't understand it," Stephen agreed. "I think it's terrible that they won't let you drive it through the Park. How old fashioned the American government is."

"Look vat zey did to my car! Took off ze wheels and my cans of gasoline and oil and put them in ze other wagon. Do you theenk zey do not trust me?"

This was Lord Billner's cue, and he dived in. "What an insult. sir. Of course you would not violate their stupid regulations. Especially when the Captain and his entire Troop are out on foot searching for a bear, and you could have my help in attaching the wheels, get some boards to make a ramp, lower the Pierce-Arrow and be on the way. By the time they return from the bear hunt, you and the automobile could be halfway to the North Entrance." Lord Billner winked at the little man.

Fritz Buschmeister's calabash pipe almost fell from his mouth. His little pig eyes examined the young Englishman for meaning. Then he sprung to life, first hitting Stephen on the arm so hard that it was tender for a week. "Bully," hissed Fritz, mimicking Theodore Roosevelt. "Heavy planks bridge that little stream," he said pointing to a brook not far off. "Get them while I get ze wheels. Ve can be on our way in fifteen minutes. Hee, hee, hee. We'll see about old Saddle-Pants. And our names will be inscribed in the annals of automobiling: 'First Auto Through Yellowstone National Park: Pierce-Arrow: Fritz Buschmeister, Owner and Driver.' Ach. To work!"

As he ran to the stream Stephen surveyed the encampment. There was the cook, sprawled in a chair, asleep. No one else was around. Quickly the Second Son fetched the planks. He dragged them to the wagon bearing the Pierce-Arrow and inclined them from the rear of the wagon to the ground, thus creating a ramp down which the car could be unloaded. Meanwhile, up on the wagon, Fritz had adjusted a jack to the rear axle and was diligently working it, lifting the car. "Here," he commanded, "you jack it up while I fetch ze wheels." Stephen worked the long handle as fast as he could, watching the rear of the car rise with each notch.

"Shouldn't we remove the tarps?" he asked of the German-American who came puffing up with a big-spoked, straw-colored forty-two inch wheel with a four-inch Goodyear tire already inflated and attached.

"Let us not arouse curiosity," countered Fritz. He fitted the wheel on and bolted it in a jiffy and was away to fetch the other wheel. Moments later that one was attached; Stephen lowered the jack as fast as he could and ran to the front, where the performance was repeated. Then Fritz lugged a twenty gallon gas can, climbed under the tarp and filled the tank. Meanwhile Stephen got the oil can and the crank. They both had to carry the folded car top, which was easily attached even though they were working under the tarpaulin.

Swelling with pride and savoring the sweet smell of success (gas and oil), Fritz and Stephen surveyed the wagon, which was pointed toward the encampment – in fact, it was right in line with the mess tent. "I tell you vat," said Fritz, analyzing the field like a general before battle, "I theenk ve vill push ze car down ze ramp quietly. You be ready to crank her. Then ve vill be on our way. I'll get in the driver's seat."

Stephen made sure the inclined planks were set just right to receive the wheels. "If you keep her absolutely straight," he said, "I think she'll coast down the ramp perfectly."

"Great," said the fat little man, clapping his hands with glee. He reached down, grabbed a corner of the tarpaulin, and with a flourish flung the covering completely over the side of the wagon. There, in all her ugly, garish, grotesque splendor, sat the new Pierce-Arrow.

It weighed over three thousand pounds. Its brass-rimmed headlights were powered by a new-fangled gadget called a generator. Its radiator was big enough to cool a room. Its shiny, jet-black hood was bolted down securely with brass hardware. Its high windshield opened from the middle, like an awning window. It had two jet-black, shiny, cushioned seats in front, a wooden steering wheel on the right side big enough to steer an ocean liner (it was right-hand drive), four black doors and a single black back seat, enormous springs, three spare tires in the rear, a tool box running along one running board and along the other a matched set of three cans, one for gasoline, one for oil, and one for water. Fenders were heavy and black, but the wheels were the car's true glory, with big, straw-colored spokes. It was a miracle of speed and comfort and power, that 1909 Pierce-Arrow with its six-cylinder forty-horsepower engine capable, as the advertisements said, of taking it anywhere, over all kinds of roads in, as they also boasted, perfect safety.

Stephen and Fritz feasted their eyes on the gorgeous monstrosity for long moments. Then sounds wafted from the woods. "Ach, ve must hurry," exclaimed the Peoria beer baron. With surprising agility he climbed on the wagon, then over the door into the driver's seat, slipped on a pair of black kid gloves, pulled down his goggles, and turned around to get the lay of the ramp.

He placed the gears in neutral position, released the emergency brake, listened apprehensively to the sounds from the woods, getting louder, and hissed to Stephen, standing on the wagon in front of the car, "Push!"

Stephen pushed. Nothing moved. The sounds grew louder.

"Harder, boy. And hurry!"

The car rocked slightly.

"That's it. That's it," shouted Fritz. "Push harder. Harder!"

Stephen gave it his best and felt the behemoth move, inches, and then it was to the ramp. It was down about halfway when its weight lifted the wagon six feet off the ground. Lord Billner leaned over the radiator and held on as the car fell three feet to the ground while the wagon shot forward like a bullet, straight for the mess tent where it overturned the big stew kettle, upset tables and brought the tenting down on the head of the sleeping cook. Army profanity emitted from under the canvas. Meanwhile Stephen had released his hold on the radiator as Fritz urged him to crank the car.

As Lord Billner bent to his task and Fritz Buschmeister busied himself with dials and handles, Tom the Curious Bear, determined to avoid capture and aware of the crescendoing sounds behind him, ran out of the woods to the Pierce-Arrow and, unbeknownst to Fritz and Stephen, jumped over the back door and crouched on the floorboards of the back seat; there he remained, quiet as a mouse.

"Oh," pleaded Fritz to some pagan German god, "please start!" For the soldiers were almost there, and the cook was cutting his way out of the mess tent with a meat cleaver. From the tone of his epitaphs, that cleaver was about to be used on flesh again – human flesh.

"Ready?" asked Stephen.

"Ready."

Stephen cranked with all his might: a sputter, a bang as the car backfired, silence.

Fritz adjusted the spark, the gas mixture, pumped some oil.

"Ready?" asked Stephen.

"Try again," ordered Fritz as troops and cook's curses grew louder.

Stephen cranked like a madman. He heard a sputter, a backfire, and a roar. The Pierce-Arrow came to life, and not a moment too soon. Out of the woods emerged Captain Freeman W. Taylor, 2nd Cavalry, United States Army, with hungry Troop K.

When he saw the Pierce-Arrow he and his men paused as if frozen in time, their mouths agape. Then the Captain roared. "Halt! Halt in the name of the US Cavalry. Halt in the name of Colonel Peavey. I order you to halt, damn you, Fritz Buschmeister. Halt, I say!"

Fritz Buschmeister chose not to hear. Stephen leaped in beside him as Fritz squeezed the big black bulb and the horn went honk-honk-honk like an angry goose. The Pierce-Arrow moved to the road, away from the camp of Troop K, US 2nd Cavalry. Close behind the auto ran the cook, freed from the tent, his meat cleaver waving menacingly in the air. At his heels ran Captain Freeman W. Taylor and his troops. Unfortunately, they were afoot. Fritz shifted gears. The Pierce-Arrow picked up speed as the pursuers lagged behind in exhaustion. It paid its respects by backfiring and leaving behind a thick cloud of blue smoke mixed with dust.

## V

Fritz Buschmeister knew exactly where he was heading: for the Norris wagon road and from there down past Roaring Mountain, Obsidian Cliff, Apollinaris Spring, Swan Lake Flats, Mammoth Hot Springs, the Gardner River Canyon and so down the road through the Roosevelt Memorial Arch and out of the Park into the hamlet of Gardiner. This was in defiance of regulations established by the

Secretary of the Interior and the Secretary of War, as administered by the 2nd US Cavalry, Colonel J. S. (Saddle-Pants) Peavey, Commanding.

Back at Canyon, Troop K, 2nd US Cavalry, was in collective rage bordering on apoplexy. "My stew! My mess tent!" shouted the cook.

"Our lunch," protested the enlisted men. Groans and curses, epitaphs and gnashing of teeth mingled in the rarefied atmosphere with the acrid odor of automobile exhaust. No one was more livid than Captain Freeman W. Taylor. Colonel Peavey would bust him, that was for sure. Transfer him to Louisiana or Alaska, maybe even have him court-martialed if that vehicle was not intercepted and Fritz Buschmeister brought before United States Commissioner John Meldrum at Mammoth. Captain Taylor hated horses and loved cars, but with his very career at stake, he had no choice.

"Round up the horses and saddle up on the double," ordered the Captain, beckoning to the bugler to sound to arms. "We've got to stop that car!"

Had the troops not been deprived of their stew by the Studebaker wagon that had wrecked the mess tent, thanks to the Pierce-Arrow, they might have been more in sympathy with Fritz Buschmeister and his defiance of the automobile ban. But around the collapsed tent lingered the aroma of beef and coffee, the men were hungry and cross for their futile search for Tom the Curious Bear, and so they obeyed the Captain – on the double. They scrambled. Troop K was lined up for inspection in jig time. Captain Taylor, splendidly attired in a fresh olive-green khaki uniform, appeared before them, astride a sleek roan.

"Atten-shun!"

Nary a horse whinnied, for the Captain was clearly in a rage.

"Now, men," he began, his voice crackling out over the pines like a prophet of doom, "a crisis is at hand. Yes, a crisis just as serious as if the Sioux were attacking an emigrant train. The very spirit, the very essence of Yellowstone is at stake. This virgin wilderness, this untainted land, this Yellowstone, is today threatened by a mechanical innovation, an automobile."

The Captain paused, then held up his free arm gallantly, lost his balance and almost fell from his horse. Somewhere, he was certain, he heard someone laugh. Repositioned in the saddle, he glared at every man in K Troop – the color bearers, the bugler, the just plain Troopers. But they were as grim as he was.

"I expect," he continued, "every man to do his duty, every cavalryman to risk his life if need me to stop that car. We'll advance double time down the wagon road to Norris, take a short cut over a couple of hills, and head off the vehicle at the geyser basin. Any questions?"

No questions, but someone just out of hearing asked, "When do we eat?"

After some difficulty, crushing such thoughts from his psyche as "bully for the automobile," the Captain got his nervous, prancing steed pointed in the right direction, checked his balance, raised his hand: "Forward, ho!" he commanded. The bugler sounded the call and K Troop, Captain Taylor in the lead, charged down the road in hot pursuit of the fleeing Pierce-Arrow.

Lingering dust, a buggy up an embankment hitched to a horse trying to climb a lodgepole pine, equestrians galloping hither and yon yelling "whoaaaaa," and a hay wagon in the middle of the Gibbon River gave Captain Taylor assurance that the Pierce-Arrow had gone that way.

"Forward ho, men!" he sang, double-timing the horses down hill – a most unwise and dangerous thing to do.

Meanwhile, in the Pierce-Arrow:

"The distance from Canyon to Norris is about twelve miles, I figure," Lord Billner shouted to his companion after examining a map the driver had given him. But Fritz Buschmeister was not listening. He was singing in German a polka from the Old Country, punctuating each verse by squeezing the big rubber bulb of a horn – honk, honk, honk. Every time he spooked a horse he roared with laughter and tossed out Wagnerian expletives and his big belly rolled against the steering wheel like a bowlful of jelly.

"Ach," cried he in joyful bliss, "ziss Pierce-Arrow, she runs like a fine watch, does she. And takes ze corners gut too." He spun the wheel as the monster skidded around a curve, raising a cloud of dust. Down the steep road by Kepler Cascades the car sped. "Aren't they beautiful?" he asked, pointing at them while the car tried to climb the embankment on the other side.

"Watch out!"

"Ach – ach," replied Fritz, twisting the wheel in the nick of time as the car angled at a single degree from overturning. Stephen heard sickening crunching and scraping as the Pierce-Arrow straightened out along the road. He looked back to see where they had been, and pronounced it a miracle that they had not turned over. Then he noticed on the driver's side that the running board was missing.

Fritz committed a similar error again, this time looking back at where he had been. The car swerved to the left, scraped some boulders and barely averted going over the side. There went the left running board with its gas, oil, and water containers. "Oh, vell," reflected Fritz. No great loss. I'm rich, you know. A millionaire. I brew beer. Lots of gut, gut beer. Ho! Me, Fritz Buschmeister. Son of the brewmaster to Count Schleslangen. Me, a millionaire. I love America. I love its thirst. You, you love America, Englishman?"

"Yes, indeed I do, sir. But I'm not ready to be buried here."

'Eh? Ho, ho, ho. Have no fear, my English friend. I have had wrecks, and I have ruined autos, but I have never been hurt." The giant machine jolted over a rock, up over a big boulder, left terra firma for an instant, then fell back *ker klud* and continued on, fast.

Lord Billner looked down the steep incline. "Your brakes," he yelled. "Use your brakes. Slow down."

"Ve iss doing fine," Fritz replied, a little annoyed at his frightened passenger. But he did apply the brakes because, as he said, "Ve iss coming to Norris Junction already."

"How do you know?"

"Because," he hissed, "I vas through here in a buggy two weeks ago. I know ze roads. Trust me, my English friend. I vill get you to Gardiner in jog time."

"Jig time."

"Jig. Jog. No difference."

The Pierce-Arrow skidded around a curve and ran another horse and buggy up the mountainside. At the junction of the Norris-Upper Geyser Basin road a line of ten Yellowstone coaches plodded along with occupants dozing in the early afternoon sun. The caravan suddenly came alive. Coaches shot up the road towards Fountain Hotel as if they had been struck by lightning or threatened by a passel of bears. "What," asked the amazed attendants at Fountain, "got you here three hours early?"

By the time the Pierce-Arrow approached Norris Geyser Basin old Fritz was bouncing up and down on his seat like a happy baboon, steering the lumbering vehicle among the ruts, honking the bulbous horn, plying the brakes, shifting the gears, and singing in German.

What he had not figured on was Alexander Graham Bell's diabolical invention, the telephone. It had conveyed intelligence about a loose automobile approaching, and a barricade had been hastily constructed across the road below Norris basin. Upcoming traffic was diverted to a campground and instructions had been given to secure all horses. Something terrible was about to happen. An automobile was loose in Yellowstone Park. It was coming this way!

Unfortunately it was a busy day on the road above Norris. The Mankato (Minnesota) Beaver Bicycle Patrol, twenty-three stouthearted scouts led by a bespectacled school teacher, was puffing its way up the road when the honk-honk-honk of an approaching vehicle caused the troop to leave the road – hastily. Not an Iver-Johnson, a Peerless, a Columbia, or a Raleigh were harmed, nor their riders, but they were covered with hot mud from a convenient mud-pot where most of them had taken refuge. Their leader expressed his anger in words new to the boys' ears.

On down the dusty road past tourists more surprised at seeing an automobile than geysers flew the Pierce-Arrow. Buschmeister was commencing to sing again, and Stephen, holding tight to any grip he could find, began smelling the odor of burning rubber. From the back seat he heard a strange sound, too, like a belch. Stephen turned around to find his face inches away from the white face of Tom the Curious Bear, who had until then laid low on the floor. The bear stared at Stephen; Stephen stared at the bear. Then Tom sat back on the seat just like a human being, sniffed at the air, bounced up and down on the black cushions, and then belched again.

Stephen turned face forward and placed a hand on Fritz's left arm.

"Vat iss it? Vat iss?" asked Fritz impatiently. "Please do not hold my arm. I need it to steer and shift gears. Oh, oh. Vat is this up ahead?"

Up ahead lay the barricade, and ahead of it along the road, Troopers of C Troop astride their steeds, a Sergeant in command. As the Pierce-Arrow approached, the Sergeant, an excellent horseman, stood his skittish mount to the center of the road and raised his hand as a signal to halt. Behind him was the log barricade, strong enough to stop a train – probably even a Pierce-Arrow automobile.

"Well, I guess this is it," sighed Stephen, forgetting the bear because of the new impending problems. He hoped the authorities would not be too harsh.

Fritz was slowing the auto, cursing in German, contemplating alternatives. The car, her big, brass headlamps like two sparkling bright eyes, her massive radiator, her huge jet black hood and plate glass windshield all creating the impression of a living, breathing monster, slowed to a crawl as it approached the Sergeant while mounted cavalrymen struggled to control their horses.

"Ach. I'm afraid it will be ze hoosegow tonight, my friend," said Fritz.

Then the Sergeant's horse saw Tom the Curious Bear, who chose that moment to hold his paws over his hairy white stomach and groan like a child, for Tom had a stomachache. The Sergeant's horse whinnied, reared, and headed northward like split lightning. This panicked all the other horses which took out in all directions. Two of them chose to hurdle the barricade, knocking over the top log, while successive horses, their riders holding on for dear life, soon had the entire barrier destroyed.

"Vell, vell, vell," said Fritz joyfully, "let us get on with our business." He shifted into low gear, gave the Pierce-Arrow the gas, clattered through the downed barricade and was once more on the open road.

"What about him?" asked Stephen, pointing to the back seat where sat Tom the Curious Bear.

"He iss our friend," replied Fritz, casting a quick glance to the rear. "He spooked ze horses. Ve keep him. Ve need him."

Trouble was, Tom the Curious was no longer enjoying life. He was drunk, dizzy, and now feeling a little sick. He held his paws over his stomach and cried like a child, as black bears actually do.

Meanwhile, above Norris, Beaver Bicycle Patrol had regrouped. "Courage, courage fellows," pep-talked their bespattered leader. "Setbacks, yes. Defeats, never." He began pedaling, at first weaving across the road, when...

They heard the clarion notes of a bugle as Captain Freeman Taylor of K Troop, 2nd US Cavalry, burst out of the piney woods at a gallop, the Captain shouting "Forward ho, men. Away!"

Beaver Bicycle Patrol from Mankato was disrupted again. Horses reared and whinnied and hooves clomped through slender spokes. No one was hurt, but the mud pot received a second visit from its unhappy guests. The horses disappeared down the road and around a curve. The scoutmaster lay in the mud, speechless.

214

From the Norris Geyser Basin the road wound through tall pines, amongst occasional springs and mud pots, and then straightened out at Roaring Mountain. This is a great, barren, yellowish mass full of steam fumaroles. Fortunately the road was unoccupied save for an occasional cursing cavalryman, *sans* steed, or a riderless, bucking horse cavorting through the forest.

Approaching Roaring Mountain from the road below was one of the enormous tally-hos such as the Snowdens had ridden from the railroad station to Mammoth. Occasionally a party leased one to take it on a swing around the Park. Six big draft horses plodded ahead of the thirty-six passenger coach, which this day was driven by an old hand at Yellowstoneing, Uncle Charlie Jordan.

It was a happy, joyous crowd aboard the tally-ho, that bright August afternoon, and the Leiderkrantz Society of Ypsilanti, thirty-six males and females strong, was enjoying the good life to the hilt. For two years they had played at Octoberfests, weddings, and German–American dances, saving their money for this one great vacation. And they were happy. They had just consumed a gargantuan lunch including Polish sausage, pig's knuckles, sauerkraut, rye bread, and baked beans, all washed down with most of a bootlegged barrel of beer. Now, aboard the tally-ho, out had come the tuba and an accordion, a drum, a cornet and a clarinet. They began toot-whomping it up while stout ladies, not one of whom weighed less than 180 pounds, raised their stentorian voices in a song of pagan, Germanic origins, their voices occasionally punctuated by beery belches as their male companions pitched in.

Uncle Charlie, in the driver's seat, felt like a damned fool with all that racket going on inside. But he sighed with resignation, knowing that in a half hour the only sounds emitting from the coach would be snores. He would have peace and quiet until they arrived at Norris, where their discomfort would raise tempers until they had all visited the 'retreat', as rest rooms were known in those days.

Sorry, Uncle Charlie. Not this day. This day would be different. Some of his passengers would hardly need a 'retreat' this day.

Up the road toward Roaring Mountain plodded the tally-ho, with the Leiderkrantz Society aboard, and down the road from Norris toward Roaring Mountain clattered and backfired the Pierce-Arrow, Fritz Buschmeister, driver. The monster was tearing along at thirty miles an hour, a cloud of dust behind, a groaning white bear sitting like a human in the back seat, and a frightened British remittance man holding on for dear life beside a fat little bearded German who manipulated the steering wheel, throttle, clutch, brakes, horn, and assorted gadgetry.

"The brakes," Buschmeister uttered, "ach, zey are weakening." His foot pumped the pedal vigorously, but deceleration was barely perceptible. Then he tried shifting into a lower gear. "Zey call zis double clutching," he said as he shifted into neutral, roared the motor, and tried to force the gears into a lower ratio. It was noisy, in those days before syncro-mesh. A series of backfires accompanied his efforts, and they were loud – so loud they made Roaring Mountain sound as weak as a one cylinder Corliss engine. Bang! Bang! Bang!

And when six draft horses pulling the tally-ho carrying the Leiderkrantz Society of Ypsilanti, already skittish from the polka music, saw that monster appearing in front of them on the road ahead, with those huge brass headlights reflecting the early afternoon sun, and – yes – a radiator now sending up little geysers of steam and boiling water...

The six draft horses were lively and young again. They leaped up like colts. They tried to go north, east, south and west. Uncle Charlie was busy supplying the services for which he was paid $75 a month. The polka band ceased playing and the singing stopped. The horses left the road with the tally-ho behind them.

"Runaway," someone shouted.

"Hyarrrrrr," yelled Uncle Charlie as the horses, together now, headed as one for a big shallow pool of hot water that trickled down from Roaring Mountain. When the horses stepped into the hot water they were startled still more and they broke into a gallop – or some of the six did – right across the pond and up the side of the steep, steaming mountain, the coach still with them.

By this time most members of the Leiderkrantz Society of Ypsilanti had taken leave of the tally-ho. The tuba player had leaped out at the cry of "Runaway!" He sat in the sulfurous, green, steaming water, still embracing the tuba, which went "obeeeeuuuummmmmphphph". The accordion player fell on his instrument, which squished and collapsed under his excessive weight; it expired slowly, sounding like a dying mule. The clarinetist and the cornetist rode the tally-ho through the water and muck until it started up Roaring Mountain, when they too departed from the swaying coach.

The women screamed like the singers in *Tristan and Isolde*, the men cursed like Woden and Thor, especially when they heard Fritz Buschmeister shouting back at them in their own language as the Pierce-Arrow passed by. A package of link sausages had burst open. The links floated in the water like oversized amoeba. Hunks of soggy rye bread bobbed up and down, and a near-empty beer barrel gurgled. Across the pond and up the mountain, some hanging onto the outside of the tally-ho, two or three inside, some about to fall off, some weaving amidst the fumaroles, were other members of the Leiderkrantz Society of Ypsilanti.

Miraculously, with the help of Uncle Charlie's horsemanship, the tally-ho remained upright. Soon he had it standing back on the road, still and inert, as he tried to calm his horses. Inside was one meek little Leiderkrantzer who had failed to get fat like his brethren. He finished gnawing on some pig's knuckles, daintily wiped his fingers on his coat pockets, and awaited the return of his lost brethren and sisters.

And the Pierce-Arrow continued onward toward the Roosevelt Memorial Arch at the North Entrance. "Ach. I theenk ve vill make it. Teddy, he vould be proud."

Words failed Lord Billner. All he could say was "Whew!" Mostly he prayed silently as the car continued cannon-balling toward the Appolinaris Spring.

Meanwhile the Leiderkrantz Society reloaded. Some of the women were hysterical. They were quite a sight. Even Uncle Charlie, now that he had everything under control, chuckled quietly at the view: overweight frauleins in huge hats cast askew by the crisis, mud bespattered, sitting in the coach at odd angles (a few behinds having received bruises as they fell into shallow water or onto the ground), lambasting their husbands who were busily adjusting their pince-nez glasses, stuffing shirt-tails into massive trousers, and otherwise rehabilitating themselves. Finally their leader ordered Charlie to proceed.

Just as a bugle's clarion notes came over the rarefied air and someone up the road yelled "Forward, men!" and K Troop, 2nd US Cavalry (with stragglers from C Troop stationed at Norris) came down upon the tally-ho at full gallop. What happened next was the subject of an investigation by the Inspector-General's Office, United States Army, Washington, DC. In the thick dossier is one letter, part of which sheds light upon the incident. It is from Colonel J. S. Peavey, Colonel, 2nd US Cavalry, Fort Yellowstone, Wyoming; the Subject is "Restitution for Musical Instruments, Damaged." The salient paragraphs read as follows:

3. Just as the horses were brought under control and the tally-ho was reloaded, K Troop charged down the road in hot pursuit of said Pierce-Arrow motor car and the tally-ho horses once more ran away, knocking all manner of tourist equipment to the road and endangering the lives of said tourists.

4. Captain Taylor's horse, in the lead, stepped on the accordion with one hoof and into the broad end of the tuba with the other, bucked Captain Taylor into the pond at the foot of Roaring Mountain and cavorted all about the area, disrupting the entire Troop, until said tuba and accordion were disengaged from said horse.

5. It is recommended that the claims for damaged equipment, viz., one tuba and one accordion, be honored, and the claimants paid.

Of course, the occupants of the rogue automobile knew nothing of this. What they were aware of, as they roared down the road, was that the Pierce-Arrow was warming up. "Ve must have more vater," Buschmeister announced. "Ze radiator must have more vater or she vill blow up."

"The Appolinaris Spring is just down the road," Stephen shouted, "and it is a cold water spring."

"Gut. Ve stop zere and feel ze radiator."

"Maybe we can get rid of our passenger, too," shouted Stephen, pointing to the back seat. At that moment Tom clasped his stomach with his enormous paws and cried and moaned as if death was imminent. Then he belched. His halitosis almost asphyxiated the humans in the front seat. It was a relief indeed when they arrived at the Appolinaris Spring.

Fritz jumped out, ran to the huge trunk at the rear and fetched a bucket. "Come. Let us hurry. The cavalry can't be far behind."

While the master brewer ran his fat body up the few steps to the spring, Stephen opened a back door. "Come on, nice bear. Let's go. The trip is over," he ordered.

Tom the Curious held his stomach with his paws and stared at him. "Get the hell out!" yelled Stephen.

Fritz came running down the steps from the spring. "Funny water, this," he commented. "It iss like soda water."

The bear watched as Fritz gingerly uncapped the radiator, then stared amazed as steam spouted twenty feet into the air. Then Tom, of his own volition, jumped out of the car and started up the steps to the spring, a little wobbly, and still groaning.

"Thank God. We're rid of him," said Stephen.

Fritz carefully poured the cold water into the radiator and threw the bucket to the remittance man to refill. "Ze radiator iss just about empty," said the driver, "but we saved her."

At the spring Stephen found Tom, up to his belly in the muddy pool below the spigot, drinking long drafts of the cold liquid. The young man filled the pail and started down. "So long, old bear," he said.

Fritz grabbed the bucket, poured the contents carefully, capped the radiator and threw the bucket in the back seat. "Let us be gone," he announced, climbing into the car. He pulled down his goggles and gave Stephen the signal to begin cranking.

The Englishman cranked and cranked, but nothing happened. Fritz adjusted the spark, wiggled the accelerator, pumped the clutch, and with a nod indicating haste, asked Stephen to try again. This time, with a backfire like a thunderclap and a cloud of blue smoke, the Pierce-Arrow started. Stephen jumped in beside Fritz, the gears crunched and smashed, and the car began moving. Just as it did, crashing down the steps from the spring, growling, leaped Tom the Curious Bear. His legs and belly were muddy and wet. Stephen had neglected to close the back door: Tom jumped in, sat up on the cushions, and looked all about him as if he was marshal of a parade.

"Oh, no!"

"Ach, ve have a true friend, I believe."

Down the road roared the Pierce-Arrow, the motion slamming shut the back door. Soon the car was passing Obsidian Cliff, rounding the curve and passing alongside the beaver dams and boggy meadows where moose were often observed.

There stood the moose.

He was the biggest bull moose Stephen had ever seen, and he was standing broadside, right across the road, chewing his cud. He stood at least seven and a half feet tall at the shoulders and his antlers were six feet across. His bell – the loose, ugly concoction of skin and gristle hanging from his throat – dangled lazily to and fro. But his ears were up and he turned an arrogant countenance in the direction of the monster that was barging down upon him. He was in no mood for an argument, was this bull moose.

It was that time of year, and Mr. Moose had not found a mate. He resented this ominous-looking animal bearing down upon him. His big, mealy nose expanded, his nostrils dilated. Nor did it help the way the brakes squeaked and the radiator, filled with Appolinaris water, burped a small geyser ever few seconds. Add to this the sight of Tom the Curious Bear who was feeling sicker than ever. "Owoooo," groaned Tom.

"Gott in Himmel," muttered Fritz Buschmeister, launching into a tirade of German profanity, for the moose had now turned to face the Pierce-Arrow head-on. From deep within his innards the beast began to emit low, angry barks. He pawed the gravel and waved his enormous antlers from side to side.

"Go around him," Stephen suggested as they slowed, and approached the great beast, which loomed larger and larger.

But Fritz had other ideas. He brought the auto to a halt within inches of the moose, so close that its head extended over the hood. The beast's eyes glared down at the car's occupants, his bell slid across the metal hood, and he breathed loudly through his wide nostrils.

"Ve shall see who gives ground," Fritz announced with bravado. He reached to the side of his seat and came up with a buggy whip. "Out of ze way, stupid moose," he commanded as he stood up in the car and flicked the whip. With a whir and a snap it struck the moose on the back. He repeated it. "Out of ze way, moose," Fritz commanded again.

The bull moose barked and came closer, until his front legs touched the hot radiator.

"Gut. Now I reach you better," said Fritz, flicking the whip straight at the moose's tender nose. "Crack!" went the whip. Stephen saw the spot where it hit throb and turn red.

That did it. The moose charged, lifting his front legs onto the hood. Fritz sat down, startled, as he stared at a maddened bull moose just inches from his face, peering at him from the other side of the plate glass windshield. Glass tinkled as one of the headlights, struck by the rear legs, shattered. Then the radiator burped and steam and boiling hot water spouted up onto the underside of Mr. Moose, striking parts of his anatomy developing into usefulness at this time of the year.

The moose barked again: "Uh, uh, uh," and swung his enormous antlers back and forth, breaking the plate glass windshield.

"Start the car moving," said Stephen. "It's our only hope."

"Yes," replied the shocked beer baron. "It's our only hope. Ve get going." He sat down and started the Pierce-Arrow moving ahead. This panicked the moose, who barked once more, swung his antlers back and forth, clearing the glass from the windshield assembly. Somehow the animal got itself off to the side of the car and began running down the road ahead of it, first on one side of the road, then on the other. Then it stopped abruptly once again in the middle of the road and turned to its protagonist. Fritz did the only thing he could do: he swung the car off the road into a conveniently situated sparsely wooded meadow.

Now in the meadow were two tents pitched within five feet of each other. They were suspended by a stout rope stretched between two pines. These were sagebrushers' tents, although the occupants were not to be seen. But they were there, for their surrey was under nearby trees and their horse was grazing nearby. Where were they?

They were in their tents, of course. Where else would two honeymooning couples from Helena, Montana, be, at 1.45 PM?

After the noon meal one of the young men had yawned and said, casually, "Golly, I'm tired. I think I'll take a nap."

And the other young man had looked at his pretty bride, and said, "Heck, the trout aren't biting in the middle of the day. May as well sack out for a couple hours."

"I'm tired too," remarked one little bride, her eyes dancing. "I was cold last night and I didn't sleep too well." She placed a hand to her mouth and feigned a yawn.

But the other bride was too aware, and too embarrassed, to disappear so boldly with her husband into their tent at midday. She said, "I've got to finish the dishes. You go ahead, dear." But she gave her husband of three days a secret, meaningful glance. He sauntered into their tent alone while the other couple brazenly disappeared into their tent and fastened the flaps. Now that they were gone the other young bride left the dirty dishes on the picnic table, feigned another yawn and nonchalantly tiptoed into her husband's tent.

"I thought you said you were tired," she whispered to her husband, playing the coy female even as she let him pull her to the cot. "In mid-afternoon. Honey, you're terrible."

Giggles came from the other tent.

Ten minutes later Fritz Buschmeister and his Pierce-Arrow came tearing through the meadow like the devil after cupid. The brakes worked only feebly now, as he weaved the car between stumps and big rocks and finally aimed at the five foot space between the tents – the only way he could see of getting through and back to the road. The Pierce-Arrow passed through the space without touching the tents but the rope that supported them caught in the broken windshield assembly. The tents were yanked from their stakes and carried off by the car. Swish! As fast as that.

Screams.

Stephen ventured a glance back, then stared wide-eyed. Even Tom the Curious Bear turned around. He placed both front paws on the rolled-down top and stared until the rope broke away from the car and the tents collapsed on the road and the vehicle continued onto Swan Lake Flats. 'What kind of cavorting was that?' thought the brute, sensing a primitive, animalistic desire to search out a female bear.

The renegade automobile spun down the road.

"Whew," said Fritz, sitting back and relaxing. "Zis has been a real adventure, ho, ho, ho. Now ve have free sailing." He gave the car gas as it whizzed northward across Swan Lake Flats. "Ve cross the Flats," he said, "then descend through Kingman Pass and Silver Gate to Mammoth, and then down the Gardner River Canyon and zipppp – ve iss out of ze Park."

Tom, who was sitting in the back seat again, began to groan and hold his belly with his two front paws.

Bang! Flap, flap, flap.

"Ach. Damn! Blowout!" exclaimed Fritz. "But ve fix fast."

He stopped the car and jumped out. It was the left rear tire. In a jiffy he had Stephen jacking up the wheel while he fetched a wrench and unbolted a spare. "See," said Fritz, "all ve do iss change ze wheel. Ze tire is already inflated and on ze wheel. No need to change tires now."

Meanwhile the honeymooners from Helena were regaining their composure – at least, three of the four were. The bride who had brazenly entered the tent with her husband thought it was sort of funny. By sheer coincidence she and her husband had been under a sheet. But the other bride – the modest one with dishes to do – had been totally bereft of clothing with no covers over her – and there was more to the story than that – and so she was screaming, sobbing, and demanding that her husband take her home to mother. Her hubby was trying to calm her by saying, "Heck, honey. They didn't see *you*, they only saw *me*. I was on top of you!"

Her screams elevated to shrieks.

Fortunately they were dressed again and repitching their tents, when the sounds of galloping horses warned of imminent company.

"Pardon me," began Captain Taylor, galloping up and halting his steed, "have you seen an automobile around here?"

"Have we!" blurted the sobbing bride. "It – it destroyed our – modesty."

"Begging your pardon, ma'am?"

"It went thataway," said her husband quickly, pointing down the road as the Captain surveyed the disheveled clothing, the cots, the tents, the youthfulness of the two couples and the words JUST MARRIED still on the surrey. Captain Taylor laughed for the first time that day. The Pierce-Arrow, he speculated, had indeed caught two and two together. Quickly he regained his military bearing. "Forward, men. Hyooooo. At a gallop."

It was just before 2 PM when the telephone rang in the office of Colonel S. P. "Saddle-Pants" Peavey. With his shiny bald head and big, white mustache, Saddle-Pants looked a lot like the kind-hearted old Emperor Franz Joseph of Austria. And he was about as progressive. His face, as he conversed over the telephone, was a study in emotions. It had been a good day, so far.

"Colonel Peavey speaking."

"Sir, this is Sergeant Tim O'Bryan at Norris."

"Yes, Sergeant."

Then, as the voice on the other end of the line continued, the Colonel's face turned pink, then crimson, then livid purple. "An au-to-mobile," he hissed. "In the Park?" Then "Captain Taylor!" as he half stood up from his chair. The words came staccato-like between his false teeth, which were clicking like castanets. "Bound for Mammoth?"

He then levied a blue-air barrage at the Sergeant, hung up and shouted for his Orderly. "Have the bugler sound 'Alert'," he ordered. "This is an emergency. I want every soldier mounted and on the parade ground in fifteen minutes. An automobile is loose in the Park!"

There was some delay. First the top Sergeant had to find the bugler, who was asleep among some feed sacks. That all-important digit in the list of job descriptions had to run back to the barracks to fetch his instrument. Then he dashed to the flagpole, raised the bugle to his lips with the Sergeant breathing down his neck, sentencing him to several years of K.P., when the bugler paused. The most sorrowful look appeared on his face. He said meekly,

"Sergeant. How do you sound 'Alert'?"

"Whadoyamean?" roared the Sergeant. "You're the bugler, ain't you?"

'Yes, sir. But – hell, Sarge, we ain't had an Alert in all the years I've been in the Army."

"Then sound something," commanded the Sergeant.

"What?"

"Reveille ought to do it. Yes, sound Reveille."

"At two o'clock in the afternoon?"

The sounds of Reveille wafted throughout the Mammoth area.

"It's to wake the Colonel from his nap," said one soldier.

"The bugler's drunk again," said another.

"Anyway, we'd best check on it," said a third.

And so it came to pass, in due time, but not nearly soon enough for Saddle-Pants, that shouting sergeants soon had young recruits and shavetails understanding what an 'Alert' was all about. Even the horses sensed that something was up as their riders appeared, breathless and still getting dressed in proper attire, and saddled them post-haste. In about fifteen minutes four Troops were assembled in formation on the parade ground. Colonel Peavey awaited them. He was mounted on his splendid Bay whose graceful lines hinted of Arabian blood. A wave of excitement and all manner of rumors swept across the visitors at the National Hotel across the way. Colonel Peavey's exhortation to the Troops assembled was equal to anything a commander ever gave to an army outnumbered ten to one that constituted the last defense of the realm.

Meanwhile, down from the Appolinaris Spring and the honeymooners from Helena galloped the Captain leading K Troop, a dusty, cursing, hungry, irritable, angry sixty-five men. Whatever their feelings about motor cars in general, they hated the Pierce-Arrow in particular. If they ever got their hands on it and its occupants...

"There it is, men," shouted the Captain as they galloped onto Swan Lake Flats. For indeed, parked at the side of the road was the Pierce-Arrow with two figures hustling about, and a strange figure in the back seat. A puncture, no doubt, or a blowout, thought the Captain. Now was his chance.

But Stephen and Fritz, hearing the commotion of 264 horses' hooves, just worked faster. "Hurry! Hurry!" urged Fritz as Stephen lowered the jack, threw it in the back seat, where Tom the Curious eyed it apprehensively. His paws were still across his belly and sobs emitted from his saliva-covered mouth. Stephen turned the crank just once and the already hot motor turned over; Fritz had the car moving even as Stephen jumped in. From behind they heard the thunder of horses, hooves and the command, "Halt! Halt in the name of the United States Army. Halt or we shoot!"

"Halt, hell," snickered Fritz Buschmeister. "Ve've got 'em licked, Englishman, if we can make it to Kingman Pass." The Pass was in sight where the road veered to the east. Stephen hazarded a glance behind. There was K Troop galloping after the car, Captain Taylor leading. Stephen was horrified to see the Captain pull a pistol from his holster and take aim. He ducked as he heard a "pow" and a whirr above his head. "Hurry, Fritz," urged Stephen. "They're shooting at us. Give her all she's got!"

Fritz shifted gears and gave her the gas. The Pierce-Arrow showed little response; then her low torque accelerated. By the time they reached the curve at the head of Kingman Pass the monster was doing fifty. It skidded around the turn so quickly that it knocked Tom the Curious Bear onto the floor. Tom crawled back up on the seat and covered his eyes with one paw while holding his stomach with the other. Skidding from right to left, raising a cloud of dust, the automobile started down through the narrow eminence of Silver Gate. The Gardner River was on the right, cliffs on the left.

"The brakes," Stephen shouted. "The brakes, Fritz. Please. Apply the brakes, sir!"

"Mein gott, I am. No response. Ach. Ve are totally without brakes!"

Faster and faster sped the behemoth, Fritz manipulating curves and holding to the road where it was nothing but a wooden trestle out from the cliffs.

"Can't you slow it somehow?"

"I try to shift into lower gear. I try."

Fritz pushed in the clutch, roared the motor, and tried to shift into lower gear. The motor backfired like cannon bursts, reverberating through the canyon walls and starting landslides on nearby Bunsen Peak. "Can't do it," Fritz announced.

"Try again!" Stephen yelled as the car emerged at the upper terraces of the hot springs, still gaining speed. Pity the horsedrawn vehicles along the way: they mounted trees and floated in the Gardner River and got their tack tangled. It was sheer chaos.

As the Pierce-Arrow skidded around a turn and straightened out into the last long hill, at the base of which was the National Hotel, Fritz tried once again. He disengaged the gears, roared the motor, ground the gears, and failed. The backfiring was like the Fourth of July.

"Never mind," shouted Stephen, viewing the stretch of road ahead. "I think we can make it now."

But hard by the road was the western boundary of the buffalo pasture where nearly a hundred bison were grazing. They were situated there, fairly close to the facilities at Mammoth, so that tourists could observe the great beasts in a natural setting.

That warm August afternoon they were bunched up at the west end nearest the road, some of them lying in the way bovines and the like have, some chewing their cuds, some washing their thick, woolly hides in big dust hollows. But unfortunately some were on edge, for the season was approaching for them. Rut! They pawed the earth. They moved about skittishly. Bulls made hostile moves toward other bulls. Other than that, however, it was an ordinary afternoon in the lives of the beasts called by mammologists *bison-bison*.

An ordinary afternoon, that is, until the Pierce-Arrow skidded into sight around the curve above the buffalo pasture and came tearing down the road beside the west fence, a cloud of dust behind it, backfiring, Fritz honking the bulbous horn. Already two or three bulls had cast their beady little eyes toward the parade ground at Mammoth where unusual doings were transpiring – a large body of mounted solders all in line, and a fat man riding up and down in front of them, speaking in commanding tones. People lined the railing of the hotel verandah, which was also strange. Not that *bison-bison* understood, for they are stupid animals. Ridiculously, unbelievably, absolutely stupid.

What could such beasts have thought of that garish black monster bearing down the road by the west fence? It was loud, cumbersome, smelly, and fast. Bang! It backfired. Whoosh! went the radiator sending up a gusher of steam and water. Carrunch went the gears. "Owoooooo," moaned Tom the Curious Bear. A human being shouted, "Slow down," another replied, "I can't." More backfiring: Bang! Bang! Bang!

That did it. Instantly one hundred *bison-bison* were on their feet. A giant buffalo bull pawed the earth and headed for the fence. Others joined, pushing. Crack! Crack! Down came the fence. The lead buffalo hit the road ahead of the Pierce-Arrow and faced it, as the moose had done, head lowered, ready to give battle. Others assembled behind him. Honk! Honk! went the bulbous horn, as Fritz squeezed vigorously. Bang! Bang! the car backfired. With incredible astuteness Fritz swung around the lead buffalo, but by the time he had manipulated a curve and was running along in front of the National Hotel, a buffalo stampede was in progress with the Pierce-Arrow in its midst.

Colonel Saddle-Pants Peavey and his men? They were part of the stampede also, and the whinnying of horses, the commands of Saddle-Pants, the blaring of the bugle, the bang! bang! of the backfiring, the honk, honk of the horn, the groans of the bear, and the tramp of four hundred buffalo hooves mixed with over a thousand horses' hooves shook through Mammoth like an earthquake. Then: down the road from the terraces galloped the sixty-five men of K Troop, Captain Freeman W. Taylor, 2nd Cavalry, US Army, commanding. When he caught up to the tail-end of the buffalo herd he angled across the parade ground in hopes of heading off the Pierce-Arrow, which had been forced to slow down amongst the beasts. "Forward, men," the Captain was heard to shout. Observers at the hotel noticed his mud encrusted uniform, his face covered with dust. "Forward!" he shouted again.

Two bison leaped onto the verandah amidst the screams of women and the curses of men. Bison charged the rocking chairs and little tables with pitchers of lemonade on them, finally departing on the other end, taking along part of the railing.

Then, like a tornado, the car, cavalry, and bison were gone; only dust remained. And broken furniture, male curses and female hysterics. The phenomenon had passed on down to the Gardner River Canyon. There the stampeding bison chose to desert the strange smelling animal in their midst (an animal that had lost both running boards, windshield, spare tires, one headlight, and its brakes, with a radiator about to burst – but which still carried two human beings and a whitish bear).

Now the Pierce-Arrow entered open country, at the north end of which were the false fronts of Gardiner's main street. Cavalrymen were still trying to get their mounts under control; others were still regrouping. Many a solder was making acquaintance with sagebrush and cactus that day.

"By Jove," exclaimed Lord Billner, "I think we are going to make it. Look. There's the Roosevelt Memorial Arch."

"Bully," replied Fritz. "Theodore would like zat. Bully for us!"

Bang! went a tire.

"To hell with ze tire," said Fritz.

Bang! A second tire blew. The Pierce-Arrow clattered along on broken tire carcasses. "We'll go under the Arch before we stop," Fritz announced like an army officer holding the line against the enemy. "Then we'll be out of the Park. And I weel be Number One automobilist through Yellowstone!"

"They're catching up with us again," Stephen warned him, glancing back. "Can't you speed up?"

"Going as fast as I can," replied Fritz. "Ze motor's so hot she won't go fast any more. Two flat tires, zey don't help."

They approached the Roosevelt Memorial Arch at full throttle doing all of twenty-one miles an hour. Just as they were about to go under it, Tom the Curious Bear groaned once more in agony, his long jaws opened, and he vomited fermented chokecherries, seeds, ham, flour, bacon, Appolinaris water, and his own fragrant stomach juices over the backs of the humans in front of him.

"What is that stench?" asked Stephen.

"Ach."

Stephen turned to face Tom the Curious, now suffering the dry heaves. They were too much even for Tom. He became quite the beast again, albeit a sick one. He leaped out of the slow moving car, turned two somersaults and, regaining his balance, ran on unsteady legs up a draw full of brambles and willows. Nor did he stop until he was far from the road. Then he turned and looked back. The Pierce-Arrow had passed under the Memorial Arch and a few bison were beginning to graze while others still ran about over the prairie. A Troop of horsemen were galloping toward the Arch. Tom's bear mind, such as it was, tried to figure it out, but Tom, whose dizziness and nausea were beginning to wear off, just nodded his shaggy head back and forth. He decided to find some cool, fresh water and lie down in it for a while. He sniffed the breeze. Was that a female bruin he smelled? Tom was intrigued, but his brute instincts said "water"; he headed for the Gardner River. He could, he thought, drink it dry.

As for Fritz Buschmeister and Lord Billner in the renegade automobile, they had coasted under the Arch and were put-putting jerkily on two cylinders down Gardiner's main street. Catching up with them, finally, was Captain Freeman W. Taylor, Commander, Troop K, 2nd US Cavalry.

"Hey," shouted someone from the boardwalk (which was on the north side of the street; nothing was on the south side), "Get off the street."

"Vy?" asked Fritz as Captain Taylor's "Halt" wafted through the air.

"Because the main street of Gardiner is still in the Park."

"Vat?" asked Fritz. "Still in ze Park?"

"Yep. It's the northern boundary."

The Pierce-Arrow sputtered, leaped ahead jerkily, then slowed as the clopping of horses' hooves grew louder and louder. From a saloon came the strains of 'The Stars and Stripes Forever' being played on a Wurlitzer with a snare drum and cymbal. Fritz did the only thing he could do to avoid incarceration in the guard house at Mammoth. He turned the Pierce-Arrow left at a forty-five degree angle, up over the boardwalk and through the swinging doors of the Lazy Horse Saloon. There it wrecked several card tables, spilled a lot of beer, and came to a stop.

The way Fritz calmed the bartender and became a hero in a town that disliked Park officials, the free beer he bought for everyone, and the shouts of derision at Captain Taylor as he and his bedraggled Troopers stood astride their mounts in the middle of the street that was still a part of the Park – sat there in utter helplessness and total misery – and observed through the broken swinging doors Fritz Buschmeister holding high a foaming mug of cold beer, in a saloon that was outside the Cavalry's jurisdiction, is a story to this day still related by Gardiner's old timers.

Napoleon's army after Waterloo did not look more bedraggled or dejected than did the men and horses of K Troop as they plodded back toward Mammoth. None were more downcast than Captain Freeman W. Taylor. Halfway up the canyon to Mammoth a Trooper approached with orders for K Troop not to return to barracks until all the bison – every one – had been rounded up and resecured in the buffalo corral. A mass groan arose from the tired Troopers. Rounding up bison, they knew, was about as difficult as rounding up trout in a pond.

## VI

Lord Billner left the rear entrance to the Lazy Horse Saloon. He had thanked Fritz Buschmeister after the German had made amends with the bartender and the customers. Both Fritz and Stephen had divested themselves of their jackets, bear vomit not being conducive to making friendships. Stephen was disappointed to notice that the odor had expanded throughout his clothing. But he had no time to worry about that. He had to be in Livingston, forty-four miles away, before 6 PM.

In futility he inquired of the schedule of the Park Branch Line, the narrow gauge railroad that ran between Livingston and Gardiner, but as he already knew, having ridden it many times during his stay at his Paradise Valley ranch, that train had left at 2 PM. He looked at his watch: it was almost 4 PM. In two hours it would be six o'clock, the post office would be closed, and Lord Stephen Billner would be bereft of his remittance.

Then he heard it – the unmistakable sound of a motorcycle. Put-put. Vroooooooooom. Put-put-put.

Britannia's abandoned Second Son sprang to life. He followed the sound down one of Gardiner's few side streets and there, at the entrance to a blacksmith shop, was the vehicle. Kneeling beside it, making adjustments, was a young man, perhaps twenty years old, wearing black oxfords and knickers, a dark blue shirt and a white cap placed on his head backwards, and a pair of goggles perched on his forehead.

Stephen checked a pocket and was gratified to discover the presence of his wallet. In it were about fifty dollars, all that were left in the way of cash until he received his remittance. *If* he received his remittance.

"I say – how much to take me to Livingston?"

The proud owner looked up at the smelly, disheveled descendant of the Black Knight's right-hand man. "What do ya' wantta go to Livingston for?"

"I must be at the post office before it closes at six o'clock. I'll pay." Stephen exposed his money.

"Livingston is forty-four miles."

"Oh, that beauty of yours could do it easily," said Stephen, playing on the cyclist's pride. "You can't beat an Excelsior."

"Excelsior? This ain't no Excelsior. This is a Harley-Davidson."

"Oh. Oh, I see. Then no wonder…"

"Whadya' mean, 'No wonder?' This machine's twice as good as an Excelsior."

"Oh, of course," replied Stephen, walking away.

"Say, you want to go to Livingston? I'll take you there on this Harley of mine for ten dollars."

"Right now?" asked Stephen, pausing. "Do you really think it can make it?"

"Hell, yes, it can make it. Put up or shut up."

Lord Billner put up and climbed on the back of the machine. Away they sped over the hills and through the dales and beside the Yellowstone River, past Corwin Springs and Cinnabar Mountain and the Devil's Slide and Chico Hot Springs. The miles slipped by. They passed Stephen's ranchland and his white frame ranchhouse. For a fleeting moment he thought of Prudence and housekeeping and the bedroom with its double bed and down mattress and how lonely he had been there and how wonderful it would be to have a wife to share it with, but the terrain passed by so quickly that his mind was soon on other things. The cyclist gained confidence as the miles passed by. His Harley-Davidson fairly leaped over the washboarded ruts, the wooden bridges, the rocky stretches. "Only about fifteen more miles," the young cyclist yelled back to him.

"Splendid," replied Stephen, using a word not commonly heard in Montana. For the first time since leaving Mr. Snowden along the Yellowstone River he began to take hope. He relaxed. Surely his remittance would be at the post office through today. It must be. It had to be. And then, with the money, he could marry Prudence. Then crowsfeet appeared on Stephen's clear forehead. Good Lord! He was supposed to meet Prudence at Artist's Point at eight o'clock! He hoped her father would remember to tell her that the date was canceled.

Quickly his thoughts were dispelled. The Harley-Davidson rounded a curve at high speed and there, broadside across the road like the moose, was a machine even larger and more grotesque than the Pierce-Arrow: the biggest Peerless Perfection Steam Tractor in western Montana! In a flash Stephen saw that it was in the process of crossing the road from the field on one side to the field on the other.

"Watch out!" warned Stephen.

The choice was of which accident to have: head-on into the side of the machine or veer to the right. Veer the cyclist did, up a two foot embankment and through the gate, into a herd of cattle, across fifty feet of meadow and up a haystack, where both riders chose to desert the Harley, which continued, unmanned, to the other side where it fell on its side.

Lord Billner lay in the hay, looking up at the blue sky. Strange sounds came to his ears. The puffing and wheezing of the Peerless Perfection Steam Tractor, the bleating of cattle, the put-put-put of the Harley-Davidson, the cyclist's agonizing moans, not for his body but for his machine, and the breathless "You fellers all right?" from the tractor man.

The first face Stephen saw was that of the farmhand standing above him on the haystack. He had an unshaven face under a greasy old Stetson, wore a blue flannel shirt, bib overalls, and sported tobacco-stained, rotted teeth. "Sorry," he apologized, "but I was crossing from the east forty to the west forty with that blamed tractor and I had to stop and close the gate or all those damned cows would have followed me. Cripes! The boss is mad at me anyway. There ain't been a hoss and buggy or a ve-hicle on this road all week. Why in hell'd you have to come along just now?"

Stephen stood up awkwardly, shook himself to get rid of the hay clinging to him and make sure he had no broken bones, and said, "Forget it." He turned to where the cyclist was digging himself out. "You all right?" he asked, and, seeing that the young man was uninjured, added, "The cycle's still running. Let's get on her and be on our way."

Even as he spoke he watched as the cyclist adjusted his cap and pulled the goggles over his eyes, then nodded his head. "Get to Livingston some other way," he whimpered. "My poor Harley-Davidson. I'm going back to Gardiner."

"But you agreed," pleaded Stephen. "To Livingston for ten dollars."

"Keep you money," bawled the younger man, sliding down the haystack and throwing the ten dollar bill at Stephen. "My poor motorcycle."

The hired man noticed first the ten dollars, then the cyclist about the leave, then Stephen. He rubbed his stubby chin. "You got to get to Livingston in a hurry?" he asked.

"Before six o'clock," Stephen answered desperately. "I've got to get to the post office by then or lose my remittance."

"Hmm," hummed the horseless cowboy. He stuck a sprig of hay in his mouth. He and Stephen slid down the haystack together and stood by as the cyclist coddled his machine to the road and then started back toward Gardiner.

"Friend," drawled the hired hand, "what's it worth to you to get to Livingston before six o'clock?"

"Do you have a conveyance," asked Stephen, looking around.

"Welllll," drawled the farmer, "in a manner of speakin'. He flicked the straw in his mouth and turned his eyes to the Peerless Perfection Steam Tractor. It had cleated seven-foot rear steel wheels, a boiler as big as a railroad engine, a massive protected cab and behind that a cavernous storage space for coal and wood. "She's all steamed up," he drawled. As if waiting for a cue, the tractor belched a cloud of steam and seemed to sigh with relief, "whoooooooooooo."

"Surely – you – don't mean—"

"How much'll ya' give me?"

"How much do you ask?"

"Ten dollars, I reckon. Enough to keep me in vittles while I ride a freight to Spokane."

"But the tractor—"

"We'll leave it in Livingston. The old man won't be out none. Besides, it needs work done on it."

Stephen pulled out his watch. It was about five o'clock. "Do you think we can make it by six o'clock?" he asked.

"Oh. Hell yes," lied the hired man, for that meant ten to fifteen miles an hour, and the steam tractor that could do that speed for fifteen miles without breaking down or blowing up had not yet left the factory.

"It's a deal," said Stephen, handing him the ten dollars.

They climbed into the cab. The noise was deafening as the operator shifted gears and backed the tractor and turned it again and again until it was pointed down the road toward Livingston. Then he gave it full throttle and away it went. To the horses, cows, sheep, pigs, and chickens along the way it looked like a primeval predator. They scampered off pounds of prime horseflesh, beef, mutton, pork, and chicken as it passed by. One thing was for sure: no one could catch up with the Peerless Perfection Steam Tractor. Every time it crossed a bridge the rear wheel cleats picked up the planks and released them as kindling wood.

"Can we go faster?" asked Stephen as he scanned a long stretch of open road. He was not sure but what he could run faster.

"Shovel on more coal," suggested the hired hand.

The remittance man, his face turning black from coal dust, perspiration running down his face leaving a trail of white streaks, applied coal to the firebox with diligence. A veritable inferno raged inside.

The Peerless Perfection Steam Tractor gained speed. It went wheez-whoosh, wheez-whoosh, wheez-whoosh. The heavy steel wheels crunched as they ground gravel into dust.

"Shore hope it don't blow up," drawled the hired hand. "I warn't plannin' on goin' this fast."

Stephen kicked the fire door shut with a clang. "There's no danger, is there?"

"Hope not. When these babies burst, they shore do save funeral expenses. There ain't a piece of man left big enough to put in a lady's jewelry box."

The tractor surmounted a big, rounded boulder, then leaped ahead. "Wheeezzzzz, wheeezzz," it went. Fear struck Lord Billner's stalwart heart.

"Where's the pressure gauge?" he asked.

"Ain't none," replied the farmer, sticking his head outside, guiding the tractor like a hayseed Casey Jones. "Gad, look at her go! By golly, Limey, we must be makin' ten, twelve miles an hour. Ya-hooooooo!"

"Ya-hooooooo," Stephen repeated without enthusiasm. The Peerless Perfection Steam Tractor ascended a low ridge, then dipped down the other side at a speed of fifteen miles per hour. It clattered across another bridge, leaving kindling wood falling into the water. Supporting beams were all that was left of what was once the bridge's floor. And the minutes and the miles passed. Then the farm hand yelled "Ya-hooooo!" again. "There's Livingston," he shouted, "straight ahead."

"Thank God," sighed Stephen, looking at his watch: 5.47. The Peerless Perfection sped alongside the railroad tracks and was soon at the town limits. "We'll have ya' to the post office in a jiffy," the hired man announced, swerving, turning, and finally driving up an alley. Then he applied the brakes. As the machine slowed, the driver leaped out. "End of the line, Limey," he shouted. "If I was you, I'd get the hell out of here fast!" The hired hand disappeared, running, around the side of a barn.

Stephen, fearful of a blowing boiler, leaped off the hot, steaming, frothing mass of cast iron and steel and ran the other way, coming out onto Main Street. Two blocks up, he knew, was the post office. And toward it he ran, coatless, dirty, grimy, desperate, just as the chimes on the courthouse clock began striking six o'clock.

Then there was an explosion like the end of the world. Nuts and bolts and a six-hundred-pound steel cleated wheel landed in the middle of Main Street. Boiler plate clattered onto tin roofs. Horses whinnied and strained at the hitching posts. Several runaways dashed by. No matter to Lord Stephen Billner. As he ran up to the post office doorway he found the postmaster locking up hastily, anxious to join the crowd hurrying down the street to where the Peerless Perfection Steam Tractor was parked – once.

"Wait. Wait, sir."

"Closed."

"Sir, this is a matter of life and death," said Stephen as he ran alongside the postmaster, who was in shirtsleeves and open vest, heading for the explosion. "Is there a registered letter there?"

"Nope."

"From England. For a Stephen Billner, Esquire?"

"Stephen Billner?" the man said, puffing as he began to tire. "From London?"

"Yes. Yes. That's it. Is there a letter for him?"

"Was."

"Wh-what?"

"Was. Ten days were up. Returned it on the St. Paul Express this morning. What was that explosion, anyway?"

The postmaster was talking to himself, for Lord Stephen Billner stood still in the center of Main Street, far more fortunate than he realized. If the crowd had connected him with the blown-up Peerless Perfection, he might have been lynched.

Dejected, suddenly more tired that he could ever remember having been, stiff, sore, a shabby, stinking mess of young manhood whom even a self-respecting tramp would avoid, he wandered over to the Northern Pacific Railroad Depot. There he deposited himself in the gloomy waiting room. He sat down on one of the hard, shiny, varnished wooden benches, placed his elbows on his knees and his face in his hands.

Besides being dead tired and despicably dirty, Lord Stephen Billner realized that he was destitute save for the forty dollars in his wallet. Forty dollars and a run-down ranch. And even Prudence, dear, sweet Prudence: she was lost. He would not be there tonight to meet her at Artist's Point. And even if, when he did see her again – if he did – and even if she forgave him, what could he offer her? He was, let's face it, just another British remittance man. In Australia they called them Sundowners because they always appeared from nowhere for grub after the day's work was over; in Africa they slept under the stars on the Veldt, and in America they expired in the back rooms of saloons with rot-gut whiskey on their breaths. And he, Stephen Billner, was one of them. One of Albion's rejects.

The plump woman, perhaps forty, possibly fifty years old, sitting opposite him and down a few feet, eyed Stephen with intense curiosity. She was wearing a drab brown dress, a modest mass of feathers on her huge hat; at her side was an old carpetbag, well stuffed. She sniffed and made a face. Finally she could control her curiosity no longer. She cleared her throat.

"Hey, sonny. What was the big bang?" she asked in a coarse voice. She gazed at his clothing. "What in hell happened to you?"

Stephen raised his head and looked at her, and smiled wanly. "Nothing," he replied. He recupped his hands in his cheeks and gazed down again at the tobacco-stained floor. About the source of the bang, he gave no answer.

"You dress that way all the time? You smell that way all the time?"

He looked up again. "Sorry, ma'am. I'll move down."

"Never mind, dearie. Just don't come closer. Say – ain't I seen you somewhere before?" She peered at him in the dim light.

Stephen studied the woman, searching for identity. The piggish face, the peroxide blond curls sticking out from under her hat. "No, madam," he replied, though in fact he did think he had seen her somewhere before.

"You never frequented the Bucket of Blood – or the rooms upstairs, did you?"

"Once, just once, I had a drink at the Bucket of Blood," he replied, "but I never went upstairs."

Suddenly her face lit up. "I know where I saw you. You were runnin' to catch the Park Line train about five or six days ago."

Then Stephen remembered. Watching Rosie was one of the reasons he had almost missed the train. It was she who had chased Hezekiah out of the saloon. Then she had been in a state of undress. And painted. Could this woman be her? He gazed at her intently.

She smiled. Then she laughed aloud, and her whole body shook. "I guess I'm an exhibitionist at heart," she said. "I have no shame. That was me, sonny, half-dressed and with a lot of paint. Now," she added, "you see me with a lot of clothes and without the paint. "I'm Rosie O'Toole, late owner and madam of the Bucket of Blood Saloon and Sporting Rooms."

Stephen welcomed some diversion from his own woes. "Quite a change, I must say," he said, scanning her clothing. "Why are you here now?"

"Let's say I've had a business reversal, sonny," Rosie replied. "When the Congregationalists bring in a 'noted Preacher from Boston' at the same time the Baptists offer a fire-eatin' evangelist, sin is in for a hard time. I saw it comin'. On Sunday they raved and ranted against demon rum and on Monday night it was the dangers of 'unclean vessels' – namely, soiled doves – and by Tuesday night they had learned that the men of this town – some of its finest citizens, I tell you – frequented my grog shop on the first floor and occasionally had doin's with 'unclean vessels' on the second. Well, sonny, I knew the boom was about to be lowered. I knew that church was out."

"Too bad," commented Stephen absentmindedly.

Rosie sighed. "Not so bad," she said wistfully. "I'm tired of being an administrator. Taking care of the girls. Keeping the peace among them. So – well, I saw it comin' and I sold out." She sniffed, choked back a sob, obtained a handkerchief from an enormous purse and blew her nose loudly. "You know," she went on, "sporting houses are different out West. We serve a purpose. All those lonesome men comin' from the mines and ranches and railroads, and from the Cavalry at Fort Yellowstone, and not one woman for ten men in the whole damned State of Montana. Most of my girls restricted themselves to a clientele of just eight or ten men. My girls weren't really whores."

"I see."

Rosie sniffed again. "Now I've bade them all good-bye. Violet married Hank McGinnis and is livin' up at Emigrant, and Lurlee is out at the Three-Bar-X Ranch and is probably gonna marry the foreman. The other girls took the train for Seattle. She sniffed once more, blew her nose again and just like that changed emotions. "Anyway," she announced, business-like, "I sold the Bucket of Blood Saloon and Rooms for $5,000. Now, so help me, I'm goin' legit. Genteel. I'm gonna be a lady, by Gawd."

"You – certainly – look like a lady," Stephen lied, though observing real improvement wrought by the dowdy dowager's clothes and the lack of paint.

"I'm goin' to open a legitimate boarding house."

"Good idea."

"Right here in Livingston. Cater to invalids and tourists."

"Excellent."

"I have a husband, you know. Well, almost."

"Oh?"

"You know him. The stage driver, Hezekiah Hotchkiss. The man I – er – ordered out of the saloon."

"Hezekiah Hotchkiss is you husband?"

"Well, he should be. Poor dear. Poor, long-suffering Hezekiah. Long years ago he hit it rich in a mine, and he gave me $5,000 on my promise to marry him. He's still tryin' to collect. I – ah – I was once a damned pretty filly, you know," she added, patting her hair.

"So that's why you and he were—"

"Yes, that's why. He comes down occasionally to collect interest and plea for the principle. Now I've changed my mind. I need a steady man around to prove to the townspeople that I'm legit. Wish I could stay here until Hezekiah comes down from the Park, but those preachers make me uneasy. I'm going up to Helena for a couple weeks until they've left and the town has gone to hell again."

"Might not be a bad idea."

She looked at Stephen thoughtfully. "Now, dearie, how about telling me just exactly what the hell happened to you?"

"I lost track of time and was in the Park and my remittance check was sent back to England before I could get to the post office here to claim it."

"A remittance man, huh?"

"As of today, an ex-remittance man."

"Girl trouble? Back in England?"

Stephen nodded. "Only trouble is, if they ever bother to figure back nine months from the birth, they'll discover that I was three hundred miles away in Scotland. And I've never heard of a girl getting in the family way by letter."

"Hmm. Who were you protecting?"

"My brother. The first born. So here am I."

"And no more remittance?"

"No more remittance."

"Flat broke?"

"Just about. I've forty dollars and a run-down ranch."

"Where?"

"About fifteen or twenty miles up the Yellowstone in Paradise Valley."

"In Paradise Valley? That's beautiful country."

Thoughtfully, the young man looked at Rosie. "Yes," he replied, "it is. And the hay is about ready for cutting."

"Sure. I hear the price of hay is up this year. You'll make out all right."

"But the place is an awful mess. I haven't been there for three weeks. I had to escort some English rotters – young fellows sent out from England to live at the ranch and dry out – all at my expense – to St. Paul and make sure they were safely on their way home. And the ranch – fences are down, ditches clogged up, house dirty..."

"It could be cleaned up."

"Yes. I suppose so."

Silence ensued for a few minutes. The old railroad clock ticked away in the dispatcher's office. They could hear the staccato sounds of the telegraph.

"I could help you," said Rosie.

"You?"

"Oh, don't be so shocked. Don't be a prude, young man. I've been a madam, not a whore. I need a place to stay until I can see Hezekiah. How about puttin' me up at your place for a few days in exchange for housekeeping?" She glanced critically at his clothing, and sniffed. "I can do laundry, too," she added.

That is how it came about that Stephen Billner, former remittance man, rented a hack, loaded it with groceries and supplies from the Bucket of Blood's pantry (the new owner not due for a week), and, with Rosie's belongings and Rosie herself, headed for the Billner ranch that evening of August 20, 1909. It took some time getting home because for the first fifteen miles all the bridges were out, and they had to ford one brook after another. But they arrived in time for Rosie to make the beds in two bedrooms while Stephen got in firewood for a cookstove on which Rosie prepared a good meal for a hungry, but tired, young man.

It was from the events of August 20, 1909, that Stephen Billner ever after marked the beginning of his redemption.

## VII

Things were nice at the big, sprawling Canyon Hotel, and the young girl had made the most of them. She had enjoyed the luxury of a hot bath and an untroubled afternoon nap on a cool bed, while in the offing were prospects of a nice meal in the dining room, followed by a meeting at Artist's Point with her lover. Prudence had decided that Daddy simply couldn't reject Lord Billner's request for her hand.

She lay on the bed in fresh cotton drawers with pink lace hems. They were the ones she had lost at Bath Lake and Stephen had returned to her that thrilling evening when they had taken their Adam and Eve bath in the hot spring. Above her waist Prudence wore a loose white cotton vest with eyelets in it and little pink bows here and there. Her golden tresses, thoroughly washed with her bath, were dry now. They spilled down onto the white sheet like a golden waterfall, in waves and curls and a few ringlets. They created a shining halo around her face as she lay on her back, staring at the ceiling. Her sky-blue eyes sparkled and her rosy lips were carved into a position of near laughter just for the joy of life. To be nineteen, to be pretty, and sweet smelling, and in love – and to be loved – no wonder she wore a perpetual half smile.

There was a knock at the door. "It's me, Madeline. Open up." The girl bounced out of bed and to the door. "Come on, young lady," Madeline ordered as she entered, "dinner's at six and it's quarter of now. Get dressed."

"Oh, Aunt Madeline. Must you be so curt with me?"

Madeline raised her head defiantly and straightened her straight back still more. "I don't know what you are talking about," she answered.

Prudence started to say something, then changed her mind. Instead she walked to the closet where, with her back to her aunt, she exchanged the eyelet vest for a stiff corset with whalebone stays. "Will you help me lace up?" she asked.

Madeline stepped to the closet and began lacing up her niece's corset. She noticed that Prudence took a deep breath. Then the girl said, "I know why you're so up tight. It's the Captain. He hasn't got in touch with you, has he?"

At first Madeline was going to reprimand Prudence and tell her it was none of her business, but something stopped her. The young lady was in love. Even though Madeline saw her as a child, she really was a young woman. Almost before she realized it, Madeline replied, "No, Prudence. He hasn't. And he has to know that we are here. Mrs. Griffin said he was ordered here. Wouldn't you think he would have left a message?"

Prudence turned her head to Madeline. "You forget that the entire Troop was called out, first to chase that old bear that disrupted us last night, and then to intercept the automobile that got away."

"Yes, I did hear about that."

"So maybe Captain Taylor's plans were so disrupted that he just didn't have time, Madeline. I wouldn't give up."

Just as she tied the corset string Madeline stifled a sob, but not quite well enough. Prudence heard her. She turned to her aunt and for the first time ever put her arms around Madeline. Always before it had been Madeline comforting Prudence. "I think the Captain is a good man," she said. "Not as good as Stephen, but a good man."

This stopped Madeline's sobs. "What?" she asked.

"Oh, Madeline. Stephen is so fine." Then she looked her aunt directly in the face and whispered, "You know we're going to get married, don't you?"

Madeline's expression changed abruptly. "No," she responded, for she had no idea that their short relationship has reached such a stage. "That's impossible. I'll not hear of it."

"Now, Aunt Madeline. Stephen Billner is asking Daddy for my hand this afternoon. That's why he got off the coach to fish with Daddy and that sloppy old Congressman." Her eyes grew misty. "Daddy won't turn him down, will he, Aunt Madeline? My happiness, my whole life is at stake. Daddy won't make me return to Elm Grove where everyone points at me and says, 'there's the girl whose bust developer got stuck on one of her pretties!' and I'll have to spend the rest of my life as a shamed woman and maybe become a schoolmarm like—" she stopped, placing a hand to her mouth.

"Like me, Prudence?"

"Oh, no, Aunt Madeline. Not like you!" she protested, hugging her aunt tighter.

Madeline wisely dropped the subject. "Young lady," she said, "you can't go to dinner in a corset and drawers. You'd better finish getting dressed."

In the first five days Prudence had worn just two skirts, and a frilly blouse or a little sailor middy above. She had worn cotton stockings and walking shoes. She had one change of clothing left. It was her Sunday best, from shoes to hat. Mother had told her she would have no use for it, but discovering a little extra space in her luggage, she had carefully packed it away, and a little straw hat and a white parasol to boot. Upon arrival at Canyon she had unpacked the dress and hung it up to get it free of wrinkles. Now she proceeded to put it on.

242

First she put on a taffeta corset cover and a petticoat. Then came the stylish white linen dress that fit her like a second skin. It buttoned all the way from shoulder to hem; at the neck she wore a light blue embroidered yoke that contrasted nicely with her pretty face. She put up her hair in a stylish, massive pile, and placed a slightly crushed straw hat on it – crushed because she was not supposed to have taken it along. It was full of artificial red, white, pink and blue flowers. She punched a six-inch hat pin through it to keep it in place. She put on expensive silk hose and little high-button shoes with bold inch-and-a-half heels. On her hands she pulled on snowy white gloves. Her costume was completed with a white, frilly, totally useless parasol. Using the mirror she set the hat just right, appraised her image, and announced that she was ready to leave.

Madeline, sitting on the bed waiting for her, reflected that Prudence's outfit was certainly nothing to go walking the canyon trails in, although she conceded that her niece was indescribably beautiful, the dress accentuating her curves, the fullness and roundness of her young body. Small wonder the Englishman was attracted to her. Prudence was a young goddess, a vestal virgin, compared to most of the women, young or otherwise, observed on this trip.

Dinner in the huge, rustic dining room with its enormous fireplace (and ludicrously small fire) was strained. The last vestiges of sunlight crept through the windows and mixed with the yellowish electric lights, creating a mood neither joyous nor sad. People talked quietly. The Snowden table was particularly quiet because no men were there, unless Rusty be considered a man. Even he was unusually quiet, not at all like himself.

Not that they were worried about Congressman Griffin or Philip or Lord Billner. Both Dolly Griffin and Emily Snowden knew from long experience what happens to men when the fish are biting. Yet being unworried was not quite the same as being pleased with their husbands' absence. In the balance, they would have preferred having them there.

"I'd like to hear the campfire lecture tonight," said Emily, "but I'm not sure I want to attend without Philip."

"Oh, a pox upon the men," replied Dolly. "We are going to hear the lecture, Emily. And so is Madeline and you, too, Prudence. After all, we women are not exactly incapable of action when our men folks are not around."

Dolly's persuasion won the day. When they returned to their rooms Emily left a note for Philip, explaining where they had gone, and within a few minutes the ladies and Rusty were ready to go. All, that is, save Prudence.

"A headache, mother. And – I feel – kind of faint." She sat on the bed and weaved back and forth, waving a fan in front of her face vigorously. Then she lay down and allowed her mother to fetch a damp cloth for her forehead. "You go on, Mother," said Prudence weakly. "I'll be all right."

"No, dear. I'm staying with you."

Prudence caught her breath. "Oh, no, Mother. I'll be all right."

"I don't really want to go anyway, without Philip," said Emily.

"But you said you did want to go, Mother."

"I was just making conversation, dear. Does the damp cloth help? Is it time-of-the-month?"

Exasperated, Prudence became tearful. "No, it isn't time-of-the-month, Mother. That was ten days ago. I'm just – tired, I guess. Leave me alone here to rest, Mother. I'll be all right."

Emily looked down upon her lovely daughter, concerned about her, puzzled at her actions. But when Dolly Griffin knocked, Emily decided, rather apprehensively, to go on. "Now you just rest, dear," she said soothingly. "I'll not be long. And Daddy should be home soon."

She was dozing off, or so it seemed, as Emily switched off the light and closed the door. "Strange," she commented to Dolly Griffin. "Prudence almost never gets sick."

"Hmm," replied Dolly. "Did you lock her in?"

"What?"

"Please, don't be offended, my dear. Feigning illness is as old as Adam and Eve. Are you sure Prudence doesn't have other plans for the evening?"

Emily glared at the Congressman's pudgy wife. "Mrs. Griffin," she replied sternly, "I'll have you know that my Prudence does not make a habit of deception."

"Of course not."

"I mean it, Mrs. Talmadge Griffin. Prudence is pure as the driven snow. And sweet. And good. I will not tolerate allusions reflecting upon her character." Strange how Emily had forgotten certain deceptions and white lies when Philip was courting her.

"My apologies, Emily. My sincere apologies. Now please – let us be friends and enjoy the lecture. Someone is going to speak on the subject of how the Grand Canyon was made." She began to smirk at what she had just said, but stifled the impulse. Down the stairs and out through the lobby and into the open, Mrs. Snowden, Mrs. Griffin, Miss Madeline Snowden, and a tarrying red-headed lad named Rusty made their way.

The group had barely started down the stairs when there was activity in the bedroom. Prudence bounced up, switched on the light and set to work getting her hair once again in place, putting on her hat again, examining herself in the mirror. She waited for what seemed an eternity, until she was sure Mother and Madeline and Rusty and that gadfly Mrs. Griffin were well on their way. Then she left the room. She walked stately, lovely, and confidently down the impressive stairway, quite aware of admiring eyes following her every move; then like a young fawn she fairly glided across the lobby. Half of her liaison had already been arranged. She was to send a bellboy to the stables to tell Hezekiah she was ready. He, with a horse and buggy waiting, was to trot up to the north end of the verandah, where she would meet him. So romantically inclined was he that he had refused to accept her dollar, saying something about going in that direction anyway. What he had forgotten, and would not remember for another few hours, was his promise to meet Rusty and get the elk antlers.

Prudence dispatched the bellboy, then slowly promenaded down the long verandah past oldsters and middle-aged couples where the roving eye put the kabosh to theories about declining virility. She distinctly heard a feminine voice say, "Walter, you're staring," and another, "Fred, it's time for us to go in now." Prudence tapped her fluffy little white parasol on the verandah floor, and hummed a gay little tune, and smiled prettily at everyone she saw. Was she aware of her beauty?

She timed it just right. Hardly had she reached the steps at the north end when up through the gloaming clattered a prim, black, one-seated buggy. It was pulled by a sleek bay horse, with Hezekiah, attired as usual in his campaign hat, linen duster, and black whip leather gloves, sitting on the right side. He brought the buggy to a stop at just the right place and would have jumped out to help his young passenger except that she was already stepping into it.

"Thank goodness you came, Hezekiah," she said as she gave him a gloved hand to help her onto the seat. "This is the most important evening of my life." She sat down beside him. "To Artist's Point, you know. That's where I'm supposed to meet Stephen."

"Giddyap," ordered Hezekiah as the horse leaped ahead; they were off at a brisk trot. "Meet who, Miss Snowden?" he asked, as if he did not know.

"Oh, Hezekiah, you know. Stephen – Lord Billner."

"Oh, him."

She studied his bewhiskered face. "Hezekiah, you know it's him."

He removed his pipe from his mouth, turned to the blue-eyed girl beside him. "Yep, Miss Prudence. I reckon I'm aware."

She hardly noticed as they clattered over the Chittenden Bridge. "He's going to be my husband," she said quietly, hands deep in her lap. "And Hezekiah, you've got to come to the ranch and have Sunday dinner with us. 'Cause I'll probably be kind of lonely there for a while."

"Eat with you and Lord Billner, eh?"

"Yes. Oh, Hezekiah, I can cook. I love to cook. I can bake bread and cakes and pies and fix a roast and fry steak and poach eggs and put up preserves. I'm a real good cook. Everybody says I am."

He glanced at the beauty beside him, then looked straight ahead. "Well, I'll be derned," he said.

"You'll what?"

"I'll be – why, of course I'll come and eat with you and Stephen, Miss Prudence."

Now the road led through a forest of dark pines, and the girl shivered in her thin linen suit. "It's chilly," she commented.

"Always like this in the evenings," he said. "You should have taken a coat."

"Mmm. He'll keep me warm."

Hezekiah was about to say something else when the horse shied, then whinnied. Curious as to what the horse had seen, or smelled, or sensed the presence of, the mountaineer scanned the woods, but saw nothing. He horse and buggy clattered on down the road.

"It's lonely here, isn't it?" said the girl.

"Will be till the moon comes up, and since it's on the wane, that won't be fer a while yet. There'll be people who want to see the falls and canyon by the light of the moon. But right now, you're right, Miss Prudence, it's dark and lonely."

"I'm glad. I don't want a lot of people around."

"Now, you look here, Miss Snowden. I ain't a party to anything illegal or immoral. You be a good girl."

"Oh, Hezekiah, of course."

He turned to her in the blackening dusk, could smell the faint odor of lilacs about her, hearkening his memories back to some incident of his own youth. "I mean it, young lady. You are not to do anything your daddy or mother would disapprove of. You promise me or else we turn around right now."

She pouted. "Oh, Hezekiah. Of course I promise. I don't think you understand. Stephen was going to ask Daddy for my hand this afternoon while they were fishing. I'm supposed to meet him here and he'll have the news." Her eyes grew misty. "Please believe me, Hezekiah. I don't think that Daddy would – ever refuse to let someone as nice as Stephen marry me. Do you?"

He did not answer, but puffed on his pipe and at one time glanced at her and gave her a reassuring wink. The buggy clattered on for a few minutes and then he said, "Well, here we are, young lady," and sure enough, the road widened into a big horseshoe which marked their destination. "Whoaaaaa." The horse slowed as they approached a surrey and another buggy parked at the hitching rail. Voices could be heard. Yet the whinnying of horses, the distant voices, even Hezekiah's puffs on his pipe, only punctuated the stillness, the dark woods, the stars appearing overhead, and the fading gold of the vanishing daylight to the northwest.

Hezekiah removed his pipe and with the stem pointed to the trail. "It leads to Artist's Point," he said. She could make out a distinct trail leading down through dark pines. "It's just a short walk to the lookout."

"I see it, Hezekiah," said the girl, rising and climbing down before he could help her. "And thank you. Thank you a million times over," she added, "and remember, Hezekiah. Sunday dinner just as soon as Stephen and I are married."

"Miss Prudence," said Hezekiah seriously, looking around, "I don't rightly think I should leave you here alone."

"Alone? Oh, bosh. I'll bet Stephen rented that horse and buggy and he's up there waiting for me right now." She ran on her toes toward the opening in the woods that marked the trail. "Thank you, Hezekiah. Bye."

He watched the whiteness of her dress until it disappeared in the darkness, lit his pipe, and puffed on it for a few minutes. Hezekiah was undecided. True, there wasn't much crime in Yellowstone. Still, he didn't like leaving her here. Then the horse hitched to the surrey whinnied and the horse hitched to the buggy stomped its feet. They reminded him that there were other people at the overlook, and that probably more were coming. He decided he was worrying about nothing.

"Tich, tich, tich," he said to the horse. "Giddyap." The bay completed the horseshoe and trotted back down the road. He had not passed far down the narrow stretch where the pines nearly enclosed the road, when the horse again shied and whinnied, just as it had coming up. The mountaineer squinted and peered into the woods, wondering what it was that had frightened his horse again – but he saw nothing and kept on going.

But Hezekiah did not return to Canyon Inn. About halfway back he spied the opening in the trees. The bay resisted when he tugged at the reins and directed her to leave the road and plunge into the dark woods. Then her animal eyes perceived the vaguest signs of a path. She reluctantly trotted through the grass, the pines brushing both sides of the buggy, until the trail ended abruptly. Hezekiah jumped down and tied the bay to a tree. He drew a pack from under the seat and set out, hiking easterly through the woods. The way he walked indicated that Hezekiah knew exactly where he was going. Soon, by dead reckoning, he was plunging through thick forest. Suddenly the forest ended and a narrow chasm appeared in front of him. The trickle of water could be heard. He'd found the place. "Hey, Lem," he shouted as he peered into the darkness, barely making out the sluice box and the little cabin nestled against a cliff. He started down.

Meanwhile Prudence hurried down the trail that ended at rough steps which she gingerly descended in her high heels until she emerged at the railed deck which constituted Artist's Point. For a few moments she gasped at the Grand Canyon and the Falls, beautiful under the starry sky. She thought she saw a tall form like Stephen's at the railing. She started toward it when she saw beside it the outline of a woman's hat. It was a tall man, all right, with a young woman close to him. She spied two other couples, but they were older. She could hear the two men discussing the potentialities in harnessing the Falls for hydroelectric power. Certainly no romance there. And the girl, embarrassed when she realized all three couples had turned to her, quietly walked to the railing and gazed at the foaming Falls, the white water, the Canyon's dim, ghostly yellow walls. She gazed, but did not see. Where was Stephen?

Minutes ticked by. The burnished orange glow that was left of the sunset quickly disappeared, and because the moon had not yet risen, the darkness deepened. First the two middle-aged couples left, still talking of hydroelectric possibilities. A few minutes later Prudence heard the diminishing talk of the young couple, and then they were gone. She was alone. Where, she thought, where oh where could Stephen be? A cold gust of wind blew down the Canyon, and the girl shivered, sweeping her hands up and down her arms to raise the circulation. And the minutes went by.

Finally Prudence decided that Stephen might not know of the trail. He might be waiting for her at the big horseshoe where the horses were tethered. So she started back up the trail, up the steps and through the pitch black pines. Only the wind, whirring softly through the trees, could be heard. She could see the star-flecked sky above, and some of the lightly colored rocks marking the sides of the trail. She was shivering all over now, and fear began to take hold. It was so lonely and dark. Where was Stephen?

She was halfway up the trail when, pausing and looking up to see where she should go, she sighted, silhouetted against the star-flecked sky, the dark outline of the upper half of a man. He was wearing a big cowboy hat and his torso was long and thin. In her concentration, she started on up the trail, fell over a root, not hard but enough to dirty her linen white suit. She stood up, said "Oh, gee," out loud, brushed herself off, and went on, inadvertently leaving her parasol by the side of the trail. When she looked up again there was no silhouette. The man had disappeared – or had he been an apparition, a figment of her imagination?'

Fear took hold. The way to the road – the only way – led up the trail past where she had seen the man. Should she go on or run back to the Point? Prudence placed a small fist to her mouth to stave off a scream, for panic and hysteria were welling up in her.

"Get yourself together," the girl told herself. "Get yourself together, Prudence. There was no one there. You just thought you saw someone. This is Yellowstone. You are safe here."

Her legs felt like lead as the girl forced herself on up the trail. As she advanced she gained confidence. She began humming a tuneless melody, when suddenly the sound of a rock falling down the mountainside, not above her, but to her side, stopped her. Terrified, she screamed "Stephen! Stephen! Is that you?"

Then from behind a gloved hand clasped tightly over her mouth, a strong arm wrapped around her waist pinning her arms to her body so tightly the girl could not struggle, and a whistling sound came from behind and above her. "No use struggling, pretty one. How lucky can I get – your comin' right past my camp down the road. Come on, now. You and me are headin' for my cabin in the Grand Tetons. And a long winter."

The girl's eyed showed her terror. The highwayman! The bandit! The holdup man with the silver disk in his throat!

## VIII

At the campfire lecture Rusty Snowden sat squeezed between the matronly hips of his mother and the girlish ones of Aunt Madeline. A geologist was droning on about the power of water, and ice, and glaciers, and of a canyon cut not once but three times in the same place. "Think of it," the scientist kept saying. "Think of it" constituted most of his lecture.

The red-headed lad squeezed between the stayed, corseted walls of mature femininity was thinking, all right. The intensity with which Rusty appeared to be listening led Emily to wonder if Rusty might want to be a geologist – and how proud of him she would be. She had never seen him sit so still, and be so well behaved under such circumstances. Dreamily she pictured her grown son discussing some newly discovered fossilized fish – *Mackerel Silverian Snowdenis* – and for all time to come her son would be remembered in geology books. And oh! She would be so proud. To be the mother of a great man! She glanced down at the tousled red hair, the freckled face. She sighed. To think that such a creature as a pesty boy could grow up to be such a man! Would miracles never cease? Rusty wondered why his mother placed an arm around his shoulders and squeezed gently. He wasn't even cold.

Of course, he was thinking. He was thinking of how he could break out of that corseted prison and find Hezekiah and go with him to get the elk antlers. Hezekiah had promised – but then, maybe, he had sort of forgotten. Anyway, Rusty knew that he would have to find Hezekiah; Hezekiah was sure as shootin' not goin' to come lookin' for him. "Darnitall," the boy said to himself, "I want those antlers."

He had contemplated feigning sickness, but then his sister had to spoil that ruse by using it for herself. He could have protested being cold, but his mother had wisely made him put on his coat. How, oh how could he get away from these women and find Hezekiah and get his antlers?

The lad wiggled enough to get his hands into his pockets. In one of them his fingers curled around his last-jawbreaker – the one his father had not found and thrown away. While it was still in his pocket the boy brushed off the dirt he could feel sticking to it. Then, when the geologist again said "Think of it" and pointed to a big chart mounted on a tripod, and the women leaned forward the better to see it, Rusty popped the candy into his mouth. He sucked it quietly as the ladies brought their sitting postures back to normal.

'Now is the time,' he thought. Rusty made his eyes as big as big marbles and held his breath until his face was livid red. Then he tapped Emily's shoulder and Madeline's too, and squirmed as if in agony, and he pointed to his mouth.

"Goodness!" cried Emily.

"What is it, Rusty?" asked Madeline.

No words, but a terrifying gurgling. "He's suffocating" cried Emily as she slapped his back. Nothing happened. The boy's face turned purplish.

"By gadfrey, let me at him," came an authoritative voice from behind. A big man with a gray beard stood up, swung down and picked up the boy, whirled him upside down and held him by the ankles. Rusty hadn't counted on this. He quickly decided the show was over and let the jawbreaker shoot from his mouth like a bullet.

"There," announced the man as a crowd assembled and the geologist kept saying "Think of it!"

"Oh, Rusty, dear, are you all right?" asked his mother, hugging his face to her soft bosom, much to the lad's embarrassment. He had been weaned ten years ago and had not yet reached the second stage of male appreciation.

"Rusty," Madeline reprimanded him. "You promised your father you would buy no more jawbreakers."

"This one was left over," explained the boy meekly as people returned to their seats. This included the big man, who received thank yous from Emily and Madeline, and compliments from others in the audience. Rusty promised him he would never suck a jawbreaker again.

"Mother," Rusty asked meekly. "Can I go back to the hotel?"

"But Rusty," she whispered, "don't you want to hear the rest of the lecture?"

"Oh, let him go, Emily," advised Madeline. "You go straight back to the hotel, young man, and straight to bed. You can get the key at the desk. Ask for room 337. Have you got that, Rusty? Room 337."

"Oh, all right," said Emily. "Straight to your room, young man. You do just as Aunt Madeline said. And your father is going to hear of this when he returns from fishing."

"Yes, Mother," the boy replied – rather too meekly, she thought.

"Think of it," was the last he heard from the lecturer.

Fast as his legs could carry him Rusty ran to the hotel, got the key, ran to the room, crossed into the adjoining room that was his, fetched his secret weapon, and was downstairs, across the lobby, and out again, leaving the key in the lock. He ran onto the verandah and was down the steps and headed for the stables as fast as his legs could carry him. "Hezekiah," the boy shouted breathlessly. When no one replied he asked the stable boys. "Mr. Hotchkiss? Where is he?"

"Hotchkiss? He took a buggy out oh, half or three-quarters of an hour ago. Said he was taking a party to Artist's Point."

"Which way is that?"

"Straight down the road, round the curve, 'cross the bridge. Why?"

But the boy was on his way. He ran down the dark road and rounded the curve and clattered across the bridge. He darted up the dark, narrow road, noticing the bright halo in the east that marked the moonrise. As he progressed away from the river the stillness grew oppressive. "Mr. Hotchkiss," the boy shouted, clutching the packaged secret weapon and refusing to give up and return to the hotel even though he was frightened. "Mr. Hezekiah Hotchkiss. Where are you?" The breeze whirred through the pines. The boy passed the narrow pathway down which the mountaineer had guided the horse and buggy. He did not hear or see a thing. "Mr. Hotchkiss. You promised. You said you'd take me to get my elk antlers tonight."

There was no reply, but the wide-eyed boy would not give up. He kept walking, crunch, crunch, crunch, and soon came to the big horseshoe-shaped end of the road. He had not shouted for Hezekiah for a few minutes, and it was a good thing. As he approached the end of the road he heard voices. He did! Like a woman pleading, and frightened, and the husky voice of an angry man. Rusty stepped into the trees at the side of the road. Through the darkness he watched a tall figure coming down the road, half dragging, half carrying a ghostly figure in white. "Please! Please let me go!"

"Shut up. Keep quiet and you won't get hurt. You scream once and I'll slam you mouth so you'll not open it again for a week. It's up to you, girlie!"

It was Prudence, his sister. Rusty opened his mouth to shout, then thought better of it as he watched the two figures disappear into the trees not far from where he was hiding. "My hat! My clothes!" he heard his sister plead. "To hell with 'em. There's a trail up here and you'll make it all right. Now hustle."

Rusty heard the sounds getting weaker as they disappeared into the pines. He looked all around, wondering what to do, where he could get help. But no one was in sight. For moments he acted like a frightened dog, running from one side of the road to another. Then his eyes fell on some cloth caught on a pine branch, and he ran to it. It was Prudence's hat. Rusty stared into the trees and by the light of the rising moon made out a faint trail. The boy, his heart beating mightily, determined to follow it.

Action gave Rusty confidence. Soon he could hear footsteps ahead, the man commanding the girl to move faster, the girl sobbing, pleading, protesting. At one place Rusty found most of Prudence's white linen dress, for the bandit had tired of her protests about it slowing her down and had forthwith torn it from her. White drawers, a taffeta corset cover and a petticoat still covered the girl as she traveled faster without the impediment of a hobble skirt. She had lost the heels to her shoes. Finally they reached a grassy space where the moon shed its soft light through the opening in the trees. The highwayman, sucking in air, gave a sigh and let Prudence fall in a heap, sobbing, her hair disheveled.

From a pocket he pulled a dirty bandanna handkerchief which he brutally wrapped around her mouth and tied behind her head. Then he grabbed a strip of rawhide from another pocket and tied her hands behind her back; he wrapped the rest of the cord around a tree and tied it securely. She was propped, sitting up against the tree.

"Ye'll stay here quiet-like while I fetch my horse, won't ye, my pretty one?" He said, kneeling close to her. She could see the silver disk in his throat, the black stubble of a beard, the tobacco-stained teeth and the odor of whiskey on his breath. "Honey," he said quietly, "I ain't goin' to hurt ye. You should feel complimented. Know where I'm takin' ye? We're goin' down an old Injun trail all the way to my cozy little hideout in the Tetons. There you and me are gonna spend the winter. Just the two of us. Heh, heh. You should be right complimented. Most gals I won't look at twice. But you – you're purty as a picture." A gnarled hand stroked her drawers above her knees. Prudence quickly moved her legs. "Not now," he said. "We got to get out 'o here now. But ye'll come around."

The bandit laughed as he stood up. "I'm just goin' back to where my horse is tethered. Won't take me ten minutes. You will wait, won't you?" He laughed as he turned and walked into the woods.

Prudence watched as the tall figure disappeared. She struggled with the cord. And then Rusty appeared. Prudence couldn't believe it. Never had she loved her brother so much. He put down his packaged secret weapon, quickly untied the bandanna and with his knife cut the leather cord. The girl hugged her little brother and kissed his freckled cheeks, but then they heard the unmistakable sounds of a horse stomping through the woods. "Come on," said Rusty. He did not need to say it twice. "Let's get out of here." He picked up his package and they started running.

Without thinking, they crashed through the woods opposite the way they had come. Prudence's petticoat caught on a limb and would not let go. "Come on," Rusty urged. "Tear it." Meanwhile the highwayman had returned and found his "purty one" gone. "I'll get ye and ye'll regret it, purty one," he shouted into the forest as he tethered his horse. Hearing him, Prudence tore off the petticoat and followed Rusty.

"Where are we?" she asked

"Just follow me," said Rusty, sounding much older than his eleven years. "We'll find something."

The boy thought he was headed for the road, but he was completely turned around and in fact was heading eastward onto the wild and untrod forest between Canyon and the Lake, east of the Yellowstone River. The boy was adept at climbing over logs, jumping down from rocks and leaping small streams, but Prudence was not. Even though relieved of her dress and petticoat, and the heels broken off her shoes, she could barely keep up. Behind them, crashing noisily through the woods, swearing and yelling, came the maddened bandit. "I'll get ye," he shouted. "And when I get ye, I just think we'll have a little marriage here and now. Ye can't get away in this jackstraw forest."

"Rusty, I've got to stop," pleaded the girl.

Hastily Rusty glanced around and saw, bathed in the moonlight, a large pile of boulders nearby. "Come on over here, sis," he directed her, holding his sister's arm. They crawled under a huge boulder. There they huddled, hoping that the bandit would not find them. They saw him appear at the edge of the timber.

"So there you are," he said. "Ye may as well come out. We've got some settlin' to do."

"Oh, Rusty!" whispered Prudence, terrified.

Rusty moved, and as he did, his package rustled. "My secret weapon," he whispered. "Hezekiah said if I was ever in danger to use it."

Quickly he tore off the wrapping, not bothering with the noise as his terrified sister watched. The bandit strode towards them. She gasped again when she saw the secret weapon – her hated Bust Developer! "I thought it was your hatchet," she said.

Rusty ignored her, but pulled out the handle and pushed it in with all his might.

"OooooooooooOOOOOooooo," it shrieked out over the night air – a shrill, piercing cry that ended in a moan. Again and again he forced down the handle. Even the highwayman stopped, puzzled at the weird sound.

Close by, unbeknownst to either hunter or hunted, was a strange geologic formation. It consisted of two narrow box canyons that merged a few hundred feet below the rocks where Prudence and Rusty had taken refuge. Small streams flowed from both canyons, but the one on the right, the one closest to Prudence and Rusty, was the more secluded. In that canyon was a sluice box and hidden just above it at the head of the canyon, in a bower, almost imperceptible to anyone more than a few feet away, lay a cabin. And there, collecting gold dust accumulated over several weeks, was a mountaineer named Lem. With him, just arrived, was his partner in subversive Park operations, Hezekiah Hotchkiss.

"My Gawd, Hezekiah. What the hell is that sound?" Lem asked.

The two men listened carefully as the sound came again.

"Good Gawd, Lem. That's Rusty's secret weapon. Either that or a bull buffalo that is mighty eager."

"Who's Rusty?" asked Lem.

"He's the kid with the party I'm takin' through the Park on the *Shoshone Belle*," replied Hezekiah. "Come on."

Quickly the two mountaineers climbed down the hidden canyon and peered through the darkness, in the direction from which the sound had come. "OOOOOooooooooooOOOOO," it came again.

Hezekiah cupped his hands. "Rusty!" he shouted. "Where are you?"

"It's Hezekiah," said Rusty. "I just knew he was around here somewhere. Come on, sis. Let's go." As they emerged from the rocks the boy yelled, "We're up here!"

The highwayman had paused, but the sounds of other voices failed to deter him. "I'm not afeerd of Hotchkiss," he hissed. "So that kid freed ya, huh? Jest wait till I get my hands on him." But the brother and sister did not reply. Instead they crawled out of their hiding place and began running away from their pursuer, only to come up to the canyon. They scrambled down the steep walls until they came to a sheer drop, about ten feet to the bottom.

"We've got to jump, sis. Jump," urged Rusty, immediately jumping and landing on his feet. He looked up at her. "Sis, hurry. Before he catches you!"

Prudence hesitated, turned around to see the highwayman coming behind her, heard the whistle as he breathed. She jumped, landed correctly on her two feet and fell on her seat. "Ouch," she groaned as Rusty pulled her up and the two started up the narrow canyon. They ran by the sluice box, heard the water, and then stopped. Bathed in the moonlight, hunting and mining paraphernalia tossed here and there, was a tiny cabin.

"A cabin?" said Prudence, surprised.

They heard sounds of rocks tumbling, and realized the highwayman was approaching. "Come on, sis, let's go in and lock the door behind us."

The door squeaked loudly as it opened. The warm air, the odors of coffee and sizzling meat, and of boots and leather, and a pungent odor a bit like a butcher shop, greeted them. Moonlight bathed part of the insides dimly, through a single four-pane window.

"Ohmigosh," commented Rusty as he closed the door. "It doesn't have a lock."

"Then let's block it with a chair," suggested Prudence.

"What chairs?" asked Rusty as the two peered at the cabin's furniture. An empty soap box and a tree stump about two feet high had served that purpose.

The two heard booted steps outside, and instinctively walked to the back wall. "Rusty," whimpered Prudence, "we're cornered." She pressed her back to the wall – and fell backwards as it gave way. Rusty stumbled after her. As they sat on the floor the wall closed behind them. "Gosh," said Rusty, "it's a secret door." They stood up and leaned facing the closed opening.

They heard the front door hinges creak; they heard the highwayman step inside.

"I know yer in here," he said. "Come on, purty one. Ye got me all wrong, ye know. We'll have great times at my hideout in the Tetons."

No response. Silence. Prudence could hardly breathe.

"I know yer in here."

Silence.

Then, the scratch of a match. Through the cracks in the boards the yellow light flickered. They heard the breathing through the silver disk. They heard him stomp around – once they were positive that he stood with his back to the wall/door, just inches from them. Then the match went out. They heard steps, heard the door open, the hinges squeak.

Prudence stepped back from the wall in the inky darkness with relief, only to bump into something that moved, something cold, clammy, and hairy. She screamed. The front door crashed open again. "So that's it," hissed the bandit. "A secret door. A false wall, eh?" They heard him stomping across the cabin towards them. But a metallic click caught him up short.

"You'd better just stay where you are," came the calm voice of Hezekiah's friend Lem from the front doorway. "You've been chasin' these kids long enough. Turn around!"

"Just as I thought. Jake Dorn, the rapist from Miles City. The Black Hills highwayman," said Hezekiah.

"You. Hotchkiss," sneered the robber. "I knew I should have killed you when I held up the *Shoshone Belle*. But I couldn't recall where I'd seen ye before. Now I remember. Ye and yer partner Lem – ye damned near saw me lynched."

"Too bad we didn't succeed."

In the darkness the highwayman had reached to the table and grabbed a piece of ore twice the size of his fist. As he slowly approached Hezekiah he timed his movements, Lem's Winchester all the while being aimed at his heart – and slammed the ore down on the rifle barrel. The bullet went wild as Jake Dorn fled out the door, past Hezekiah and Lem.

Lem took out after him. "I'll get him, Hezekiah. You stay with the kids," he said, running down the canyon. After several hundred feet the highwayman reached the junction of the two narrow canyons, paused, then ran up the other canyon.

"Don't go up there, ye damned fool," yelled Lem, in return for which he heard a pistol shot and the whir of a bullet so close that it knocked his hat off. "There's poison gasses up that canyon. They'll kill you."

But the bandit did not hear. It smelled of sulfur, as did so many areas of Yellowstone, and of something else that he could not identify. Jake Dorn climbed over rocks, noticed the carcasses of a big bear and the skeletal remains of several coyotes, possibly a wolf, and assorted small mammals – rabbits and chipmunks. Dead birds in various conditions of deterioration lay all about. Dorn paused and rubbed his forehead. All of a sudden he had a terrible headache, and he felt faint. He looked back and saw by the moonlight that he was not being followed, realized how tired he was, and crept between some boulders that hid him from view. He sat down to rest. He closed his eyes, breathed deeply, relaxed, went to sleep, and never woke up.

When Lem returned he explained to Hezekiah how, since the tremors of two nights ago, the gases up the other canyon had become very lethal. "It's always been dangerous," he explained, "but now there's fresh corpses up there," he said. "I've gone in a little ways but in almost no time I get a headache and I feel faint and I ain't takin' any chances. I guess I hope old Dorn climbs out and high-tails it for the Tetons. But if he don't, well, I shouted a warning to him."

They turned to re-enter the cabin. "God rest ye, Mr. Highwayman," said Hezekiah, casting a last glance in the direction of the deadly canyon.

Hezekiah lit a candle. "Just a minute, kids, and I'll be with you." He cupped the candle in his hands to keep it from drafts and stepped through the secret door. The girl sat on the floor sobbing.

"Hello, Mr. Hezekiah," said Rusty. "Boy, are we glad to see you. Did you hear my secret weapon?"

"Sure did," said Hezekiah, rubbing the boy's red hair. He reflected that without Rusty's warning the highwayman would have caught Lem and him unprepared, and would probably have killed both of them and Rusty too. Hezekiah raised the candle high in the four-foot wide secret room at the back of the cabin. Rusty turned to see what the light revealed, besides his terrified, half-dressed sister. It was a butchering room for poached deer and elk. The gutted carcasses of two elk hung from hooks on the back wall. In the pitch darkness Prudence had touched one of them, felt the cold flesh and the hairy hide. No wonder she had screamed.

"Holy mackerel," gasped the boy, ignoring Prudence entirely. "My elk horns!" He darted to the side of his sister, who sat in a heap, one shoe missing, stockings falling around her ankles, a long slit in her drawers revealing a creamy thigh, the corset cover above her chest torn to shreds, and her golden tresses falling over her eyes.

Hezekiah knelt beside Prudence, holding the candle. "It's all right, Miss Prudence," he began, separating her hair from her eyes. "There's nothing more to be scared of. This is my partner Lem's butcher room."

"Elk horns!" exclaimed Rusty from a corner where they were piled high. "Can I have my choice, Mr. Hezekiah?"

"Shore, Rusty," said the mountaineer, still kneeling beside Prudence. "Come on, now, young lady. You've got too much pioneer stock in ye to let this get the best of ye. Let's see if we can find some clothes for ye."

That diverted Prudence, woman that she was. Although the sobs still came, they came more slowly and less audibly; she was on the road to recovery already. "I'm a terrible mess," she wailed. "You must think I have no shame."

"Oh, bosh," replied the coachman. "What you need's one of Lem's doeskin huntin' shirts that come halfway down to the knees. Come on, now, give me your hand. Stand up and let's get some real mountaineer's clothing fer ye."

Soon she was standing, walking through the secret door, casting a final last glance at the elk carcasses. "Why don't ye pour some coffee for us while I see what I can find?"

Hezekiah knew it was good therapy to put the girl to work. Sure enough, he soon heard the sounds of tin cups and when he came back to her, holding a doeskin shirt, she was pouring coffee from the stove, which still held glowing coals, and was rapidly regaining her composure.

"Hey, sis," said Rusty excitedly, emerging from the secret room. "Look at these. Ain't these the biggest elk antlers you ever did see?"

"Aren't, Rusty. Not ain't." She looked at them. "If you say so."

"Can I take these, Mr. Hezekiah?"

"I reckon so," replied Hezekiah. Then he turned to Prudence. "Here, Prudence. Try this on."

"Oh, it's so soft and – it looks warm and comfortable," said the girl.

"It goes on over your head," Hezekiah volunteered, embarrassment in his voice. "Say, Lem. Hadn't we better get some wood?" The two men went out the door, saying that they would be right back.

Prudence kneaded the soft, piney-woods-smelling garment with its fringes on the hem and down the sleeves. Her feminine mystique admired it. In a jiffy she slipped it over her head and let if fall over her body. It fit her remarkably well, falling halfway down her thighs. She examined the fringed hem and noticed the torn lace of her drawers below it. On down were her stockings, fallen about her ankles, and one scuffed shoe, without a heel; she did not know where she lost the other shoe. Her eyes rebelled at such shabby raiment. "Turn your head, Rusty," she ordered the boy. Then she pulled off the shirt again, tore off the remainder of the corset cover and then tugged at the corset, finally getting it off. Then she reached down to her drawers and, with the dexterity all women display towards clothing, ripped off the lower part of each leg so that nothing but tiny shorts remained. She kicked off the scuffed white shoe and removed the torn stockings. For a moment she stood in the white drawers-cum-shorts and nothing more. Now Prudence slipped the hunting shirt over her head once again, let it slip down, tightened the belt at the waist. Then, she swept her golden tresses behind her ears so that once again her cameo face showed forth. Unfortunately redness from tears marred those blue eyes, but even they were rapidly recovering their natural beauty. When she said "Okay, Rusty", and the men subsequently reentered the cabin, it was evident that Prudence was already recovering from her ordeal.

"I think we better clear out, Lem," said Hezekiah, very businesslike, to his partner. "I've got to get these children back to the hotel. There're goin' to be a lot of questions asked."

"Seems too bad," Lem replied, looking around. "All the work that went into these diggin's. This nice cabin hidden in the canyon. The secret butchering room."

"I know," said Hezekiah, "but we've taken out about all the gold dust, I think."

"I have enough saved to set me up with a ranch over in the Big Hole country," said Lem. "I don't know what you've done with your share. Besides, Hezekiah,. Why push our luck? We've been poachin' and placer minin' and you've been bootleggin' on this Reservation long enough to get sent up for life. You just know they'll catch us sooner or later. Even at this hidden place. So let's git."

"Agreed. They must be havin' conniptions over at Canyon by now, lookin' fer these kids."

"I expect they'll tell the soldiers all about this place."

"Probably. But by the time the soldiers get here, Lem, you should have bagged your gold dust and your belongings and skedaddled out of here. As for me – they ain't got nothin' on me 'cept a charge of bootleggin', and I suspect I've got a friend at court to defend me, namely an imbibing Congressman."

"They're the best kind," said Lem, winking at Hezekiah. "Say, Miss Prudence," he said, looking at the girl's bare feet, "I wonder if we've got some old boots for you."

"Are we leaving?" asked the girl, who was sitting on the stump chair. "I'm afraid Mother and Daddy will be missing us." Then her eyes filled with tears again. "Even if Stephen Billner doesn't miss me. I hate him!" She blew her nose into a red bandanna handkerchief

Hezekiah had given her and then agreed to try on the woolen socks and old miner's boots that Lem had fetched.

Mother and Daddy and Madeline? Indeed they were in a state of worry, fear, and near frenzy that night.

Neither Philip nor the Congressman had joined them at the campfire lecture, nor had Lord Billner made his presence known. After the lecture, with "Think of it" running through their minds, the ladies had strolled back to the hotel engrossed in their own thoughts. It was nearly ten o'clock and no sign of the men. Mrs. Griffin's thoughts were: 'Has that bulbous-nosed old walrus got drunk again?' and Emily was thinking, 'What has that dirty old man done with my Philip? Philip's been so grumpy lately. If he comes back his usual well-behaved self,' she resolved, a far-off look in her eyes, 'he'll not be grumpy another day.' She thought of their nice room at the hotel with Rusty's separate room and a door between. And Madeline was thinking, 'I should quit fantasizing about Captain Taylor. I was just a passing female in his life.'

Philip had not imbibed and he had done his best to get to the Canyon Hotel. He had left Talmadge Beauregard Griffin asleep on the grass overlooking the River while he, Philip (Stephen having left for his flight to Livingston) worked the stream, as fishermen do. The trout were biting just enough to keep him interested, so that when he noticed the position of the sun and looked at his watch, Philip was disturbed to discover how he had overextended his time. He folded his tackle and started back to where he had left the M.C. recovering from his near drowning, and almost tripped over the sleeping form. The Honorable Talmadge Griffin was snoring, his hat over his face, an empty bottle of Old Quaker Rye cradled in his arms. Mosquitoes were feasting on his arms while ants were exploring him like Lilliputians examining Gulliver.

"Oh, for—" Philip grunted disgustedly. "Congressman," he said, leaning over and shaking the Solon's shoulders. "Wake up. We have to catch a coach to the hotel."

It took a while, but Philip's demeanor was so serious that the Congressman immediately tried to obey him. Philip finally had him on his feet, unsteady but upright, just as the last Yellowstone coach came by. When they reached the hotel Philip held up, hauled, pulled, pleaded, tugged, taunted, insulted, and nearly carried Congressman Griffin inside the hotel, where at last Mr. Griffin became sober. "You go on up while I go in the men's room and tidy up and drink a gallon or two of water," he said, "and if you are my friend, Snowden, do not divulge to my darling Dolly my escapade with the Yellowstone River and John Barleycorn."

Philip trudged up the stairs, discovered a key in the lock, which puzzled him slightly, and found Emily's note – that she was attending the campfire lecture. Philip lay down across the bed. When Emily arrived a few minutes later she apologized for turning on the lights, for he had dozed off and the lights awakened him. "You poor dear," she said, noting his fatigue. "Is the Congressman to blame?"

Speak of the devil: within minutes, into the room bounced Congressman Talmadge Beauregard Griffin, fresh as a daisy, smelling of SenSen. His arm was around Dolly's waist. "Come on, you-all," he said. "There's a beauty of a moon tonight. Let's all go look at the Grand Canyon."

"Oh, no," pleaded Emily. "Philip is tired."

"What, Judge? You tired? You mean that little fishin' expedition tired you out? No wonder it took you Yankees four years to lick us Confederates."

Philip shook with rage as he sat up, thinking of the Congressman's narrow escape and long nap after consuming the bottle of Old Quaker. He was amazed and angered at how the Southerner had snapped back to life.

"Shhh," Emily indicated, pointing to the closed door leading to the adjoining room. "Rusty's asleep. He almost choked on another jawbreaker. He was so tired I let him come home with orders to go right to bed."

Dolly tip-toed to the door, opened it and peered in. "Rusty isn't in there," she announced. "His bed hasn't been slept in."

"What?" exclaimed Emily, dashing to the door just as Madeline entered from the hall. "Where's Prudence?" she asked. "She's not in her room."

Mrs. Talmadge Griffin expanded her already generous bosom; she placed her hands on her fleshy hips and began nodding her head up and down. Puritan Emily, defensive of her children's virtue, was fairly well ready to start a hair-pulling match then and there.

"I'll bet," ventured Dolly, "she's out seeing her young Englishman."

"Can't be," replied Philip. "Stephen Billner raced down to Livingston this afternoon. Something about his remittance being in jeopardy."

"Then where is she? And Rusty?" asked Emily. "This isn't like my children at all."

First they inquired at the front desk, where they picked up information that implicated Hezekiah Hotchkiss, who had not been seen for several hours either.

By eleven o'clock they had notified the Cavalry, a detachment of which was called over from Lake, the local unit having left in pursuit of a Pierce-Arrow motor car. At midnight a private came in with Prudence's parasol. Suspicions of foul play, and of the highwayman who had tried to force Prudence to accompany him at the time of the holdup, began to be rumored around the Canyon Hotel. Philip and the Congressman set up field headquarters, Philip at the front desk and the Congressman at the soldier station. It was from the Congressman that Madeline heard about the Pierce-Arrow's successful run and of the stampeding buffalo herd. She envisioned Captain Taylor galloping all over the mountains after the wild beasts – a remarkably accurate image.

Emily by now was fighting off hysteria. A hefty, bewhiskered doctor-tourist, the same person who had flipped Rusty upside down, was considering giving her a sedative.

"Do you think," he asked of Madeline, who was calm and self-contained, "the lad could have just pretended he was choking? To get away from the ladies, you know, and be up to some mischief? I thought he spat out that jawbreaker mighty quick."

"Rusty would never do such a – I don't think he – Doctor, perhaps Rusty would!" replied the boy's aunt. The doctor's eyes twinkled.

Dolly Griffin, sitting nearby, rolled her eyes. "Children put all kinds of things over on their mommas and daddys," she said. "I put it over on my momma and daddy so many times," she boasted, "that Daddy finally blurted out – at Sunday dinner, of all places – 'Dolly, why don't you marry Talmadge and quit trying to deceive us!' And so I did."

Emily smiled wanly in spite of her worries.

About twelve thirty a soldier reported a horse and buggy coming up the Artist's Point road. A few minutes later it appeared out of the darkness, a tired "whoaaaaa" was heard, and Hezekiah Hotchkiss looked up on a verandah at the relieved faces of a hundred guests. For they all saw, seated beside him sound asleep in each other's arms, brother and sister, Prudence and Rusty Snowden. A pair of antlers stuck out from the back of the buggy. The long wait was over.

## Chapter Seven

# The Sixth Day

## I

It was afternoon of the next day, and the sixth of their stay in the Park. Hezekiah, having driven the *Shoshone Belle* with the Snowdens and Congressman and Mrs. Griffin down to Mammoth where they proposed to rest for a day and a night before leaving for home, was riding an old Appaloosa toward Lord Billner's ranch. After that, perhaps he would return to Mammoth or maybe he would go on to Livingston. First he had to see how young Lord Billner was doing. He was going to tell him how his decision to rush to Livingston had resulted in Prudence almost suffering a fate worse than death. 'Probably,' he mused as he shook out his corncob pipe and filled it with fresh Prince Albert, 'he's not even there. He's most likely lying in a gutter or a filthy cot in a back room somewhere, sobering up from a royal fling that cost him his entire quarterly remittance. That's the way it is with remittance men. Feast or a famine. Get drunk when the remittance arrives, go begging when the money's gone.'

He lit the pipe and savored the taste of the strong smoke. 'Then again,' he thought, 'maybe not. Billner's a clean-cut young feller. A notch above the general run.' Truth was, Hezekiah thought Stephen would be at the ranch. Never call old Hotchkiss a Cupid's helper, but if he ever saw a handsome young couple in love, it was Prudence Snowden and Stephen Billner, and damnit, they oughta' be wed.'

The Appaloosa trotted along the road at a satisfactory pace, and Hezekiah relaxed in the saddle as only an experienced horseman can do. He thought of the excitement of the past few days. By gadfrey, he'd sure never had a bevy of passengers like this last one. Take that rebel Congressman, Talmadge Beauregard Griffin, and his wife Dolly. Couldn't say he didn't like 'em. Friendly as first cousins, no

shame about 'em – but think of someone like old Griffin bein' in Congress makin' laws for these United States!

Then he thought of Captain Taylor, and that cute little old maid, Miss Madeline Snowden. The Captain shore did look at her as if he'd found the love of his life. The way they talked so much in the coach. And there shore warn't any doubt about how she felt about him!

Hezekiah rubbed the stubble on his face, swatted away a horse fly. Something strange about that little old maid, though. Sort of a vague, haunted look. Somewhere in her past, he figured, there's a story. Probably a sad story.

Then he smiled, for now he was thinking of Rusty. That carrot-topped freckle-faced kid! He'd go far, Hezekiah wagered. Gettin' out of his mother's sight by makin' believe he was chokin' on a jawbreaker. Hezekiah removed his pipe and laughed out loud, startling the Appaloosa. "Hy'ar! Behave yerself, Nellie!" commanded the mountaineer.

And Philip and Emily, the father and mother. Stability incarnate. Hezekiah wondered how many Philips and Emilys he had escorted around the Park. Two – three hundred of 'em, anyway, two or four or six at a time, week in and week out for ten weeks each year. God bless 'em. America can't have enough of 'em. Especially people like the Snowdens – they were, he thought, just about the handsomest family unit he'd ever taken 'round the Reservation.

The Appaloosa rounded a curve and there, by the Yellowstone River, was the white frame house Hezekiah was seeking. Squinting the better to see it in the distance, he made out not one but two figures, one of which was dumpy, he thought, and wearing a skirt. Immediately (he didn't know why) he thought of Rosie. The Appaloosa, seeing the figures or perhaps the white horse in the nearby pasture, whinnied loudly. The figures turned toward the lone horseman.

The man dropped what he was doing and ran up the path toward the gate. "Just a minute. I'll open it."

When Stephen saw who it was, he broke into a smile. "Why, it's Hezekiah Hotchkiss. Say, we're glad to see you." He opened the gate. "I've got a lot of things to ask you."

"I reckon you do, young feller," replied Hezekiah, urging his horse through the opening, "and I got something to tell you."

"Come down to the house and have some coffee and cherry pie."

"Don't mind if I do. Say, don't I smell new mown hay?"

"Yep. Got quite a crop coming in, and the price is good this year."

"Who'd ye get to cut it?"

"Oh, Rosie knew a couple of hands who agreed to do it for room and board."

"Rosie?"

"Oh, yes. Rosie is here. She'll be glad to see you."

Hezekiah rubbed his mustache. "I ain't so sure of that."

"Oh, yes," Stephen reassured him, looking the stage driver squarely in the face. "She's sold the saloon – and rooms, you know."

"What?"

"Yes. She's out of business."

"Well, I'll be—"

"Hello, Zeke." He was dismounting now. On the front porch was Rosie, but it was not the Rosie he had known. She was wearing a gingham dress and a neat white apron. She was plump but still curvy, her hair was stylishly rolled upward in the newest fashion. No paint covered her face – or was there the faintest trace of rouge? "Come on in, Zeke, and have some coffee and cherry pie," she said cheerfully. Hezekiah relaxed: Rosie hadn't called him Zeke in years.

Bewildered, he was escorted into a kitchen that was sunny, cheerful, and spic and span. Stephen and Hezekiah sat down at the oil-cloth-covered table, and Rosie served.

Hezekiah was speechless. First he looked at Stephen, who was wearing a tan work shirt open at the collar, sleeves rolled up. The stage driver noticed the broken, painful calluses on the young man's hands, and grime that even soap would not entirely remove.

"You been workin'?"

"Oh, my yes. Since five this morning. I've fetched the hired hands, cleaned and oiled the hay rake, borrowed draught horses from Colonel Prescott across the way, mended the fence in two places, cleaned out part of the irrigation ditch, and just now Rosie is having me apply some leftover white paint to the front door. If I can keep this up, the ranch will be the showplace of the valley," he frowned, "provided we can make it through the winter."

"I've always liked this spread," said Hezekiah. "It's well drained, got good hay fields that stretch right up to the grazing lands on the hillsides, got the Yellowstone at your front door. Got beautiful

Emigrant Peak and the other Snowy Mountains to look at whenever ye get tired of civilization."

"I love it too, Hezekiah," Stephen replied. "I don't ever want to leave it. And what you say about looking at the mountains when you are tired of things..." Stephen paused, then changed the subject. "You know," he began seriously, "I've had an idea for a long time."

"What he really means," said Rosie, sitting down with them, "is for the long time since losing his remittance."

"Eh? You lost your remittance?"

"Yes. I lost my remittance, Hezekiah."

"Good. Now maybe you'll make somethin' of yerself."

If this was a slur, Stephen let it fall. "Back to this 'being tired of civilization'," he continued. "This beautiful valley here. I've an idea for a new kind of summer resort."

"Wait a minute, Stephen," said Hezekiah, holding up a hand. "This is workin' land, and this should be a workin' ranch."

"Oh, I know, Hezekiah. But listen to this," Stephen leaned over to Hezekiah and lowered his voice. "What would you say if I could get ranch hands to *pay* for the privilege of working?"

"Pay for workin'? Now what kind of nonsense is that?"

"Hear him out, Zeke," commanded the ex-madam.

"Look, Hezekiah," Stephen continued, his face becoming more and more expressive, "you've taken rich people on hunting trips and excursions through the mountains. Weren't there always some who wanted to do the chores?"

'Oh, sure. Pilgrims. Dudes..."

Stephen slapped a hand on the oilcloth table. "That's it, my mountaineer friend. We've going to have a *dude ranch* here!"

"A what?"

"A dude ranch. We're going to advertise in the London *Times*. We'll register with Cook's Travel Agency. 'Holiday on a Working Ranch in Paradise Valley, Montana.' They'll pay, Hezekiah, they'll pay to put up our hay, dig our ditches, herd our cattle, milk our cows—"

"Castrate the calves?"

"Hotchkiss," broke in Rosie, "there's a lady present."

Hezekiah slapped a fist into his palm. "Gadfrey if you ain't got an idea, son. The dudes always want to work. We'll let 'em. I'll haul 'em here from Livingston fer ye at cost plus a dollar."

"I see no reason why we can't do it," said Stephen enthusiastically. "Why, I have an uncle who's a director of the Canadian Pacific. He can help sell the idea. We could fix up the bunkhouse—"

"Wait a minute," said Hezekiah, holding up a hand. "What is this 'we'? Who else is in on this?"

A cloud settled over Lord Billner's face. All the life went out of him. "Oh, Hezekiah, I guess I'm just day dreaming. There's nobody else. Rosie just came out here for a few days."

"I'm going to run a respectable boarding house in Livingston," she said to Hezekiah.

"In other words, young feller," said Hezekiah, ignoring Rosie for the moment, "you're goin' to try it alone."

"I guess so." He looked pitifully at the coachman. "I've lost her, haven't I?"

"Well," he drawled quietly, "let's just say she ain't very happy with ye. She near lost her – she was kidnapped by the highwayman – same one that held up the *Shoshone Belle* – at Artist's Point 'cause you warn't there to meet her. See, her daddy didn't get back to the hotel in time to give her yer message." Hezekiah then recounted the happenings of the night before.

"But – then – it really wasn't my fault, was it?"

"Guess not. To tell the truth, Stephen, they're a very mixed up family right now."

"Couldn't you do somethin', Zeke," cut in Rosie. "You've always been so romantically inclined."

Hezekiah looked perceptively at her. Her face was softer and kinder than he had seen it in years; he realized this was no barb. "What can I do?" he asked. "Look, Stephen, she ain't the only girl in the world. She may be only nineteen, have golden curls and blue eyes and white teeth and a peaches and cream complexion and a body cuter than a baby antelope, and a musical voice purty as a meadow lark's, and besides that she can cook, but—"

"Please!"

"All I was about to say was, there are a lot like her. But I ain't so sure." Hezekiah pulled his beard. "Anyhow, the loss of a gal shouldn't stop ye from makin' a good dude ranch here. It's a disgrace, the way ye let it go down."

"I know," he said, lacking enthusiasm.

"One thing. Purty fillies don't marry town drunks. You stay out here and stick to business."

"I'm going to."

"See that he does, Rosie."

"I will until I move back into town, Zeke."

"Fine."

"Zeke."

"Yes," replied Hezekiah.

"What are you doing this winter?"

"Oh, I dunno. Go into the Tom Minor Basin north of the Park and do some poachin', maybe. Go out to Cooke City or up to Emigrant and do some minin'."

"Oh. Just wondered."

Hezekiah complimented Rosie for the coffee and pie. "Gotta be gettin' back," he announced, rising from his chair. "New coachful comin' in. They haven't expelled me yet. See you. Maybe in a week."

He walked out, mounted the Appaloosa, and waved good-bye. It was hard to tell whose replying wave was the weaker, Stephen's or Rosie's.

## II

Night following the terrible night came on at Mammoth. The Snowden family ate in dismal silence in the big National Hotel dining room, while all about them excited tourists, eagerly awaiting the Park tour, gushed with enthusiasm. Only Rusty was contented. He had his elk horns stashed safely in his room.

Philip was worried. His after dinner cigar didn't even taste good. News in the two-day-old *Denver Post* about a court case involving a woman who had her husband submit to a blood transfusion with an octogenarian to cool his ardor barely aroused his lawyer's mind. Damnit! He was concerned about every member of his family except Rusty.

Emily, who hadn't slept a wink last night, remained so wrought up that the doctor had given Philip sedatives to administer to her – and to the other ladies if necessary. Madeline, poor Madeline, was suffering terribly, in silence, but she did not fool her brother. Philip was well aware of her infatuation with Captain Taylor. Perhaps it really was love, which made it all the sadder. The way she was constantly glancing around, it was clear that she still retained hope that he would appear. But appear he had not. This bothered Philip because the Captain had seemed so sincere, such a decent fellow. Philip hated admitting to himself that his judgment had been wrong about the Cavalry officer.

And then there was Prudence. Good Lord! She hadn't eaten a thing all day. She looked like a Dresden doll, for if there was blood in her veins, it certainly didn't show. She gazed off into nothingness, as in a daze. She cried easily. She had nothing to say. Philip, who blamed it all on the experience of the night before, feared now for her health.

They finished their coffee (milk for Rusty) and rose from the table. They sauntered onto the verandah but as it grew dark the ladies suggested that it was time to go to their rooms. At Philip's urging, all three women agreed to take a sedative. Rusty did not need one – he was asleep, with the antlers at the side of the bed, almost as soon as he got under the covers.

Philip remained downstairs in the lobby. Truth was, he too was restless and ill at ease. He walked to the Haynes Studio and purchased some hand painted photographs of Old Faithful. He was returning to the hotel when he met Hezekiah.

"Jes' the man I've been lookin' fer," said the mountaineer.

"Glad to see you once more, Hezekiah," replied Philip cheerfully. "I can't thank you enough for all you've done for us."

"Aw, fergit it, Mr. Snowden. How's the little lady?"

"Which one? Emily, Prudence, or Madeline?"

"I was thinkin' of Prudence, Mr. Snowden."

"Prudence?" Philip removed his cigar and exhaled. "Frankly, Hezekiah, she's got me worried. I've never seen her so sad, so despondent, so sickly looking. I'm afraid that kidnapping might have affected her both physically and mentally. I'm concerned."

"The kidnapping? Bosh," retorted Hezekiah. "She's all right, Mr. Snowden. Why, she even dressed herself purty-like in that huntin' shirt when the trouble was over. And she talked a blue streak in the buggy, till she fell asleep."

"Then what's bothering her?"

Hezekiah paused, then said, "I saw someone just as hang-doggish as Miss Prudence, not four hours ago."

"Who?"

"Young Stephen Billner."

"Oh. Him." Philip put his cigar back in his mouth.

"Now, you wait a minute, Mr. Snowden. Stephen Billner's a promising young feller. Works hard. Well educated. Good family connections."

"Once a remittance man, always a remittance man," replied Philip. "I'm glad we're through with him."

"Stephen Billner ain't a remittance man no more. He's lost it."

"Oh."

"So now he goin' to work. He's got a good spread up in Paradise Valley 'tween here and Livingston. He's goin' to have guests in the summer on top of raisin' hay and cattle."

Philip took several fragrant puffs on his cigar.

"This is new country, Mr. Snowden," Hezekiah continued as they walked slowly toward the hotel. "Montana's the most beautiful, most wonderful country in the world. A man's got a future here. Business, politics, ranching, mining – it's a great country for an ambitious young man."

"Go on," said Philip, flicking ashes from his cigar.

"And young Billner's got everything goin' fer him, Mr. Snowden. Except one thing..."

"What's that?"

"That's a healthy young woman by his side." Hezekiah paused to let his statement sink in. Then he added, "I didn't save Miss Prudence so she could throw herself at some flabby-muscled dude back East. Stephen and Prudence – they love each other, and they both know it. That's why they're the two most miserable youngsters in the world tonight."

They had arrived at the steps to the verandah. Philip removed the cigar and stared blankly at it.

"Let her marry him, Mr. Snowden. She's a strong-willed, well-balanced young woman. She knows what she wants. She's more mature than you think. Why, together they'll make it here in Montana. Make it big. I tell you, Mr. Snowden, Prudence is all Stephen Billner needs to become a very successful man."

There was a long silence, then Philip replied, "Let me think about it overnight, Hezekiah. Thanks for telling me. I'll let you know my thoughts in the morning."

## III

At the same time Madeline Snowden was retiring to a cold, cheerless bed and a restless night, even with a sedative, Captain Freeman W. Taylor, who hated horses but had ridden the hurricane deck of three mounts and been bucked off four times over the past thirty hours, fell into his own bed at Bachelor Officer's Quarters. He was so tired that he could hardly stay awake long enough to pull off his mud and dust caked clothes. All the previous night and all that day he had pursued buffalo. He had yelled so many commands that he was hoarse. Yet, he was so apprehensive of what the next day would bring that he could not sleep soundly. For Captain Freeman W. Taylor was ordered to report to the Office of the Commandant, Colonel S. P "Saddle-Pants" Peavey, the coming morning at 9 AM sharp.

He knew that Saddle-Pants was not going to compliment him on rounding up the buffalo. Oh, no! Captain Taylor knew Saddle-Pants better than that! Colonel Peavey was calling him on the carpet for allowing that Pierce-Arrow automobile to get through the Park. 'And there,' thought the exhausted Captain, 'goes my career.' He would be the laughing stock of his West Point Class of '01. 'What happened to Taylor?' 'Didn't you hear? He was court-martialed.' 'What for?' 'He let a Pierce-Arrow get away! Ho, ho, ho.'

The Captain's thoughts occasionally turned to the cute little thirtyish school teacher, Madeline Snowden. She'd understand. Cripes! She was the only person who showed real interest in those internal combustion engines! He wished she was with him right now. Not for sex – though sex with her was a pleasant thought – but for sympathy. And encouragement. She'd agreed with him about old Saddle-Pants.

"Man," the Captain told himself, "ask her to marry you. Marry me? A failure? The most unsuccessful graduate in the Class of '01? She'd never have me. Yes she would! She's a tarnished woman. You aren't exactly a priest yourself. God, she'd be pretty in bed. She's exquisite in three-quarter size. Go ahead. Ask her to marry you. Do you want to end your years as an aging bachelor in a rocking chair at the Old Soldiers' Home? Marry her!" The Captain's thoughts about Madeline helped him get some sleep that night. Some sleep: again and again he roused just enough to envision Saddle-Pants sending him to the guardhouse. And he turned and tossed some more.

Morning: Poor Captain Taylor. He felt more fatigued than he had the night before. He belted down two cups of black coffee, shaved and bathed and dressed at his immaculate, military best. It made his obligation no easier. The stairs of the big sandstone building were like thirteen steps to the gallows. Why was he short of breath? Why was his heart beating so fast? He reached the second floor and walked to the Office of the Commandant. A sergeant sat in the outer office, shuffling papers.

"Captain Taylor to see Colonel Peavey."

The sergeant stood up, saluted, opened the door to the Colonel's office, spoke a word or two to the person inside, and then stepped aside in the doorway. "You may enter, sir." The sergeant rolled his eyes and shut the door behind him.

"Captain Freeman W. Taylor reporting, sir." The Captain saluted smartly. He looked down upon a shiny bald head which slowly rose to reveal a man in his late fifties with a thick, white mustache and leathery skin. He was a big man, was Colonel Peavey, fat but with his girth well contained in an immaculate uniform with a polished Sam Brown belt encasing his belly. On his left breast were campaign ribbons denoting action against Geronimo and the Apaches, heroism in the Battle of Wounded Knee (when his unit ran down, shot, and sabered women and children), action in Puerto Rico during the Spanish–American War (his unit had installed a sewer in a filthy town) and service in the Philippines (some said that it was he, Colonel Peavey, who coined that oft-repeated statement: "We'll teach the Filipinos democracy if we have to shoot every one of 'em to do it"). He had also commanded troops during the Pullman strike, running down impoverished strikers and crippling several anarchists for life. Ahh, a veritable Colonel Blimp was he, and a towering pillar of strength in the West Point Protective Association.

The Colonel did not put the Captain at ease. Instead, he placed his fists on his desk, leaned on them as he rose from his chair, and stared into the face of Captain Freeman W. Taylor, 2nd US Cavalry. "Well, Captain Taylor," he hissed, "what have you to say for yourself?"

"We – well, sir—"

"*Speak up!*"

"We got the buffalo all back in the pasture, sir. All but six or seven of them, anyway."

"Fine. But now tell me, Captain, *why were the buffalo outside the pasture?*"

"Oh, you already know why, sir."

"*Why?*" roared Saddle-Pants. "*Tell me why.*"

"Because of the Pierce-Arrow, sir. We were pursuing it, and it apparently lost its brakes, so the driver tried to slow it by shifting into a lower gear, which caused it to backfire - you know, bang! bang! bang! - and that alarmed the bison, and they broke through the fence and—"

"Enough. Enough. Now tell me, Captain Taylor: Where were you? Where was K Troop?" The Colonel's steely eyes were squinting, sending daggers through the Captain's own.

"We were in pursuit, sir."

"Pursuit of the au-to-mobile?" The Colonel spat out the last word so that it sounded obscene.

"Yes, sir."

'Why?"

"Why - er - because it was not supposed to be operated under its own power in the Park, sir."

"And who was ordered to secure said vehicle, and escort it out of the Park in two wagons?"

Flustered, Captain Taylor shifted his stance.

"You are still at attention, Captain."

Quickly the Captain restored his stance. "I was, sir. The vehicle in question got away because I was leading K Troop in pursuit of a troublesome bear. We - ah - didn't get it, either."

"Taylor," hissed Saddle-Pants. "It's too bad we're not at war. If we were, I'd have you shot at sunrise. You", he pointed a finger at the Captain and shook it vigorously, "are a disgrace to the Service, sir. You are a total incompetent. You have less brains in your cranium than the horses you ride. The Second Cavalry simply cannot have such men as you in command, Captain Taylor."

"No, sir."

"I gave you orders, Captain. You were not to let that au-to-mobile out of your sight. That au-to-mobile was not to operate in this Reservation under its own power. Simple orders, Captain. But no. Not for you."

"Yes, sir."

"Captain Taylor, do you know what I would like to do to you?" the Colonel asked, sitting down. He leaned back in his chair and looked up at the miserable countenance of the man standing in front of him.

"N-no sir," the Captain replied meekly.

"For punishment, I would tie you to that au-to-mobile with your face over the exhaust. And I would parade you back and forth before all the troops at my command. In due time the fumes would kill you, Captain. But not too soon, I trust."

"Yes, sir."

"Wait. I am not through."

"No, sir."

"Then I would have your carcass drawn and quartered into separate and equal parts, and each section thereupon placed on a stake at each entrance to Yellowstone National Park with a sign attached: AUTOMOBILES KEEP OUT. What do you think of that?"

"Yes, sir."

Colonel Saddle-Pants Peavey frothed, fought for words, and gave all signs of breaking into a sob. Horses were his life. Noble, dumb, stupid, beautiful four-legged beasts. To have to live to see the horse put to pasture gave him pangs of sorrow. He could not bear thoughts about the end of the age of the horse. Finally the Colonel regained control. Quietly he said, "Unfortunately, Captain, I am prohibited from doing that to you. Or anything else. You are no longer under my command."

"Begging your pardon, sir?"

"Orders came through by telegram yesterday. You are to report for duty at Aberdeen Proving Ground, Maryland, as of September first to participate in research upon the military potential of the internal combustion engine."

Captain Taylor could not believe it, but clearly, from the look on Colonel Peavey's face, it was true. Somewhere, somehow in the channels of the Army someone had been persuaded of the validity of his thesis promoting the internal combustion engine for use in warfare. Someone in the Army besides himself was living in the Twentieth Century! Like a flash he glimpsed all the brass in the Army he had ever met, but he failed to come up with a single far-sighted officer. 'My God,' he thought, 'who could have done this for me?'

The Colonel ended Captain Taylor's reverie. "Here are your orders, Captain. You are relieved of your command as of midnight last. And I suppose," added Saddle-Pants, "as an Academy man, I should shake your hand and wish you well." He stood up and held out his hand and gave to the flustered and hesitating Captain a firm handshake. "But if ever you are at an Officer's Club, and you hear I am there – don't bother to look me up."

"Don't worry," replied Captain Taylor cheerily, "I won't – I mean—"

"Oh, one other thing, Captain. Dispense with the usual formalities of saying good-bye to the other officers. I suspect they would prefer you to use the time in preparing to leave the Reservation."

"Yes, sir."

"You are dismissed."

Captain Taylor saluted, swung on his heels, and stomped out, slamming the door – unintentionally? – behind him.

Left alone, Colonel Saddle-Pants Peavey turned to the open window, hands clasped behind his back, and surveyed the big, sandstone stables in his view. He breathed deeply of the intoxicating aroma of horseflesh, hay, and manure. His weather-beaten eyes grew misty. Two nights before, after the defeat of his troops by the Pierce-Arrow, he had strolled down to those stables and visited with the horses. They had seemed as restless as he. Nostrils of their big muzzles were dilating. He suspected that they smelled the odor of automobile exhaust, and were fidgety about it. Or did they smell the acrid odor of animal rendering plants and dog meat factories?

The Colonel, in his office, heard a horse whinny. He returned to his desk, sat down, buried his head in his hands, and sobbed.

## Chapter Eight

# The Seventh Day

### I

The Snowdens breakfasted silently. Madeline drank her coffee and played with two pieces of dried toast. Emily had slept, but was still groggy from the sedative; she consumed two cups of black coffee but still felt tired. Prudence, wearing a brown skirt and a white blouse, stared straight ahead, her thoughts far away. Rusty's unbounded interest in the world about him simply irritated the rest. Only their curtness restrained his enthusiasm. "What a way to end a vacation," he commented.

Philip finished, and lit a cigar which he puffed on silently. Thoughtfully he looked at his daughter Prudence. Then he made his decision. He put out the cigar even though it was hardly a quarter smoked – a most unusual thing for him to do – and said, "Prudence, let's you and I take a stroll over to the Haynes Picture Shop. I want to show you some Indian jewelry they have there."

"Yes, Daddy."

"Can I come too?"

"No, Rusty. You stay here."

An argument ensued, but Philip and Prudence got away without the boy. They began walking up the path.

"Prudence," her father began, "you look unhappy."

"I am, Daddy," she replied meekly. "But it's nothing. I'll get over it." Daintily she dabbed tears from her eyes with a little handkerchief.

"Is it Stephen Billner?"

"I'm afraid so, Daddy. I'm afraid I'll never see him again."

Philip unwrapped a new cigar. "You know, Prudence, marriage is for keeps. Wouldn't you be lonely, living up here in this wild country?"

"Oh, no, Daddy. Stephen and I both love it. And he has a ranch – not a farm, Daddy, but a ranch. And he's educated and kind and handsome and – so much fun!"

"But marriage, my dear. Do you realize its implications? You've hardly known him a week."

"Oh, Daddy," she said in that way young people have, with a measure of disgust and irritation. "He was with me more than twelve hours a day for four long days. That's forty-eight hours, not counting the hours we were on the train. An average Saturday night date in Elm Grove lasts what? Three hours? That's – let's see – that's the equivalent of sixteen dates, Daddy. That's a four months' courtship in Elm Grove. That's not too short a time!"

Judge Snowden smiled at her logic. A chip off the old block, by gad. He halted at a hitching post. "And you really love him, Prudence? Really, truly love him?"

She placed her head on his shoulder. "Oh, Daddy. So much. He's the one. The only one."

Philip nuzzled his daughter's soft curls and patted her back. "Well, then, Prudence," he said softly, "don't you think you'd better run down to his ranch and tell him so?"

She raised her head and searched her father's face for meaning, her blue eyes widening.

"Hezekiah says Stephen is even more hang-dog than you. And speaking of Hezekiah, there he is, Prudence. With a horse and buggy." Hezekiah waved.

Prudence's joy was unbounded. "Oh, Daddy. I love you!" she gushed, kissing him on the cheek and then dashing to the buggy. Philip walked hastily behind her. "Hezekiah," he ordered, "telephone the stationmaster at Livingston what happens. There's either to be a marriage, or Prudence will return East with us. One of the two. I'm not leaving her here unattached. You hear?"

"Trust me, Mr. Snowden."

"Come on. Hezekiah. Let's go!" she implored him even as she sat down in the buggy. She pounded his arm, "Hurry!"

"Kickickickick," Hezekiah spoke to the horse. Horse and buggy clattered down the road toward Gardiner and Livingston.

The girl kept telling him to hurry. She sang and she commented on how beautiful the day was and how blue the sky was and aren't the antelope graceful and did the mountains ever look more majestic and please, please Hezekiah, hurry!

"He can wait," muttered the mountaineer. "It's quite a distance down there, young woman."

"But hurry."

"As I said, he can wait."

"He can. But I can't. Please hurry!"

Hezekiah had a dismal thought that maybe his measure of the young ex-remittance man was wrong, that Lord Billner had tired of work and thrown the whole thing over and headed for town and got totally drunk. He thought of what a discovery like that would do to the sweet young thing sitting beside him.

"Maybe he ain't thar," drawled Hezekiah, taking the corncob pipe from his mouth. "Maybe he's gone back to England."

"Oh, no, Hezekiah. No, no, no! He mustn't. Hurry, hurry, hurry, hurry." She grabbed the buggy whip and swung it. "Giddyap," she commanded.

Hezekiah sighed. By golly, he hoped Lord Billner was there. And still in love with this young filly. He smiled, recalling a common statement out of his youth. "There's nothing like a virgin-on-the-verge."

Somehow – it seemed an eternity to Prudence – they reached the ranch. Hezekiah opened and shut the gate and the buggy clattered up to the front porch. Prudence was out of the conveyance before Hezekiah had a chance to help her down. Now she was running up the steps. Rosie appeared at the door.

Prudence stopped short. "Wh-where is he?" she asked, trying to place where she had seen the woman.

"You must be Prudence," said Rosie cheerfully. "Hello, Zeke."

"Where is he?" the girl demanded.

"Over on the other side of that knoll, dearie. He's choppin' wood."

The girl jumped from the steps and dashed toward the knoll.

Stephen, meanwhile, stripped to the waist, perspiration glistening on his manly chest, was busy chopping at a cottonwood log. He had paused to rest a moment when he heard her.

"Stephen!"

His heart skipped a beat as he looked up on the knoll from whence the voice had come. There she was, framed against the blue sky and a white cumulus cloud, the breeze whipping at her skirt, revealing her graceful form. Her face was wreathed in a 'come hither' smile, her golden tresses, having fallen down during the wild ride and the run up the knoll, waved backward in the breeze. Her arms were held out to him. To Stephen in a flash she was energy, and power, and force, and mystery, and life. Small atom of humanity that she was, Prudence appeared, silhouetted against the sky, as a giantess. For Stephen Billner knew – knew that very instant – that she was all he needed to give meaning to his life. She held the power within her to make him a veritable man among men.

He was not aware that he was running up the knoll, but he did say, "Prudence," and she ran to him and they met halfway. He hugged her and lifted her off her feet and swung her around. She felt the muscles of his bare arms and the perspiration on his strong back and desire rose in her loins and her breasts and her body through and through. And he smelled the faint odor of lilacs, nuzzled the soft thick golden hair, felt the softness of her woman's body and an urge as old as Adam came over him and he had a floating vision of planting seeds in a fresh-ploughed furrow.

"Do you still want me?" she asked between kisses.

"If you will still have me," he replied. "Now. Right now."

"Not so fast, young 'uns," warned Hezekiah, who had appeared at the top of the knoll. "You put on a shirt, thar, young feller, and make yourself respectable, and you young 'uns come into the house."

"Hezekiah, we're not children," Prudence replied.

"Ye shore ain't," he said. "Come on, now. Come with me."

The lovers walked down the knoll arms around each other to where Stephen's shirt was flung over a low branch. She watched as he put it on and buttoned it up. He started to turn around before tucking it in his trousers, but Prudence said, "No, Stephen. Tuck it in facing me. Let's make him angry."

"Righto, sweetheart," Stephen replied with a wink as he unbuttoned his fly, tucked in his shirt, rebuttoned it and buckled his belt as Prudence watched. Then they marched to where Hezekiah waited. As they strolled towards the house he muttered, "Ye young folks ain't got no shame, have ye?" Prudence giggled.

In the kitchen the decision was made to get married that evening in Livingston. "Rosie," Hezekiah ordered, "don't let them out of yer sight, not fer more than five minutes." Then he turned to the young couple. "I'm goin' over to Colonel Prescott's to phone Livingston. I'll get the preacher and make arrangements fer you folks to be married afore the east bound train leaves tonight. I'll be back in an hour, and ye better be ready to leave. Stephen, let's take your surrey. It'll hold more people than the buggy."

Hezekiah clattered off in the buggy. Rosie shifted into high gear, showing Prudence all about the house over which she would soon reign as mistress. They chatted in a strange tongue about problems female, while poor Stephen was left alone to work up a fine state of apprehension.

## II

Had Captain Taylor known the Snowdens were at Mammoth, he would have run to the hotel to tell Madeline his good news. But if they had gone by their itinerary they would have left Mammoth the previous afternoon. Because he knew nothing about the highwayman two nights before, he assumed their departure had taken place according to schedule.

It took him until early afternoon to get together his gear and take care of the thousand and one items one must look after when leaving a residence for a permanent change. He was also telephoning to have his ticket include a stopover in Elm Grove, Michigan. He was determined to look up the cute little old maid school teacher there. It was only by coincidence that the last Trooper he talked with at Fort Yellowstone told him about the attempted kidnapping at Canyon.

"Too bad you didn't know about it," said the soldier, "since you know the family. They stayed overnight at Mammoth. I suppose they're catching the two o'clock Park Line out of Gardiner."

Captain Taylor snapped his fingers. "I'm taking that train," he said, "and Madeline must be on it. By gadfrey, let's go!"

It was one of the quieter afternoons for the Park Branch Line. The passenger cars were mostly empty. Philip and Emily had climbed aboard and settled in seats midway down a car, Emily tearfully but bravely accepting the probability of Prudence's marriage.

"You are positive, Philip, that all that was wrong with Prudence was her love affair with Stephen?"

"Positive, Emily. Don't worry. Stephen will be a good husband. I've explained to both you and Prudence why he was not at Artist's Point to meet our little girl. It was a legitimate excuse."

"It all seems so sudden, though," she said. "Less than a week's courtship..."

"Well, now Emily, that depends on how you look at it," replied Philip. "Now let's see. Prudence saw Lord Billner for four days, say, fourteen hours a day. That's fifty-six hours, Emily, not counting the hours she saw him on the train. Now an average Saturday night date in Elm Grove lasts about three hours. That's the equivalent of, mm, eighteen dates. Now at once a week, that's a four and a half month courtship. Why dear, that's longer than I courted you!"

Emily twisted a handkerchief nervously, analyzing her husband's arithmetic. "Well, dear, when you look at it that way – oh, he does seem like a nice young man."

Rusty sat alone with his antlers and package and souvenirs. He was looking out the window, sucking a jawbreaker, bored but happy. Life has few enough successes, but at age eleven Rusty Snowden had already chalked up a big one. He came to Yellowstone to get elk antlers, and he got them.

Madeline sat ramrod straight near the front of the car, prim and alone. She was dressed stylishly in an off-white linen skirt, a frilly blouse covered by a tan matching jacket and, as was the style then, by another thin coat overall. Every wisp of her soft brown hair was in place, and a huge hat topped her coiffure. She wore heavy black veiling. Beside her on the seat was her parasol, neatly closed. But her lips were thin and pale, and her mouth tightly closed. The lines of age were clearly drawn about her eyes and forehead, and sorrow and hurt were revealed in her face. "You fool," she told herself. "You fool, Madeline Snowden. To lose your heart to a Captain!" She knew she could bear up under it, but why, oh why, must she be called upon to carry such a burden?

So they all sat. The narrow gauge engine, steam up, and the coal car, baggage car, and passenger cars, awaited the conductor's "All Aboard" to begin the journey north to Livingston. Suddenly two riders appeared far off on the plain south of Gardiner. As they approached it was obvious that an officer was riding the horse, the other, an enlisted man, was riding a mule and carrying a Gladstone bag. Just as the horseman reached the road running alongside the railroad the saddle slipped and the officer fell awkwardly to the ground.

'Oh! It can't be!' thought Madeline. She was both exhilarated and frightened. Her gloved hands went to her lips. Only one Cavalry officer rode a horse as badly as that! She watched him stand up painfully, shaking his fists at the horse which whinnied sarcastically, kicked up some turf and headed back to the stables at Mammoth.

"Never again," she heard him shout. "Never, never, never again will I ride thee, four-footed beast from hell! I'll see you rendered into glue, you bloomin', bloated, four-legged...!" She saw that he had run out of words, watched as he brushed himself off and ordered the Trooper to stash his Gladstone in the vestibule of the very car she was riding. It was almost unbearable for Madeline as she watched him approach the car, wave the Trooper adieu, and climb in. It was Captain Freeman W. Taylor, all right. "Oh, dear God," prayed Madeline, "what is he going to do?"

The three-quarter size English teacher lowered her eyes, so hopeful of things to come that it hurt, so apprehensive that she wished she could die. And out of the corner of those lowered eyes Madeline saw first the shiny olive brown boots standing in the doorway from the vestibule, take two steps and halt by her seat.

"Madeline."

Madeline raised her aristocratic head. She smiled. Trying to control her voice, and succeeding quite well, she said, "Why, hello, Captain Taylor."

He removed his hat and placed it under his arm, being militarily correct even at a time like this. "Madeline," he repeated, sitting down and crushing her parasol. He grabbed her gloved hands and cupped them in his. He looked straight into her face, at her eyes. Firmly he said, "I love you, Madeline. Will you marry me?"

"Why—"

"Oh, let me tell you. I've been ordered to Aberdeen Proving Grounds, Maryland. Experiments with internal combustion engines."

"Oh, Captain. How wonderful!"

"And I'm on my way now, routed through a little town in Michigan called Elm Grove. To see the most wonderful girl I've met or ever want to meet. But why wait? We could be married in—"

"All aboard!" cried the conductor.

"Married in Livingston, Madeline. There's a two hour layover there."

"Captain—"

"But most important of all," he added, placing a hand on her delicate chin and turning her face to his, "I love you, Madeline."

The thin, tightly pressed lips swelled and rounded and reddened, the lines on her forehead and around her eyes disappeared as if by magic, the straight back relaxed, the icy expression melted, the brown eyes softened with tears. "And I'll love you, Captain Freeman W. Taylor, forever and ever!"

Carefully he lifted her veil and they kissed, long and hungrily. They were oblivious of the train's jerky start and the engine's whistle. They were barely aware of the sounds of people entering the vestibule and coming through the door.

"By golly, we made it, Dolly," said the Congressman.

"We'd have been on the way yesterday if you hadn't stayed in that poker game for so long."

"But them fellers, they had Southern antecedents, Dolly," he countered. "I couldn't leave 'em in the lurch."

"You mean, you couldn't leave as long as you were winning."

"Well, now, glory be, I did win a minin' claim up at Emigrant, wherever that is, and part interest in a cattle ranch. By gadfrey, Dolly, this trip ain't gonna cost us a cent. We'll just have to come up here again. Hey, look here. The passengers from the *Shoshone Belle!*"

And Dolly said, "Why, I do declare. There's Emily and Philip Snowden, and Rusty and", she looked down from where they stood, "and Madeline and Captain Taylor." Madeline and the Captain broke their embrace.

Dolly smiled. "I told you you'd see him again," she said. "I knew he loved you-all."

"And Captain," cut in the Congressman, "you've been transferred to Aberdeen Proving Grounds."

"How did you know, sir?" asked Captain Taylor, his hands still embracing Madeline's.

"Connections, laddie, connections. Politics. The night of the Antelopes, you told me about your ideas for internal combustion engines for military uses. And I ain't a member of the House Military Affairs Committee fer nothin'. I telegraphed from the Fountain Hotel to have you transferred. Gotta have somebody promotin' new ideas. If we left it to the Army, they'd still be fightin' with maces and swords. You've got good ideas, Captain. Best of luck!"

"So he's responsible for my transfer," said Captain Taylor to Madeline. "I didn't think it could be anybody in the US Cavalry."

### III

"Brother Van" Arsdale was the most honored and respected clergyman in all Montana. A Methodist Circuit Rider, he knew his parishioners – their needs, fears, weaknesses, strengths, and especially their sins. All manner of preachers had come and gone in Montana during his decades there, but not a one had ever contested Brother Van's place in the hearts of the Montana people.

One of the days he loved to reminisce about in his later years occurred on August 22, 1909. It was his only triple wedding, and he always took pride in boasting that, so far as he knew, the three couples had all lived happily ever after.

The stationmaster had alerted him that a young couple were coming by surrey from up the Valley to be married, and that relatives would get off the Park Branch Line to see the honors done. So Brother Van had waited in the little white Methodist Church. As the sun began to sink in the west, the surrey appeared.

In it was Hezekiah Hotchkiss, looking dignified in a black Prince Albert coat borrowed from the local undertaker, a white shirt, and a string tie. Sitting beside him was a conservatively dressed Rosie O'Toole. In the back seat sat the young couple. Lord Billner was dressed in a black western suit, white shirt, and blue cravat. The bride wore a form-fitting silk dress that Rosie had obtained from – well, Hezekiah knew but would not tell. It accentuated her slim waist, firm young breasts, and tender rounded hips. It revealed rather more of Prudence's breasts than Emily would have approved of, but Emily had not been present to protest. Only a cad would have mentioned the faint, lingering odor of cheap perfume – for indeed, it had come from a closet on the second floor of the Bucket of Blood. Its owner, now practicing in Seattle, had left it behind. In her hands Prudence held a small bouquet of real violets that Rosie had fetched from a flower-loving acquaintance in Livingston.

"Good evenin', Brother Van," said Hezekiah.

Brother Van bowed low. He knew Rosie and had heard that she had sold out and planned to go legit. "It is indeed my pleasure, Rosie.

And good evening to you, Brother Hotchkiss. And this is the young couple?" Prudence and Lord Billner were duly introduced. To prevent embarrassment during the ceremony, they informed Brother Van that a wedding ring would have to come later.

Then a hired hack arrived from the depot. Seated in it were Philip and Emily, Madeline and Captain Taylor, Rusty, and the Honorable Talmadge Beauregard Griffin and his lady. Introductions were made, plans for a second marriage – of the Captain and Madeline – were explained, and all entered the church to get on with the business at hand.

Hezekiah stood for Stephen Lancaster Billner and Philip Snowden gave away his lovely daughter Prudence. In the nearly empty church, the setting sun casting bright rays through colored glass windows and across the pews, Rosie O'Toole sniffed as she sat alone on the groom's side of the aisle. The vows were taken, Stephen kissed his bride passionately and she returned his ardor, Emily thought, just a little too much. They hurried down the aisle and out of the church – but then came back in. Emily was tearful, remembering dreams she had had of her daughter's beautiful wedding in Elm Grove. But she could not help but admire Prudence's choice of a mate: Stephen Billner was a fine looking young man. She liked him. She had always liked him – for all of seven days – in spite of herself.

Congressman Griffin stood for Captain Taylor and Philip gave away the bride, his sister Madeline. The marriage of the dashing Captain (except on a horse) and the exquisite thirtyish Miss Madeline Snowden was itself sufficient to bring tears to the eyes of Dolly, Emily, and Rosie. The affection of Captain Taylor and Madeline for each other was obvious, two mature people who have found true love in a meeting of minds as well as of bodies. There was something touching about that.

Even Rusty, spruced up and with his red hair brushed, was impressed. For once, Emily sighed with relief, he behaved himself.

When the ceremonies were over, and congratulations were being exchanged with Brother Van, Rosie and Hezekiah remained seated, one across the aisle from the other.

"How much do you have to pay a preacher to get married?" asked Rosie.

"Oh, a couple of dollars, I reckon."

"Isn't that strange?" mused Rosie. That's all we charged at the—"

"Shhhhhh. We're in a church"

"You mean," she said, "it only costs a couple of dollars to be legitimate?"

"Yep. You know, Rosie, that's all I ever asked of you. Only I gave you $5,000 and still you refused to marry me."

"I guess I best start livin' up to my part of the bargain," said Rosie. "Here's two dollars, Zeke," she said, at the same time beckoning to Brother Van.

"Two dollars?" said the astonished Hezekiah. "Rosie, Brother Van won't marry *us!*"

"And why not?"

"Rosie—"

Brother Van approached them. "Did you want something, Rosie?" the parson asked in a low, gentle voice.

And Rosie said, "Brother Van, would you marry a couple of old sinners like Zeke and me?"

And Hezekiah said quickly, "Fergit her, Brother Van. She don't really mean it. We don't aim to start no trouble."

"Of course," said Brother Van. "Outside every church there should be a sign saying SINNERS WELCOME. Of course I'll marry you."

So the Snowdens, the Taylors, and the Billners filed back to the pews and heard Rosie O'Toole pledge her troth to Hezekiah Hotchkiss. When the preacher had pronounced them man and wife, there was a long pause.

"You're supposed to kiss me, Zeke," she whispered.

"But Rosie," he pleaded, "in front of all these people?"

"Hell, yes," she replied.

"Well, okay," he said. As befits older lovers, he leaned over stiffly and gave Rosie a peck on the cheek.

Outside they heard the first whistle of the east bound Yellowstone Special. But just before they broke up, Congressman Griffin asked, "Where's the photographer?"

There was none, as he knew.

"You know," he said, "to take the weddin' picture. The one with the bride standing beside the groom who sits in a chair. You know why they pose that way, don't you-all?"

"Talmadge," pleaded Dolly. "Please. This isn't Loosiana."

"Because the groom's too tired to stand up, and the bride's too
sore to sit down. Ho, ho, ho!"

That broke up the festivities.

## IV

The Yellowstone Special stopped long enough in Livingston for a
change of engine and train crews. By the time the party had returned
to the station, less than an hour remained.

It developed that Hezekiah and Rosie were taking the westbound
train. Rosie all along had planned that they would be married and a
few days in Helena would constitute their honeymoon. Their train was
due out a half hour later than the east-bound. This left the surrey to
Lord and Lady Billner, who would return with it to their ranch. First,
however, they were going to see their relatives off on the eastbound
Yellowstone Special.

"Hezekiah, I'm counting on you to keep an eye on the young
couple," Philip said with Emily standing by. "I'm giving them a nice
cash wedding gift that should help them get through the winter. That
idea of a dude ranch makes sense. You let me know how things are,
won't you?"

"Oh, more than that," Rosie cut in. "Zeke and I will stay with
them – after our honeymoon, of course – while we look for a boarding
house to buy in Livingston. Zeke will help Stephen get the ranch
looking up to snuff again, and I'll help Prudence learn what it is like
to be a rancher's wife. She'll need some help."

Emily thanked Rosie profusely. For the life of her, Emily could
not remember where she had seen that woman before.

Captain Taylor and Madeline made strained conversation with the
Billners, but it came hard. Both had too many thoughts of their own.
Finally Prudence hugged her aunt and said, "Oh, Aunt Madeline. I'm
so happy that you are going to be having what I am about to be
having." She paused, thinking of what she said. "Marriage, I mean.
We want you and Captain Taylor to come out next summer."

"Only if Saddle-Pants has been reassigned," the Captain
commented.

Soon the east-bound Yellowstone Special with its fresh engine and
crew churned to a stop. Too soon, it seemed, the conductor shouted
"All Aboard". Final hugs took place. Then Rusty Snowden showed
emotion for the first time. He ran to Prudence and wrapped his arms

around her. "Sis, I don't want you to stay here!" he sobbed as no one had heard him sob before. Then he broke from her and ran to his Aunt Madeline and hugged her. They consoled him, though, Stephen promising him his own horse when he came to visit, and Captain Taylor promising to teach him how to ride it. Madeline looked devilishly at her new husband. "How to ride a horse? You, Captain?"

Captain Taylor laughed.

The Snowdens, the Taylors, and the Griffins boarded the Yellowstone Special for points east, and home. Awkwardly, the Hotchkiss's and Billners remained on the platform. Hezekiah made some suggestions for improvements Stephen could make at the ranch until he and Rosie returned, in about a week. As their train arrived, Rosie could not quite overcome habit. "Honey," she said to Prudence. "don't you be scared of Stephen. And Stephen," she said sternly, squeezing his arm hard, "you be gentle with this beautiful filly, you hear?"

On the train and on their way, Rosie asked Hezekiah, "How long will it take Prudence and Stephen to get to the ranch? An hour and a half?"

"Let's see," said Hezekiah. "First, the bridges are out and it takes a bit longer to ford the streams. Then there are two buffalo robes in the surrey. And there's about three stacks of fresh mown hay near that lonely road. It's a beautiful, star-filled night. Oh, I reckon it'll take 'em about six hours."

Rosie elbowed his ribs. "Hezekiah. They wouldn't."

"Betcha they would."

They did.

## V

On the Yellowstone Special the Captain Freeman Taylors had their wedding feast, such as it was, in the diner with Philip and Emily, Rusty, and the Griffins. The Congressman, it turned out, was a real power on the Military Affairs Committee and, surprisingly, proved to be a serious student of the subject. The friendship Captain Taylor and Madeline made with him would help the Captain's career in years to come.

Dinner over, Captain Taylor and Madeline left the others and walked to the observation platform at the end of the train. While hugging and kissing and pledging their troth, they watched the variegated colours of the fading Montana sunset. They had a compartment, and before nine o'clock walked down the aisle, announcing that they were tired. They paused to speak briefly to the Snowdens. Then Philip received the shock of his life. "Have a good night's sleep, Madeline," said Emily. "You, too," Madeline replied. And then, out of the corner of his eyes, Philip caught the women exchanging winks – knowing winks! 'My Gawd,' he thought, 'what is this world coming to?' Emily and Philip – Philip's mouth open with shock – watched the newlyweds disappear into another car.

"Why are they goin' to bed so early?" asked Rusty, whose emotional outburst at the loss of his sister and aunt had ended as abruptly as it had begun.

"Because they are tired, dear," said Emily.

"Ho, ho, ho."

"Rusty!" Emily cast a quick glance at Philip for support. But Philip just smiled.

Not much later and the porters came through to make up the berths. Emily retreated to the ladies' lounge to change and Rusty and Philip changed into night clothes in the men's room. They met at their berths, where Emily announced that she and Philip would occupy the upper one.

"Hop into the lower bunk, Rusty," ordered Philip.

The boy yawned and settled under the covers, his elk antlers above his head so that as he lay there, he looked as if they were attached to his head. Emily leaned over to kiss her freckle-faced son good night, and her hand crunched a package she had not seen.

"What's that, Rusty?"

"Just my secret weapon, Mother."

"Oh, my goodness!" She looked at Philip, who roared.

"Shouldn't we throw it out, Rusty?"

"No, Emily," interjected Philip. "Keep it, Rusty." Then he turned to Emily. "Know what? I'm going to take it down to Charlie Jacobs, the cabinet maker in Elm Grove, and have him mount it on a big, walnut plaque. Then I'm going to give it to Prudence and Stephen to mount above the fireplace."

"You wouldn't."

"I would."

She paused. "It would make quite a conversation piece," she admitted.

Even as they talked, Rusty's eyelids were getting heavy. He was sound asleep before they closed the curtains. Philip whispered: "I'm going to take the antlers and the package down to a luggage compartment at the end of the car. I'm afraid they could interfere with Rusty's sleep."

When Philip returned he found that Emily had already climbed into the upper berth. Philip climbed up and, on his knees, closed the curtains.

"Hurry, dear," said Emily. "It's cold here." She flounced the covers and Philip – constantly frustrated Philip – caught an exciting glimpse of his lovely wife, her nightgown ruffled up about her arm pits, and all of pretty Emily – all of her – exposed momentarily to her husband's eyes.

"Er, Emily," he said as his heart beat faster and he squirmed out of his robe.

"Yes, dear?"

"Are you sure you want to be closest to the wall? The berth slopes down toward it, you know. I'm afraid I'll roll over onto you."

"I know," she cooed.

He said no more. The porter came through the car turning down the lights, and in darkness Philip crawled into the berth.

Up ahead from the engine came a long, low whistle as the east bound Yellowstone Special sped through the night.

# Author's Note

*Yellowstone Holiday* is a work of fiction and as such needs no explanation or apologies regarding authenticity. Yet perhaps something should be said about where the facts do lie, and the fiction begins.

Save for references to Larry Mathews, who ran the lunch counter at Norris, Judge John Meldrum, the United States Commissioner at Mammoth, and "Brother" Van Arsdale, the Methodist Circuit Rider in Montana, every character is sheer fiction. Incidents relative to the above persons are also products of my imagination.

There were several stagecoach robberies in Yellowstone.

"Package Tours" were popular before the day of the automobile. Most of them probably did not stop at the Fountain Hotel, as did the characters in *Yellowstone Holiday*, because it went into virtual disuse after Old Faithful opened. Many "couponers" returned to Mammoth by way of Tower Falls. There really was a McCartney's Cave. The *Zillah* was the real name of the steamboat that plied the waters of Yellowstone Lake for many years, and by all accounts it was an unreliable old tub.

There is a Bath Lake and it was used by skinny-dipping men and was therefore prohibited to women.

Automobiles were not allowed in the Park until 1915. There is a recorded incident of one vehicle being mounted on a wagon, covered with a tarpaulin, and hauled from the South Entrance to the West Entrance.

With regard to the behavior of Tom the Curious Bear, see Philo Skinner's *Bears in Yellowstone* (Chicago, A.C. McClurg & Co., 1925). I acknowledge that Tom's antics with the flour bag and his bawling from a bellyache come from this source; his other antics are figments of my imagination.

I have seen a poacher's deteriorating cabin in Yellowstone. Unoccupied for many years, the roof had fallen in, and it will soon have disappeared. The Snowshoe Cabins were for real. In the Tom Minor Basin, north of the Park, I have seen a free-standing garage with a false back wall, behind which was a four foot wide space for hanging and dressing poached deer and elk. Gold has been discovered in the Park, most especially during road construction, but knowledgeable laborers have been told to keep it quiet. Gases wafting down the Yellowstone Canyon sickened workers on the road above Lamar Junction and Ernest Thomson Seton's grizzly bear hero Waab expired in a gulch full of poisonous gases.

Controversy surrounds the first dude ranch in the American West (it was probably the Eaton Ranch in North Dakota, later out of Sheridan, Wyoming) but one story backed by substantial proof has at least one of the first dude ranches operating in Paradise Valley, just north of Yellowstone Park.

And for discerning readers, the town is spelled Gardiner, and the river, Gardner.